The Missing

The Missing Sister

DINAH JEFFERIES

PENGUIN BOOKS

PENGUIN BOOKS

UK | USA | Canada | Ireland | Australia
India | New Zealand | South Africa

Penguin Books is part of the Penguin Random House group of companies
whose addresses can be found at global.penguinrandomhouse.com.

First published 2019
004

Set in 11/13 pt Dante MT Std
Typeset by Jouve (UK), Milton Keynes
Printed and bound in Great Britain by Clays Ltd, Elcograf S.p.A.

A CIP catalogue record for this book is available from the British Library

ISBN: 978–0–241–98543–4

www.greenpenguin.co.uk

Penguin Random House is committed to a
sustainable future for our business, our readers
and our planet. This book is made from Forest
Stewardship Council® certified paper.

Rangoon, Burma, 1936

Belle straightened her shoulders, flicked back her long red-gold hair and stared, her heart leaping with excitement as the ship began its steady approach to Rangoon harbour. Think of it. The city where dreams were made, still a mysterious outline in the distance but coming into focus as the ship cut through the water. The sky, a shockingly bright blue, seemed huger than a sky ever had business to be, and the sea, almost navy in its depths, reflected a molten surface so shiny she could almost see her face in it. Even the air shimmered as if the sun had formed minute swirling crystals from the moisture rising out of the sea. Small boats dotting the water dipped and rose and she laughed as screeching seabirds swooped and squabbled. Belle didn't mind the noise, in fact it added to the feeling that this was something so achingly different. She had long craved the freedom to travel and now she was really doing it.

With buzzing in her ears, she inhaled deeply, as if to suck in every particle of this glorious moment, and for a few minutes she closed her eyes. When she opened them again she gasped in awe. It wasn't the bustling harbour with its tall cranes, its freighters laden with teak, its lumbering oil tankers, its steamers and the small fishing boats gathering in the shadow of the larger vessels that had gripped her. Nor was it the impressive white colonial buildings coming into sight. For, rising behind all that, a huge golden edifice appeared to be floating over the city. Yes, floating, as if suspended, as if a section of some inconceivable paradise had descended to earth. Spellbound by the gold glittering against the cobalt sky, Belle couldn't look away. Could there be anything more captivating? Without a shadow of a doubt, she knew she was going to fall in love with Burma.

The heat, however, was oppressive: not a dry heat but a kind of damp heat that clung to her clothes. Certainly different, but she'd get used to it, and the air that smelt of salt and burning and caught at the back of her throat. She heard her name being called and twisted sideways to see Gloria, the woman she'd met on the deck early in the voyage, now leaning against the rails, wearing a wide-brimmed pink sun hat. Belle began to turn away, but not before Gloria called out again. The woman raised a white-gloved hand and came across.

'So,' Gloria's cut-glass voice rang out, breaking Belle's reverie. 'What do you make of the Shwedagon Pagoda. Impressive, no?'

Belle nodded.

'Covered in real gold,' Gloria said. 'Funny lot, the Burmese. The entire place is peppered with shrines and golden pagodas. You can't walk without falling over a monk.'

'I think they must be splendid to create something as wonderful as this.'

'As I said, the pagodas are everywhere. Now, my driver is waiting at the dock. I'll give you a lift to our wonderful Strand Hotel. It overlooks the river.'

Belle glanced at the skin around the other woman's deeply set dark eyes and, not for the first time, tried to guess her age. There were a number of lines, but she had what was generally termed handsome looks. Striking rather than beautiful, with a strong Roman nose, chiselled cheekbones and sleek dark hair elegantly coiled at the nape of a long neck . . . but as for her age, it was anyone's guess. Probably well over fifty.

Gloria had spoken with the air of someone who owned the city. A woman with a reputation to preserve and a face to match it. Belle wondered what she might look like without the thick mask of expertly applied make-up, carefully drawn brows and film-star lips. Wouldn't it all melt in the heat?

'I occasionally stay at the Strand after a late night, in fact I will tonight, though naturally I have my own home in Golden Valley,' Gloria was saying.

'Golden Valley?' Belle couldn't keep her curiosity from showing.

'Yes, do you know of it?'

Belle shook her head and, after a moment's hesitation, decided not to say anything. It wasn't as if she knew the place, was it? She simply wasn't ready to talk to someone she barely knew. 'No. Not at all,' she said. 'I simply liked the name.'

Gloria gave her a quizzical look and Belle, even though she had determined not to, caught herself thinking back. A year had passed since her father's death, and it hadn't gone well. The only work she'd found was in a friend's bookshop, but each week she'd pored over the latest copy of *The Stage* the moment it arrived. And then, joy of joy, she'd spotted the advertisement for performers wanted in prestigious hotels in Singapore, Colombo and Rangoon. Her audition had been in London, where she'd stayed for a gruelling two days and an anxious wait until she heard.

Belle had done her reading. She'd discovered Rangoon had been under British rule since 1852 and had grown from a small town of thatched huts to a vast city and thriving port, of which she was now to be a part. As Gloria pointed out imposing government offices, private houses and stores, Belle felt the stifling heat of the car and longed to get out and feel the air against her skin. Gloria had been right. The saffron-robed monks milling along the street were everywhere, and a few women too, though they were dressed from head to toe in faded pink.

'Nuns,' Gloria said, clearly not impressed. 'Buddhist monks and nuns. Though the nuns are fairly rare.'

Gloria went on to tell her the Strand had been the first area to be developed by the British and, together with the block at Phayre Street, was the best business address to be had. Belle didn't really care. There would be time to explore later. All she wanted now was a long cold drink and to feel solid ground beneath her feet.

'You'll like Phayre Street,' Gloria added. 'Named after the first Commissioner of Burma. Runs along the river just like the Strand. It's lined with beautiful rain trees and, more importantly, it's where one finds all the jewellers and silk merchants.'

Belle didn't speak, but ran a hand across her brow where beads of sweat were already dripping from her hairline.

'Here we are,' Gloria was saying as the drive came to an end and the driver pulled up in front of an elegant portico with a large palm tree growing resplendently on either side. 'But, heavens almighty, let's dive beneath a fan.'

Two silent porters came to fetch their cases and when they reached the massive glass doors a turbaned doorman bowed and held them open. Inside, the lobby was high ceilinged and refreshingly cool.

'I love to see the river shimmering through the tall bamboo opposite the hotel,' Gloria said as she turned to face the doors. 'Look.'

Belle looked.

'I suspect you'll be in one of the small back rooms in the new extension or in the attic. One hears talk that they might cover the swimming pool to build more rooms, you know, but it hasn't happened yet, and I hope it won't.'

She drew out a packet of Lambert and Butler cigarettes from her crocodile-skin handbag and offered one to Belle.

Belle touched her throat. 'I can't. My voice. I have to protect it.'

'Of course. Silly me.' Gloria paused. 'Word of warning. I'd keep away from the harbour and the narrow streets along the riverfront, especially after dark. It's where the Chinese live in an absolute maze of hidden alleyways. One takes one's life in one's hands.'

A short, rather stolid and officious-looking man with a pencil moustache and florid complexion marched over to welcome Gloria.

'Mrs de Clemente,' he said, with an obsequious bow, and speaking in what seemed to be a northern accent he was attempting to disguise. 'And your lovely guest. My apologies for intruding but if your companion requires assistance I can book her in straight away.' He turned to smile at Belle.

'Oh no,' Belle said, keen to put right his misconception. 'I'm not a hotel guest, I'm a performer. Singer, in fact.'

His jaw stiffened and, ignoring Belle, he addressed Gloria. 'As you are no doubt aware, Mrs de Clemente, there is a separate servants' entrance. I would respectfully ask your companion to use it.'

Gloria's eyebrows shot up and she gave him a gracious but icy smile. 'But, Mr Fowler, Miss Hatton is not a servant. As a performer and, I might add, as a personal friend of mine, she has certain rights. I shall expect to hear they have been adhered to.' She spun on her heels dismissively and stalked over to the reception desk.

Fowler had turned an even brighter red and, glaring at Belle, hissed that she should follow him.

'I'm sorry,' she whispered, guessing the short interaction was not going to help.

After he'd led her away from the lobby, he stopped and drew himself up to his full height. 'I'm sure you will be able to find a way to make it up to me. Remember, I am the assistant manager and, as such, you answer to me.'

As he'd been speaking Belle had willed herself not to smile at his excessively mobile eyebrows. Eyebrows that might at a moment's notice strut off and demand a life of their own. She could tell he was a man who would not take kindly to being a figure of fun and managed not to giggle.

His smile was taut. 'I make it my business to have eyes in the back of my head. All seeing is what I am. And may I say you don't seem to be the typical performing type.'

She shrugged.

'So where are you from? Home counties?'

'Cheltenham.'

'Same difference. Well, I don't know how you'll get on with the other girls. Most of them come from the East End of London. I hope you don't consider yourself too good for the job.'

She frowned. 'Others?'

'The dancers.' He raised his brows and gave her a look. 'Airs and graces won't get you far here.'

'I hope I can manage to fit in,' she said, wanting him to go and pleased when he took a step away.

'Well, I can't waste any more time chatting,' he muttered, and with that he turned a corner, took her up three flights of a narrow staff staircase and then stopped outside the first of four painted white doors lining a dark corridor. 'This is you,' he said and handed her a key. 'You'll be sharing with Rebecca.'

Sharing? Her spirits dipped a little bit. But then, she thought, it might turn out to be fun.

2

It was the next morning before Belle met her room-mate. As she had lain in bed the night before, waiting for the girl to turn up, she'd fallen into an exhausted sleep, only lurching awake when the sound of buzzing roused her. Eager to start her new life, she sat bolt upright and stared at the window where a couple of gigantic flies – at least she thought they were flies – were batting at the glass angrily. Without any qualms, she threw back the thin cover, swung her legs to the floor and leant across to open the window.

The small attic room was painted off-white and furnished with two single beds – one, beneath the small window she'd just opened, was clearly already reserved. So, Belle had slept in the other. A single chest of drawers, a small desk and one wardrobe constituted the rest of the furniture. But when she'd pulled open the wardrobe door to hang some of her own things, she'd found it jam-packed with her room-mate's clothes.

At a washbasin in the corner she splashed her face and hoped her pale skin would not turn into a mass of freckles in the harsh Burmese sunshine. Her compelling looks – sea-glass-green eyes, symmetrical oval face, wide mouth and straight nose – meant she stood out from the crowd and that had served her well when she'd auditioned for this job. Still in her nightdress, she brushed her hair, probably her best feature, and thought of her mother's hair, a bit darker than her own, though Belle couldn't say how true her memory was. It had been so long.

Now, while her room-mate was still absent, Belle opened the wardrobe again, wondering if her clothes might give an insight into the girl's character. There was an awful lot of shiny red silk and she pulled out a skimpy dress to take a closer look.

The door flew open and someone burst in.

Belle twisted round to see a blonde girl of medium height, who stood with hands on hips just inside the room, glaring at her.

'Like it, do you?' the girl said.

'Yes. It's nice,' Belle replied and, determined not to be put off by the girl's hostile attitude, she gave her a broad smile.

'Nice? It's bloody lovely. Saved a whole month for it, so if you don't mind I'd prefer you kept your mitts off.'

Belle hesitated. 'Sorry. I . . .'

The girl narrowed her eyes. 'Best get things straight from the start.'

'Yes, of course. I was only wondering where I'd hang my things.'

The girl glanced at Belle's enormous trunk. 'Blimey, did you bring the kitchen sink an' all?'

Belle shrugged. 'My father's,' she muttered pointlessly.

'Rebecca,' the girl said, and held out her hand.

Belle shook it. 'Annabelle . . . everyone calls me Belle.'

'I'm a dancer,' Rebecca added. 'There are four of us.'

Belle nodded and took in the girl's dishevelled appearance – smudged make-up framing large blue eyes, an upturned nose, full lips painted red and a clinging cotton dress doing little to conceal a voluptuous figure.

'You must be the new singer. I hope you can bloody sing. The last one was right useless, always crying, miserable as sin and light-fingered too. Up and effin' left, taking my favourite earrings with her.'

'Was she homesick?'

'What do I know, or care? Hope you're not a whinger too.' She paused and searched Belle's face as if for signs of feebleness. 'First time away from home?'

'No. I've lived in Paris and London.'

The girl nodded. 'So, where you from then?'

'West Country. Cheltenham.'

'Posh.'

Belle sighed. Was it always to be like this? Perhaps she should have lied and claimed Birmingham instead. She'd worked there briefly.

'You got family?' Rebecca asked.

Belle shook her head.

'You're lucky. Our house is crawling with kids and I'm the eldest. Course I love 'em all, but I couldn't wait to get away.'

'Maybe they'll come and visit?'

Rebecca laughed. 'Not likely. Haven't got the cash. Poor as church mice.'

'Ah.'

'Anyway, as long as you don't interfere in what I do. Your predecessor came from Solihull, thought she was better than the rest of us. If there's one thing I can't abide . . . Anyway, I need to get some kip now. You goin' out?'

'I was rather hoping to unpack.'

'*Rather hoping*, were you?' she said, mimicking Belle's accent. 'Well, jolly dee. Now give me a few hours with my head down and do it after.'

'Fine, but I need to wash and get dressed before I can go out.'

The girl merely shrugged.

'I waited up for you,' Belle said. 'It seemed a bit rude to go to sleep without having met. Where did you get to last night?'

Rebecca tapped the side of her nose. 'Least you know, less likely you'll be telling tales.'

'Oh, for goodness' sake . . .'

'Not a goody two-shoes then?'

Belle bristled. 'Of course not.'

'We'll see. Bathroom's opposite. But you need to get in early. All five of us share it and the hot water runs out.'

Belle choked in surprise as a foot-long lizard with a wriggling tail suddenly ran up the wall and behind the wardrobe while making a strange inhuman sound.

Rebecca laughed. 'They live indoors and keep you awake at night. We see insects inside too, larger than at home, and maybe the odd squirrel.'

'Inside the room?'

Rebecca simply tugged off her dress and, leaving it in a heap on the floor, slid into bed in her underwear. Scarcely a moment later, as Belle was about to open the door and head towards the bathroom, the girl raised her head.

'Bloody lovely hair you've got, an' I bet it's natural, that red in it,' she said, and then she turned over and faced the other way.

Belle smiled to herself. Perhaps it wouldn't be too bad sharing with Rebecca after all.

The day before, soon after she'd arrived, Mr Fowler, bursting with self-importance, had given her a tour of the hotel. From the grand entrance hall with its mirrored walls, dark leather sofas, polished hardwood floors and glass coffee tables, he'd led her through to the plush dining rooms. Pale-pink silk lamps dotted the room and paintings of Burma decorated the walls, alongside portraits of dignified white men and their bejewelled women. The tables were already laid with crisp damask tablecloths.

She'd murmured her admiration volubly enough to satisfy him, and in truth she really was impressed, and more than happy to be working there. He'd shown her more of the place, telling her the hotel had been totally renovated in 1927. 'Of course, I wasn't here then.'

'How long have you been here?'

'Not long,' he'd said, brushing her question aside and continuing, 'We're the most comfortable, up-to-date hotel in Rangoon – we even have our own post office and a jewellery shop owned by I. A. Hamid and Co.'

A prettily dressed room followed which, he'd told her, served as the breakfast room, doubling later for afternoon tea. She'd glanced at the wicker chairs and dainty place settings. It was nice, she'd thought, with a more relaxed atmosphere than the grand dining room. They were famous for their afternoon teas, he'd said, with a note of pride in his voice.

'There are sometimes cakes left over for the staff,' he'd added, smiling magnanimously, as if leftover cake had been bestowed by him alone.

The storerooms came next, then a large high-ceilinged kitchen opened on to a small room where the staff took their meals, and finally they'd ended up where the Strand concert hall had been built behind the annexe, with a girls' changing room and a small garden behind it.

'We used to rely on visiting orchestras, dancers and singers. A resident band and performers are a recent thing. We've yet to see if things really work out.'

'Is it only the English who come here?'

He'd nodded, then added, 'Well, and the Scots. A lot of Scots.'

'And what about the people who work here? All British?'

'Course not. We have Indian kitchen boys and you've seen the doorman.'

'No Burmese?'

He'd shaken his head. 'The Burman – the menial class, I mean – does not like to work.'

'At all?'

'For us.'

'Oh.'

'There are plenty of the more educated Burmese in governmental departments.'

Here, as in the main building, the public areas were extraordinarily lavish. Once they were back in the entrance hall she'd pointed at the velvety carpeting of the wide staircase sweeping up to the floors above, but he'd shaken his head. 'Guest bedrooms, suites and lounges,' he'd said. 'No need for you to go up there.' And she had immediately longed to see.

Catching the curious look on her face, he'd pushed open a swing door leading to a dark corridor. After they had gone through he'd taken her right hand in his and placed his other hand on her left shoulder. She'd squirmed out of his hold as he tried to push her back a little. 'It's possible for the right girl to *see* an unoccupied bedroom from time to time, you know, between guests, if you get my drift. Are you one of the right girls, Miss Hatton?'

She'd stepped away from him. 'I doubt it, Mr Fowler.'

He'd inclined his head and narrowed his eyes slightly before saying, 'Well, we shall see, shan't we.'

She wasn't worried. There had been men like him before.

Now, with a day to herself, ostensibly so she could settle in and generally stake out her bearings before a busy rehearsal the next day, she decided to explore the town. As she came out of the hotel, she nodded at the turbaned doorman and blinked as the haze of dust in the air stung her eyes. She passed the offices of a shipping agent, followed by an ornate red post office, but then, changing her mind, turned back on herself and headed in another direction.

She inhaled the heavy air, bursting with mysterious Eastern scents. What could smell so aromatic, she wondered? Then she paused, listening to temple bells ringing from every direction. In the street, the swarm of rickshaws, bicycles, automobiles and pedestrians forced her to frequently dodge out of the way. Judging by the differing languages she heard – possibly Hindustani as well as Burmese and, of course, English – a broad mix of races lived here. The Indians looked busy and vigorous, the Chinese anxious to sell you their wares, but it was the Burmese who enchanted her. The men smoked cheroots and tilted their heads at her as she passed, and the women, dressed in immaculate pink silky clothing, were tiny and doll-like in their beauty. They wore their hair tightly coiled and decorated with a flower at one side, but she was surprised to see they had painted their faces with some thick yellow stuff. Charmed by the sweetness of their smiles, she grinned back at them. She was fascinated to see that men and women all wore skirts with short jackets – she'd already found out the skirt was called a *longyi* – although the women's version was more bunched at the waist. She also noticed the men generally wore pink turbans while the women often seemed to drape a gauzy silk shawl around their shoulders.

Further on a faint odour of drains mingled with the distinctive spicy aromas stemming from the various stalls and traders. She stood at a crossroads and listened to the iron-tyred wheels of the horse-drawn *gharries*, no more than old-fashioned boxes on wheels for hire, and marvelled at the way past and present coexisted in these streets. After a moment she turned left into Merchant Street.

All along the Strand Road, and beyond, evidence of British building dominated the town, but Belle was yearning for something more thrilling than these monuments to colonialism. She turned right, passing the ornate high court building, where she believed her father must have worked, then she turned again and, with a sharp intake of air, saw what she'd been looking for. This had to be the one they called the Sule Pagoda, smaller than the Shwedagon Pagoda she'd seen from the ship. Delighted to have come across this shining golden apparition in the centre of downtown Rangoon, surrounded by the bustle and noise of everyday life, she stopped to look. The receptionist at the hotel had informed her it was 2,200 years old and had always been at the centre of the city's social activity.

As she stared, the gold sparkled and shimmered seductively but, dizzied by the scorching heat, she glanced about. She hadn't remembered a hat or an umbrella, and as the flies buzzed around her face she batted them away and looked for somewhere to have a drink. The tea stands lining the streets looked none too savoury, so where? She looked again and spotted Gloria coming out of Rowe and Co., a large cream and red department store with a corner tower, curved top-floor balconettes and ornate windows. Belle called and waved.

3.

Diana, Cheltenham, 1921

At last I've received a letter from Simone. I'm so pleased I could dance about the room. I think of her kind amber eyes, pale blonde hair and peaches-and-cream complexion; remember, too, the terrific fun we had. My doctor's wife and my best friend in Burma and, although her news is sad, of course it is, for her husband, Roger, has died, she says she'll be coming back to live in England. Somewhere in Oxfordshire, which isn't so far. I run downstairs, pick up my gardening scissors and trug from the little hall at the back of the house and nip outside, angling my face upwards for a moment – I love to feel the sun on my skin – and then I cut some roses for the dining room.

I recall the brilliance of the flowers in Burma and my life there, *my life*! Crammed with excitement and laughter. Cocktails, dinner parties and those lavish night-long garden parties. The sheer joy of a Parisian silk dress skimming my skin – and my darling husband holding me so tight I felt as if I was the bee's knees. Then, having drunk too much champagne, watching pink and orange lanterns swaying in the breeze as the sky turned indigo just before dawn.

But oh, the garden, with its perfumed flowers and the huge canopies of trees where monkeys swung in the branches. We both laughed to see them, our arms wrapped around each other, young – well, I was – and so much in love. And our own special secluded place where nobody could see what we did and could never know how my stern upright husband wanted me so much it stopped his breath.

I bring myself to a standstill.

Don't think about the garden.

4.

Gloria crossed the street, handbag swinging, a broad smile on her face as she strode over. Belle smiled back and Gloria kissed her on the cheek, her film-star lips painted crimson.

'How's our little songbird liking Rangoon?'

'Haven't had time to see much yet, but yes, I love it. There's so much going on.' She paused for a moment and wiped a hand across her brow. 'But, golly, it's hot! I was wondering where to go for a drink. I'm dying of thirst.'

'I know a little place. And, while we're at it, we'll buy you a hat. Rowe's will have one. Just the ticket, I'm sure. While we're there you must pick up a copy of their catalogue. You can literally get anything.'

'Sounds terrific.'

'And it's beautiful inside. Fans everywhere, cool black-and-white marble floors throughout *and* only Britishers serving. Harrods of the East, darling.'

Belle grinned. 'You're very kind.'

'My dear, you are misguided. Truth is, you intrigue me. I get so easily bored, you see.' Her sigh was long and languorous as if to prove her point. 'And you seem like you need someone to look after you.'

Belle felt she might become something of a toy to the older woman and would as swiftly be put down as picked up, and as for being looked after, she had long been used to looking after herself. Still, if that was what Gloria wanted to think, so be it. She matched her step to Gloria's and they walked off, crossing the gardens of Fytche Square and turning back on to Merchant Road.

'The yellow stuff on their faces?' Belle asked. 'What is it?'

'It's called *thanaka*. They believe it's good for the complexion and prevents sunburn too.'

'Looks terribly drying. Have you tried it?'

'Not my cup of tea, darling.'

And Belle could see her friend's chiselled cheeks would never be sullied by native remedies.

Inside the bar, Gloria ordered two long cold Pimm's.

'Oh, not alcohol,' Belle said. She didn't trust alcohol. If it could change you for the better, it could also change you for the worse. She'd become accustomed to denying herself since the age of eight, when she'd cottoned on that with a little self-control she could eke out a single chocolate bar for longer than anyone. 'It's . . . relatively early,' she added. 'Can I have a pot of tea?'

Gloria laughed. 'Tea! Utterly revolting here unless you like it with condensed milk. I know some do.'

'Why condensed milk?'

'The Burman population think it disgusting to milk a cow. Anyway, you wanted a drink and in my book a drink means only one thing.'

Belle gave her a determined look. 'Just lemonade. Honestly.'

Gloria shook her head and contemplated her with faux sad eyes. 'You're missing out. The Pimm's here is the best in town. But never mind, tell me what you've been up to.'

'Not much. Getting my bearings, really.'

Gloria smiled with a look that suggested she was pleased with herself. 'Well, I have something to tell you that might well be of interest.'

'Go on.'

The next evening, before her first performance, Belle was checking the running order in her head while applying her make-up. She stared at her reflection in the brightly lit dressing-room mirror and applied a burgundy lipstick that highlighted the red-gold of her hair, though what she would do with her hair she hadn't decided. Loose? Up?

Was she feeling nervous? A little, but she'd learnt to use her nerves when she sang. More importantly, she felt a wild new kind of happiness and was absolutely determined to make a good impression. They would be kicking off with some of her favourites – a good omen. She loved Billie Holiday, of course, but also Bessie Smith, the queen of blues. Any of their songs were firm favourites but she'd chosen 'Nobody Knows You When You're Down and Out' and 'Careless Love'.

After saying hello to the dancers, she'd been concentrating so hard she hadn't taken much notice of them changing on the other side of the room. But now she became aware of her name being mentioned in overloud whispers, intended most certainly for her ears. She gave no sign that she'd heard and carried on applying her make-up.

The whispers continued, and Belle worked out they were saying she had only got the job because of her connection with Gloria de Clemente. She twisted round and stared at the scowling faces of the four girls.

'I barely know her,' she said with a smile, hoping to dispel the ill humour. 'Really.'

Rebecca stared at her. 'You would say that, wouldn't you? Annie here was in line for the job and then suddenly up you pop, arriving on the same boat as Mrs de Clemente.'

'And I saw you in a bar with her yesterday,' the girl called Annie added. 'Very chummy.'

'I met Gloria for the first time on the boat.'

'Gloria, is it? She never lets us call her *Gloria*.'

Belle felt her anger rise as she got to her feet. 'Oh, for goodness' sake, this is ridiculous. I saw an advert for the job and I applied like anyone else.'

'Oh yes, and I'm the king of England,' Rebecca retorted.

Annie snorted with laughter and Belle felt her jaw clench as she spun round to face her. 'Maybe *you* didn't get the job because you bloody well weren't good enough. Ever occur to you?'

'Easy for you to say. We've seen your type out here be–'

'My type? You know nothing about me. Nothing!' Belle felt her cheeks inflame so calmed herself before speaking again. 'Now, if you don't mind, I have a performance to prepare for.'

She sat down stiffly, trying not to show her upset, and attempted to detach from them. Floating off in her mind had always been her way of escaping conflict and she was good at it. But she had hoped her relationship with her room-mate would be friendlier and the unpleasant exchange bothered her. After a few slow breaths she regained her self-control but couldn't help worrying that the unpleasantness might harm her performance. Of course, it was exactly why they'd done it. Well, she was blowed if she'd come all this way only to let some vindictive jealous girls ruin things for her. She would go out, smile, and sing her heart out.

5.

Diana, Cheltenham, 1921

As I stare out of the window at Pittville Park and watch the pigeons – small black shapes lining up on the roof of one of the houses on the opposite side of the wide expanse of the park – I hear my daughter calling her father. She must be hungry. I am flooded with energy, so I grab my dressing gown and rush down the three flights of stairs to the bowels of the house. There are eggs and bread, I'm sure. I'll make her boiled eggs with toast fingers; her favourite. But when I burst into the kitchen, tripping with anticipation, the aroma of beef stew greets me, and I know I'm interrupting when I see her sitting at the scrubbed pine table with Mrs Wilkes, our housekeeper. They are close together, and both stare at me. I blink back at them and want to point out it is me who belongs. Me who has lived here the longest.

My mind switches and the years peel back to the old days when the house belonged to my father and then to me after my mother died from the dreadful influenza. My father went to live in Bantham in Devon where our summer residence was, and he remains shut away there. He misses my mother and I really did try to visit, until travelling became too tricky. But before, when I was a child, I was happy enough in this old place.

I long to keep that window into a much safer past open for longer, but Mrs Wilkes gets up and as she does the window slams shut and I am jolted back to the present.

'I stayed on. I hope you don't mind, madam, but the girl needed feeding.'

I nod at her but feel the judgement in her voice.

'Darling,' I say, turning to my child. 'Would you like me to read your bedtime story tonight?'

She raises her head and looks directly at me. 'No thank you, Mummy, Daddy has promised to do it.'

I bite my lip and swallow. Then I turn on my heels and head for the stairs, moisture pricking my lids.

People here give me anxious looks and tell me it's my nerves. Once I heard our housekeeper gossiping with the delivery boy – the delivery boy! 'She's a martyr to her nerves.' But it's not my nerves: I fear the voice.

Back upstairs in my room the rain is buffeting the window and the park looks bleak as dusk darkens into night. But I can still make out the lights in the houses on the other side of the park, and those little rectangles of gold, shining like beacons, give me hope. I imagine happy families, the husband coming home from work, throwing down his hat and embracing his wife. The children, maybe three of them, scooting down the stairs with cries of, 'Daddy, my daddy is home.' And the wife shooing them into the playroom, so Daddy can read his freshly ironed newspaper while enjoying a Laphroaig whisky in peace.

'Drink, darling?' she will say, with no idea of the frailty of things.

6

On the evening of her second performance, before the other girls came back to the dressing room after their first two dances, Belle dipped into her bag for her notebook, then drew out the newspaper clippings. When she'd read the news item the first time she'd been intensely curious and, if she was honest, she still was. A year ago, when her father died, she'd had the unenviable task of packing up his extensive library. The brittle and yellowing newspaper cuttings had been well hidden within a dusty book and if they hadn't slipped out when Belle was finishing packing, she'd never have known. She had tucked them between the back pages of her own little notebook for safekeeping, and there they had remained. As she read the first of the two clippings again now, she shook her head, still finding it hard to believe.

The Rangoon Post 10 January 1911
STOLEN FROM THE GARDEN – THE CASE OF THE VANISHING BABY

It is with great sorrow and regret that this correspondent is tasked with reporting the disappearance of a newborn baby girl. The child, Elvira Hatton, just three weeks old, is the daughter of our esteemed member of the justice department, District Magistrate of the Rangoon area, Mr Douglas Hatton, and his wife, Diana. The baby disappeared yesterday, from her pram resting in the shade of a tamarind tree, in the Hattons' Rangoon garden in Golden Valley. The police are appealing for witnesses to come forward as a matter of the greatest urgency.

As the other girls entered the room, buzzing with energy, Belle glanced at her watch and slipped the cuttings back inside her bag. With five minutes to spare, she settled on an ivory floor-length dress in rayon crêpe, beaded at the neck and waist, and quickly slipped into it. She checked her reflection and appraised her performance look. It had taken her a while to become accustomed to wearing so much make-up; left to her own devices she wore very little and allowed her hair to hang loosely to her shoulders in its natural wave. Now she finished the look with glossy red lipstick and pinned her hair at the sides with two diamanté clips.

A few moments later she stepped on to the stage tingling with excitement and knowing the knot in her stomach would quickly dissolve once she began to sing, exactly as it had the night before.

The first number was enthusiastically received, although she was disappointed at the size of the audience. But it was only a Thursday evening and afterwards in the bar, Gloria, dressed entirely in black satin with a real ruby at her throat, told her the big crowds only turned up at the weekends. When Belle had seen her in town she had mentioned how her brother, who was something high up in the British administration, would be coming specially to hear Belle sing on Saturday. And now she revealed the exciting news she had only hinted at the other day: her brother had contacts in the entertainment world in America, so if Belle played her cards right . . . well, anything could happen.

'Really? Do you know who they are? These contacts?' Belle, unable to conceal the thrill she felt, wondered what the cards might be.

'Afraid not. But, darling, you were wonderful. The way the orchestra burst into sound, especially the trumpet, and then your voice. I swear your voice is like honey and the way it swings! Fabulous. Everyone up on their feet. And look at you! Eyes sparkling, skin glowing. You've found your passion, I'd say.'

Belle tingled with pleasure but only said she was relieved it had gone so well.

'All one has to do to get on in this world is believe in oneself and if you can't do that . . . well, believe in me.' Gloria laughed and Belle joined in, but as she did so she spotted Rebecca watching with a spiteful look. Belle gave a quick smile, but the other girl frowned before turning away.

'What?' Gloria said, noticing.

Belle pulled a non-committal face. 'The other girls are being a bit tricky. It's nothing.'

'They'll come around.'

'They think I only got the job because I know you.'

Gloria arched her brows. 'Maybe I can sort it out?'

'Honestly, I'd prefer to deal with it myself.' Belle hesitated before continuing. 'Actually,' she eventually said, having decided it was worth a try, 'there is something you might be able to help me with.'

Gloria gave her a warm smile. 'Nothing I like better than helping a friend. Fire away.'

'The thing is, my parents used to live in Burma. I wondered if you might be able to put me in touch with anyone who might have known them.'

'You didn't say before!'

'No.'

'And their names?'

'Well, Hatton, of course, like me.'

Gloria's eyes narrowed barely a touch. 'Ah yes. I did wonder if the name might be familiar.'

'Douglas and Diana, they were.'

Gloria looked taken aback. 'Then you've lived here before too? I didn't realize.'

'No. This was before I was born. It was extremely sad,

actually.' She paused, uncertain about continuing, but then went on. 'They lost a baby.'

Gloria gave her a knowing look. 'There are so many infectious diseases out here.'

'No. I mean they lost a baby. Literally. It disappeared from their garden here in Rangoon in 1911.'

'Good God, how shocking!'

'So, you hadn't heard about it?'

Gloria seemed to falter, as if suddenly unsure of herself, then she dipped her head and rummaged in her bag for somewhat longer, it seemed to Belle, than was strictly necessary, eventually extracting her cigarette case and a lighter.

'We-e-ell,' she said, drawing out the vowel as she lit a cigarette. 'I wouldn't have been here then, but you know it does ring a bell. Must have seen it in the paper. My brother, Edward, would probably remember. You'd better ask him.' There was a tiny waver as she stopped suddenly and scrutinized Belle's face. 'Goodness, is that why you've tipped up here?'

'No. It was purely the job. And what happened was so long ago. Twenty-five years, so I didn't think there'd be any harm in coming.'

Belle decided not to say more about her parents, but she couldn't escape the memory of rattling around their enormous house with only her mother and Mrs Wilkes for company. And the times she'd hated her mother with such trembling unstoppable rage it had always ended badly. Had even told her mother she wished she was dead.

'Penny for them,' Gloria said.

'Oh, nothing much. Tell me about you.'

'One thing you need to know about me is that I never tell the truth. On principle.'

Belle laughed.

'And my one aim in life is to break all the rules.'

'I always seem to get caught if I do.'

Gloria, mistress of the dazzling smile and the sardonic raised brow, smirked. 'Oh, I get caught, darling, all the time. The trick is not to care when you are. Bravado, sweetie, that's the ticket. I simply do not give a fig.'

Belle laughed again, thinking of the bravado she was in fact already so familiar with.

7

On Saturday night Belle met Edward, Gloria's brother, who, on first sight, seemed an affable sort of a man. When Gloria introduced them, during the interval, he regarded Belle with dark, glittering eyes, then held out his hand. Though not tall – their eyes were on the same level – she found herself feeling flustered. She couldn't exactly put it into words, but there was a look about him she'd seen before, something a bit old-fashioned, reminding her of one of her father's most charming friends. Accustomed to a privileged life, Edward had the resultant presence and confidence, plus, she guessed, an inborn sense of entitlement. His dark hair, greying at the temples – a distinguished feature – and something about his face and the chestnut colour of his eyes reminded her of a glamorous fox. He must be about fifty, she thought. Having taken all that in within an instant, she wondered what he might be observing in her and raised a hand to smooth her wayward hair.

'So,' he said. 'Finally, I have the honour of meeting my sister's latest protégée. I'm delighted.'

Belle could feel the heat spreading from her chest to her cheeks. Apart from freckles, this was the main disadvantage of her colouring. 'Pleased to meet you,' she said, and flapped a hand in front of her face. 'Gosh, it is hot, isn't it?'

'We could try the garden. Or maybe stand closer to the fan, although it's near the bar and considerably noisier.'

She nodded. 'I only have half an hour before the next set.'

'And congratulations on your performance. Simply splendid. The world is your oyster, my dear.'

'Didn't I tell you?' Gloria interjected.

Belle smiled modestly.

While he ordered their drinks, whisky for Gloria and lemonade for Belle, the two women accompanied him to stand beneath the ceiling fan. But the packed hall, echoing with laughter and raised voices, was reaching a crescendo around the bar.

'On second thoughts,' Gloria shouted into Belle's ear, 'let's go outside. We can hardly hear ourselves think here.'

'Your brother?'

'Will find us. Anyway, I wanted a word.'

'Oh?'

As they went into the courtyard, Gloria turned to Belle. 'I spoke to Fowler about the other girls.'

Belle was horrified, her hand flying to her mouth. Precisely the trouble with being taken under somebody's wing, she thought. If you weren't careful they started acting as if they owned you.

'Don't be silly. He's going to keep an eye out, that's all.'

'If he says anything it will only make things worse.'

Gloria reached out a hand just as Edward appeared with a waiter in tow. 'Sorry to interrupt girl talk.' He paused, then gently laughed. 'Now, my dear, don't let Gloria interfere – because she will, you know.'

The smile on his sister's face slipped ever so slightly and Belle wondered if she'd spotted a touch of animosity between the pair. Perhaps these two don't always get on, she thought, though it could be normal for brothers and sisters. She didn't know.

'Come on, sis,' Edward was saying. 'Have a drink.'

While they sipped their drinks, Belle observed the siblings and particularly Edward. His slim build was more athletic than skinny, and he had elegant hands. He smiled at her – he was quick to smile – but had he read her mind? Something about his eyes too. Seductive eyes, drawing you closer than you might wish to be. She could even imagine wishing to be close, despite the age gap. Or – remembering her affair with Nicholas, who'd been the producer of her last show and also older than her – she *almost* could. Edward nodded greetings to various friends, emphatically, in the same way Gloria had.

'You seem to know everyone,' Belle said.

'I suppose so,' he concurred. 'Now, listen, Gloria tells me you'd like to meet people who might have known your parents.'

Belle nodded.

He glanced up at a spot above her head before looking right into her eyes. She felt disconcerted. When she'd met Nicholas, she had felt the same way, with a kind of tingling in the pit of her stomach. Although they'd been together for the best part of a year, they had lived separately, and she had still wanted to travel, see the world. So, when he'd wanted her to settle down and become his wife, she'd turned him down. She knew most girls would have given their eye teeth for such a match, but her father had brought her up to be independent-minded and she valued that. With Nicholas she'd have ended up thinking what he thought, believing what he believed. Though if she was honest, it wasn't only that: she really hadn't loved him enough. So, when the show came to an end, Belle had walked out of his life. Any earlier and she might have risked her job.

'Is there a Mrs de Clemente?' she asked, the words slipping out before she could stop herself. Oh God, why had she said that?

He blinked for a second in surprise. 'Well, actually, yes. There's Gloria, of course, who has reverted to her maiden name since her marriage ended –'

Gloria grinned as she butted in. 'Causes no end of confusion as you can imagine when newcomers conclude I am Edward's wife.'

Edward raised his brows as if to say that causing confusion had been Gloria's aim all along. 'And there's my wife who lives in England with my children.'

Now, as Gloria looked on in amusement, Belle stuttered a reply, fully aware her cheeks had turned beetroot.

'Don't let my brother fluster you, child. He only does it to entertain himself.'

Edward shook his head. 'Belle, my dear, you will discover that my sister, who is, of course, a fine woman in many ways, can be a touch fanciful.'

Gloria sighed. 'Believe that and you'll believe anything.'

'Anyway, what were we talking about?' he said.

Belle stepped in. 'People who might have known my parents.'

'Ah yes, Gloria mentioned.'

'So, do you think there's anyone?'

'Well, it was so long ago, many of the older folk have retired and gone back to Britain.'

She gave him her warmest smile. 'I'd love it if you could find out.'

He nodded. 'Do my best.'

'Just a thought, but were you here yourself in 1911?'

'I must have been but could have only recently arrived back. I imagine it must have been a rum do. I'd been working in London but then a job offer over here in the military police wasn't something I could refuse.'

'And you still work for them?'

He twisted his mouth to one side. 'Not exactly.'

'Enough,' Gloria said, interrupting. 'What you need are friends. Lots and lots of friends. There's a party soon at the swimming club. Why not come as my guest when you've finished here?'

'I'd love to,' Belle said. 'Won't it be too late though?'

Gloria laughed. 'How old are you, Belle? Twenty-one? Twenty-two?'

'Twenty-three.'

'Well, you've a lot to learn.'

'What my sister means is that because of the heat our social activity tends to start – and go on – later than at home.' Edward touched her on the arm. 'It would be nice to see you again.'

While he and Gloria turned to hail a friend, Belle continued to watch them from the corner of her eye, but then her father came to mind, perhaps because they'd been talking of the time when her parents had lived in Burma. She could see him so clearly, the sparkle in his eyes when he saw her, the set of his jaw when he was concentrating on a book. He was a good man but there had always been something inflexible about him, even then, and she had learnt not to argue.

She noticed Gloria was looking at her with a quizzical expression.

Belle pulled herself together and pasted a smile on her face. 'Simply remembering,' she muttered.

'I never remember. Make a point of it. Life is to be enjoyed and I damn well intend to.'

Belle laughed but then grew serious. 'What happened to your husband?'

'Who says I remember?'

'But you know?'

'Like I said . . .' And then she let out a long peal of laughter, her eyes glittering with mischief. 'I'll make a deal with you. Promise you'll come along to the pool party and I promise to reveal my sordid history.'

Belle laughed too. 'How can I possibly refuse?'

Later, on her own in her shared bedroom, Belle was still thinking about her father. She recalled the time she had been about to tap on his study door when she heard raised voices. With her mind in turmoil she'd stood completely still, listening to her parents arguing.

'What are emotions?' she heard him say. 'Nothing but something you make up. There is no reason to be so out of control.'

At this point her mother must have hurled something across

the room because Belle heard an almighty crash and then her mother weeping.

Her father carried on speaking but in a louder voice. 'It's a product of your own mind, Diana. Why can't you see it?'

Belle didn't believe he'd said it to be cruel; it was simply the way he'd learnt to cope with the world.

She let the memory fade and changed into her favourite Liberty lawn nightdress, ready for bed. Rebecca still hadn't turned up and had last been seen propping up the bar along with one of the band members. Despite a decision not to look again, Belle took the opportunity to flip open her notebook to the back where she had slipped in a second newspaper clipping. She reached out a hand to catch it as it fluttered out and then stared at the words.

The Rangoon Post 15 January 1911
MOTHER ACCUSED – THE CASE OF THE VANISHING BABY

In an unprecedented move, Mrs Diana Hatton has been taken into police custody for questioning in connection with the disappearance of her baby daughter, Elvira. Furthermore, this correspondent has received information from an undisclosed source that Mrs Hatton had been acting in a suspicious manner prior to the child's disappearance. According to our sources there are worrying indications that she will shortly be charged with murder. More details will no doubt be forthcoming, and *The Rangoon Post* will always be first with the news.

Belle wished she'd never found the damned newspaper cuttings and was annoyed with herself for bringing them with her. She didn't want to think about why her parents had concealed what had happened. Nor did she dare consider how the loss must have affected her mother. She simply could not. Because if she did . . . well, she might have to reconfigure her entire childhood. She shook her head. This wouldn't do. She was here for one reason only: to sing. Of course, she was curious, who wouldn't be, but she absolutely was not going to dwell on the past. The world was her oyster, that's what Edward had said, and she was going to make the most of it.

8.

Diana, Cheltenham, 1921

When they accused me my world split apart, just as if an axe had cleaved right through it. The day of the fire, a storm had been closing in. I'd fallen asleep in the summer house at the bottom of the garden. Whatever it was that Roger, Simone's husband and our doctor, had given me, it was strong enough to sedate me. Anyway, I must have accidentally knocked over the oil lamp. I don't know how. But I remember waking and feeling drowsy before falling asleep again. Maybe I stood for a moment before? Maybe I knocked over the lamp then? I don't recall. I do, however, remember the smoke and Douglas dragging me out of there. Just in time, they said.

Simone sat with me afterwards.

The fire was my undoing. The police believed I'd started it deliberately to conceal my poor baby's dead body. They'd previously searched the summer house, of course, but hadn't taken up the floorboards. Once fire had destroyed everything, nothing could be found.

They questioned me all over again.

'Did you see anything unusual on the day *you say* you found the pram empty?' the sharp-eyed, bald policeman asked.

I shook my head. 'I've already told you I did not.' I looked into his eyes in the hope of finding some compassion there, but there was none, merely a blank expression he used to disguise what he really thought of me.

My skin prickled. It wasn't only the heat of the day. Although I struggled against it, I jumped up and felt anger exploding inside me. 'Why aren't you looking for the person who took my baby? Why won't you leave me alone?'

He put out a hand as if to push me back down but when I flinched he stopped short.

'Now, now, Mrs Hatton . . . Diana, I've told you before, such a belligerent attitude will not help your case. Please sit down.'

'Case?' I whispered. 'I have a case? Are you charging me?'

'As of now you are simply helping us with our enquiries. Now to go back to the day in question. Did you sense something might be wrong? You were in the summer house that day too, weren't you, with the pram in full view? Surely you were keeping an eye out for your child? Are you really saying you did not hear or see anything?'

I shook my head, numb with exhaustion.

All day the questions went on. Round and round. What time did you come out to the garden? How long had the baby been alone? Who did you see in the garden? Why didn't you call for help immediately?

Beware the darkness hidden within the mind. The thought was so loud in my head, for one moment I was certain I had spoken, but the policeman was staring at me with a disingenuous smile, the type that stops short of the eyes.

'Humour me, Mrs Hatton,' he said, arms folded now, antagonistic, the smile gone. 'What about cracks in your marriage before this happened?'

I dared not look him in the eye.

I had thought I had everything: a beautiful house in Rangoon, a caring husband, my old childhood home in England, and a garden I had laboured over day after day. I knew nothing of cracks within our marriage, except for the one noticeably large one, but I was not about to admit an indiscretion to the policeman.

'Mrs Hatton?'

'Yes?'

'Do you love your husband?'

The silence went on a fraction too long.

The servants must have told him I'd been acting strangely since Elvira's birth. It's hard to remember clearly. All I know is I loved her so much I thought my heart might burst and yet . . . those bouts of crying I was unable to soothe. They tore me in two. No matter what I did, I could not comfort her, nor could I control myself. I wept continuously and felt so ashamed I would often go to the summer house to hide my face.

As for what happened to Elvira . . . I don't know.

9.

Gloria hadn't mentioned it was to be a moonlight party and Belle was thrown when she noticed the poster on the front gate also stated admission was by formal invitation only. She could hear the muted hum of conversation drifting, she guessed, from the other side of the building. As she pushed open the gate a Chinese woman stepped out from a gloomy office and held out her hand.

'I haven't got an invitation card,' Belle said. 'But I was invited.'

The woman shook her head. 'Card only,' she said in heavily accented English.

Belle wondered what to do. 'Mrs de Clemente invited me. Could you maybe go round and look for her?'

The woman shrugged but didn't move.

It had been an exceptionally long day and Belle was tired. She'd woken early and, although she had invited Rebecca to have coffee with her, the girl hadn't turned up at the café. Later there'd been long rehearsals with the band and the dancers. Most nights the dancers performed their routines with the orchestra but on show nights they worked up a routine to go with the numbers Belle sang. She had to dance with them too and the rehearsal had been tough. They had been professional but distant and she'd experienced a few moments of panic when she'd thought they might deliberately wrong-foot her, but in the end the show had gone well and, glad it was over, Belle felt relieved.

But she'd expended a great deal of nervous energy and, as the Chinese woman had now turned away, she decided to cut her losses, return to her room and go straight to bed. It didn't matter.

As she turned to make her way back, wondering if there

might be a rickshaw nearby, a tallish man approached. In the blue light of the moon it was hard to make out his colouring, but she could see he had angular features and a wide smile.

'Hello,' he said. 'Aren't you going in?'

She explained what had happened.

'No problem. I can take you through as my guest.'

'Are you certain?'

He gave her a lopsided smile. 'Sure. I'm Oliver, by the way, Oliver Donohue.' And he held out his hand.

'Well, thank you. I'm –'

He didn't let her finish. 'I know who you are, Miss Hatton. I saw you singing tonight. Scat singing at one point. Mighty impressive.'

'Ah.'

'So, shall we?' He flashed his invitation card, then held out his arm as if to shepherd her through.

'You're American,' she said, as they walked around the building towards the sound of the party which was growing louder now.

She didn't hear his reply because as they turned the corner she surveyed the scene in surprise. It was much prettier and more festive than she'd expected. The pool sparkled with coloured reflections from paper lanterns hanging from trees circling the water. On the terrace oil lamps lit the animated faces of people gathered together in knots, and fairy lights hung across the entrance to the pool house itself. As Belle took in the softly playing music, she noticed a few couples dancing cheek to cheek.

'I hadn't expected it to look so lovely,' she said.

'The British never stint.'

She looked up at him, wondering if there had been a hint of criticism in his voice, but he was smiling broadly. Now the light was better she could see his luminous blue eyes, fringed by impossibly long dark eyelashes. She forced herself not to stare at those eyes. He had a strong, straight nose with tousled, rather unruly light-brown hair and a deep tan. He's different, she thought, as she noted his barely concealed amusement, as if life provides him with endless entertainment.

He went to the bar for drinks and while he was gone she glanced around, spotting Gloria and Edward laughing at something on the other side of the pool. When Gloria waved and began to make her way over, Belle, acknowledging she'd hoped to spend a little more time with the American on her own, felt a spark of disappointment.

'You made it. I'm glad,' Gloria said. 'How was the show?'

'Good, thanks.'

Oliver returned with a glass of champagne for Belle and a beer for himself. She hesitated, weighing things up, but in the end held out her hand and took the glass.

'Oh,' Gloria said, 'I see you've met our resident American journalist.'

Oliver bowed in mock formality. 'Foreign correspondent for the *Washington Post* at your service.'

'And the rest,' Gloria added with a touch of sarcasm in her voice.

Oliver shrugged and, ignoring Gloria, addressed Belle. 'What Mrs de Clemente is referring to are my columns in the *Rangoon Gazette*.'

'Which are none too complimentary about us, I might add,' Gloria pointed out.

'Us?' Belle asked.

'The British, darling. You and me.' She waved an arm around the gathering. 'All of us. He believes Burma should be for the Burmans. Anyway, I have people to see.' She turned to Oliver. 'Don't monopolize our new angel. She has people to see too.'

She kissed Belle on the cheek, gave Oliver a cursory nod, then walked away.

'I'm surprised she didn't drag you off with her,' he said with a wry look.

'Not your greatest admirer, it seems, but was she right?'

He gave her a smile. 'Sure. I don't hide the fact I'm not a fan of

39

British pride in their Empire, nor do I approve of their blindness to the moral issues inherent in colonialism.'

'Ah,' she said. 'So, in that case, if you don't mind me asking, why are you here?'

'Well, there you have it. Conundrum, isn't it?'

She narrowed her eyes as she looked up at him, then shook her head. 'Not an answer.'

He grinned and as he did so his eyes lit up. 'Maybe I want to watch as Rome burns.'

'Really?'

He shrugged. 'Burma fascinates me. It's the source of the best rubies in the world, plus endless teak, oil and rice from which, I might add, the British have made colossal fortunes. But times are changing, and I want to be around.'

'How do you mean?'

'I mean the days of the British are numbered.'

'Don't seem to be numbered,' she said, gazing around at the carefree faces of the crowd.

'Blinkered, the lot of them. But stick around. You'll see. The university student strike sixteen years ago pointed the way.'

'A strike?'

'The council and administration staff were all British and nominated by the government. The students resented it.'

She shrugged. 'Can't really blame them.'

He nodded. 'Exactly. So, despite threats from the government, the strike spread and was only partially settled when changes were made.'

As he looked at her a long pause ensued, and feeling her colour rising, she touched her cheeks. Such a direct look he had. Perhaps useful in a journalist.

'And since then?'

'The Burmese who work at the Secretariat are paid far less than their British counterparts and that too is a source of discontent.'

'I can imagine.'

'Can you?' he said.

'Of course.'

'You'd be one of the few. Many Brits still believe the only way to maintain authority is to treat the Burman as an inferior. And some British who have lived here most of their lives don't even speak a word of Burmese.'

She shook her head. 'That beggars belief.'

'Sure does,' he said. 'Being accused of being pro-Burman is considered an insult.'

'And you are pro-Burman?'

'I guess. Things are changing but I can't stomach the way some Brits still treat Burma as if it were a little England.' He paused as if deciding whether to say more.

'And?'

'Well, if you really want to know . . .'

'I do.'

'There's the brutal repression, the exploitation, the forced labour, the suffering of the dispossessed. It's wrong. All of it.' He paused again. 'But don't get me started. Tell me, instead, what's your story?'

She felt a moment of unease. The man worked for a newspaper, after all, and her father had always mistrusted journalists. 'Everything's a story to you?' she finally said.

He laughed. 'Sorry, I'll put it another way. Why not tell me about yourself?'

She silenced the doubt and as they talked a little about their backgrounds she felt more and more drawn to him. He was from New York but hadn't wanted to go into the family import–export business and had instead made a point of seeing the world and writing about it, eventually picking up freelance work for various papers. He'd been lucky, he said, a small inheritance had been enough to fund the first two years while he'd made his way.

She told him about Cheltenham and about her career, then,

completely without intending to, found herself talking about her parents and the sister she'd never known. He listened intently, as if there were only the two of them there, and something about that meant she wanted to say even more. His focus seemed to draw the words from her without his even trying, and she felt happy to have found someone she really liked and who seemed to like her. She even told him her parents had once lived in Golden Valley.

It went quiet between them. He appeared to be thinking and she hoped she hadn't said too much.

'If you like we can take a wander around the area where they once lived. Maybe see if anyone remembers anything. You'll like it. Golden Valley is the garden of Rangoon and from parts of it you can even see the Shwedagon Pagoda.'

She nodded, touched by his kindness. 'I'd love to. But there's something else. I haven't told you everything.'

'You don't have to.'

'I want to. The thing is, my mother was arrested in connection with my sister's disappearance. I've got the newspaper cutting.'

He raised his brows. 'Your parents must have offended someone for it to be reported. The Brits usually close ranks, especially back then. It sounds fishy. You could check it out with the police. They'll have records and I can put you in touch with one of my contacts.'

'Really?' She paused. 'To be honest, I'm not sure how much I want to know, but it would be nice to see where they once lived.'

'I'll drop you a note at the hotel with my contact's name. What's your day off?'

'Wednesday.'

'So how about then for a trip to Golden Valley?'

She smiled up at him but saw his eyes were trained on something going on behind her.

'Early?' she said.

'Sure. Look, Gloria's brother is on his way over. He and I . . .

'Good,' he repeated and patted her on the shoulder. 'Well, have a wonderful week. Enjoy yourself.'

'I will.'

'And I'll call for you next Sunday at twelve. And, don't forget, if you need anything at all you can always give me a call. The hotel will give you my number.'

She thanked him but what had really caught her imagination was the American journalist and his offer to accompany her to Golden Valley.

well, let's say there's no love lost.' He touched her hand for a second and his eyes sparkled. 'See you Wednesday morning. Eight okay? Before the heat builds up.'

She nodded, pleased with herself.

'And, by the way, I don't know if anyone has warned you but keep clear of the dogs. Some are rabid. And take care near the bars lining the docks. Most are fronts for opium dens and brothels.'

'Good Lord, nobody said.'

'They should have. The town was originally built on a swamp, so cholera epidemics have been annual events. Not my thing to advise you to stick to the British areas and the centre of town, but on your own you should.'

As Oliver left, Edward approached her, looking smart in a relaxed kind of a way. He gave her his usual charming greeting, but she had caught the hint of an odd expression she felt he was now trying to conceal. Had it been something more than simple dislike of Oliver?

'So,' he said, 'I'm glad you're here. I wanted to let you know that the best place to meet anyone who might have been around in your parents' day is likely to be the Pegu club. It's the stronghold of the senior civil service. Shall we say next Sunday lunchtime?'

'You're very kind.'

'Not at all. Now I know my sister would like a word. She wants to take you to Gossip Point.'

Belle laughed. 'Sounds hideous.'

'Delightful spot actually, overlooks the Royal Lakes. Where the women meet.' He squeezed her arm and spoke warmly, his eyes fixed on hers. 'Look, I know it must be tricky to come to terms with, but you don't want to live in the past.'

She frowned. 'I don't . . . really. I was simply curious, nothing more.'

'Well, that's good.'

She glanced at her feet and didn't add anything.

10

Diana, Cheltenham, 1921

I loved our private back garden in Golden Valley. The roses in June and July, the huge poinsettia bushes with the bright-red flowers, the anthuriums, the purple asters surrounded by big drifts of pale-blue butterflies, and the lovely orchid tree with its heart-shaped leaves and flowers of white and pink. The birds too, especially the luminous green ones and the hawks swooping across the clear blue sky high above the ancient padauk tree which had been there long before the house was built.

When we moved in I'd asked the Burmese gardener what the padauk was called in English. He said it had no English name but told me it was a member of the pea family and it produced a hardwood a bit like rosewood. He offered to chop it down, but I told him no. I'm so glad I did because in April, when the weather was so hot and dusty I thought I'd never survive, it burst into blossom and turned gold overnight. And, as the delicate fragrance of the padauk hung in the evening air, Simone and I would sit out, watching for the snakes living in the trees and batting our hands at the flying insects. We'd drink our gin and tonics and laugh about our husbands' quirks and sometimes end up quite drunk. We rose at five in the morning back then to escape the heat and I slept most of the day.

The gardener also told me it was Thingyan or water festival time, and Burma's new year, when everybody who dares go out is met with a bucket of water thrown over the head. Not a bad thing, I thought, given the weather, although Douglas cautioned against it and it was never wise to disagree.

Our house was beautiful. Painted white, the airy bedrooms caught the breeze from the veranda circling the house, and I often spent the afternoons resting on a chaise longue in the upstairs day room where a through draught gave some relief from the heat. All the hardwood floors were dark and polished to such a sheen I swear you could see your face in them. The wooden shutters, originally bright green, quickly faded to a subtler paler green which I preferred. Tall palms shaded the front of the house and tropical bushes and plants lined a curving pond at the side.

Among the other trees we had one bodhi tree, an acacia and a shady tamarind where the ayah would park my darling's pram.

I will never forget the day they dug my precious garden up and dragged the pond, killing the fish and destroying the planting, and what did the police find for their trouble, digging for all they were worth in that terrible burning heat?

Early on Monday morning, and against her better judgement, Belle set off for the police station. She thought about her conversation with Oliver Donohue and, remembering those piercing blue eyes, realized she was looking forward to seeing him again on Wednesday. Despite his anti-colonial stance there had been something generous about him she felt she could trust. He'd been true to his word too, leaving a note for her at reception with the name of his contact: Norman Chubb. She'd already found out most of the lower ranks in the police force were occupied by Sikhs but the British filled the managerial posts and this man was a detective, so that had to be good.

She entered the imposing building and scrutinized the hallway. Four doors stood closed and forbidding. She tapped on the largest, hoping this heavy sombre-brown affair was the correct one. Silence. She waited then tapped again but was dismayed when an angry voice yelled at her to *bugger off*. Her breathing sped up and her heart began to thump but, not to be deterred, she tried again, and this time opened the door to find a small office where a large man with thinning bright-red hair sat slumped at an enormous desk piled high with papers in an appalling mess.

'For Christ sake,' he said, without looking up. 'What the hell is it this time? Can't you see I'm trying to catch forty winks?'

She coughed. 'Excuse me.'

His head shot up and, now she could see his face, she reckoned he had to be in his mid-fifties.

'Who the devil are you?' he demanded.

'I'm Annabelle Hatton. I'm looking for Mr Norman Chubb.'

'Are you indeed. And may I ask the nature of your relationship with Detective Chubb?'

'No relationship. I was given his name by an acquaintance.'

'And who would that be?'

'Oliver Donohue.'

'Ah, the American journalist.'

'You know him?'

'What do you think?' He paused then added, 'We all know Oliver Donohue.'

'Is Detective Chubb here?'

'No.'

Belle hesitated, feeling hot and incredibly sticky, unsure whether to leave now and come back when Chubb was around, but in the end decided to speak to this man instead. 'Would it be all right if I sat down?' she asked politely and gave the man what she hoped was a winning smile.

His response was to jerk a finger at a chair opposite his desk, so she seated herself, smoothing her damp dress down nervously and feeling the way she had at school when hauled up in front of Mrs Richards.

'Your business?'

She gawped at his bright-red cheeks and bristly moustache. Such an overweight man, she thought, with a piggy look about the eyes, nestled as they were between folds of flesh. She circled the question she really wanted to ask by at first enquiring if he was busy.

'Always, Miss . . . er?'

'Hatton.'

'Ah yes. Well, Miss Hatton, I am always busy.'

'I'm really sorry to interrupt.' She paused. 'Would you mind telling me your name, please?'

He sat up taller in his chair, running a hand over his damp forehead and then his hair. 'I am Inspector Johnson, Chubb's superior officer. Whatever you were hoping to say to him, you may say to me.'

'It's a little delicate.'

'Just get on with it, miss. As I said, I am rather busy.'

Belle doubted that, but she smiled apologetically and got to the point, telling him she wanted to know if there were any records about a baby who had vanished from the garden of a house in Golden Valley.

He shifted his bulk and rifled through the papers on the desk at a snail's pace.

'I don't recall,' he said eventually. 'Was this recent?'

She shook her head. 'In 1911.'

His jaw dropped, he turned even redder and then he choked with laughter. 'Let me get this right?' he said, once he'd controlled his mirth. 'You are asking about something that happened twenty-five years ago?'

'Yes.'

He pursed his lips. 'And why do you want to know?'

She glanced at the bright sunlight streaming in through the small window, protected by bars, she noticed, then she turned back to the man. Best not be too strident with him, though it was hard to take this foolish-looking man seriously. 'The parents were my mother and father. The baby would have been my older sister.'

'Ah, I see, and the purpose of your wanting to see the records? Parents still alive?'

'No. My father died recently, but I've been wondering about what happened here.'

'Well, Miss . . . Hatton, I can tell you I was here then and I do remember a little about it. If I recall, the case went cold, although there were theories. And rumours. Oh yes.'

'And they were?'

'I believe the most convincing idea was that a witch doctor

from one of the head-hunting Wa tribes had paid for the baby to be taken.'

'But why?'

He puffed out his cheeks. 'Are you sure you want to hear?'

She nodded.

'It is thought he wanted to use the organs for medicine.'

She gave an involuntary shudder.

'Another idea was that a criminal gang had stolen the baby to sell to a rich Siamese family. Nothing conclusive. Some rumoured it might have been a revenge killing by someone your father had convicted.'

'You think the baby died?'

'Afraid so.'

She chose her words carefully before she spoke. 'And my mother?'

'If I remember correctly, your mother was placed under house arrest.'

'Was she proven innocent?'

He twisted his mouth from side to side. 'It was somewhat odd actually. I believe she was to be charged, but then suddenly she and your father upped and left Rangoon. Nobody knew what had happened. Well, I say nobody, but somebody must have. All extremely hush hush.'

'In that case would it be possible to see the records of the investigation?'

He gave her a sorrowful look. 'Sadly not. A fire a few years later destroyed them. The entire station had to be rebuilt.'

She wondered for a second if it was true, but then dismissed the thought. What reason could he have for lying? She stared at him, hoping he might reveal more. But he gave nothing away, took a deep breath and then puffed out his cheeks, letting the air out in a noisy burst.

'It has been a pleasure to meet you, Miss Hatton,' he said.

Taking the hint, and not wanting to push it too far, she automatically rose to her feet.

He appeared reassured that she was happy to leave, hauled himself out of his seat and then ushered her towards the door.

Belle hurried back towards the hotel feeling irritated by her meeting with the policeman. He had seemed to be helpful, but she couldn't rid herself of the thought he hadn't been telling the whole truth about the events of that day in 1911. She shrugged the feeling off and then, passing a bustling shopping area, she paused. She longed to encounter something not the slightest bit British and although Oliver had warned her to take care, this was in the middle of one of the main streets, and so she felt it ought to be safe.

The frontage looked like a row of shabby food stalls, so at first she hadn't even been aware it was the entrance to a bazaar, but something about the spicy smells wafting from within tempted her to explore. Divided into multiple dark alleyways inside, the dirt, noise and crowds should have been off-putting. But as she walked ever deeper into the centre, jostled and pushed, but never aggressively, she saw it was more like a huge raftered warehouse than anything else. Every alley, lined with stalls, was packed to the hilt with goods including beautiful *longyis* and shawls as well as other fabric and silks. These she loved, but whenever she touched one the mainly Indian stall owners, dressed in white shirts and trousers, would rather frighteningly burst out from where they had been squatting on a bench behind and beseech her to buy. Of course, she didn't actually know what they were saying but it stood to reason. She muttered something about returning later and carried on in search of the spicy smells that had drawn her in.

Next came an area where prettily dressed Burmese girls in *longyis* and short jackets hovered behind huge sacks of differing grains. The girls dipped their heads demurely and then giggled behind their hands. Belle had no idea what the grains were and when she tried to ask for directions to the spices they giggled even more and, arguing among themselves, pointed in opposing directions. She passed stalls selling the pieces of wood from which *thanaka* was made, the strange yellow paste the women coated their faces in, as well as stalls selling seeds and nuts.

Led mainly by her nose, she eventually stumbled across the intoxicating spice stalls. The huge baskets of powders, glowing in colours of yellow, red and orange, drew her eyes, as well as the sacks of chillies in every size and shape. Strange brown knobbly spices sat next to bowls of roots, and when she held a piece of one to her nose and sniffed, it reminded her of ginger biscuits. There were stalls selling tiger skins too, plus skulls of animals and other parts of various skeletons, though she had no idea what they were.

But the heady scents thrilled her, reminding her she was in Burma and that it really didn't feel the tiniest bit British. She bought some ginger and a little bag of red powder with the most gorgeous aromatic smell and then looked around for the way out. But the colossal market was deceptive, and she was unable to identify the way. After a momentary panic, she decided she would just choose any direction and keep going until she spotted daylight ahead. Eventually the smell of charcoal burning told her she was close and when she reached an opening she stumbled on stalls displaying fruit and vegetables, some of which she'd never seen before. She bought a large green melon, intending to share it with Rebecca. Then, bypassing the rough peasant-like woman reeking of rice wine and selling grubby squares of what looked like solid rice pudding, she found herself back on the street. A blue bird with a large orange beak sat self-importantly on the hood of a rickshaw. Feeling considerably proud of herself, she hailed the driver and asked him to take her back to the hotel.

In the dark corridor outside their room a tall man was striding towards her. As he passed he nodded and then walked briskly on. Maybe a member of staff, she thought, though a bit odd to see a man, especially a Eurasian man, in the girls-only corridor. When she stepped into her room it was to find Rebecca sitting cross-legged on the floor, reading Belle's own notebook, the place where she recorded her private thoughts from time to time, and where the newspaper cuttings were hidden. She darted forward and, feeling a rush of fury, snatched it from the other girl's hands.

'How dare you?! That's personal.'

Rebecca stared up at her. 'Don't get your knickers in a twist. I found it lying open on the floor. Sorry, didn't think you'd mind.'

'You're a bloody liar. I didn't leave it on the floor.'

'I swear.'

'No. You may not be the brightest button in the box, but it doesn't take a genius to realize a notebook with my name on is private. Or don't people write where you come from?'

Rebecca rose to her feet. 'No need to be rude. I said I was sorry.'

Belle felt her cheeks warm up and then, without any warning, tears started to slide down her face. She swiped them away angrily, but they kept on falling.

Rebecca came closer, placed a hand on her shoulder and gently squeezed. 'Hey, don't take on. It's only a book.'

'But it's . . .' Belle sobbed, not wanting to say. 'Just for me and there's things . . .'

Rebecca shepherded her towards the bed. 'Now sit. I'm going to get you a brandy.'

'I don't really –' she began, but the other girl had already left the room.

Belle still couldn't staunch the tears as she tried to unwind her tangled thoughts. What if Rebecca had read the accusation in the newspaper clipping? She berated herself, wishing she'd left the cuttings in her trunk. What if Rebecca knew everything? As images spooled through her mind, it was as if everything she'd been holding in was now pouring out. Her father's death, the awful discovery of the missing sister, the policeman, the way the other girls had been with her.

As a child she had needed someone who could tell when she was feeling sad, but there had been nobody. Mrs Wilkes had done her best, but she'd been a bustling kind of a woman who brooked no nonsense. Keeping occupied had been her way to deal with an unjust world. Belle recalled her sparkly eyes and ample backside. Dear Mrs Wilkes, who made delicious pies with the Bramleys that grew in the little orchard at the bottom of the garden, which she also preserved in Kilner jars. Feeling a bit better, Belle wiped her eyes and for the first time tried properly to picture the sister she had never even known existed. A baby. Just a little baby.

Rebecca returned, sat beside Belle and pressed a glass of brandy into her hand.

As Belle gulped, the warmth flooded her veins. Perhaps it was time to change her mind about alcohol – after all . . . she was not her mother.

'Now,' Rebecca said gently. 'What's all this about?'

'I thought I'd left the notebook under my pillow.'

'Honestly, it was on the floor.'

Belle nodded. 'I left in a hurry. It might have fallen, I suppose.'

'So?'

'Everyone hates me.'

'The girls?'

Belle sniffed miserably. 'Yes.'

'Don't worry. I'll sort the girls.' Rebecca handed her a handkerchief. 'It's clean. Now come on, what's the matter? It can't only be that.'

Belle listened to the drone of traffic rising from the street below. Then, for the second time that day, found herself recounting the time when her father had died, and she'd discovered the story of the missing baby. She sniffed, surprised that despite her best efforts not to care, it had suddenly become more real to her. Rebecca was a good listener and waited quietly until Belle had finished.

'So, tell me about the notebook,' she said eventually. 'I'd hardly read anything when you came in.'

'There's stuff about my mother.'

'She's still alive, right?'

Belle couldn't find a way to reply.

'Brothers or sisters?'

'Nope.'

Rebecca put an arm around Belle's shoulders. 'You poor old thing. And now you've come over here and we're mean to you.'

'It doesn't matter.'

'It does. And that's going to change. Promise.'

Belle smiled weakly. 'I'm such a sop. Sorry.'

'You've a lot on your plate.'

'I met a man who says he can take me to my parents' old place.'

'Who?'

'Oliver Donohue. A journalist.'

'A tasty one at that,' Rebecca said and then laughed. 'And one for the ladies, I've heard.'

'Is he?'

Rebecca shrugged and stood up. 'Your guess is as good as mine. Come on, dry your eyes, splash your face and put on a pretty dress. We, young lady, are going out.'

'But I'm blotchy and I've got rehearsals.'

'Not for hours and hours. Come on. Oh, I almost forgot, it's for you,' she said, picking up an envelope and holding it out to Belle.

'Who's it from?'

'Blowed if I know.' She grinned. 'Try opening it.'

As Belle tore it open she hoped it might be from Oliver. It was not. She read it a couple of times before looking up.

'You've gone all white,' Rebecca said, frowning. 'What does it say?'

Belle passed it to her and Rebecca read it aloud. *'Think you know who to trust? Look harder . . .'*

'Oh God!' Belle said, and a shiver of fear slid through her. 'What does it mean?'

'Means someone is out to rattle you.'

'But who could they be referring to?' Her voice had turned croaky.

Rebecca shook her head and then glanced up at Belle. 'Could be a genuine warning, I suppose.'

'But you don't really think so?'

'No. Like I said, I think it's some idiot trying to rattle you.'

Belle felt unsure. It had certainly rattled her. More than that, it had scared her, and now she didn't know what to think.

'The question is why,' Rebecca said. There was a short silence before she added, 'So, out of everyone you've met so far, who do you trust?'

Belle didn't reply but thought about it. After a few moments she looked at Rebecca. 'I saw a man in our corridor. Eurasian, I think. Did he deliver it?'

'Didn't see. It was slipped under the door.'

'Pity.'

'Come on, let's forget about the stupid note.'

'Should I go to the police?'

'Go bleating to them and say what? "Someone sent me a mean note." They'd laugh in your face.' She paused for a moment. 'Look, after my special treat for you, I don't half fancy getting sozzled. Join me?'

'I've never even been tipsy.'

'Blimey!'

12.

Diana, Cheltenham, 1921

They found nothing when they dug up my beautiful garden in Burma, nothing at all, except for the bootee, so what was the point? Here, as the first blush of dawn filters through my curtains, I hear the chorus of birds greeting the day. I stand at the window for a long time gazing out as the sun tints the treetops gold. When I peer down from the window I see a man wearing a grey trilby and navy-blue mackintosh turn into our front entrance. I falter. It's still early. Have they come for me already? When I hear voices lower down in the house, I steal across to my door and open it slightly, acutely aware of the tread of my footsteps on the creaking floorboards. The front doorbell chimes and after it has been opened I hear voices again. This time from the hall and a little louder than before, although still muted, and not loud enough for me to hear what they are saying.

I grip the door frame and although I feel dizzy with anxiety I step out on to the landing. Then, leaning on the bannister rail, look down the stairwell. An internal door closes and the hall empties – it's completely silent. I breathe a sigh of relief and go back to my room. Maybe the man is one of Douglas's colleagues and nothing to do with me.

This top-floor room with sloping walls has become my prison – or perhaps a source of solace? Either way, I am safe up here. If I swallow the tablets our housekeeper gives me with a glass of water morning and evening, they say I am not a danger to myself . . . or anyone else. I smile. If I remember to swallow and don't merely put them under my tongue . . .

I hear voices again and tiptoe back to the landing. From my vantage point I see the man who had been wearing the navy-blue mackintosh. Now he is staring up at me. He smiles, inclines his head and begins to climb the stairs.

Despite the fog in my brain there is one thing I am sure of.

I am not ready to go.

13

Belle stopped outside a temple and stared. She could see a large space inside where red pillars, decorated with Chinese script and imagery, held up a wooden raftered roof. She glanced over to where Rebecca had gone on ahead.

'What's this?' she asked.

'Chinese temple. Go in if you want.'

Belle nodded and took a few steps inside but was instantly assaulted by an overwhelming smell of incense and smoke rising from bowls stuffed with joss sticks. She coughed and spluttered as she tried to acclimatize, eyeing a golden canopy surrounding images of Chinese lions and various idols she couldn't identify. Maybe Confucius and Buddha? Yellow and red chrysanthemums stood in vases on carved ebony tables and, above them, lanterns in the same colours hung from the rafters.

A man in robes approached Belle and, in broken English, asked if she'd like her fortune told. Encouraged by Rebecca's vigorous nods, she agreed, and was told to frame a question. She hadn't been able to forget the note, so asked if there was anyone she should not trust in Rangoon. Telling her fortune turned out to be a complex business involving wooden sticks and a round object made of red painted wood composed of parts that looked like the segments of an orange. The answer was simply that she had asked the wrong question and she would soon be going on a journey.

She exchanged looks with Rebecca, who only shrugged and said, 'Lucky you.'

Leaving the temple, they ignored the street-corner tea shops and food stalls, eventually reaching the noisy area behind the waterfront, where Gloria had told her the Chinese lived. As she encountered the maze of hidden alleyways, thick with the scent of jasmine and fried rice, Belle couldn't help remembering the older woman's warning.

One takes one's life in one's hands.

'Is it safe?' Belle asked, feeling nervy among the swell of people crowding the steaming, claustrophobic streets.

Rebecca laughed and tossed her blonde hair. 'On your own perhaps not but stick with me. It'll be fine, I promise.'

'Why are we here?'

'For one, you are going to taste the best Chinese food you've ever had and, for two, you are going to treat yourself.'

Belle didn't say she had never in her life eaten Chinese food.

She stared at the many shuttered shophouse blocks where narrow wooden houses squashed up against each other, most with a shop on the ground floor – selling cooked food, vegetables, fish, ornaments and so on – with living quarters above. Confused by the unfathomable high-pitched language of Chinese street hawkers, she watched as squawking chickens and squealing piglets sealed in bamboo cages added to the din. As they dodged the many dogs snaking the streets in search of scraps and the reckless children racing between bicycles and the legs of pedestrians alike, the whole place pulsed with life.

Once they dived into the heart of the quarter, the fragrance of jasmine faded and now the streets sweated beneath the mixed odours of burning charcoal, fried fish and drains. Rebecca was striding ahead without glancing back and again Belle worried if she really could trust her room-mate. What if she were to vanish and leave Belle stranded here? But then Rebecca stopped and took a bow in front of a tiny shop tucked inside a backstreet threading behind a wider alley.

'Tra-la!' she said with a grin and a flourish.

Belle gazed at the window, astonished to see row upon row of neatly folded, brilliantly coloured silk, ranging from the colour of a Burmese sunset, shimmering in rose pink and yellow, to gentle pearly blues.

'It's the best but also the cheapest in Rangoon. The British don't like it here so they pay over the odds at Rowe's. Shall we?'

'You bet.'

Rebecca pushed open the intricately carved wooden door and a small bell tinkled.

Inside Belle stood transfixed, then trailed her fingertips over the bales of patterned silk, her senses on fire.

'I'd love some, but what would I do with it?'

'That's where I come in. I have a Chinese friend who works as a waitress in the Silver Grill . . . have you been there yet?'

Belle shook her head.

'Well, we must go, but the thing is, this friend of mine introduced me to the owner of this shop and her daughter is a brilliant seamstress. She can copy anything the top designers come up with.'

'And where is she?'

Rebecca laughed. 'Upstairs. And she has loads of magazines. She'll give you local rates too, or very nearly. You go up, choose the style, she tells you how many yards to buy and then you pick your fabric.'

'We can go up now?'

'Knew you'd be keen. I haven't told the other girls about this place.'

'Why tell me?'

'You were so miserable. There's nothing like a new dress is there, especially if it doesn't cost the earth. No guilt. And I wanted to make it up to you.'

Belle could have hugged her.

They climbed the narrow wooden staircase and upstairs Belle met Mai Lin, the seamstress. After flicking through several editions of *Vogue*, she settled on a sheath-like halter-neck dress, cut on the bias, gently skimming the hips and revealing a daring, completely bare back. She chose an evening jacket to match in a sweet boxy shape, for cooler evenings or after-show drinks.

After being served green tea in tiny porcelain cups, Belle was measured, and then they went back downstairs to choose her silk. Bewildered by all the gorgeous colours, Belle couldn't decide. After much deliberation and several changes of mind, she chose a plain but beautiful silvery silk shot through with the palest blue.

'Now for the food,' Rebecca said, as soon as Belle had paid.

'Aren't you buying fabric today?'

Rebecca shook her head. 'Not this time. I only paid for a new dress last week.'

As they left the shop, Belle surveyed the street.

'Come on, slow coach,' Rebecca called out, already ahead, but something had caught Belle's eye, or rather *someone*. On the opposite side of the road Edward was walking with a red-haired woman. Belle was about to lift a hand and wave to him but, deep in conversation, he hadn't seen her. As they walked on, Belle felt there was something familiar about the woman but couldn't quite put her finger on it. And then she realized the woman reminded her a little of her mother. But was that all? Could there be the slightest chance? Could it be possible she might be Elvira? She dismissed the thought as far too unlikely.

14

On Wednesday Belle wore a kingfisher-blue cotton dress and laughed when Oliver turned up in an identically coloured shirt that made the blue of his eyes sing. They took the tram and reached the tree-lined stretch of road where her parents had once lived. As they passed large colonial houses built all along one side and facing woodland on the other, she was keeping up with Oliver's long strides in silence. The buildings had been developed at the turn of the century for the great and the good and were set well apart from each other in extensive gardens with high fences. Through the gated driveways Belle saw Indian gardeners watering the lawns, while young Chinese women swept the terraces and wiped down wicker garden furniture.

'Did you see Norman Chubb?' Oliver asked suddenly, giving her one of his lopsided smiles.

She shook her head. 'He wasn't there. I spoke to an Inspector Johnson.'

'Ah, not too helpful, I imagine.'

'He told me a fire had destroyed all their records.'

He snorted. 'How convenient.'

'You don't believe it?'

He shrugged. 'What do you think?'

They had reached number nineteen.

'Almost there,' he said. 'Twenty-three, you said?'

As they walked on she nodded but couldn't speak. It felt weird to know her parents must have once walked down this street precisely as she was doing. What part, if any, was she about to play in their story?

When twenty-three loomed into sight, she stood rooted to the spot.

'But it looks abandoned,' she said, gazing at the tall palms shading the front of the house. 'I hadn't expected this.'

'I'll try the gate,' Oliver suggested, but closer inspection revealed a rusty padlock holding the ornate but heavily corroded iron gate in place. 'Another entrance, maybe?'

'Someone might still be living here.'

He puckered his chin. 'I guess, though it looks pretty unlikely.'

They both took in the blistering paintwork of the doors and windows and the stained plaster of walls that must have once been pristine white. A first-floor veranda circled the upstairs, now shattered in places, and wooden shutters hung at awkward angles, no longer protecting the grimy windows. In fact, they looked as if they had not even been closed when her parents departed.

'Must have been stunning once,' Belle said, and felt a wave of sadness.

'A mansion. They lived well.'

She glanced across at him and could see it in his eyes. 'I know you don't approve.'

'It isn't about individual people, it's the system I don't like. We come to these countries and take over, as if with a God-given right.'

She watched him walk beside rusting railings overgrown with greenery. After a moment he called out, 'There's an opening here.'

Uncertain about following a man she barely knew into this deserted place, a man with a reputation at that, her footsteps slowed. She had expected to see an occupied, immaculately maintained residence like all the others, had expected to observe it from the street.

'Will you go in first?' she said.

'Sure.'

This forgotten place unsettled her, but eventually she moved towards the opening through which Oliver had now vanished.

'Careful,' he called out. 'Brambles.'

She spotted he'd made something of a pathway through and, though she couldn't see him, he was now urging her to follow. Still she hesitated and after a few moments he burst back on to the street again.

She stared at him. 'You know, it seems wrong. As if I'll be spying on my parents' past life.'

He walked towards her and held out a hand. 'You can go through or we can turn back. Either way it's okay.'

She took a deep breath, while thinking, and then exhaled slowly. 'Let's go in.'

Entering the garden, they went up to and then stood on the steps leading to a once-grand but now sun-bleached front door: hardwood but in desperate need of oiling. At the top of the steps Oliver knocked and then thumped the door.

No answering sounds from within.

Suddenly energized, and jumping from the steps, Belle set off at speed, glancing back at him only once. 'Come on! I'm going to look round the back.'

He caught up and they ran, side by side, along a pitted gravel path leading right round the house. A dry pond followed its contours, completely choked by weeds, and at the back of the house they found a wide terrace overlooking extensive gardens.

'Dear God,' she said, stopping and staring at them. 'It's a jungle.'

Oliver was now peering through the one unboarded dusty window. Like the rest, it must have been boarded up too, but somebody had already prised the boards away. 'We're not the first, it seems.'

'Can you see anything?'

'Still some furniture inside.'

She joined him. 'Surely nobody can be living here?'

He glanced at her questioningly. 'I'll try one of these back doors. Okay?'

She acquiesced and he went for the larger one and then another smaller one to the side of the building. He turned the handle, but it didn't budge, so he put his shoulder to the peeling door and gave it a hard push. This time it shifted.

'Not locked,' he said. 'Jammed. I think I can free it.'

She gave him an encouraging smile.

He pushed several times and eventually the door flew open with a shrill creak.

'Come.' He held out a hand, but she hung back, pulling a reluctant face.

'There's nobody here,' he added. 'I'm sure of it.'

'It's not that . . . I don't know. I feel as if I'm prying.' She shrugged and gave him a wry smile.

'Like I said before, we can leave. And it may not have been your parents who last lived here.'

She shook her head. 'Something tells me it was.'

They entered the gloomy room.

'A torch,' he said, and dipped into his pocket. Suddenly a beam of light lit up a wall of grimy shelves at the back. As he pointed the light towards different parts of the room, Belle gasped. Cobwebs hung in heavy drapes from the ceiling light and darkened the corners too. A few broken chairs rested haphazardly on a rickety table and a heap of rubbish had accumulated on top of them. The tiled floor, blackened with a thick layer of dead insects and dust, needed scrubbing. Old newspapers, odd shoes and some filthy packaging lay abandoned, and the air smelt musty. Dead.

They wandered through the ground-floor rooms where plants from the exterior had invaded the interior, climbing and winding across the window frames. Exotic bindweed, Belle thought, or at least something that had been able to force its way through the narrowest cracks. So hard to imagine how this place must have looked before. The wooden flooring would have once been polished to a sheen but now they stepped over missing floorboards and had to watch out for the rotten ones. Forgotten furniture lined the walls of the high-ceilinged grand rooms at the front, heavy, difficult-to-shift stuff, so nobody had bothered. Here the windows hadn't been boarded and they could see that anything portable, like coffee tables or lamps, was gone. They spied more weeds creeping through small cracks in the internal plaster of the stained walls.

The smell of mildew and decay followed them from room to room and in each one Belle stood sniffing the air. Sad. So inexplicably sad. As soon as she'd realized the house was abandoned, she'd expected a place packed full of secrets which, considering how many years had passed, had been unlikely. But there wasn't even a hint of the awful tension that must have flooded the place, only a lingering melancholy.

Oliver had gone ahead but now came bounding back to her full of enthusiasm, and she found herself smiling as he ran a hand through his unruly hair. I can't help liking him, she thought, whatever Rebecca had said about him being one for the women. He was so alive. Freer, more open than the British colonials with their duty and honour and doing the right thing. For a moment she considered telling him about the anonymous note.

She glanced around again. It looked as if her parents had left in a hurry. Perhaps they'd had to flee? The thought gave her the shivers.

'All right?' Oliver said, and she saw that despite his easy-going manner there was a tenderness in his smile.

They were now standing in the huge entrance hall facing a sweeping staircase.

'Mahogany,' he said. 'Awful to see it like this. Shall we go up?'
She nodded.

Gingerly they made their way up to a large galleried landing with six open doors leading to sunlit rooms.

'This is better,' she said with a smile.

In the first room the windows were smeared with grime, but the place was still furnished with a large bed, no mattress, and two heavy-looking wardrobes. Belle imagined one of these rooms must have been her parents' bedroom. In the second room she saw glass doors opening on to the veranda. Maybe this was the one? She tried the handle and as the door opened with a squeak she stepped out, taking care to avoid holes in the veranda floor. The view was fabulous, and Belle visualized her parents standing in exactly the same spot while gazing out at what had once been their beautiful garden.

Back inside, Oliver had opened a door at the side of the room. 'Come and see,' he said.

She walked over and stood at the threshold of a small empty room leading to a bathroom. Could this room have been the nursery? There had been no sign of her mother in the house so far, but this? This was different. Here she felt her mother's presence so strongly it was hard to believe she wasn't there. There was something about it. Something scented.

Oliver had opened the fitted cupboard doors but found nothing within except some dried petals and leaves. He crushed them between his fingers and as they crumbled and fell, there was the scent.

'Herbs, I think,' he said, 'and roses, maybe.'

She joined him and surveyed the cupboard.

'What about that?' She bent down and pulled at the ivory handle of a narrow drawer at the bottom. It appeared to be locked. He took out a pocketknife from his jacket pocket and after a few minutes of jiggling managed to open the drawer. He pulled it partly open.

'Nothing,' he said.

'Let me try. I've got smaller hands.' Belle reached right into the back of the drawer and felt something soft that appeared to have been jammed there. She pulled gently and then more vigorously and brought out what must have once been a baby's white muslin square, yellowing now, and wrapped around something solid.

'Christ,' she said as she held it in her hand. 'This is so old.'

'What's inside?'

She gently unwrapped the muslin and, when she saw what she was holding, the tears came.

15.

Diana, Cheltenham, 1921

As the man in the blue mackintosh comes up the stairs I find myself desperately wishing that Simone were here. She gave me a gift for Elvira when I was feeling downcast – a beautiful silver rattle – and it was so pretty I believed her when she told me the dark times would pass. She'd been a nurse and was always seeking ways to look on the bright side. She'd know what to say to this mackintosh man – all I can think is to run and conceal myself in my bathroom. Even I know that wouldn't be the right thing to do, although I can't help feeling the madder I prove myself the better it will be for everyone else.

The man reaches the top of the stairs and holds out his hand. 'Mrs Hatton, I'm Doctor Williams.'

'I know who you are,' I say, recognizing the weaselly, grey-haired man with the watery pale-blue eyes. 'We've met. You're the madness man.'

'I am indeed, although we do tend to prefer the term psychiatrist. Shall we?' And he points at my door, then smiles, arms folded, studying me.

We go in and he settles himself on one of the two chairs beside my coffee table.

The room feels suddenly stuffy and I want to look out of the window, so I walk over there and face away from him, my back stiff.

'I'm wondering how you are coping with the new medication. Although a little bitter, the Veronal is usually tolerated better than the bromides, and has less of that strong unpleasant taste. You are taking it daily?'

I twist round and nod. Well, everybody lies, don't they?

'It makes me feel drowsy,' I then say, remembering the effect the few times I really had taken it.

'Anything else?'

I shake my head. He looks at me and I think, *I don't trust you.*

'You have been unlucky,' he says.

I take an angry step towards him. 'Unlucky!? Is that what we are calling losing a child, now? "Oh, how unlucky, well never mind, you can always have another, can't you?"'

'You did have another.'

'That's not the point.'

'Won't you come and sit down with me? Tell me what the point is?'

I think about it. Strange, isn't it, how you can usually tell who to trust? This conversation does nothing to make me change my mind.

'Mrs Hatton?' He smiles a difficult, uneasy smile as if smiling is a little alien to him.

'Very well.' And I come to sit opposite him with my back to the window, all the while scrutinizing his face. Pleasant enough, I suppose, but drearily ordinary. In a studied, delicate manner, he lifts and then settles his spectacles on his nose again. How I long for beauty, I think, but still manage to smile at him.

'Your husband tells me you haven't been out.'

I try to contain my response but, in the end, lose the battle and stand up, bristling with irritation. 'Telling tales again? Well, he's wrong. I've been out to the park. Often, as it happens. I like to watch the nannies pushing their perambulators.'

'Really?'

I feel his irritation although he doesn't show it visibly.

'You think I'm lying?' I snap, for how can I possibly tell him the truth? How can I say I dare not go out, that even the thought of it makes me shake so much I must sit on the floor and cling to the legs of my chair to make me feel I am still attached to the earth?

He shakes his head. 'Of course not. Won't you sit down again?'

He is too careful with me, wary even, and I don't like the feeling of . . . of his condescension, that's it.

'I'm fine,' I say and move towards the door, but with my head half turned, watching for his reaction.

He clears his throat and does that ghastly smile of his again.

'Would you answer my question, please? When have you been out?'

I gawp at my feet and mutter. 'I've been to the park. Nobody saw me go, that's why they don't know.' I realize I sound like a petulant child and try to moderate my tone. 'Sorry, I didn't mean to be cross.'

He stares at the floor before glancing up at me again. 'These voices, what do they say?'

I hesitate in surprise. No one has pressed me on this before, so I sit. Usually they want me to pretend they aren't real. 'Oh, you know . . .'

'But I don't, that's why I asked.'

'They say different things.'

I don't want to tell him sometimes they frighten me, or laugh at me, or accuse me of dreadful things. Sometimes they whisper, and I must stand perfectly still because I have to hear them. I absolutely have to. There's nothing worse than knowing they're there but being unable to properly hear the venom they spout.

He twists his mouth, and there is a longish silence until he speaks again.

'I wanted to have a word with you about the Grange. As you may already know, it's a private institution at Dowdeswell. I –'

So, there it is. What he has really come for. How I need Simone now. When, oh when is she coming?

'No,' I burst in. 'I won't go.'

'Nobody is forcing you to go. It's simply that your husband and I feel you are too much alone up here.'

'And if I refuse?'

16.

The golden pink of the cool early morning had turned into a blisteringly hot day. Belle felt dizzy and a sickly wave of heat passed through her as she stared at the silver and ivory baby's rattle. The silver ball had tarnished a little but not as much as one might have expected, and the ivory handle, though yellowed, remained intact. She held it to the light.

'Look, an inscription.' She traced the tiny letters with her fingertips. 'Three hearts and the letters, *D* and *D* and *E*. Diana, Douglas and Elvira. My mother, father and sister.'

On one side of the silver ball was a tiny dog with the words *Bow-Wow-Wow*. The other side was engraved with a bird and the words *Who Killed Cock Robin*. She supressed a sob. This lost sister had suddenly become so real.

Oliver touched her hand gently. 'Let's go outside. You need air.'

She was glad to leave the damp heat of the house. Outside it was still hot but a little fresher. She regarded the tangled profusion that had no doubt once been a glorious garden.

'Is this all there is, do you think?'

He shrugged. 'Hard to say.'

Her eye was drawn to a gap in the bushes that seemed to create a barrier at the back of the long grass.

'Do you think . . .'

'It might lead somewhere?'

The sun was now burning her neck and she could feel it on her back too through her thin cotton dress. As they began to pick their way across the grass, something about being in the garden tugged her into the past. She saw her mother walking in front of her, bathed in sunlight and heading for the same gap between the bushes. Belle longed to lay a hand upon her shoulder and speak her name. Might everything have been different had she been able to?

The moment passed.

Oliver was ahead of her now, pulling back the ivy and overgrown vegetation. 'There's a path,' he called out in an excited voice.

As Belle followed him she hardly felt the pain as sharp thorns in the dank undergrowth scratched her bare arms and legs. Then, as beating wings alerted her to the presence of birds, she could feel herself getting closer to something that mattered.

Beyond the path, as she came out into the light, her gaze wandered over the expanse. They attempted to circumnavigate this part of the garden, but their progress was impeded by a wilderness of tropical plants. Trees too, lots of trees. He pointed out a large, sprawling acacia, its marbled trunk seeming to twist and turn in the air until it finished in a spreading crown that shaded the ground beneath.

'What's that one?' she asked, pointing at a tree thirty feet high at least and about forty feet wide.

'They call it the Pride of Burma. It's an orchid tree.'

She nodded and continued to inspect the garden, brushing the buzzing insects from her hair and eyes. Over in one corner a vine with red flower clusters crept upwards through the canopy of another tree in search of the sun. And beyond lay the remains of a building that looked black and broken.

'Must have been a summer house,' she said. 'Destroyed by fire. What a shame.'

A little further on she gasped at the sight of a tree with the largest girth of all.

'The tamarind,' Oliver said.

She gaped at the bright-green feathery foliage of the massive tree, at least eighty feet high. Its trunk had divided into three which meant the canopy had grown gigantic. So much shade for a baby lying in its pram.

He noticed she'd gone quiet. 'You okay?'

She nodded and walked closer to the burnt-out summer house. Oliver followed and began to rip away the creeper.

'You won't find anything there,' she said.

'Maybe not.' But he carried on, only stopping to wipe the sweat from his brow.

'I'll help,' she said. He'd rolled up his sleeves and the sight of his tanned, muscled arms as he worked made her smile. It had been so long since she'd enjoyed being with a man as much as this, and she realized his presence was helping her feel grounded – to have been here on her own might have been a little too much. There was more to him than the easy-going man she'd first met, and that pleased her.

As she stood gazing at the secret garden the noises of the city faded and only the sounds of the birds accompanied Oliver as he worked at pulling more of the creeper away. Feeling soporific, and forgetting her previous offer to help, she watched drifts of yellow-winged butterflies hover over the bushes at the back of the garden, where she spotted the remains of a gate, now smothered by climbing plants. Just then she heard Oliver shout her name.

She ran over and he held out a blackened metal box.

'Wedged in the earth beneath what remained of the floorboards.' He passed it to her.

She attempted to open the lid, but it wouldn't give.

'I've got the pocketknife,' he said. 'Might do it.'

'Are you actually prepared for everything?'

'Depends. I might be.' And he gave her a wide smile.

He passed the pocketknife to her and gradually she prised the lid open. When she glanced inside, the first thing she saw was a yellowing photograph of her parents with their arms wrapped around each other, broad, happy smiles on their faces.

She felt a hot flash of resentment battling with the longing she'd always tried so hard to hide. She did not love her mother. She had persuaded herself of it. Steeled herself. Nor did she care that her mother did not love her. But she'd been living with a lie.

As she thought of Diana, she stared at the gently drooping branches of the tamarind tree and shaded her eyes from the narrow shafts of piercing sunlight streaming between its leaves too brightly. The intensity of the light, plus the loud buzzing in the air, made her feel strange and she reached out a hand to Oliver.

As he held her hand for a moment, there was one thing she knew without question. Whatever had happened in this garden, whatever had happened beneath this self-same tree, it had changed her mother, and in doing so it must have altered her father too. She had a sudden uneasy sense of how her mother might have once been before the tragedy destroyed her life and her mind. She wrapped her arms around herself, feeling the ache of it because, however much she might have thought otherwise, however much she'd longed for it to be otherwise, their story *was* her story too.

17.

Diana, Cheltenham, 1921

The longer I am not myself, the harder it is for Douglas. He still smells the same as he always has, of Trumper's Wellington Cologne. I'd know the mix of cumin, orange and neroli anywhere. But we don't speak to each other now except to argue and I have no chance of winning against his logical mind. That cuts deep. The more I think about it, the more the thoughts tangle in my head. To make them stop I go down the stairs and out to the garden by the French windows in the drawing room. Despite the biting cold of the afternoon, it soothes me to see the birds ruffling their feathers in the birdbath on the terrace. I love my birds. Their song lifts my spirit and I even dare to hope a little. Hope. How wonderful is that little word?

Maybe things can change. Maybe I really will remember what happened in Golden Valley. And if I do, maybe it won't be as bad as I fear.

The sun is fragile today, pale behind a wispy grey sky. How strange that on this chilly winter's day, with even a forecast of snow, all I can think of is the bright yellow sun of that Rangoon day. Huge, round, blisteringly hot. It still blinds me now and, even though I close my eyes against it, it remains trapped behind my eyelids.

As for Douglas. Well, one minute I was loved and then I was not. He hides it, of course, but I see beneath the anxious smiles and brevity of his words to the place where grief has burrowed deep inside him. He is empty now too, full of holes, but I remember his lips on mine and the tenderness in his eyes and the way he loved me until I felt we had dissolved into one being.

I tell myself I want to remember what happened, I truly do, but whenever I try a band of pain circles my head and my mind becomes a slippery mess. All the doctors say the same thing. Whatever happened, I cannot allow myself to see it and have blocked it from my conscious mind.

I still dream though. And yet the dreams provide no clarity, as each one is different from the last. I have no recollection of returning to England. All I remember is that one minute I was under house arrest in Rangoon and then the next, or so it seemed, I was back here.

18

For the visit to the Pegu club on Sunday, Edward wore a well-cut pale linen suit and Belle a blue-and-white-spotted day dress, cinched in at the waist by a red leather belt. She'd tied back her hair and topped it off with a white wide-brimmed hat with a red ribbon to match the belt. Although she hadn't fully decided what she felt about Edward she still wanted to look her best and create the right impression.

On their way they passed the usual colonial edifices, their facades decorated with ornate arches, corbels and pilasters – buildings absolutely reinforcing power and invincibility over others. Then there came the private houses with deep eaves designed to provide shade from the harsh Burmese sun for delicate English skins.

'Pretty wonderful, isn't it?' Edward said, and before she had time to collect her thoughts, he went on to enquire about how she was getting on, so she recounted her interview with Inspector Johnson.

He narrowed his dark eyes, frowned and then thought for a moment. 'He's a sound chap but you really should have consulted me first. I'd have given you a formal introduction. I have considerable contacts, as you can imagine.'

'You work for the police?'

'Not exactly. I'm advisor to the Commissioner, among other things. In any case, you'll be pleased to hear I've done a bit of digging.'

'And?' she said, thinking he looked pleased with himself.

'It seems your mother was acting strangely around the time of the baby's disappearance and that gave rise to accusations of guilt and her eventual house arrest.'

'How strangely?'

He puckered his chin then rubbed it as if reluctant to speak.

'Please?'

'I believe she was discovered scrabbling about in the earth while in her nightdress.'

He went on to explain that her hands and nails had been black with earth, which led to the suspicion she had been searching for the spot where she had buried the baby. Belle pictured the awful scene, her mother on her knees and weeping.

'The ayah reported that the child had cried incessantly, and the child's distress disturbed your mother terribly, so much so that more than once she'd flown into a rage. The inference was she had tried to quieten the baby but went too far.'

Belle shook her head in dismay.

'The police dug up the entire garden and found nothing save for a single pink baby's bootee.'

'Elvira's?'

'I imagine so. I haven't been able to establish what eventually happened, except that your parents went back to England. Didn't even sell the house before they left.'

'So, my mother was proven innocent?'

He shook his head and winced. 'Not exactly. The case remained open for a while. It seems nothing was proven one way or the other.'

'Why did they let her go?'

'I reckon the whole affair must have been causing such a stink the powers that be concluded it was the only thing they could do. There was no solid evidence, or at least I haven't come across any. I think whatever there may have been was swept under the carpet a long time ago.'

Belle sighed.

'Inspector Johnson told me a fire had destroyed the police records.'

'Correct.'

'So how do you know all this?'

He raised his brows. 'As I said, I have considerable contacts.'

She nodded. 'I went to see the house, you know.'

He looked surprised. 'On your own?'

She shook her head, but for reasons she couldn't explain didn't want to tell him she had gone with Oliver. Nor did she reveal their plans to meet again on her next day off. 'It was in a terrible state,' she said instead.

'Yes, I believe so. You realize it may well be yours now.'

'Really?'

'As I said, they didn't sell it.'

'How do you know?'

He hesitated for a second. 'Pretty much common knowledge. You'd have to go through all the legal channels at the office of the registrar, of course, prove you are who you say you are and provide a certificate of your father's death, that sort of thing.'

Belle struggled to take it in. One minute she was a stranger here and the next she could be the owner of that huge house.

'You'll probably want to sell up. Just tip me the wink if you do. I wouldn't mind buying it myself. Of course, it needs work. A lot of work.'

She nodded and, wanting to change the subject, asked who she might be likely to meet at the Pegu club.

On the outskirts of town, they approached the club. Belle saw a vast Victorian building, surrounded entirely by trees and encircled by a shady veranda, the air heavily scented with the flowers of jasmine and frangipani. Edward explained it had been built predominantly of teak in the 1880s to serve British army officers and civilian administrators. And it had the reputation of being one of the most well-known gentlemen's clubs in Southeast Asia, rather like the Tanglin club in Singapore.

'Members only,' he added, 'and mostly senior government

and military officials and prominent businessmen. Sadly, it's a bit of a relic these days. Times change, don't they, and sometimes more's the pity.'

'Gentlemen only?'

'Not any more, at least not at weekends. People used to refer to this place as the real seat of power in Burma.'

They went into the clubhouse where highly polished parquet floors shone and large ceiling fans blew warm air about.

With a hand firmly on the small of her back, Edward shepherded her past a billiards room and then a large dining room and into a dark but cosy room at the back of the building. She took in the bored faces of middle-aged men puffing on cigars or hiding behind their newspapers while their wives smiled blandly at the air and sipped their iced gin.

When they had made themselves comfortable, both seated on worn brown leather armchairs, he suggested she try the Pegu Cocktail before lunch.

'It's our signature drink. Gin and Roses lime juice.'

She nodded, having already worked out that being teetotal in this country was an impossibility, but she vowed to limit herself to one drink only. She hadn't got drunk with Rebecca the day they'd gone to Chinatown, didn't dare go that far, but she'd downed two bottles of beer and that had been enough.

The drinks arrived served in chilled glasses with a slice of lime and when Belle sipped she thought it tasted of grapefruit. 'Very refreshing,' she said as the gin fizzed in her blood and went straight to her head.

While they fell silent for a few minutes, Belle glanced around at the clientele. They were exactly as Edward had described and even on a Sunday were dressed formally. The few women, wearing mainly high-necked and noticeably drab cotton florals, were talking in hushed tones, while the louder hum of voices was decidedly male.

'The club was named after the Pegu, a Burmese river,' he said.

'Is this place only for the British?'

He frowned. "Fraid we're somewhat old-fashioned. No Asians. I know things are changing and there are those who feel we should change with them, but . . .' He spread his arms out, palms uppermost, in a shrug.

She thought of what Oliver might say. This would be exactly what he detested about the British colonials, and perhaps he'd be right. She didn't condone the blatant anti-Burmese attitude either and she could see these insular people felt obligated to uphold British power and superiority, no matter what.

Edward cleared his throat and ran a finger around the inside of his shirt collar. If she hadn't known better, she could have sworn he looked a bit nervous.

'Look here, Belle,' he said, 'I was rather hoping you'd allow me to take you for a quiet dinner one evening. Just the two of us.'

Surprised, she stared at him.

'Get to know each other better,' he said with a broad smile on his face. 'Would that be so bad? On your next evening off?'

'No . . . I mean, of course it wouldn't . . . it's just . . .' She didn't finish her sentence.

'Or maybe you'd prefer to accompany me to the next dinner at the Governor's residence?'

She began to reply but Edward gave her an apologetic look as he rose to his feet. 'Ah, here's old Ronnie Outlaw. He may be able to help you.'

Belle stood up too.

The man who approached the table was clearly retired. He walked with a slight limp and carried a silver-tipped cane. A huge grey moustache made up for the lack of hair elsewhere, but he stood to attention as Edward clapped him on the back and then explained that Belle was hoping to meet people who might have known her parents, the Hattons, back in the day.

Ronnie Outlaw narrowed his watery blue eyes as he shuffled into an armchair. 'Knew them slightly, but was posted in

Mandalay back then, so our paths didn't often cross. Had something of a bad end here?' He raised his brows and glanced at Edward, who nodded. 'Upset a few important people with his rulings when he was presiding over the chief court?'

Edward nodded again.

'So where are you from, young lady?' Ronnie continued.

'Cheltenham,' she said, with as much grace as she could summon.

'Ladies' College?'

She nodded but all the time was wondering whom her father had upset.

Ronnie was silent for a few seconds and Belle wondered if that was all he'd reveal, but then his eyes suddenly lit up. 'Tell you what. When we did eventually move to Rangoon, my wife, Florence, became a friend of this woman, Simone something . . . Simone . . . drat it, what was her name? Doctor's wife. Anyway, I'm almost certain this Simone was close with your mother.'

'Do you know where she lives?'

'Not the foggiest, but I think Florence still maintains a correspondence. Tell you what, why not get Edward's sister to take you up to Gossip Point. All the girls meet there. You can have a good chinwag with Florence – tell her you went to school at Cheltenham and she'll be your friend for life.'

'Oh?'

There was the slightest pause before he spoke again. 'Our daughter, Gracie, was a boarder there for four years.'

'Does she live in Cheltenham now?'

Ronnie looked down at the floor and then back up at her. 'Sadly, no. Came down with malaria over here. Never made it past fifteen.'

'I'm so sorry.'

'Thank you.'

There was a silence during which Belle wondered what to say. Luckily Edward stepped in, thanking Ronnie for his help and offering him a stengah, a drink made of equal measures of whisky and soda water, served over ice.

'Gloria tells me you have contacts in the entertainment world,' she said after Ronnie had finished his drink and then left them alone.

'Yes, yes I do. I can put in a word for you if you like.'

She grinned at him. 'I'd like that very much. You know, for after Burma.'

'So, tell me your dream?'

'To travel and keep on singing for my supper, of course.'

'I like an independent girl,' he said with a laugh, and leant forward to give her shoulder a squeeze.

As Belle turned into the corridor leading to her room, she paused. She'd asked Edward to drop her a short distance from the hotel, to carve out a little time to think. Too hot, it had been a mistake. So far, apart from Rebecca, nobody knew about the anonymous note, but it was still on her mind. The fortune teller had told her that the question she'd asked about who she should trust had been the wrong question and that she would go on a journey soon. So far, no sign of that. Probably a load of bunkum anyway.

She'd hoped for a breath of fresh air, but in the sweltering climate she ended up staggering back with a sweat-sodden dress. The afternoons were utterly impossible. It was little wonder most of the British slipped home for a nap, although the heat still seeped through even the thickest walls. Before Edward had left he'd reminded her of his invitation to accompany him to a dinner at the Governor's residence. When she had thanked him and agreed to go he had looked genuinely delighted and said he'd let her know the date in due course. She decided she might tell him about the note then.

19

On her next evening off, Belle stood waiting for Gloria in the hotel lobby. They were about to be driven to Gossip Point, although Belle had mixed feelings about it. While she wanted to know if Florence Outlaw was in touch with her mother's friend, Simone, at the same time she was feeling weary of the whole thing. Earlier in the day she'd called at the offices of the *Rangoon Gazette* where she had agreed to meet up with Oliver and had been disappointed to learn he was out of town on a story and they didn't know when he'd be back.

Think you know who to trust? Look harder . . .

She had trusted Oliver, hadn't she? Liked him a lot. What about Gloria?

Belle shook her head, then sat on one of the striped sofas, sipping the iced water she'd ordered, and before long her friend was waving jovially from the doorway in a flurry of hat, gloves, high heels and perfume. Her dress today was scarlet with a wide white collar and a nipped-in waist.

'Darling. Do hurry. We'll miss all the good stuff,' she called to Belle. And then added in a stage whisper, 'Though to be honest with you, I only go because if I didn't it would be me the old biddies would be gossiping about.'

Belle smiled ironically. 'Surely not! Whatever could they find to say about you?'

Gloria laughed. 'Stick with me, kid, and I'll tell you.'

The doorman held open the door for them and as soon as they were settled in the back of the car they carried on their conversation.

'Actually,' Belle said, 'you did promise to tell me your history if I went to the swimming pool party. I kept my side of the bargain.'

Gloria rolled her eyes. 'So I did. And all that happened was that you met up with that Donohue man.'

'Oliver.'

'The very one. I grant he is outrageously attractive . . . those come-to-bed blue eyes! I admit I did have a minor flirtation – haven't we all? But he's not . . .' She paused.

'Not what?'

'One of us.'

'I didn't think you'd care.'

Gloria looked scornful. 'Well, I don't, not really. But I wouldn't spend too much time with him. You have seen him again, haven't you?'

Belle observed her keenly. 'And you know how?'

'The irony about Rangoon is that in a place as full of secrets as this, it's also impossible to do anything without people finding out.'

Belle frowned. 'Why would anyone give a hoot?'

'Oliver Donohue has a reputation.'

'With the ladies, I know.'

Gloria laughed. 'Good Lord. That's par for the course. Everyone here has affairs. It's practically mandatory. No, I wouldn't want to put the kibosh on a budding friendship, but he's been mixed up in some shady business.'

'Shady? What kind?'

Gloria shrugged. 'It's only rumour but shall we say you could be putting yourself in danger.'

'You can't just say that.'

'I really don't know any more, though my brother might.'

'Did you know Edward asked me to have dinner with him?'

'He likes you.'

'But he's married.'

Gloria roared with laughter. 'And?'

Belle felt herself redden.

'Come on, darling. His marriage is in name only. And he's an important man. You could do a lot worse.'

'Than be someone's mistress?'

'Don't be so strait-laced. It's only dinner.'

'Did he ask you to work on me?'

'Now that's plain mistrustful.'

'Anyway, in the end I agreed to dinner at the Governor's residence.'

Gloria's eyes widened. 'Well, you are honoured.'

They slipped into silence and then the car pulled up at the lakes and the driver opened the back doors. As she climbed out, Belle gazed about her. She'd already discovered Rangoon sprang to life soon after tea, with or without condensed milk, and today was no exception. The sun had lost its fury, but the sky was still a glorious blue and from a pavilion in the distance the sounds of a military band greeted the women as they arrived. As more women alighted from chauffeur-driven cars, it was clear that these were the wealthiest and most privileged of their type. Gossip Point really was in a stunning spot overlooking the Royal Lakes, and at a rough guess Belle thought at least twenty women were already assembled while dozens of Indian gardeners were still at work.

'I can't believe how green it is,' Belle said, gazing at the vast expanse of emerald lawns where birds like English starlings hopped about. 'Every time I think I'm getting used to things, something new surprises me.'

'They use water from the lake to keep it green.'

Trees in various stages of bloom surrounded the huge lake, and a profusion of flowers and vines lining the banks shone vibrantly against the astonishing stretch of blue water.

'What do the women talk about?' Belle whispered as they began to move forward.

'Often it's the latest news. You know the kind of thing. What's happening across the world. It helps us keep in touch. Local news too of course.'

'Not more personal?'

'Why don't we say hello and you'll find out.' Gloria gave her shoulder a little squeeze as if to encourage her to move forward. 'They won't bite.'

Most of the women wore pretty hats and were dressed fashionably in discreetly patterned slim-line dresses with mid-calf hemlines and elbow-length sleeves. Sadly, the style didn't really suit some of the larger more mature ladies who were a good deal older than Gloria and who, Belle felt, would look better if they didn't slavishly follow the latest styles. Among the group there were a few younger women who, like colourful butterflies, hovered and then moved on.

'Darling, this is Annabelle Hatton,' Gloria said again and again as she introduced Belle to one woman after another.

When they seemed to settle in a small group of five the conversation turned to the story of a barmaid.

'Deplorable,' one of the older women proclaimed as she fanned herself with increasing speed, unable to conceal the tone of glee in her voice.

'Think of it. An Englishwoman soliciting in the street,' another added.

'Whatever next. And did you hear . . . I can hardly bear to say it.'

As the woman paused Belle could tell she was desperate to steal a march on her friends.

'Oh, do tell, Wendy.'

'You can't keep us in suspense.'

Wendy looked from one to the other. 'Well, I have it on good authority she was soliciting Indian coolies.'

While the other women gasped, Gloria winked at Belle, who couldn't help smiling.

After that Gloria steered Belle away, towards a small round

woman who had arrived a minute ago and was making her way to the water's edge.

'Florence,' Gloria called out, waving madly, and then whispering to Belle, 'It *was* Florence Outlaw you wanted to speak to? Edward mentioned it.'

Belle nodded.

Florence Outlaw had grey hair neatly pinned up and a soft, rosy complexion. She gave Gloria a broad smile as she made her way over with a slow, rolling gait, accompanied by a little white dog on a lead.

'Florence, this is my lovely new friend, Belle.'

'My husband mentioned you. Something about Simone. Such a pretty woman. Amber eyes, you know. So unusual.'

'Your husband said you were still in touch,' Belle said. 'I'd love to meet her.'

'Oh, my dear, she's not here.'

Belle frowned. 'But she is alive?'

Florence looked happy. 'Thank goodness, yes, but didn't Ronnie tell you, she's been back home for some time?'

'Home?'

'England. The Cotswolds. I wrote down the address for you.' She delved into a large tapestry bag and rifled through the contents. 'Now where the devil is it?'

'She knew my mother well?' Belle had no memory of her mother ever having any friends.

Florence glanced up and nodded. 'Best friends, although we're going back a bit. Heavens, do you mind holding the bag open while I search?'

Belle held the bag and after a few moments Florence located a folded piece of paper. 'Hurrah! At last. Here you are, dear. I'm sure she won't mind you writing. Just mention my name.'

'Thank you. I'd be keen to ask if she remembers what happened when my sister disappeared.'

A little later Belle found herself without Gloria and in a small group of women who were discussing the few eligible men who still lived in Rangoon. One of them turned to Belle and, glancing at her ring finger, stared witheringly.

'Dear me. Not engaged yet?'

'No,' Belle replied with pride. 'I'm a singer at the Strand.'

The woman visibly paled. 'Oh no. No, no. Won't do at all. Find yourself a husband double quick. You don't want to be working for a living, although if you really must I'm sure we could find you a family.'

Belle frowned. 'Sorry, I –'

'A family who require a governess, dear, something respectable.'

One of the other women nodded, and Belle, laughing at the loathsome old-fashioned attitudes, quickly took her leave and walked over to the water's edge. She would write to Simone that night and hope she'd be more enlightened than these women.

She noticed the flush of rose in the sky and as a flock of black birds crossed the lake she glanced at the sun setting behind the golden Shwedagon Pagoda. The pagoda, now a deep burnished copper, enchanted her and seemed as if it were a living thing, changing colour depending on the time of day. Completely absorbed by the spectacle, she continued to look and only gradually became aware people were bidding each other farewell – the sunset a signal for the women to return to their cars. She watched the sky, lilac at the top, then yellow, orange, pink, and finally the deepest burgundy. This is the colour of Burma, she thought. Then she spotted Gloria surrounded by fireflies flashing like tiny diamonds in the growing darkness and she watched the older woman's languid swaying gait as they walked towards each other. Above them the emerging stars seemed twice the size they had been in England.

Think you know who to trust? Look harder . . .

On the evening Belle met Edward to go to the dinner at the Governor's residence, she hoped the gown she'd had made up in the Chinese quarter was smart enough. The evening dress Edward wore made the most of his slim, athletic build, somehow accentuating the distinguished slice of silvery grey hair at his temples. She hadn't really been terribly keen to go, and had worried that it might be stuffy, but when she and Edward arrived at the opulent building it totally confounded her – and not in an especially good way.

'Completed in 1895,' Edward said, noticing her astonishment as they got out of the car. 'The architect, Henry Hoyne-Fox, described it as being in the "Queen Anne Renaissance Style".'

She nodded and continued to stare up at the grand domed towers and extravagant architecture as they stood together. 'Do you like it?' she asked cautiously.

He roared with laughter. 'Like? No! I think it's the most hideous example of overwrought building I've ever seen.'

Despite her earlier reservations about coming, and appreciating his honesty, she laughed too.

'Shall we go in? There are drinks on the terrace I believe and then I have some news for you.'

'Why not tell me now?'

He hesitated but then inclined his head. 'It's a bit of a long story.'

'I don't mind.'

'Well, the thing is, a chap I know found a misfiled memo in the police records.'

He talked as they walked and he told her that at one point a Burman had been accused of taking the baby but was later released. However, it turned out the police must have found new evidence and decided to charge him after all, but before they could do so he had been killed in a motorbike accident.

'None of this appears to have been released to the press, but from what I can gather, there is a strong suggestion the police remained convinced he was involved in the baby's disappearance, at least in some way.'

'What was the evidence? Can I see the memo?'

'Unfortunately, we can't allow it. Police records protected, and so on. But I've told you everything you need to know. Soon after that your parents went home to England.'

'And that was that?'

Studying her at arm's length, he inclined his head in agreement. 'Yes. That was that.'

She wanted to assent but something stopped her. 'Except it wasn't, was it? I still don't know what really happened.'

He nodded. 'But doesn't it put your mind at rest to at least know your mother was released without charge?'

'Yes, of course,' she said, but couldn't help thinking about Elvira.

He moved closer and held her hand in his. 'Look, I do wonder how you can hope to find out what happened to your sister all these years later when the police drew such a blank at the time. Does it matter so much to you?'

'Well, no, at first it didn't but now . . .' Her voice trailed off.

She could see him suppress a smile. 'Now, young lady, no buts.'

He'd spoken cheerily and there was a short silence before she spoke again.

'Thanks for this,' she said eventually.

He gave her a broad grin and she found herself warming to him. 'Now, I rather think it's time to enjoy the evening, don't you?'

She hadn't been expecting to have fun at such a formal dinner but to her surprise she was enjoying being with Edward. As well as knowing everyone, he was a bright, intelligent man, extremely attentive and excellent company. However, as soon as it was over she knew she would have to face the challenge of writing to Simone again. It was problematic writing to someone she didn't know and, so far, she'd made three futile attempts. All of them ending crumpled up in the waste-paper basket. Tonight, she would be straightforward and simply ask her what she remembered about her mother and the events of 1911.

20.

Diana, Cheltenham, 1922

When Simone walks through the door, I feel myself welling up. Although I had vowed I wouldn't cry, I am so relieved to see her I can't stop. She drops her bag on the floor and within a moment I'm enfolded in her arms. I can't explain how grateful I am that she still cares.

'Diana,' she says and, pulling away gently, scrutinizes me. 'How are you?'

'Come to the window,' I say, wanting her to understand how this precious window on to the world is my lifeline and I don't want anyone to take it away. 'My whole world is out there.'

We walk over to look out at the park. It's turned into a beautiful spring day with a generous blue sky and fluffy white clouds. So still. So soothing. Like the sea on a sweet summer's day when the waves roll in so lazily the whole world feels at peace. Every summer I remember our cook packing a hamper filled with cream buns, cucumber sandwiches, chicken pies and jam tarts. All my favourite things to take down to the beach at Bantham in Devon.

I glance at Simone's perfect straight-nosed profile as she stands waiting for me to say something.

'Have you spoken to Douglas?' I ask, hoping the answer is no. 'I have.'

'So, he has told you about the dreaded Grange?'

She nods and puts an arm around my shoulders. 'Darling, don't you think it might help to be away from here for a while? I don't think being cooped up for hours on your own is doing you much good.'

I scowl at her, more aggressively than I intended. 'I'm not going.'

'It might help. You'd receive expert nursing care. There'd be things to do.'

'Basket work,' I snort and shake my head. I don't tell her I've heard about these terrible places where husbands send their once-loved wives. 'I would be left to die.'

'That can't be true. Douglas wouldn't let it happen.'

I try to halt it, but pain rips through my chest. 'Douglas wants rid of me and you know what he's like. Once he's decided on something he never changes his mind.'

'Darling, he doesn't want rid. He loves you.'

I look for the truth in her tone and shake my head again. For the first time I notice the grey in her blonde hair. 'I'm so sorry about Roger,' I manage to say. 'He was a good husband.'

She nods. 'I miss him terribly.'

We exchange looks and I feel comforted that we still understand each other.

'He loved you,' I say.

'Yes.'

'And Douglas used to love me. Now he wants me locked away. I'm an inconvenience. They want something to call my illness, so they say I have psychotic depression, you know, because of . . .' I stumble over my words.

'Because of?' she says gently.

'The voices I hear.'

I stare at her. She's always been such a good friend to me so I reach out a hand. 'Talk to Douglas for me. Tell him I'm taking the Veronal.'

Her brow puckers. 'And are you? Truly?'

I can't lie to her and suck in my breath before I own up. 'It makes me feel terrible. But I will take it, I promise.'

'He's worried about you going off somewhere unaccompanied or wandering the house at night while everyone is asleep.'

I feel a flash of rage and my heart speeds up. 'I'm not a child.'

'He's afraid you might fall. At least at the Grange there would be somebody on duty.'

There is a short silence and I wonder what else she's thinking. Eventually she asks me if I feel awful all the time and I tell her it comes in waves. She smiles and looks hopeful.

There is a short silence while I wonder whether to speak.

'He had an affair,' I say eventually, and look into her beautiful amber eyes, so kind, so loyal, and wonder if she knew, but her hand flies to her mouth and she looks genuinely shocked.

'When I was pregnant with Elvira.'

'You never said.'

I think back to the day I confronted him when he came home smelling of another woman's scent and with an awful look of shame in his eyes. I'd thought he could do no wrong until then. At least he had the decency to look embarrassed at being caught out but, in a way, I wish I hadn't known because once he'd so diminished himself in my eyes I couldn't feel the same. There was always the feeling from then on that something had been broken. I don't know if Douglas felt it too. I suspect he did. But even when I screamed at him he wouldn't tell me who the woman was.

'It was the shame,' I say.

'His shame?'

'Both our shames. I was a woman who couldn't keep her husband.'

'So, did he confess? How did you find out?'

I shrug. I had suspected all the women in Rangoon, all but Simone, even that bloody awful woman, the Governor's wife. So damned self-righteous, the very worst kind of Englishwoman.

'All water under the bridge now,' I say. 'Lots of men had affairs, didn't they?'

Simone sighs.

'He used to write me a note every morning, you know, and

I'd find it in an envelope popped on to the tray when the silent-footed butler brought my early tea and toast.'

And, at the beginning, life had been sweet indeed. Nothing could touch us, cocooned together as we were. Douglas, my rock, my love, my everything. But in time I had felt horribly constricted, had begun to feel as if I couldn't breathe.

'Oh, those early days,' I whisper.

'You miss them and yet you don't.'

'That's it. That's it exactly.'

We are silent for a while.

'Darling, you're not even dressed,' Simone says at last, interrupting my thoughts. 'Shall I wash and set your hair, and then pick you out something pretty to wear? Maybe afterwards we could go out to the café in the park for afternoon tea.'

I smile at her and, although I am terrified, I tell her I couldn't ask for anything better. But going out? I breathe in. I breathe out. Breathe in. Breathe out. And then, in that moment, and entirely unexpectedly, I feel I might be able.

'How long is it since you were last out?'

'Weeks. Months maybe.'

'Too long. Darling, you really could do with someone to watch over you.'

'Maybe you could do it?' I laugh as if I hadn't really meant it.

She regards me carefully, choosing her words. 'Diana, I honestly believe you can get better. We underestimate what the mind can do.'

'You think?'

'I more than think. You'll see.'

I smile at her and a bubble of hope rises in me.

'There. You're already feeling better. I promise we will find a way. All you need is a better place of safety.'

Simone's cheerful presence has lightened my heart and, infused by the sudden startling wish for something new, I see the slanting shadows of the trees. *A place of safety.* Was there such a place?

21

After posting her letter to Simone and having braved the seething mass of rickshaws, cars, bullock carts and bicycles, narrowly escaping a collision with an electric tramway carriage, Belle arrived at the spectacular offices of the citadel-like Secretariat. This was the administrative seat of the entire colonial government. Set in extensive gardens on Judah Ezekiel Street, the sprawling complex of buildings was built of red brick in the Victorian style. Once inside, Belle faced a confusing labyrinth of halls and corridors. Each department was signposted, from Revenue to Judicial, to Sanitary, plus many, many more.

An army of clerks, secretaries, record keepers and so on scurried from one place to another, giving her brief and confusing directions while on the hoof, so it took Belle an age to locate the office of the registrar. She worried she'd be late for her meeting with Oliver. He'd turned up unexpectedly the night before to hear her sing and although the words on the note – *Think you know who to trust? Look harder* – had played on her mind, because they might well refer to him, they'd agreed to meet today for another visit to Golden Valley, this time with the keys.

When she finally located the registry, a bored, badly dressed man glanced up from his desk and indicated she should sit. Odd that crumpled suit, she thought, because his fingernails were carefully manicured, so he clearly cared about some aspects of his appearance. While she explained her situation, he didn't meet her eyes, his gaze resting on a spot inches above her right ear.

'You'll need your father's death certificate and his will.' He'd spoken quietly, in the way of people who force you to lean forward so you have to put in all the effort.

She withdrew the documents from her bag and passed them across the desk. He studied them and nodded.

'I see you are the sole beneficiary to his entire estate,' he said, his voice thin and bored.

She nodded, the emotion of dealing with her father's death once again catching in her throat.

'I need your birth certificate and passport to prove you are who you say you are.'

She pulled herself together. 'I have those.'

'And something to prove your father is the same Douglas Hatton as this one on the deeds.'

'How do I do that?'

He gave her an excruciating look, as if the whole experience of working at the registry was insufferable. 'Well, first, we need to conduct an official search for the land registration documents and the deeds. There may be a deed of sale attached which should include his previous address in England.'

'Can we look for it now?'

'There is a fee. And if everything is in order you will also need to prove your residence here.'

'I have a contract of employment.'

He nodded and as he bent his head to look at the will again she noticed a bald patch ineffectively disguised by a thin combover of hair.

'A contract of employment should suffice,' he said, looking up again.

'What about the keys to the house?'

'With the solicitor, I imagine. We will need to retain an authenticated copy of the will. Once we've located the deeds, the solicitor's name should be on the deed of sale. If the solicitor is also a notary public, he has authority to sign it off.'

'And I get an authenticated copy how?'

'The solicitor's clerk can do it.'

'Gosh, it's a lot to have to sort out. I was hoping to have the keys today.'

He gave her a condescending smile. 'Come back in a few days and we'll look at the registry details.'

Back at the hotel, unsure if Oliver had already been and gone, Belle waited beneath the porch. She was late, very late, but hoped he still might turn up. The Indian doorman noticed her pacing back and forth and offered to help. When she asked if he'd seen a tall man with piercing blue eyes and light-brown hair, he beamed at her.

'Mr Donohue?'

She grinned. 'You know him?'

'I do indeed. A good man. Got to the bottom of a burglary at my wife's shop when the police did nothing. Helped a lot of us local people get justice. As I say, a good man.'

He went on to tell her that Oliver had not been seen outside the hotel during the last few hours.

When three of the dancers came out, giggling and laughing, they greeted Belle with waves and smiles. Rebecca had been good for her word and Belle's relationship with the dancers had lost its sourness. She rolled her shoulders and waited a little longer, but then, feeling disappointed, was just turning to go back to her room when she heard Oliver call her name. She spun round and felt a burst of pleasure as she saw him striding towards her, more deeply suntanned than ever.

'Hello,' he said, blue eyes sparkling, she hoped, with the same satisfaction at seeing her that she was feeling at seeing him. 'My editor insisted on some last-minute changes. I didn't think you'd still be here.'

Even more relieved to see him than she'd expected to be, she smiled broadly.

'Shall we take the tram?' she said.

'Sure, let's make tracks.'

As they sat close together on the tram she felt his presence intensely and found it hard to articulate her thoughts. Was he feeling it too? Or was it only her? Either way she felt invigorated at his proximity, although a little bit shy too. She shifted a little to defuse the tingling sensation going on all over her skin and after a moment or two managed to explain she didn't have the keys. They could enter the same way as before and, while they were in the area, they might also find some neighbours to question. Whatever Edward had hinted about it being a waste of time, she increasingly wanted to find out what had happened to the baby. And you never knew, someone might remember something.

Although she was excited to see the house for a second time, Belle couldn't help thinking about her mother again. But not the one who lived in the upstairs room and who'd once woken her at midnight insisting they put on their wellington boots and slip out to the garden to cut flowers. Instead, a different and magical version of her mother occupied her imagination. She smiled at the thought and Oliver glanced at her.

'What?'

'Oh, silly memories. That's all.'

'I'm sure your memories aren't silly.'

You might not say that if you knew, she thought, as the mother of her imagination helped her with her arithmetic while they sat at the kitchen table together, teasing each other and laughing at the silly mistakes they both made. This mother made up delicious picnics they shared sitting on a tartan rug beside the lake, before throwing the crusts to the ducks and geese.

'You lived in the countryside?' Oliver said, interrupting her thoughts.

She shook her head. 'A town. A Regency town in Gloucestershire.'

'I grew up in the city too.'

She laughed. 'I don't think Cheltenham compares to New York. But we went to the countryside and sometimes to the sea.'

The only time she had actually been to the seaside in the summer was to stay with her grandfather in Devon. Her mother found the beach too untidy, the sand scratchy and too unforgiving, the sea too wild. And it had given her a headache, so they'd gone home early. *Home* for the week had been her grandfather's sweet little cottage in Bantham, although he was a quiet and solitary soul who wouldn't play games and spent most of the day alone in his study. They'd only gone there once again, and that had been for Christmas.

Oliver's voice broke into her thoughts again.

'We're here,' he said. 'You keep drifting off.'

Once inside the house, Belle felt suddenly awed. Everything was exactly as it had been the last time they had broken in and yet it was different too.

'You sure you're okay?' he said, picking up on her mood.

'Of course. I'm excited.'

But she wasn't simply excited. She was full of questions too. How had they kept so much from her? How was it possible she had never known she'd once had a sister? And now, because of what had happened here, her mother's illness began to make sense. Had she spent her whole life judging Diana Hatton unfairly?

'You never explained what happened to your mother,' Oliver was saying with such a perceptive look in his eyes. Had he known what she'd been thinking? He was certainly shrewd enough.

'I know your father died, of course,' he added.

Belle hesitated. This was not something she usually discussed.

He put a hand on her arm. 'Sorry. You don't have to.'

'It's all right,' she said, but all the same waited a little longer for her emotions to subside. They didn't and she continued to feel edgy as she glanced around her. The room smelt stale and it seemed as if her lungs were preventing her from breathing properly. For a moment she felt as she had done as a child when things became too hard to bear.

'She went,' she said rather sharply.

'Where?' he asked, unperturbed by her tone.

'Nobody knows.'

'Must have been tough for you.'

She looked right into his eyes. 'No. It was a relief. Well, mainly it was. Is that awful?'

He held her gaze and shook his head.

'And then she died. Eventually. My father was the one who told me.'

She paused, wishing she could shake off the wretched memory of the rainy day her father had passed on the news. True, it had been a relief in a way, and she'd never hinted how frequently she still dreamt of her mother standing at the foot of her bed with a strangely significant longing in her eyes. Nor did she ever reveal she'd woken day after day with wet cheeks. It would have upset her father to know the truth, and so she'd lied.

She dug her fingernails into her palms. 'Look, do you mind if we change the subject?'

'Of course. Shall we go outside?'

She had the sense he'd wanted to comfort her, hug her maybe, but she didn't want his pity. She'd never really come to terms with her conflicting feelings about her mother and doubted she ever would.

When she'd written to Simone the night before, a wave of homesickness had caught hold of her and an echo of it still lingered today. And yet there was no longer a home to go to, no longer a family to which she belonged. She was on her own.

As they made their way through the tangles of tropical plants surrounding the house, Oliver asked what she intended doing with the place once it was hers. The truth was, she had no idea.

Sell it at a knock-down price to Edward perhaps? He'd already expressed an interest and she hardly relished the responsibility of its restoration. Apart from anything else, how long was she likely to remain in Burma? Her plan had been to travel and keep on singing. And yet the house was so beautiful – or at least it could be.

She thought again of the letter she'd sent Simone. When she'd asked the clerk at the post office how long it would take to reach her, he'd said it was fortunate she'd used airmail paper as it would only require about nine days. By sea and rail, it would be at least fifteen, possibly even a month. So, she'd be unlikely to hear anything back for at least twenty days and that was assuming Simone replied quickly.

Once away from the house, she glanced at the little green birds lining the telegraph wires threading along the road, birds with yellow heads and long tails, looking so sweet. Despite her earlier unsettled feelings she now felt buoyant and relaxed. This place had done it . . . this place with its beautiful old houses and lovely gardens. But then she remembered something and in a flash her mood changed.

'My father upset someone important,' she said suddenly as the memory returned. 'An old boy I met at the Pegu hinted at it.'

'You went there?'

She nodded. 'With Edward de Clemente.'

The skin around his eyes tightened but he only asked if she knew what her father had done and who he had upset.

When she told him she wasn't sure, he hesitated as if he was deciding what to say and she felt there might be something he was keeping from her.

She spun around and took one last look at the house. 'I'll be back, you lovely old place,' she whispered, 'and then we'll work out what to do with you.'

'I think you've fallen in love,' he said.

She could feel herself blushing furiously.

They passed a middle-aged Indian man standing in front of the gate to the nearest house. A gardener, she thought, judging by his clothes.

She and Oliver exchanged glances and then stepped towards him.

'Good morning,' she said, and the man inclined his head. 'Does he understand me?' she asked Oliver, who just looked amused.

'Yes, madam, I speak English for many years now,' the man said.

She felt herself blushing again. 'Of course. I'm sorry. Do you mind me asking how long you have worked here?'

His smile was proud. 'All my life, madam.'

'So, you started here when?'

'As a boy. I was fifteen and so it must have been 1895.'

'Quite a while then.'

'Indeed.'

'I don't suppose you remember the time when a baby disappeared from the garden next door?'

He frowned and then with a solemn look he spoke. 'A terrible time it was. The police were everywhere.'

'And what did people think had happened?'

'Many of the British thought it was the lady herself.'

'And you? What did you think?'

He shook his head. 'I knew the poor lady. She was always polite to me, enquiring after my family and such. No, I never could believe such a thing of her.'

'So, what did you think happened to the baby?'

'I do not know, but the local Burmese people said the baby was taken by supernatural forces summoned by the angry family of a man the lady's husband had convicted.'

Oliver glanced at Belle and nodded. 'The Burmese are highly superstitious.'

'In what way?'

'Well, they believe in *nats*. Spirits, if you like. They erect magic-al devices outside their houses to prevent the evil spirits from entering.'

'But what exactly are *nats*?'

'Anything from a spirit living in a tree to a Hindu deity. We could probably find out if your father had ever been threatened with a *nat*.'

'Oh, come on, Oliver. What would be the point?' She turned to the gardener. 'Thank you for talking to me.'

He bowed, then opened the gate and walked through.

'So,' she said. 'What now?'

Oliver hesitated for a moment. 'Coffee at my place? I have something to show you.'

And I you, she thought. Intrigued, she said she'd be delighted.

His apartment was in a purpose-built Victorian block. The sit-ting room was painted a soft white and, equipped with rattan furniture, comfy emerald-coloured silk cushions and beautiful blue and green Persian rugs, felt unexpectedly homely, as if it had enjoyed a woman's touch. Four tall oriental-looking lamps stood in the corners of the room casting a soft patterned glow on to the parquet flooring. Billowing white curtains framed a fine view of tall trees in the street beyond, a polished coffee table sat in front of a sofa and a small desk was pushed up against one wall. Another wall boasted floor-to-ceiling shelves of teak packed tightly with books almost to overflowing. Pleased to be in his apartment, and smiling to herself, she felt at ease. She walked along the length of the shelves, glancing at the book titles and running a finger over their spines.

'You have eclectic tastes.'

'I have to in my game.'

'Game? Is that what journalism is to you? A sport?'

He grinned. 'You're very hard on me.'

She laughed. 'Am I?'

He went into another room, and she could hear the clunk of china and cutlery as he prepared their coffee. After a few minutes he came back carrying a tray with the coffee already poured into dainty white cups, accompanied by a selection of unusual biscuits, or maybe they were cakes.

He saw her looking. 'They're Indian. Try one.'

She picked one and bit into the scented sweetness.

'So what was it you wanted to show me?'

22.

Diana, Cheltenham, 1922

Douglas rarely comes to my room, but today he has, and I can't imagine what he wants. No, that's not at all true. He must be here to talk about the Grange. Again. I resolve to remain as calm as possible, give him no excuse to send me away, but in my agitation I can't stop walking back and forth.

'I've been talking to Simone,' he says, and I notice how stooped he has become. There had always been a hint of it because he is so tall, but now it's more pronounced.

'Oh?'

'She seems to think being here in this house is doing you no good.'

I stop in my tracks, chest constricting. 'I won't go to the Grange.'

He frowns. 'Don't glare at me, Diana. I understand you don't want to go but, my dear, I fear Simone is right. Your being here is not helping.'

I smell the hint of cumin and orange on his skin as I pass and I stare at his beautiful deep eyes behind those spectacles and the once dear face, but I don't speak. Why should I make it easy for him?

'It's not doing Annabelle any good either.' He pauses. 'I know you are suffering but she is too. I don't mean to be cruel, but I wonder if you realize she fears you? She insists on having her bedroom door locked at night and sometimes won't rest until she comes in with me.'

'Why?' I say, shocked to hear it.

'Oh, my dear, you must know she is scared when you wake her in the middle of the night with some madcap idea.'

'I merely thought it would be nice to pick some flowers.'

'That was only the most recent incident. There have been others and, darling, she's now a little girl who's too anxious to go to sleep. Our lovely child has become a terribly nervous little girl and it isn't fair. You must see.'

My eyes heat up because I know it's the truth. I've seen her helpless wide-eyed shock and it has frightened me.

'Things cannot go on as they are. If our daughter hears you about the house during the day she hides, makes herself scarce.'

I cover my face with my hands, not wanting to see him as he tells me this.

'Only last week Mrs Wilkes found her in the broom cupboard. The lock had jammed, and she'd been trapped in there crying her eyes out. I have my work and can't be here to watch Anna-belle. Mrs Wilkes is unable to stay for more than one night each week, so the upshot is Simone has suggested another possibility for you.'

I suck in air. Please. Please. Surely Simone hasn't betrayed me? Don't let him send me to the Grange.

He narrows his eyes and doesn't attempt to hide the despair I see in them. 'Please will you sit down, Diana. It's hard to concentrate with you pacing the room.'

Determined to maintain the right impression, I do as he asks and take the chair opposite.

He sighs deeply. 'Simone has kindly offered to care for you.'

'Here?'

He shakes his head. 'In her village.'

My heart lifts and I smile at him. 'Live with her, you mean? How wonderful.'

'No.'

'Then?'

'Let me explain. You know Simone was a nurse before she married and that her husband was a doctor?'

I nod, silently urging him to get to the point. Of course, I know.

'Her idea is for me to buy you a little cottage close to her –'

'No!' I interrupt. 'I can't.'

'Simone believes that with her help you can. She will be with you every day until you feel you can cope.'

'And what if I can't, you know . . . go out?'

He looks at me steadily. 'She'll take care of things. This way you are free of the strain of being here.'

I make a strangled snorting noise and can't meet his eyes. 'You mean *you* will be free of me?'

'No. I mean the burden of worry about Annabelle will be gone. You will have all the time and help you need to get better. It will be better for Annabelle too. You do see I have to put her first?'

I nod, stare at the floor for a minute, and then glance up at him. 'Can I think about it?'

'Of course, but if you agree to go ahead there will be certain conditions.'

'And they are?'

'Think about it first and then we'll talk again. But don't take too long. A darling little cottage has recently come on the market and we will have to move quickly to purchase it before somebody else does. Simone has already viewed it and she's certain you will adore it.'

I search his eyes for signs of falsehood. This was the man I once would have trusted with my life. Now I sense a nameless undercurrent. What is it that he's not saying?

'And you will visit?'

He shakes his head. 'No. That will be one of the conditions.'

'How many conditions are there then?'

'As I said, just think about it first.'

While Oliver rose to his feet and walked across to the polished teak desk littered with papers and all the usual paraphernalia of writing, Belle continued to smile.

'I love your place,' she said. 'Have you lived here long?'

'A couple of years.'

'You've made it so comfy.'

He grinned at her. 'Glad you like it, ma'am.'

At the desk he pulled open a drawer and extracted a brown cardboard folder.

'So,' Belle said. 'What is it?'

He took a deep breath, then exhaled slowly. 'You said someone had hinted your parents must have offended somebody important, that something might have happened.'

'Yes.'

'Well, I spent an hour in my newspaper's archives and found something that may well confirm it.'

'You did that for me?'

Before he went on, he looked directly at her. She couldn't help thinking how much she liked his lopsided smile and easy-going ways. And how his presence always seemed to instil a sense of . . . of . . . what was it? A sense she was in the right place, maybe?

'Any wrongdoing by a British colonial is usually hushed up, even now, but more so back then, so for your mother to be publicly accused there must have been a damn good reason.'

'Was it something my mother had done?'

'Partly, but it began with an unpopular ruling of your father's.'

'Heavens! What was it?'

'It's not the usual run of things.'

She sighed. 'For goodness' sake, spit it out.'

'Your father committed to prison a British officer for the rape of an Indian woman. The entire British community was so outraged that the ruling was overturned, but the result was your father's reputation was severely dented.'

Belle pictured her father's solemn expression and kind eyes and the thought of him being treated so unfairly really hurt her.

'And you think that's why they accused my mother?'

'Maybe. But there's more. During a formal function at the Governor's house, your mother threw a glass of champagne at the Governor's wife. Right in the face. No idea why but she was seen by a doctor and sedated. Look, here are the cuttings.'

Belle leafed through the various pieces but, though reeling from the news, something else was troubling her. What it was she couldn't fully grasp, but it made her feel uneasy. She got to her feet and went to lean with her back against a cool wall to think about it.

'What?' Oliver asked.

When clarity came it brought the realization she was feeling doubtful about Edward's story. He'd told her about a man who'd been about to be charged, and had then been killed in a motorbike accident, but she felt unsure about it now. It seemed a bit too convenient, a way of swiftly wrapping up what had happened so it could be brushed under the carpet and forgotten.

And she wasn't interpreting things in the same way as Oliver was either. Oliver had suggested her mother might have been accused because of an unpopular ruling of her father's. But if her mother's behaviour had been extreme enough to throw champagne in the face of someone so important, even before the baby was born, maybe that proved she had been crazy enough to have hurt the baby. Such an act, equivalent to throwing champagne in the face of the monarch . . . well, nobody in their right mind would dare.

Belle walked over to contemplate the fine view of tall trees and thought about Edward. Had it been an act of kindness? Had he been trying to protect her from the truth that her mother really had been guilty? He'd given such a vague excuse about why she couldn't read the memo herself. Or might his story be true after all, because had her mother really been guilty, surely they wouldn't have let her go? It was all so confusing and her mind circled the different possibilities until it spun. Then, remembering the anonymous note, she picked up her bag, fished inside for it and turned to Oliver.

'I have something to show you too. It's just a stupid note,' she said dismissively, to hide the fact it had really bothered her.

He took it from her and read it out loud. '*Think you know who to trust? Look harder.*' Then he glanced up with concern in his eyes. 'When did you receive this?'

'A while ago. In an envelope pushed under my door.'

'Any idea who sent it?'

She shook her head.

'But ever since then you've been wondering who you can trust?'

'Well, yes. A little bit.'

'Including me?'

She shrugged but couldn't meet his gaze as she replied, 'Not really you.'

He came closer and put a warm hand on both her shoulders. 'Whoever was responsible, it's a damn cruel thing to do.'

Self-conscious, she shifted slightly, but then looked right into his shining eyes and felt better. She saw such decency and transparency, she wanted to hug him and then keep on hugging him for a long time. So much about Rangoon felt slippery and unknowable. This thing between them, whatever it might turn out to be, was different and she welcomed it.

'You're not alone, Belle. I'm on your side. I promise you.'

And the strength of his look convinced her – but if he was on her side, then who was the one who wasn't?

24.

Diana, Cheltenham, 1922

In the moment I am losing myself in a memory of Rangoon, Douglas walks into my room again. I blink rapidly and force myself back to the present.

'How are you today?' he asks.

I study his impenetrable face. So calm and controlled that I take my cue from him. 'I'm well, thank you.'

'Shall we sit?' he says, indicating a chair. Then he gets straight to the point. 'Have you thought about Simone's offer?'

I nod but don't admit how challenging this decision has been for me and still I'm not entirely sure. I take a sharp breath.

'So?' he says.

'Well . . . all things considered, I think it might be for the best.'

'I'm glad.'

I'll bet you are, I think, but do not say. I try to speak, explain myself, but losing track, break off mid-sentence.

'I would not send you if you didn't agree, but you will love the cottage,' he says as if he hasn't heard my mumbled words.

'You've seen it now?'

'Indeed. It's Cotswold stone, only a few steps from Simone's, and with a lovely garden encircling it on three sides.'

I smile, delighted by the thought. I do love my flowers.

'The village is perfect too. Minster Lovell. Quiet. With a river running alongside it. Simone knows a good doctor who will visit you at home. There's a pub, a mill, a small corner shop, and a wonderful bakery delivers to your door.'

I nod.

He bows his head for a moment and, before he looks up, I notice how thin his hair has become. My darling is entirely bald at the top.

'But now we need to discuss the conditions,' he says.

His face is solemn, and I pick up a hint of anxiety in his eyes. He must be worried about these conditions of his.

Outside it's noisier than before. I rise from my seat and walk over to the open window. A wind is getting up and I see it beginning to lash the trees as if a storm might be on its way. I spot lamps already casting their golden light in the drawing rooms of the houses on the opposite side of the park, even though it's only mid-afternoon.

'Diana?'

I turn towards him. 'Yes?'

'Come and sit down again, please?'

I do as he bids and stare him in the face. Why is he looking anxious?

'So, the thing is, I feel the decision we are making is in the best interests of Annabelle. I hope you understand.'

'Of course.' I make my voice sound reasonable.

'It might seem harsh.'

I blink rapidly, worried now.

'But I don't feel any contact with you is helpful for our daughter.'

'Elvira,' I hear myself say.

'Diana, it's Annabelle, you know that.'

Stupid, stupid mistake. I feel momentarily flustered and want to cover my face with my hands. But we all make mistakes, don't we? I realize he's waiting for me to speak.

'Of course. Of course. That's who . . .' I trail off, unable to finish.

His eyes soften for a moment. 'It's better if I bring her up alone. The instability, you know, it upsets a child. She doesn't understand why you don't care for her.'

I feel the heat pricking my eyelids. 'I care.'

'I'm sure you do, but it's not enough, and we've already said it can't go on like this. I propose to set up a trust for you to be administered by Simone. I do believe this is the best solution, not only for Annabelle, but also for you.'

I bite my lip and scrutinize the floor and I know it's he who wants me away from here.

'Being away from here will help you,' he says, echoing the words in my head. 'We will tell Annabelle you have gone but that I don't know where. That you left a note saying it would be better for all of us. And then, at a much later time, when she has all but forgotten you, I will tell her that her mother has died.'

I gasp. 'That's the condition?'

He nods. 'It must be a clean and total break. I want her to grow up free from, well, free from –'

I interrupt. 'Me.'

His voice takes on a note of resignation. 'I wouldn't have put it so bluntly, but yes, I suppose that is the crux of it. You will not be confronted daily by your failure as a mother and neither will she. It really is best she forgets you. Naturally you will revert to using your maiden name.'

It is a statement, not a question.

I think about leaving this house where I grew up. My house. Though it's his now. The few months we lived here before going to Burma, everything lay before us and we were so happy. I want to tell him how I feel. How I've felt for years. I want to give voice to the hurt he's caused me and the hurt I have caused myself, yet I remain silent. But then, suddenly, as if I have no choice, the question I want to ask slips out.

'When did you stop loving me?'

His eyes are so sad I can hardly bear to see them.

'It isn't about that,' he says and observes me for the longest time. 'I never stopped loving you.'

'But?'

'No, my dear. You stopped loving yourself.'

'And that's what you really believe?'

He stares at me as though he knew I had been referring to the affair he'd had, because after all, how could he if he'd still loved me? After a moment or two he opens his mouth and I wait. He says nothing, but his eyes give him away and it is shame I see. Shame fighting with his pride.

After he has gone I pace the room, hearing the rhythm of the rain beginning to pound on the roof, resounding like the beating of my heart. His decision seems so callous, but I can't argue with the facts. I've been no kind of mother to our daughter but I do want to make her life better. So, will my going do that?

An hour later Wilkes brings me a tray of soft-boiled eggs and toast soldiers, and treats me as if I were the child. She looks at me pityingly and I wonder if she already knows I am to be banished. At least it's not to the Grange, I think, at least. But never to see my daughter again? I don't eat the eggs and toast. Instead, I curl up in a ball on my bed, pull the blankets over my head and, cocooned in the darkness, I cry myself to sleep.

25

Belle stood in the porch outside the hotel in a desultory mood, watching guests arriving and leaving. Two businessmen first, wearing pale linen suits, who both nodded at her as they headed out. They were followed by an overdressed middle-aged matriarch dragging an unwilling child by the hand as she marched into the lobby. It was already mercilessly hot, and Belle knew she really ought to find somewhere to sit beneath a fan, but she felt confused by Oliver's recent revelations about her father and mother and couldn't settle. Oliver was proving to be a true friend, but she was still no closer to uncovering what had happened to the baby and felt unsure of her next move. After a few minutes she noticed the Indian doorman was watching her with a curious look on his face so she walked up to him.

'Can I assist you in any way, Miss Hatton?' he said in a lull between guests needing his help.

She considered it. Could he help her? Guests sometimes forgot the staff were people and a man in his position might well hear gossip.

'Maybe.'

'If you do not mind me saying, you do look rather troubled.'

'I didn't sleep well.'

'That is a shame. Would there be something particular on your mind?'

She gazed at him, sniffing air laden with the smell of salt and oil from the docks. 'Well, yes, there is.' And, after a momentary hesitation, she went on to explain about her parents and the baby who disappeared in 1911.

During a short silence, his brow furrowed.

'She would have been my sister, you see,' Belle added by way of explanation. 'I'd like to find out what really happened.'

He nodded, and she thought that was that, but then he spoke. 'My father worked here before me as night watchman. He used to tell a story about a baby he heard screaming one night. Terrible screaming it was. He had been drifting off, I imagine, and the baby's cries had woken him. For a few minutes he felt disorientated and thought it must have been a nightmare. But the screaming continued. At first, he couldn't make out where the baby was, but as it went on he realized the cries were coming from somewhere inside the back entrance of the hotel. By the time he ran round there, he saw nothing except a black car accelerating away at breakneck speed. He often spoke of that night. Said it haunted him. That screaming baby.'

Belle stared at him. Could it have been Elvira? Or was she being ridiculous? There might have been several babies staying here.

'There had been no babies staying at the hotel,' he said, answering her question before she had posed it.

'Was it definitely 1911?'

He nodded. 'Oh yes, I remember it most distinctly.'

'Did he tell the police or ask the other staff about it in the morning?'

'He asked, of course, but no one knew anything and if anyone did know they were not saying. Of course, he'd seen the story about the missing baby – it was in all the papers – but my mother convinced him not to involve the police. Worried for his job, you see.'

'Is your father still alive?'

'Yes, but he is not well. And I don't think he would be able to tell you any more than I have. He recounted the story many times. He had no proof, but instinct told him something had not been right. The expensive car racing away. The distraught screams. The time of night it happened. There had been something clandestine about it.'

She nodded and thanked him, her thoughts churning. What if

Elvira really had been kidnapped, and by somebody wealthy? At least that might mean she was still alive, though how Belle would ever find her, she didn't know.

She was about to go back inside when Fowler, the assistant manager, stepped out looking puffed up and self-important.

'Miss Hatton. You may have friends in high places, but we do not encourage staff to gossip on the doorstep in full view of the guests.'

'It was quiet.'

He inclined his head. 'Well, off you trot now. We have some important guests arriving any minute.'

She glanced at the doorman and winked, then turned back to Fowler. 'Don't blame him,' she said. 'It was entirely my fault.'

'I don't doubt that,' Fowler said, casting her an annoyed look, and then he turned his back on her to greet a newly arrived guest in his usual sycophantic manner.

Later Belle went to the reception desk to see if there had been any post for her. The head receptionist, a smart middle-aged Glaswegian man, handed her an airmail envelope postmarked Oxford. At last this was it – a reply from her mother's old friend Simone. She took it straight to her room, hopes rising. Much as she liked Rebecca now, Belle wanted privacy to read this and luckily the girl wasn't there. She unfolded the letter and, scanning the tiny handwriting, devoured every word. Then she read it again more slowly.

Dear Annabelle,

It was a great surprise but also an enormous pleasure to hear from you. How extraordinary that you find yourself in Rangoon. Life can be so strange with all its twists and turns, don't you agree? But what am I saying? You are still a girl and, although I'm sure parts of your childhood may not have been easy, you cannot have experienced many twists, as yet. Thank you for informing me of dear Douglas's death. He, like my darling husband, Roger, was a fine man.

Now on to the main topic of your letter. Yes, I do remember when baby Elvira disappeared. How could any of us forget? It was a desperate time for all of us, but most of all for your mother who suffered terribly at the hands of the police. My husband and I were outraged that a woman such as your mother could have been accused in the way she was. Of course, we both did what we could, with Roger going through all the official channels, while I did my best to comfort Diana.

She had been unwell during her pregnancy with a terrible sickness that continued virtually all the way through, but it was after the baby was born when things went so badly wrong. It was as if the birth had drained Diana of life. It worried me. She hardly ate, could not sleep and cried all the time. The baby cried too, incessantly Diana said. Roger gave her something to help her sleep, but her mood remained desperately low. Nothing seemed to help, and I was concerned for her sanity. It is true some women go through a difficult time after giving birth but, Roger assured me, this was far worse. It was as if Diana had completely given up on life. The light had gone from her eyes and all she could see was darkness. Douglas could be a difficult man, stubborn, and I believe he became increasingly so as he grew older. Like so many men, he found emotions impossible to deal with and thought he was always in the right, no matter what, so there could be no arguing with him. I'm sorry to speak of your father like this. At heart he was a good man who did what he could, but he simply did not comprehend how the birth of their longed-for child could have brought about such a drastic change in his wife. Nor did he understand his role in it all.

On the day it happened, as far as I can tell, Diana had been alone in the garden while Elvira slept in her pram. One of the servants spotted your mother kneeling on the grass in her nightdress beside a recently planted flower bed and reported that she had been digging up the earth with her bare hands. This was the reason she was later accused, along with her inability to care for the baby. The police concluded that Diana wanted the baby dead, and when they began digging up the garden they found one bootee exactly at the place where your mother had been digging. She never could give a reason for her actions that day, which to the police was highly suspicious, but to me were a direct consequence of a troubled and distraught state of mind.

The questioning went on for days and then suddenly your mother was let go and your parents left for England in the middle of the night without even packing up the house. I always felt they had been ordered to leave from somebody right at the top. Oh, I almost forgot, there had been an incident with the Governor's wife. Douglas had dragged Diana, while she was pregnant and feeling unwell, to a dinner at the residence. The Governor's wife, a stupid, vacuous woman in my opinion, had made a remark in Diana's hearing about how pregnant women should put up and shut up. Nobody believed in their stories of extended sickness. Diana marched up to her and threw a glass of champagne in her face. Oh, the hue and cry! though privately I thought the woman deserved what she got, but it didn't do your mother's reputation any good. Even before the baby she had become regarded as unstable.

After your parents left I realized your mother's name had not been cleared. The case remained open for a short while and in the end was never resolved. My suspicion was somebody had to know what had happened but had made sure the whole awful affair was hushed up. In my opinion your mother was simply a scapegoat.

Anyway, dear Annabelle, that's all for now. I hope you can read my writing.

With best wishes for your health,
Simone Burton

26

Diana, Cheltenham, 1922

I wake up with the most terrible headache I've ever had. It's as if someone has beaten me about the head with a cosh. The room is bright, too bright, and when I look about I realize it's entirely tiled in white and there is a sickening smell of carbolic in the air. I'm not at home.

I am blinded by the light and, as panic grips me, I long to escape back into the dark. Then a thought hits me. A terrifying thought. This must be the Grange. I try to move and find I am bound to the bed, not too tightly but tight enough that I can't get out. Why has he had me brought here? He promised he would never send me without my permission. I begin to shout Douglas's name, until I am screaming, but he does not appear. Instead a young woman dressed in blue, who I think must be a warden, walks in and tells me if I'm not quiet I will disturb the other patients.

She walks out again, and I begin to shake with fear. Why have they brought me to the Grange? My head still aches, and my thoughts are spinning so fast I can't catch hold of them. I try to remember but nothing comes clear. My brain is a fog. Where was I yesterday? What was I doing? I screw my eyes shut in the effort of remembering and try to force the images to return. Then I hear a voice, an actual voice, asking me a question. I open my eyes to see that the young woman has returned and I wince at the smell of body odour as she looms over me.

'I asked if you could hear me,' she says, prim, full of self-importance, and clearly looking down her nose at me.

When she tells me I'm in the Cheltenham General Hospital and Dispensary, not the Grange, there's something I can't put my finger on and I don't believe her.

'Why am I tied to the bed if I'm not at the Grange?' My voice comes out as a husky rasping sound and my throat feels raw.

'It's for your own safety,' she says, and leaning over me again, whispers, 'We had to pump your stomach.'

'I don't understand. I want to go home. Why can't I go home?' Tears fill my eyes and I can't prevent them from falling and dampening the sheet.

She purses her lips. 'You have caused everyone a great deal of trouble, but I imagine you probably will go home.'

'Have I . . .?

'What?'

'Damaged myself?'

She shakes her head. 'The doctor is speaking to your husband now and they will make the decision.'

'Decision?'

'Whether you are safe to return or not.'

'Why wouldn't I be safe?'

'Mrs Hatton. It's not for me to say. Now you must rest. Do you need the bedpan?'

I shake my head even though I do.

Once she has gone I try to remember and then I have the most constricting feeling in my chest. I gasp, close my eyes and cover my face with my hands. The Veronal pills. And me stuffing them in my mouth as if they were sweets. So many of them. So many.

My eyes fly open when I hear a tapping on the door and then a doctor walks in followed by Douglas. I am overcome with relief and hold out my arms to my husband, but he stands a few feet away and that confuses me. I look at Douglas and see dark exhausted bruises beneath his eyes.

I turn my gaze to the doctor. 'Can I talk to my husband alone?'

He nods. 'For a moment or two.'

As I lie still and silent, I am surprised when Douglas takes my hand and begins to talk rapidly and in not much more than a whisper. 'We haven't got long,' he says. 'You must tell them it was an accident. You had forgotten how many you had taken. Diana, it is a crime to commit suicide, and anyone who attempts it can be prosecuted and imprisoned. Luckily the doctor has listened to me and understands you were not exactly yourself yesterday, that you had a bad headache and had not slept much. I told him you became confused. Do you understand? You must insist it was an accident.'

Once we are back at home, Douglas accompanies me up to my room where fresh daffodils have been placed in a vase beside the window. I instantly feel myself relax, though I notice they have taken my mirror away. Do they think I am going to stare myself to death?

'Thank you for organizing the flowers,' I say, still shaken, and focusing on slow and steady. Slow and steady. Slow and steady.

He nods, and his face is soft. 'Mrs Wilkes will bring up a tray soon.'

'I can't remember,' I say. 'What happened?'

He sighs deeply and bows his head for a moment.

'I know you told the psychiatrist you had been out to the park but we all know it isn't the truth. You used to spend time in the garden but increasingly you remain up here.'

I bite my lip.

'I thought if you were to be strong enough to undertake the move to Minster Lovell we ought to try to acclimatize you to the outside world a little.'

'Oh God,' I say as the memory returns and I squeeze my eyes tightly shut. Sweat gathers on my brow and at the back of my neck. Sticky, damp. The sensation of being crushed beneath this merciless thing robs me entirely of rational thought. I feel hot and terribly dizzy. My chest tightens and it hurts so much I feel

I can't get any air, that I am choking, that I will die. I reach out to Douglas in panic and begin to shake uncontrollably. The panic rises and rises. Overwhelming me. I can no longer hear Douglas although I know he is speaking. His mouth moves as I stare at him. It moves and moves until I want to wail. Then everything blurs.

Douglas holds me, whispers in my ear soothingly, and I hear him now. 'It's all right, Diana, you're at home. It's all right.'

I open my eyes. I really am in my room.

'You're just remembering how you felt yesterday. You are safe. I'm so sorry for what happened.'

'It's not your fault.'

'Ah, but it was, and I blame myself. I should have realized how it would affect you. But, you see, you were fine at first when we were in the garden. And then we went out into the park, almost as far as the pond, but that's when it all went wrong. It was too much too soon. I encouraged you to go further than you were able.'

'And when we came home?'

'Even though it was still the afternoon you went straight to bed. I blame myself for that too. You should have had someone with you.'

The memory returns. Douglas had left me. I was happy to be alone and as I lay in bed staring at the four walls I felt as if I'd become the keeper of the past and it was time to let it go. All the emotion, the regret, the lost hopes and the dreams. Everything. When I closed my eyes, I saw the faces of those who had gone before me and then, when the past melted away, an extraordinary calm came over me. I'd been told what to do. It was time to allow myself to fall through the hole in my life and leave the pain behind. And so I decided to take the pills. I was smiling, happy. I'd finally made a choice.

'Mrs Wilkes was worried,' Douglas was saying. 'She couldn't rouse you when she brought up your supper.'

'I thought it would be best for everyone. I'm so sorry for the trouble, Douglas.'

He pats my hand. 'I have sent Simone a telegram asking her to come and stay with you until you are well enough to move to the village. I've already exchanged on the cottage, so it will be ready, all furnished and waiting for you.'

I focus on his eyes. 'I'm still going there?'

'I think it's for the best, don't you?'

'I'm not sure,' I say and my mind wanders.

'I won't force you, but the alternative is to employ a nurse to look after you day and night here, and you've already said you don't want that. I am terribly worried about how all this is going to affect Annabelle.'

I drag my attention back to him. 'Do you know when Simone will come?'

'No, but I emphasized the urgency.'

I hope he'll let me stay until I feel stronger. I don't say it, but I know he's read my mind when he speaks.

'Don't worry. There's no rush.'

I look at him with blurry eyes. 'It was as if a voice told me I had to do it.'

His brow furrows although I am not sure if it is with concern or anger.

'Precisely why you cannot be left alone and why I cannot be sure some "voice" will not tell you to hurt Annabelle. What might tomorrow bring if you don't go?'

I avert my gaze. It's a serious question and the truth of it bites into me, but I wish I had not mentioned the voice. Had I really felt so lost I couldn't envisage any way back? So lacking in hope, so broken by the past? Or had it been the voice taking its chance? I have yet to accept the voice might be me.

27

As Belle left the stage at the end of her set she'd been planning to read Simone's letter again and then have an early night, but when she walked outside for a breath of air she found Edward waiting for her.

'Walk with me?' he said and gave her one of his seductive smiles. 'It's a wonderful evening. And I have good news.'

She glanced up at the sky, midnight blue and scattered with stars, the air so surprisingly cool after such a blistering day, and she heard the night birds flitting from tree to tree.

'Of course,' she said.

'You look very beautiful tonight. Lovely dress.'

'Thank you. It's the second one I've had made up in the Chinese quarter.'

He stopped walking and put a hand on her arm to halt her too. 'Really? It can be dangerous there. Their secret societies cause us no end of problems. The place is riddled with money lenders and even the Chinese themselves dare not report the atrocities.'

'Gloria said it might be tricky there, but I went with one of the girls.'

'I avoid the place like the plague. Rather too cut-throat for me.'

'So, you never go there?' she asked, recalling how she had seen him there with the red-haired woman who had looked so uncannily familiar.

'Not if I can help it. On another note, I've been wondering if you've come to any conclusion?'

'About?'

'Your mother. The baby. What happened. All of it, I suppose.'

Well, I don't think my mother was guilty, she thought but did not say. 'Not really,' she replied. 'I think I'm just going to get on with my life.'

He smiled but she caught something else in his look. And she wondered why she had lied. 'Mind you,' she added, 'I did hear a story about a baby heard crying in or near the hotel at the time.'

'Who from?'

'The doorman mentioned it.'

'That old tale.'

'So, you know about it?'

'I have heard it before.'

Belle thought it a little odd. The doorman had said his father hadn't reported it to the authorities, but then again there would have been gossip. Maybe Edward had caught a whiff of it?

'Ah well. It was so long ago,' she said. 'People get muddled up, don't they?'

They continued to walk in step with each other along Phayre Street where the air was scented with night stocks and the dappled light of daytime had been replaced by trees standing stark and black against the starlit sky.

'I do have something for you, but if you're not going to pursue it, perhaps – well . . .' He paused. 'It doesn't matter.'

'Now you've made me curious.'

He laughed. 'Curiosity killed the cat.'

She rolled her eyes. 'Am I the cat?'

'You've got the green eyes.'

'So?'

'I found a police report about a white baby having been seen with a Burmese couple.'

'Where?'

'On a steamer going up the Irrawaddy river to Mandalay. It's probably another something and nothing story.'

'Intriguing. Did the police follow it up?'

He shook his head. 'They had closed the case. There had been too many red herrings, I guess, and there would have been other more pressing calls on their time. Just as there are now.'

'What do you mean? What's happening now?'

'Unrest is bubbling up. A shooting in the Indian quarter last night. Two men and a woman killed. It's only a matter of time.'

'Until?'

'Until it becomes unsafe for all of us.'

'I thought you said you had good news.'

'That's something else, but really I wonder if a trip up the Irrawaddy might be a jolly sound idea. It may not be too safe here in Rangoon for a woman alone and, you never know, you might be able to pick up a clue or two about the white baby seen on the riverboat.'

'But it was so long ago. Surely nobody will remember?'

'Maybe not, but it might be worth a try.'

'Are you proposing to come with me?'

He laughed. 'Sadly no, although, well . . . you must know how fond I have become of you.'

She didn't know what to say and cast about for a way to change the subject. After a short silence he spoke.

'I'm sorry. I've embarrassed you.'

'You haven't. It's fine.' She paused and put a hand on his arm as she went over their previous talk in her mind. 'I wanted to ask you something.'

'Fire away.'

'The story you told me about the motorcycle man, the one who was killed in an accident. The man who was to have been arrested.'

'Yes?'

'Was it true?'

She couldn't see his face as they walked beneath a tree but noticed a hint of hesitation. 'Look, I can't lie to you – the truth is, I wanted to make you feel better.'

'So, it wasn't true?'

'Not exactly. You were troubled by what your mother might have done.'

'You lied?'

'I worried it might become an obsession, and I didn't want to see you ruin your best chances for a great career. And, as I said, I'm very fond of you and I thought you might get hurt.'

'And this story about the white baby?'

'That's true all right. I can show you the report. But, look, I still haven't told you the good news.'

'Which is?' she asked, realizing he had adroitly steered the conversation in a different direction.

'There's a man I'd like you to meet. A theatrical agent who may have a proposition for you. He's dropping by Rangoon on his way back to Australia. Not sure of the date yet but it won't be too long. Maybe a few weeks.'

On her next night off, Belle joined Gloria and some of her friends for an evening regatta at the Royal Lakes. The entire place was enchantingly lit by thousands of brightly coloured Chinese lanterns and Belle watched as a procession of illuminated boats made its way past, then wound in and out of the many little bays. The British were gathered at Gossip Point where the best view was to be had and Belle was telling Gloria about Edward's idea that she should take a steamer up the Irrawaddy.

Gloria's deep-set dark eyes brightened as she clapped her hands. 'What a splendid idea – but I wouldn't go alone.'

'I was thinking of asking Oliver Donohue.'

As Gloria waved her hand in a dismissive gesture, Belle focused on her friend's chiselled cheekbones and haughty expression. There was something else too. Maybe a touch of wariness?

'Darling, haven't I told you before? He's only ever after a story. Utterly ruthless actually and you really cannot trust him.'

Belle frowned. 'I thought he was relatively nice.'

'Nice! Such a damning word, but I assure you he is a dangerous man and about as far from nice as you can get.'

The noise from a terrific blaze of fireworks startled Belle and she turned from Gloria and stared, wide-eyed. The fireworks crackled and boomed and then, as suddenly as the show had begun, it had ended.

'Well, I wasn't expecting that. What's the occasion?'

'Don't you know?'

Belle shook her head.

'It's the Governor's birthday. Now, about that boat trip. I know just the person who should accompany you. Harry Osborne. He's a governmental surveyor and what he doesn't know isn't worth knowing.' She looked right and left. 'He'll be here somewhere. Don't move. I'll have a little look see.'

Belle glanced around for Edward, wondering if he had any news about the agent he'd mentioned. If he wasn't arriving for a few weeks she'd still have time to take the steamer up the Irrawaddy to Mandalay and be back in time, if she went at all.

She stood on her own and surveyed the gleaming faces. At first the sheen looked glamorous but then it dawned on her it was mainly down to sweat. Feeling a little self-conscious, she moved away from the lanterns into a dimmer light. Although she recognized some of the men and women clustered in knots around her, she felt excluded and without the confidence to break in to one of the groups. Ridiculous thought, as so many of these people would have heard her sing – though maybe that was precisely the issue.

'Penny for them?'

She recognized Oliver's American accent immediately and felt herself blushing with pleasure. Stupid really. But thank goodness he couldn't see her face in the gloom.

'All alone?'

'I'm waiting for Gloria.'

'Heaven forbid! That's a fine reason to allow me to steal you away from this joint.'

She laughed. 'Where to?'

He stepped closer. 'Anywhere not swarming with the British.'

'I'm British,' she said, but with her heart beating riotously against her ribs she didn't feel it. Instead she had become a wild new thing. Unruly, unrestricted, uncontrolled. Time, my girl, to be mad and bad. She paused, remembering her mother. Perhaps not mad, but bad. That would do. Who cares what these people think of Oliver, I like him and *that's* what matters, she told herself.

'Yes, you're British all right, but I suspect you are not one of them. You, my dear, are cute as a bug's ear.'

She laughed. 'Is that your idea of a compliment?'

He pulled back and narrowed his eyes to better study her face. 'Coming? I know you want to.'

It was a disarmingly intimate moment. She glanced over at the direction Gloria had melted into and, despite the reservations the woman had shared about Oliver, she instantly made up her mind. She allowed him to grab her hand and they left the lakes in a run, laughing like children, and weaving between the astonished British matrons and their stuffy husbands.

Once away from the crowds, breathless and exhilarated, Belle came to a stop, doubling over and clutching her side. 'Wait,' she called out. 'I've got a stitch.'

'Dawdler,' he said with a laugh.

'Not fair. I'm wearing heels.'

'Take them off then, take everything off!'

She laughed. 'And get myself locked up.'

'On a night like this I'd join you.'

'In jail or in taking everything off?'

'Which do you think?'

She straightened up. He was right. An intoxicating night, balmy, scented, and with a gentle breeze caressing her bare arms, parting her lips and tempting her to touch his warm skin.

Burmese nights are irresistible, she thought. It's as if all rational thought drains away: the stars sparkle in their thousands, the moon seems golden rather than silver, and the air fills with mysterious sounds. Best of all is the cool. The wonderful, glorious cool. She wondered what he might be like as a lover. Her lover. Pictured their legs entwined in white rumpled sheets, heat and sweat and warm skin gluing them together. Then she told herself not to be so stupid. She wasn't here to fall in love. It would be better if they were to remain friends. Fellow conspirators. No, not that. Fellow detectives.

As they began walking again, slowly now, he raised her hand to his mouth and kissed each of her fingers one by one. She didn't say a word but leant towards him and, with her mouth against his, pressed herself close. His skin smelt masculine, of lemon and sandalwood soap, though most of all he smelt of himself. As they kissed, she blamed it on the extraordinary soft air of the night. And when sweat ran down between her breasts, there was nothing she could do about it, except give in to this wonderful tingling feeling of being fully alive . . . So much for remaining just friends.

After a few minutes they pulled apart.

'Are you hungry?' he asked, scrutinizing her face under the light from a street lamp.

She beamed at him, happy to prolong things. 'Utterly famished.'

'You and me both. Fancy Burmese? There's a terrific place immediately round the corner.'

'I've not tried it.'

'Dear God, you need educating. Come on.' And he held out a hand to her.

Within minutes they arrived at a lantern-lit restaurant and were shown to a quiet table at the back where a strange fishy smell hung in the air.

'You'll have to order for me. I have no idea what anything is.'

'Ginger salad to start with. *Gin thoke* they call it. What do you say?'

She focused on his eyes and felt she'd agree to anything he might suggest.

'They make it with pickled ginger, plus lentils and lima beans which are soaked overnight and then crispy fried and mixed with shredded cabbage, peanuts, sesame seeds, lime juice and fish sauce.' He waved a hand about. 'Fish sauce is what you can smell, and it tastes a lot better than it smells.'

She grinned.

As he ordered she watched his hands tapping out a rhythm on the table.

'What's that?' she said.

'Just a tune. You know the way they get stuck in your head?' He paused. 'So, after getting to know the food – next time we'll have tea leaf salad – I shall introduce you to Burmese culture, music and so on, starting with the most important pagoda.'

Next time, she thought. There will be a next time. And she felt thrilled at the thought.

28.

In the early evening, two days later, Belle and Oliver made their way to Sanguttara Hill and the Shwedagon Pagoda. Hectic market stalls selling fabric, sticky cakes, wooden goods and flowers lined the way, while brightly coloured umbrellas protected the traders from the heat. The whole place teemed with people flocking to buy and, here and there among them, Belle spotted young women sweeping the ground.

'They volunteer,' Oliver said. 'It's central to their beliefs to gain merit by charitable work and good deeds, thus increasing the chance of a favourable reincarnation.'

'And the pagodas? Why are there so many in Burma?'

'Well, the wealthy pay for pagodas to be built to increase merit. Each of those is an *Odeiktha zedi*. But there are other kinds of pagodas too with holy relics inside.'

Belle nodded. They moved on and soon reached a stall packed with bamboo cages, each with a tiny green sparrow-like bird confined within. 'Look!' she said, aghast.

'Would you like one?' Oliver asked.

She shrank back. 'A bird in a cage? No thank you.'

'It isn't what you think. Come on.'

Reluctantly, she followed him as he stepped up to the stall.

'So, how many?' he asked, twisting round to her.

'Are you crazy?'

He grinned at her. 'Trust me.'

As he bartered with the trader Belle stood watching anxiously. After a few moments an agreement seemed to have been reached and the man placed three cages on top of a makeshift table.

'All yours,' Oliver said.

She raised her brows but didn't move.

'Go on.'

'But I don't want them.'

'Just open the cages. You can let the birds go now. That's what they're here for. It will gain you merit.'

She shook her head and laughed. 'Honestly, Oliver, you let me think . . .' Her words trailed off.

'I couldn't resist it.'

She opened the cages one by one and watched in delight as each little bird took to the air and flew off, soaring higher and higher.

They carried on up the steps towards the colourful central compound which Oliver called the *aran*. Until she was actually standing there, staring at the multiple edifices before her, Belle hadn't realized that the huge central pagoda stood in the midst of a complex of so many smaller pagodas dotted among trees. Nor had she realized how busy it would be or what a social event it was to visit the pagoda. All of Rangoon seemed to be out. First, she concentrated on the families promenading in their smartest clothes while small children slept in little heaps guarded by elderly grandmothers. Then she watched young couples praying on their knees and groups of people sitting together sharing food. Most intriguing of all were the saffron-robed monks she saw scrambling up the lower terraces of the Shwedagon itself.

'Whatever are they doing?' she asked Oliver.

'Checking the surface for problems.'

'It looks precarious. Surely they don't climb all the way to the top?'

'I believe they do, all three hundred and twenty-six feet of it.'

'Good God!'

'Come on,' he said. 'We need to see it properly before the sun sets.'

He linked arms with her and they went on, passing huge bells hanging within stone structures, decorative pavilions protecting shrines and magnificent lion-like statues. She loved the bustle going on around the main concourse, which seemed in complete contrast to the quiet shady corners where monks prayed beneath the trees.

'It's covered in jewels,' she said, gawping at the astonishing scale of the Shwedagon.

'Yes, though some are glass.'

As the sky turned gold and dense black shadows began to dissolve the light within the pavilions, she gasped in awe at the dazzling brilliance of the Shwedagon illuminated by the dying sun. With light refracting through coloured glass the whole thing glittered and sparkled: a multi-jewelled marvel like no other Belle had ever seen. The arena, now glowing with oil lamps, candles and limited electricity, shimmered in the breeze. The atmosphere had changed too, becoming more enthralling and less excitable, as if a magical mantle had descended with the night, muffling the chatter and intensifying the religious significance of the moment. She shivered slightly, and he wrapped an arm around her shoulders.

'So,' he whispered, his head close to hers. 'You like?'

She nodded, 'I like very much,' though whether she was referring to her feelings about him or the sight of the pagoda, she couldn't say. She leant against him for a few minutes, absorbing the peace. Then, as they began to walk away, he held her hand.

She felt his energy sweep her entire body and longed for him to kiss her again. The first time it had happened on her initiative but now she wanted him to take the lead. She stopped walking, then lifted a hand to touch his cheek. When he took her in his arms and skimmed her lips gently with his own, it electrified her. He teased her, and she teased him back, her lips barely touching his but searching for the moment when it would become more. She felt the power of her own feverish appetite, until she was ready to dissolve. Fluid like water, or molten like mercury. It was a wonder. A joy. Then – and she didn't know how it turned from one thing to another – when she rested her head on his shoulder for a moment, unexpected laughter erupted from her. It was laugh-out-loud happiness and perhaps the only way to deal with the intensity of her heightened senses while surrounded by so many other people. He joined in the laughter.

'Come,' he said, when they stopped, and he pulled away a little, holding both her hands. 'We'd better move on. People here are offended by public displays of affection.'

'Affection?' She laughed again. 'Is that what it is?' But she looked around and saw a few women were staring at them.

She felt altered by being with him on such an intensely romantic evening but was also curious about what she'd witnessed. Once her emotions had subsided and she had calmed herself she asked him to tell her about the religion.

'Buddhism,' he said, 'blended with *nat* worship.'

'*Nat* worship?'

'Remember I said before?'

'Oh yes. Spirits.'

She listened to the sounds of the evening, the noise now more subdued.

'And the monks? I often see them in the streets.'

'Yes, they go out usually early each morning with their bowls to collect alms. Food for the day.'

'And it's all they have?'

He nodded. 'The role of Buddhism has changed so much since the British took over. The laws used to be built around Buddhist teaching and the monks were protected. Now, of course, the connection between government and Buddhism has been lost.'

'What do they believe in?'

He frowned as he thought about it. 'Very simply, they believe in showing respect for parents and elders. They're naturally curious and think ignorance is a sin. And they emphasize the need for forgiveness and caring for family and community.'

She glanced up at him. 'Sounds pretty good to me.'

'But there's an odd kind of contradiction because this type of

Buddhism is highly individualistic. Each person is responsible for their own salvation, despite the emphasis on community.'

'It must lead to a peaceful life.'

He laughed. 'Maybe. Anyway, after all that, I think it's time to come back down to earth. Ready for a drink?'

29.

Rangoon, 1937

Over the following months Belle spent most of her time working, and, if not working, she spent it with Oliver. When she wasn't actually with him, she usually found herself thinking of him. On one of their evenings together they had been drinking champagne beside the Royal Lakes, watching the fireflies, laughing at nothing, and slowly becoming a little drunk. Since she had given up resisting alcohol there had been several nights like this.

'So,' she had said, 'will you stay on in Burma?'

'I suppose that depends. They will achieve independence from the British sooner or later and who knows how things will be after that.'

'But you do like living here?'

'For now.'

'And you came here because?'

'I think I told you when we first met. There is change afoot and that's newsworthy.'

'But what about after?'

'I don't know, Belle. There are worrying rumblings going on in Germany, suspension of civil liberties and elimination of political opposition, that kind of thing, and I foresee trouble ahead.'

'But surely that won't affect us here?'

'Maybe. Maybe not. Hard to tell at this stage.'

This had been followed by a long silence, after which he'd gently turned her head towards him. 'Let's not talk about depressing things,' he'd said and then he'd traced the outline of her lips with his fingertips.

Happy to steal every possible moment together, they went to the races, too, where they lost money, watching keenly as Gloria did rather well, while her brother shook his head in gloom when the horse he part-owned came in last. They went to the Silver Grill for delicious dinners, and the park for walks in the evening when the heat of the day had faded. They ended up in his flat for coffee when they were tired and wanted to put their feet up. It was as if each was biding their time in an unspoken agreement that whatever this was, it must not be rushed. She was glad of the time getting to know him. To understand his funny turns of phrase, and then tease him over the American murder of the English language. He took it in his stride and never did she feel as if he was pushing her.

This was so different from her first and only real relationship, the one she'd had with Nicholas Thornbury. As a producer he'd promised her the world and had wanted to move so quickly. She'd tried to be what he asked of her, a serious girlfriend, but it hadn't felt real. It would never have worked, although maybe she should have told him to his face, rather than just leaving a letter. She was sorry about that. He had been clever, and she'd found him stimulating. Had enjoyed the way he knew his way around town and associated with all kinds of exciting and un-usual people too. But the truth was she'd been swayed by the glamour and, overly impressed that he'd been interested in her, she'd gone along with it. Only later had she realized she was with him for the wrong reasons and had felt a little ashamed.

After that, men had sometimes taken the view that because she was a singer her morals would be loose, that she'd be ready for anything. But Belle was not like that at all, with a reserve most failed to recognize. Oliver was different – sensitive – and increasingly she felt she could trust him. She loved that it felt a bit like coming home.

She'd written back to Simone, thanking her profusely for such a detailed letter. In fact, it had finally put her mind at rest about her mother. Clearly, the events of 1911 had affected her mother's state of mind and for the first time Belle wished there was some way to make up for everything. They say sadness doesn't kill you, she thought. But it does. It can. She was sure it had killed her mother. Yet there was something Belle still couldn't work out. What had Simone meant when she'd said her father hadn't understood his role in her mother's illness? What had he done?

Nor could she figure out why her own birth had not been enough to redress the balance, or at least go some way to defuse the pain caused by the loss of Elvira. It still hurt. Though she'd never spoken about it with Oliver, she felt he'd somehow picked up on it, and had been able to sense her distress.

On the day she finally took possession of the keys to the house in Golden Valley, she thought of asking Oliver to accompany her again but then decided she preferred to go on her own this time. Now it was hers, she longed for something that she couldn't totally explain. She needed space to touch its surfaces, feel the texture of its walls, and maybe sense whatever might still linger from the past. And she wanted to do it alone. There were decisions to be made about its future and, although she quite liked Edward, she wasn't sure she wanted to sell to him.

She took the tram again and then walked the last part, passing the luxurious colonial homes, looking the same as they had before. Her house though – and a little quiver ran through her at the thought of 'her house' – looked different. On hearing she was to shortly receive the keys she'd employed a gardener to cut back the undergrowth. Now, as she opened the gate, she could see the change. It was as if the front garden had been unwrapped, making the house appear larger and lighter too. She glanced up at the incandescent sky and felt a surge of happiness.

Although the front door was stiff and at first would not budge after she turned the key in the lock, she was determined to enter the house the way her parents would have done, and not by illicitly sneaking in through a back door. She placed her shoulder firmly against the peeling door and pushed and pushed until a creak and then a groan hinted at its imminent surrender. When it suddenly did she fell into the hall and wobbled before reaching a hand out to steady herself. *Sorry, old place*, she whispered. It had not been the most elegant entry to her new home. She paused, taken aback by her train of thought. Was it really to be a *home*?

She left the door wide open. This house needed fresh air to blow the cobwebs away. Now she could see the hall properly she inspected the floor, a black-and-white-checked marble affair lit by shafts of light and, luckily, still largely intact. Then, walking through the rooms again, she began to see it with new eyes, and a spirit that longed to coax it back to life, though it became obvious the rest of the downstairs needed a great deal of work if the ghosts of the past were to be truly expunged. She opened any window that wasn't jammed and then climbed the stairs, going directly to the room she believed might have been her parents'. From the veranda she looked out at the garden. The hired gardener had been at work there too and, now much of the jungle had been cut back, she could see how much her mother must have loved it.

The few good memories she had of her mother were of when they had been together in the garden of the Cheltenham house, but they were hazy images and Belle couldn't really tell if they were merely a child's wishful thinking. She did know her mother had loved flowers. That much was true.

After opening the upstairs windows, she went back downstairs and then out through some French windows to what had been the patio. It was treacherously patchy, most of the paviours broken and some missing altogether. As she picked her way, armies of ants scurried from her footsteps and a family of tiny lizards ran for shelter. She walked across the mown lawn, terribly uneven still, but no longer knee high, and headed for the entrance to the hidden part of the garden. Before she went through she turned to glance back at the house. It looked golden in the sunshine and a lump grew in her throat as she absorbed its faded beauty. It wasn't hard to imagine her parents living here before everything went so wrong. She felt a moment of intense sadness, but it passed, and she went on through and headed for the tamarind tree. She lay on the grass beneath it to gaze up through its shady leaves and, although she had never lived in Burma before, she felt a connection, as if she'd finally found the place she really belonged.

Could she live here? Restore the house? Bring it back to life again? Was it possible?

The next evening, two minutes before going on stage, Belle received a note from Edward asking her to meet with him and another man straight after the show. Belle had spent so much time with Oliver she'd almost forgotten about Edward's mention of the agent – or, if not forgotten, she'd certainly taken it with a pinch of salt and had put it to the back of her mind. However, here he was. A Mr Clayton Rivers, Australian, and an international theatrical agent. It was a pity she'd have to stand Oliver up, but it couldn't be helped. She'd tried calling but there'd been no reply. They had agreed to meet at the Silver Grill for a nightcap and she'd been planning to tell him about her recent trip to the house. She knew he'd understand why she couldn't keep their date but, at this late stage, there was now no way to let him know.

Despite a mixture of excitement and nerves the show went well and at half past eleven she adjusted her hair and make-up, put on her highest heels and headed past the few remaining drinkers to the bar where she could see Edward, looking relaxed and at ease in an open-necked shirt, sipping a whisky with another man. They both rose at the sight of her and, with a beaming smile, Edward introduced Belle to the theatrical agent, a tall, broad-shouldered man with a deep tan and white-blond cropped hair.

'Pleased to meet you, Mr Rivers,' she said, holding out a hand.

'Clayton, please.' He gave her a dazzling smile. 'How about you and I make for a quiet table over there?'

They left Edward at the bar and settled themselves at the corner table. Clayton Rivers went on to say he was from Sydney and was currently travelling to all the top hotels and theatres in the East on the hunt for new acts to represent. As Edward, an old friend from his London days, had praised Belle so effusively, he'd felt obliged to make a slight detour. Hadn't been disappointed either and would be prepared to accept her on to his books with all the usual terms and conditions, if she was interested.

Belle felt elated to hear all this and, listening intently, nodded as he explained that the paperwork would clarify all the details, although it wouldn't come through for a couple of weeks or so. The only condition was that she'd have to be in Sydney at the end of the following week to audition for an understudy role in a successful musical for a sixth-month run.

'No promises,' he said. 'You realize there will be others auditioning too, but . . . you're good. Very good. It costs, but Imperial Airways will get you there in three days with a stop at Singapore and Perth.'

Apparently, the star of the show was struggling with personal and health issues and although she hadn't given up the role just yet, a breach of her contract was very much on the cards. The current understudy had got herself caught out, by which Belle understood the girl was pregnant, and already showing, so time was of the essence, Clayton explained.

Belle nodded eagerly, at the same time feeling an undercurrent of hesitancy. Having an agent on her side would mean she'd be considered for jobs she might never have heard about, so why dither?

'Could I have a couple of days to think about it?' she eventually came out with.

He raised his brows in surprise. 'Really? You need to think?'

'I have some things I need to sort out, that's all.'

It wasn't exactly true. She felt torn about leaving Oliver precisely when they were truly getting to know each other, and also her house in Golden Valley, in all its faded glory, was playing on her mind. The house was a potent link to the past, to her parents' past, and although the way she'd felt so at home there didn't really make sense, it had felt like a part of her. And what of Elvira? There was still the story of the white baby seen travelling upriver with a Burmese couple to investigate. True, her missing sister hadn't been at the front of her mind lately, but would Belle ever come back to Burma if she left now? Would she ever know the truth about what had happened? She took a long, slow breath. This was a terrific opportunity. How could she even consider turning it down?

She glanced across at Edward, who'd been joined by Gloria, and when she saw who was with them she hesitated. It was the red-haired woman, the one she had seen with Edward, and she was smiling across at Belle. She stared at the woman with questions spinning in her head. Who was she? And why did Belle feel as if she knew her? Could it be anything more than her resemblance to Diana?

'Shall we join the others?' Clayton said.

As they approached the bar Gloria beckoned Belle forward. 'Come and meet Susannah.'

The other woman smiled and, in a moment of understanding, Belle realized the apparent familiarity was exactly as she'd previously thought: the woman *did* resemble her mother, who of course was no longer alive. When the woman spoke, Belle was surprised by a strong Scottish accent. And, though well preserved, with only a network of fine facial lines, she was older than Belle had first thought. Her upright posture and modern dress had, from a distance, given the impression of a younger woman but, face to face, she must clearly be in her late fifties. If Belle had harboured even a shadow of suspicion that she might have been Elvira, which of course she had not, not really, it was now quickly dispelled. The woman's age made it impossible. Belle shook her hand.

'I tracked Harry down the night of the regatta,' Gloria was saying, 'God, it seems ages ago, but when I looked for you you'd vanished. You never did say where and I've barely seen you since the races.'

'Oh,' Belle said, thinking rapidly and remembering how she'd made her escape with Oliver. 'I had a headache that night so headed home. And since then . . . well, I've been rather busy.'

Narrowing her eyes, Gloria gave her a funny look.

Belle felt her colour rising. 'Sorry, I did look for you at the regatta to say.'

'Did you, darling?' Gloria paused, clearly not taken in by the lie. 'Well, never mind now. Harry went off to the wilds soon after the regatta, so there was no point bringing up the subject again, but he's back now, and he and I will be at the Golden Eagle at eleven for an early lunch tomorrow. It's the bar I took you to when you first arrived. You remember it?'

Belle nodded but couldn't help feeling she'd been caught out. Now, wanting to get away, she muttered something about having had a long day but she'd see her in the morning, then bid them all goodnight.

30.

Harry Osborne turned out to be a serious man fluent in Burmese, whose job it was to survey the country and compile a report for the government detailing land use and activity in the far reaches of Burma. An overly neat, sandy-haired man with wire spectacles continually slipping down his nose, he seemed oddly out of place in the bar, quietly sipping a lemonade and refusing Gloria's offers of alcohol.

A strong scent of incense emanating from the corner of the room made Belle's eyes smart and she began to cough. After she'd recovered and explained her quest to discover the truth about her sister, Harry nodded slowly, glancing about him as if to ensure no one could overhear.

Then Gloria spoke. 'Harry knows everybody in the villages en route. The Burmese, I mean. If anyone saw anything he'll be the one to winkle it out of them. Nobody better and it's enormous luck he's about to set off. I'll let Harry explain.' She flashed him a smile.

'If you wish to accompany me to Mandalay . . .' he said, speaking in such hushed tones Belle was forced to lean so close they were practically nose to nose and she could even smell the fish on his breath.

'I leave in three days,' he continued, 'and won't return for ten months. After Mandalay I go north-west, you see, up to the rugged border between the mountains and the Chindwin River. I'm sure I can arrange useful meetings for you in Mandalay. Maybe even with the District Commissioner. Give me a day or two and I'll come up with a plan.'

Belle gulped. Three days. She'd have to decide quickly. Now

that she'd finally met Harry and the river trip had become more real, the story of the white baby, seen with a Burmese couple on the riverboat, was tempting her to go. And if Harry really could persuade a top official to see her, there might be a chance of getting near to the truth – or at least turning up some kind of lead. It was a long shot, naturally, but if luck was on her side, she could possibly meet someone who'd seen them.

'How long does it take to go upriver?'

'Two weeks.'

'Two weeks!' She had naively been hoping for a couple of days, which would still leave her time to get to Sydney.

He gave her a wearied look. 'And then the train back to Rangoon isn't always fast either, can be over twenty hours unless there are floods, in which case it's anybody's guess. In fact, if you plan to come back by train you'll need to be ready well before the monsoon comes.'

'And when is that?'

'At the beginning of June usually.'

So enough time before the rains at least, although it was undeniable this whole trip might result in a complete waste of time: a red herring that would cost her the chance of acquiring an agent.

Obviously noticing her hesitancy, Gloria stepped in. 'Darling, you should seriously go. It'll be perfectly safe, although Harry, poor thing, might not hang on to his head.'

Not understanding, Belle frowned.

'He's hoping to reach Nagaland. The Naga are infamous headhunters.' She let out a peal of laughter that, Belle noticed, Harry didn't share.

'Actually, Gloria, I'm slightly more worried about the tigers,' he said, 'and as far as the Naga are concerned, I'm only there to survey the land, although we do need to know if there's a chance some of them might be persuaded to join our military.'

During all this Belle had been thinking, and not about

headhunters or tigers either. 'What about Clayton Rivers?' she said, giving Gloria an anxious look. 'He won't wait.'

'From what I hear, it's only an understudy role. There will be other better chances. Maybe he'll still represent you at a later date?'

'He insisted that I have to be in Sydney at the end of next week.'

Gloria snorted. 'Don't believe everything you hear, especially if it's anything to do with my brother. Mark my words, it will come to nothing. I've seen this sort of thing before. Anyway, I'm fairly sure Edward may be able to persuade Clayton to take you on regardless. The man owes him.'

'Why?'

'Edward lent him money some time ago when Clayton was finding his feet in the entertainment world.'

Belle puffed out her cheeks and glanced at Harry Osborne, who was staring morosely into his empty glass. She could see there was something indefinably sad about him. But what was she going to do? Take up his offer or take up Clayton Rivers' offer?

An hour later that morning, Belle called at Oliver's apartment. A few minutes passed before he answered her knock, so when he finally did, she was about to leave. He looked the worse for wear, with tousled hair and shadows under his beautiful, dark-lashed eyes. Clearly, he'd just tumbled out of bed and, wearing only a towel wrapped round his waist, he stretched and yawned.

'What happened to you last night?' he said, his voice gravelly, and she winced at the coolness of his tone.

'Am I keeping you up?' she said, trying not to stare openly at his naked torso, where his belly button was revealed plus the hint of a curl of hair beneath it. Her emotions pitched and rolled, his golden skin tugged at her heart and she reached out to touch him. But then, spotting what looked like lipstick smeared on his neck, she froze.

He frowned. 'As you can see, I'm not exactly in a state to receive visitors.'

'All right,' she said, feeling confused and wondering if he had a woman concealed in his apartment. 'I'll see you another time then.'

He put a hand on her arm as she made a move to leave. 'Sorry. Come in. I'll jump in the shower, then make some coffee, if you don't mind waiting.'

She followed him in and didn't speak for a moment as she stood at the kitchen door and watched him make the coffee.

'I thought you were having a shower first,' she said.

He turned his head to look at her. 'You're right, I was.' He handed her a cup of what was clearly strong coffee and drank his own in one swift gulp. 'I won't be long.'

'Take your time. I'm not in a rush. I wanted to explain about last night.'

He nodded, then walked through the living room to his bathroom. She listened to the grind and creak of plumbing and the sound of water flowing. She could have phoned but had been dying to see him in person, and now the sight of that lipstick bothered her. Although she tried to rally innocent reasons for its alarming bright-pink presence on his neck, she failed miserably. What did it signal? Or, rather, who did it signal? She tried concentrating on the pale sitting room, taking in the rattan furniture, the emerald-coloured silk cushions and beautiful blue and green Persian rugs, just as before. After placing her empty cup on the polished coffee table, she rooted around in his pile of magazines, then stepped over to look at the view of tall trees again.

'Nice view, isn't it?' he said, and she spun round, not having heard him come back in. Pale beneath his tan, he hadn't shaved, the shadow of stubble on his chin still showing.

'I wanted to explain.'

He shrugged. 'It really doesn't matter.'

Her eyes widened. 'But it does. I am sorry. Something last minute happened.'

'Obviously something important,' he said in an unusually reserved tone of voice.

'Well, yes.'

He reached out a hand. 'Come on. Let's sit down. I'm absolutely bushed.'

'Heavy night?' she asked, flinging down the magazine.

'Yeah. I bumped into an old friend.'

As they sat on the sofa, she spoke, sounding bolder than she felt. 'A woman?'

His blue eyes widened. 'How did you know?'

She lifted her chin and gave him a peevish look. 'The lipstick on your neck. A bit of a giveaway, I think, don't you?'

Instead of retaliating, he simply laughed. 'Jealous?'

'Don't be ridiculous.'

Aware that suspicion had flooded her face and annoyed with herself for her petulance, she quickly rose to her feet. 'I'd better go.'

'You haven't explained why you stood me up.'

'Oh, it was nothing much, merely an international theatrical agent Edward had brought to meet me! You know, the sort of thing that happens every day . . . Anyway, I'll . . .'

'If you wish to leave, be my guest.' He turned up his palms and shrugged.

'I will.' But she didn't move. Instead, to her horror, her eyes began to sting, and as the tears sprang out, she angrily brushed them away with the back of her hand. He was instantly by her side, wrapping his arms around her and holding her to him. She felt his heart beating against her chest and heard him whispering in her ear.

'Come on, honey, let's not quarrel. I simply got drunk with an old friend. There's nothing going on, I swear.'

She pulled away and sniffed. 'And the lipstick?'

'A peck aimed for the cheek but must have landed on my neck

as we parted. Nothing more. I was pissed you'd stood me up and drank more than I'd intended.'

'Old friend or old girlfriend?'

He scratched the back of his neck. 'The latter. Over years ago. Happily married now.'

His sincere look, completely without guile, reassured her. Knowing she'd overreacted, she nodded. After all, they hadn't promised anything to each other, hadn't even publicly acknowledged they were a couple. She had no right to be upset. He was a free agent and so was she. It had been a bad start to the day, but they could get over it.

She ran a thumb across her chin and rubbed it, still wavering over what to do about the river trip. 'I have a decision to make,' she said. 'I did want to discuss it . . .'

'Well, you can.'

They both sat down again and, while he held her hand, she explained it.

'Do you trust Edward?' he asked, looking unconvinced. 'Is this agent kosher?'

'Why wouldn't he be?'

'Look, I don't want to put the dampeners on it, but in my experience, Edward can be tricky.'

'In what way?'

A shadow passed across Oliver's face. 'I have no proof, but the word is he has interfered in the due process of the law more than once.'

She stiffened slightly, her mind overactive. 'But that doesn't mean the agent isn't legitimate. Anyway, how do you know about Edward?'

He gave her a lopsided smile. 'A good journalist never reveals his sources,' he said drily.

'What exactly does he do? His job, I mean.'

'Well, the story is he's a powerful advisor to the Police Commissioner.'

'You don't believe it?'

His shrug was non-committal.

'So, what are you telling me?'

'He's been the brains behind a number of shady dealings. He and others have silenced more than one of my stories when it suited them to do so, and people who have challenged him have disappeared. He, like many others, is unprincipled when it comes to preserving British power and dignity.'

Belle frowned. This wasn't the Edward she'd got to know. He'd only ever been helpful and kind. In fact, she'd become quite fond of him.

'In any case, surely finding out what happened to your sister is the most important thing?'

'Well, yes. Maybe. But –'

He interrupted her. 'And what did you make of Harry Osborne?'

'Do you know him?'

'I know of him. He's a regular kind of guy, I hear, highly regarded in his field.'

'I quite liked him, although he's a little quiet.'

Oliver grinned, and his eyes lit up. 'It's the quiet ones you have to watch.'

'Well, I can't accuse you of being one of them.' She poked him in the chest as he pulled a face. 'Are any Americans truly quiet?'

He laughed but then grew serious. 'This white baby on the boat is the first decent clue you've had. And if you can get to Mandalay there might be more to find out there, especially if you're able to talk to a top official, chief of police, someone like that.'

He was voicing exactly her own thoughts but it was still a tough choice to have to make. If she went on the river trip she wouldn't be able to meet Mr Rivers' deadline. It was as simple as that, and although Gloria had suggested there might be other opportunities, was she right?

With a look of excitement, and rising to his feet, Oliver began to pace the room. 'Just think! If we stick with it and something comes of this – if you find out what happened, maybe even find Elvira alive – what a wonderful story it will make. Imagine the headlines: *Beautiful young Englishwoman solves the case of the vanishing baby. Nightclub singer solves the mystery.* It would be the story of the year. Might even go international or – get this – maybe it could become a film. Our fortunes would be made!'

There was a long silence.

'Belle?'

She gulped a mouthful of air. How could she have been so naive? How could she have put her faith in someone who would think it was acceptable to sell her personal family history, their tragedy even, and make it the subject of gossip on the streets? A film for heaven's sake! She felt a chill and stood abruptly.

'Story?' she stammered, too upset to say anything more.

'Belle, I –'

She shook her head. 'I can't do this.'

As disappointment eddied around her in painful waves and the truth sank in, the heat in the room grew more intense. 'That's what I am to you? A scoop?'

'No. I didn't mean –'

'Stop right there.' She backed away. 'They warned me about you.'

His jaw stiffened and he stood completely still as he gazed back at her. 'They?'

'I chose not to believe them.'

Her chest tightened. She had been so stupid. Now she only wanted to get away quickly, and never be reminded of his duplicity again.

'It isn't Edward I shouldn't trust, is it? It's you.'

'Belle, you're overreacting –'

She held out a hand to silence him. 'You're spending time

with me because you're after the big story. You need me to help unravel the truth. Oliver Donohue's big scoop!'

He gave her such a curious look she felt her heart might break. Then he shook his head. 'You've got this all wrong,' he said with a hollow laugh, 'but I guess you're more of a Brit than I thought. Be it on your own head if you put your trust in Edward and his cronies.'

She felt sad and lonely and terribly disappointed but, mustering her courage and determined to preserve her dignity, she gulped down the lump in her throat. 'I'm sorry my friendship with Edward doesn't meet with your approval. I shan't bother you any further. You don't care about me. I was a fool for thinking you did . . .'

He stared at her for a moment in disbelief and then shrugged.

As Belle left the building, she made an instant decision. To hell with the *story*! To hell with the river trip. That was not going to happen. Not now. Not ever. Blinded by the angry tears which fell the moment she reached the street, and fuelled by the hurt of having been duped, she was shocked by the savagery of her own response to what had happened. The nonchalance of his final shrug had sealed it. Now the pain whipped through her. How? How could he have been so uncaring of her feelings? So insensitive to her family sorrow? It was hard to have to face the fact that the person you had put your trust in wasn't who you thought he had been. And then she remembered the anonymous note. *Think you know who to trust?*

31

Diana, Cheltenham, 1922

Simone has been staying with me for three weeks and I must say I've never felt better. Once I recovered from the reckless stunt that had landed me in hospital we started to take short trips outside, beginning with standing in the front garden for two minutes while gazing at the park. She holds my hand and moments before the point when I feel everything is about to fold in on me, she seems to sense it, and we go straight back inside. Each day we have walked a little further and each day I've endured a little longer.

Simone is the most accepting person I've ever known, never judging or hinting at anything to make me feel worthless. She has absolute faith that one day I will recover completely, and her calm and soothing presence is exactly what I need. I try to believe it will happen, but yesterday the whispering voice sent me spiralling down again and, even after only a few minutes outside, my heart felt as if it would leap from my chest. Simone told me to keep my breathing slow and encouraged me not to run back indoors but to concentrate on the flowers lining the beds in the front garden. And I did it. I actually did it.

She's helping me pack up all my possessions ready for the move. We hope before long I'll be able to withstand the journey by car. I'm not so worried about being in the car if someone is with me. It's being in the open that makes me feel as if I'll be swallowed up.

She's sitting on the floor now gazing at the few photographs I have from our life in Burma. Simone believes I shouldn't avoid the thing that terrifies me. She tells me avoidance only makes matters worse and she thinks that's why I hear the voice. She thinks the darkness I refuse to face or even acknowledge must find its way out. So now, each day, to try to defeat the voice, we take control by spending fifteen minutes looking back. There's no map to show me the way. I have no choice but to take it as it comes. Dead ends and all. So, we attempt to weave in and out of the past, even though it seems mad to me and I only do it to please her.

As I join her on the rug, she pulls out one of only two photographs I have of Elvira and even before she hands it to me I feel the panic rising and turn away.

'Come on, Diana. Take a look. It won't hurt you.'

Her expression is hard to read but I eventually agree and glance down at the blurred younger version of myself cradling my firstborn. As I gently trace the image with my forefinger a strangled noise escapes from my throat.

'Diana?'

I look up in anguish. 'But I don't know what I did.'

'Do you think you would have hurt your child?'

I shake my head. 'I loved her,' I say, but my voice is little more than a whisper.

'Are you worried the voice told you to do something? Is that it? Had the voices already started then?'

I sigh. 'I can't remember. If not then, soon after.'

There's a long silence as images from the past come hurtling back. The pram, always the pram beneath the tamarind tree and me gazing up into the branches and listening to the birds. I'd drunk two large pink gins over lunch and was feeling tipsy. I didn't tell the policeman, though one of the servants might have done. I remember I'd been feeling relieved that at last Elvira had gone to sleep. I won't pretend I didn't find her crying hard to bear. It wasn't the sound so much, although it could drive a mother crazy, it was the fact that no matter what I did I couldn't help her. The doctor said it was probably colic and it would pass but I felt helpless listening to her pitiful cries.

'You've done well,' Simone says and tucks her arm into mine. 'Are you all right?'

I'm only half listening, but I come back to the present, nod, and then hand back the picture.

'Tomorrow,' she says with a confident smile as she helps me up, 'I think we might get Mrs Wilkes to donate some stale bread and then we'll feed the ducks on the pond. What do you think?'

'Lovely,' I say. But what I mean is *really*? Can I really get as far as the pond?

32

Righteous indignation fuelled Belle's footsteps as she marched away from Oliver's apartment building. Silently fuming, she barely noticed the usual mix of people, vehicles and animals in the streets, nor was she aware of the sun high in the sky and the sweat trickling down her back. All she could think was that she would definitely go to Sydney after all, leave everything else behind – leave *him* behind – certain now it was the only thing to do.

By the time she'd regained her composure she glanced about and found she had ended up in an unfamiliar area of the city riddled with alleyways. She came to a stop when a huddle of Burmese men, dressed only in skirts, blocked her path. One man was painting black signs on the bare chest of another and more waited in line, eager to be ornamented. Engrossed in this strange activity, they paid Belle no attention. As more men attached themselves to the group Belle sidled past and headed for what she hoped was the road leading to the Secretariat. She wanted to find Edward to tell him she was delighted to accept Clayton Rivers as her agent.

As she rounded a sharp corner and then headed towards a crossroads she heard a throbbing, rhythmical sound. The hairs on the back of her neck pricked up. What was this odd noise? She stood still and listened to the *thump, thump, thump*, and then it dawned on her. Marching feet. She was listening to marching feet. A moment later dozens of Burmans wielding swords, iron bars and axes came into sight. 'Jesus,' she whispered. What on earth was happening? She spun round trying to figure out the best way to get out but now men seemed to be pouring from every direction. In a flash she knew she was hemmed in. She flattened herself against a doorway, heart pounding, fear stealing her breath. As she stared, the mob tripled in size and a huge number of men were now beating a path towards her.

Rooted to the spot, she attempted to scream. Nothing came out. She willed herself to move but, glancing about, could not see a route through. She squeezed her eyes shut in a hopeless effort to block out the petrifying sight. Dozens of men, bent on attacking her, were brandishing their weapons, gesticulating and shouting. Marching. Thumping. In a state of shocked disbelief, she had frozen. Was this how her life was to end? Was she to be beaten to death on a street corner? She desperately wanted her mother, her father, anyone to come, but could only take a ragged, terrified lungful of air and wait for her fate.

When, after a few moments, nobody had touched her, she opened her eyes and realized the men leading the charge had begun pounding on the door and windows of a house two doors further up from where she cowered. She vaguely recalled being told this was the area where the Indians lived, and looked up to see Indians hurling bricks from the windows of the houses on the opposite side of the street. Panicked by what was happening, she scanned the street in the hope of spotting a policeman who might be able to get her out of there, but there was none.

She watched as a group of Burmans began crawling up the outside staircase of one of the Indian houses opposite. Aware the inhabitants were in terrible peril, Belle searched again for the presence of the police. At the top of the stairs the men hacked at the door until it fell open and then, even above the roar of the crowd, she could hear the terrified screams of the people within. She felt sure they would be slaughtered. Still unsure if it might yet be her turn, Belle wanted to weep, but now the crowd had shifted across the street she had to grab her chance. At first, panting, she slipped behind the backs of the men still gathered in the road and then, with only one thought in her head, she broke into a run with no sense of direction in mind.

As she ran she passed more and more armed Burmese men with painted chests, brandishing crowbars and bludgeons, and advancing on the Indian quarter. In one of the narrow side streets she picked her way around a few unarmed constables facing a mob of angry Indians bent on retaliation. Clearly this riot was something between the Burmese and the Indians, though she didn't know why. Unable to understand why the authorities were largely absent, Belle knew it was even more important to reach Edward and alert him to what she'd witnessed.

When she arrived at a row of tenements in a narrow street leading off the docks, she realized she had set out in the wrong direction. The whole place reeked of drains and fish but there was something worse. Far worse. Stricken by the sickly-sweet smell of blood, she felt her throat close. The street itself, eerily silent, was empty of life and she backed away in shock as she saw the twisted corpses of half a dozen Indian men, women and children splayed out on the ground. She gazed about her in horror but saw that nobody had come to move them. She stared at the horrific purple bruising spreading across the face of one of the men and the dark congealing blood where the side of his head had been caved in. Then she saw his empty black eye sockets and felt sickened. They had gouged out his eyes. She closed her eyes and, holding her stomach, retched over and over. When she was done, she heard the buzzing of enormous flies and squinted up to see them already gorging. She looked away to where one woman lay in a pool of shining blood, her clothing ripped and with gaping stab wounds to her chest. A small child lay at an awkward angle close to her bare feet. Belle wanted to help but there was nothing, absolutely nothing she could do. No one had been left alive. She glanced over to where another man had clearly had the life beaten out of him. Horrified by the savagery, her one thought was to get away. The Strand Hotel couldn't be far, and she twisted round to figure out the right direction. But then, hearing a baby crying, she faltered.

She had assumed everyone had been killed and longed to make her escape from this terrible carnage, but how could she leave a baby to die alone? She tried to work out where the baby might be and made her way along the street, forcing herself not to glance at the blank eyes of three more men she found lying beaten and dead on the ground. She stopped in front of one of the tenements where the crying had become more insistent but wavered in fear of the bloodshed she might discover within.

The front door was hanging open and she shouted out in the unlikely hope someone might still be alive. Fear settled in her stomach and in her bones. Get a grip of yourself, she whispered, get a grip. Then, avoiding the worst of the slippery blood-sodden wooden steps, she cautiously picked her way up, and with every step felt more and more nauseous, unable to prevent herself from heaving.

The three rooms leading off the landing were empty but for one old man sitting against a wall with a serious wound to his head and glassy, dead eyes. She let out a sob but carried on up to the next floor, the baby's cries weaker now. Just before she reached the top she felt her legs slip from beneath her and she slid down to the landing below. She lay still for a moment, but when she tried to move a searing pain shot through her left leg. Still she tried again and eventually managed to haul herself upstairs step by step. Only now the crying had ceased.

In the first room two women lay dead on the floor and Belle was just wondering if she could bear to try for the third floor when she saw movement. She limped over to one of the women and, bending down, gingerly lifted the corner of a thin blood-soaked blanket to see a baby curled up inside it. With a sinking heart, Belle checked to make sure the woman was dead and then gently lifted the child. It blinked, and she gasped. The child was alive. She stared at its huge brown eyes then examined it for injury, stroking its soft skin and hair, before wrapping it in the soiled blanket again and cradling it to her. What was the right thing to do? Should she leave the baby in the hope the authorities might find its relatives, or should she take it to safety? If she left the baby it might die, or the murderous mob might return. She made a snap decision. After stumbling to the stairs, she held the baby tightly and slowly edged down.

Outside, she glanced about so she'd be able to identify exactly where she had found the child, and then she began weaving through the alleys, finally ending up in an empty street, the pain ripping through her leg now so excruciating she shouted out. She stopped to catch her breath, all the while terrified and watching for the return of the armed men. Dizzy and sick, her leg burned with a ghastly pounding throb. On the verge of fainting, it became so overpowering she knew she was about to keel over, so steadied herself against a wall before stumbling on. The baby whimpered and tried to wriggle free. Belle considered putting her down beneath the shade of a tree, just for a moment, but heard a car travelling at speed towards her. As it drew up she saw it was a police squad car from which three uniformed men alighted followed by . . . She blinked. It couldn't be. But the fourth man, this one not in uniform, ran towards her. She wiped a bloodied hand across her eyes, the world tilted and then she dropped to the ground.

She woke in darkness. For Belle, unable to differentiate one hour from another, time drifted. A thing, blacker than she could ever imagine, hovered in the night-time shadows of the room. A light from the nurses' station slid under her door. The fear had changed her. Made her cringe at sudden noises, startle when a shadow moved. Made her tight inside herself. Small. Her whole being made up of fear. She did not call out.

Her mouth felt impossibly dry when she woke again and opened her swollen eyes. Lying very still, Belle saw a clean white room with gauze curtains gently blowing in the breeze from the open window. Strangely light-headed and stiff, she sniffed the air. Disinfectant and something floral. A uniformed nurse, arranging some pink peonies in a vase on the bedside cabinet, noticed Belle was awake.

Lungs constricted, painful, breath rasping and raw, Belle forced out the words. 'How long have I been here?'

She squinted in the brightness for a moment before a wave of nausea turned her stomach as memories of the massacre began racing back. She covered her eyes and groaned. Images of blood and death swam in her muzzy head. The women lying dead in the house, the people in the street, the killing, all the killing. And the baby . . . The poor little baby. Oh God! She remembered the feel of her warm soft skin and silky hair. And her eyes, her huge eyes. What had happened to her?

The nurse handed her a bowl and Belle sat up and retched into it, but there was hardly anything for she hadn't eaten, had she? She couldn't entirely remember the order of things. There had been the row with Oliver. Yes, she remembered that but what had happened directly after? Too weak to sit up for long, she fell back against the pillow and the nurse wiped her face with a cool, damp cloth.

'Thank you,' Belle murmured, then struggled to sit up again. 'How long have I been here?'

The nurse passed her a glass of water.

Belle drank it and then the nurse gently helped her back down. 'You need to rest.'

'I need to know about the baby.'

'Plenty of time for that.'

'So, how long *have* I been here?'

'Almost forty-eight hours.'

'I think I woke in the night.'

'Maybe, though the doctor gave you a sedative. You might have been dreaming.'

'And can I go now?' she said, wanting to get out of bed, stretch her legs and sort everything out. Wanting, too, to find a way to escape from everything she'd seen and the fear that had twisted her stomach and almost made her heart stop. Gin should do it. A few very large gins.

'The doctor will see you later but now you have a visitor. He has been waiting most anxiously.'

Oliver, Belle thought, forgetting their quarrel, but when the nurse opened the door she saw with mixed feelings that the man was Edward. But she was grateful he'd come and attempted a smile.

'I hope you like the flowers,' he said with a broad smile.

She nodded distractedly and tried to peer through the open door to see what was happening in the corridors beyond. 'Thank you. But the baby? Is she here?'

'She's safe and sound.'

'Did you find her relatives?' she asked, urgent in her need to know.

He gently closed the door and then explained they were taking care of the baby and she was not to concern herself.

'I can tell you exactly where I found her if it helps. I'm sure I can tell you if you take me there. Please help me to get up.' She began to shuffle up the bed. 'I'm sure I can walk.'

'Belle, there's no need. We're already making enquiries. Hopefully we'll find a relative soon.'

'Are you sure? I can't bear to think of that tiny child ending up in an orphanage.' She gulped back a sob. 'Edward, can you imagine how terrible it must have been for her to be there when her mother was stabbed?'

He pulled out a chair and, after settling himself, took hold of her left hand and stroked it gently. 'Now, now, no need to worry. I've already said the baby is fine. How are you feeling? That's the important question.'

She frowned. 'Grateful to be alive but extremely light-headed. I can't quite remember everything.'

'Possibly a good thing.'

'But how did I get here? What happened to me?'

'You know we found you close to the Indian quarter?'

'Yes. I didn't mean to be.'

'I should hope not. You fell and injured your leg on some broken glass – at least we think so.'

She glanced down at herself. 'I can't feel it.'

'They've given you painkillers.'

Tears began to fill her eyes and then spill down her cheeks. He quietly handed her a clean handkerchief and she wiped her face.

'Better now?' he said.

'It was awful, Edward. Awful. The things I saw. Why were they killing Indians?'

'I'll explain it all when you're feeling better.'

She pulled her hand away. She needed to get it straight in her head. Why had it happened? Why had it been allowed to happen? But she could see he wasn't going to tell her now. She pressed both hands down on the mattress for leverage and pulled herself up the bed. 'I must get up. I don't want to be here any more. Please help me. Please. I have to see Clayton and get to Sydney.'

He shook his head and his eyes darkened. 'Out of the question, I'm afraid. You've had a traumatic experience. The doctor wants to keep you here for at least a week, possibly longer.'

'But Clayton?'

Edward's mouth twisted to one side as he pulled a regretful face. 'Sorry, my dear, but he fled as soon as the trouble started.'

She shook her head, disbelief bubbling up inside her. 'No! I don't believe it. You mean he isn't going to take me on?'

'Not at the moment. They've already hired a new understudy, I hear. I'm sure he will be back though.'

'Couldn't they have waited for me?' Her voice had come out thin and high pitched and, in her weakened state, she struggled to prevent her disappointment from showing. Although, after everything she'd been through, she had the notion that disappointment over an agent was an awfully trivial thing. Did it really matter so much?

'It seems they could not wait.' Edward reached for her hand again. 'I know you must be frustrated by this but show business does appear to be a somewhat cut-throat world.'

She gazed at him. 'It was you, you know, who . . .?'

'Yes. Lucky I came across you, especially as you were losing blood. But what on earth were you doing there?'

She shook her head. 'I'm trying to remember but it's all a blur. I just found myself caught up in the trouble and then in my panic I lost my way.'

He nodded. 'You poor old thing.'

'What was it all about? Please tell me.'

'As I said, I'll explain it when you're feeling better. At the moment we're still trying to piece it all together. Now you need to rest.'

For the next couple of days Belle did little but eat and sleep, although when awake she felt choked by the cloying scent of the flowers in her room. She had gleaned a little of what had happened from the nurse, but Edward hadn't yet returned. Had she even thanked him for rescuing her?

But then the image of the man with no eyes swam before her . . . Oh God! She covered her own eyes with her palms.

How had it all come about? And why? What could have been the cause of such terrible carnage? Edward would come back and tell her – surely, he must – for nothing had ever seemed so important as her need to understand. Without understanding there would be no respite from the violence and brutality she had witnessed on the streets. The sleeping pills they mercifully gave her at night made her woozy and unfocused in the morning but without them she wouldn't have slept at all. In the daytime, still with the awful stench of blood in her nostrils, she continued to weep over the sound of buzzing flies and the appalling silence of the dead looping round and round. Her sorrow for the baby with its enormous dark eyes did not abate and she prayed the authorities would do their best for her. She vowed to ensure the little baby girl was safe and cared for, as soon as she was better.

One morning, when all Belle wanted to do was hide from the world and bury her head under the pillow, Gloria turned up.

'Darling, you really have been in the wars. Silly girl, whatever were you thinking?'

At the tone of her friend's voice Belle felt herself tensing. She forced a weak smile and saw Gloria was looking especially glamorous in a black-and-white suit with a matching hat, and she was armed with chocolates and wine. But really Gloria was the last person she wanted to see right now.

'Won't you sit down?' Belle managed to say.

'Actually, I have to dash, but I wanted to bring you these.' She placed her gifts on the already crowded cabinet. 'But, darling, you don't seem terribly pleased to see me. And I am the herald of extremely good news too.'

'Sorry. I don't feel so good. It was terrible, Gloria.'

'I'm sure it must have been and, naturally, you don't feel well. Only to be expected.'

Belle shifted herself into a more upright position and ran a hand over her hair. 'I saw such awful –'

'Of course, of course.' Gloria waved her hand dismissively and then tilted her head and seemed to be scrutinizing Belle's appearance. 'Hmmm. You could do with a trip to the hairdresser. I'll arrange it. But now for the good news.'

'Well, I could certainly do with some,' Belle said despondently, wondering how anything could make her feel better.

'Tra-la! Listen to what I've got. Harry has postponed his trip. He'll wait until you're well enough to go.' She winked. 'After I had a few well-chosen words in his ear, that is.'

'Oh God, what did you say to him?' Belle asked, unsure how she was expected to take this.

'Let's simply say I reminded him of a little indiscretion I had witnessed.'

'You blackmailed him?' Belle was horrified.

Gloria smiled complacently. 'Only a teeny-weeny bit.'

'But he'll absolutely hate me.'

'Of course he won't. He'll hate me. The difference is, I couldn't care less.'

Belle looked away, completely unconvinced and certain the man would resent her.

'He's actually managed to arrange a meeting with the District Commissioner of Mandalay, just as he promised. The man's been there for donkey's years apparently and if anyone knows anything it'll be him. Say thank you nicely.'

Belle managed another weak smile. How typical. Of course Gloria didn't want to hear anything about what had happened. Belle couldn't help thinking of Oliver and wishing they could talk.

'Anyway, as I said, I have to make tracks.' She leant across to kiss Belle on the cheek. 'Bye, darling. Get well soon.'

And with that she swept from the room in a cloud of scent infused with jasmine, rose and sandalwood. Chanel No. 5, Belle thought as she picked up the novel somebody had kindly left for her. *The Murder at the Vicarage* by Agatha Christie. She read for a few minutes but still found it hard to escape the dreadful images in her head. As she laid the book down a slip of paper fell out and landed on the bedcover. She picked it up and read it, then, with a gulp, tore it into shreds. She could not let this touch her. And though she wanted to see him, there was no chance she would make the same mistake again. Oliver had sent his love and hoped she was over her horrific ordeal. He had expressed the wish she would soon be feeling better and suggested they might meet up for a drink. In the aftermath of the massacre Belle felt vulnerable, as if the shock had shaken something loose within her and all the insecurities she had tried so hard to conceal were now slipping out. She badly needed a friend, but it couldn't be Oliver. It just couldn't.

She was remembering more and more now, reliving the immobilizing terror she'd experienced when she'd believed the men were going to attack her. It lodged inside her stomach, this fear, and it kept her tightly coiled, had become part of her, inseparable from who she was. She pressed a hand hard into her stomach as if to force it out, but it only made her choke and splutter. In the end she managed to doze out of sheer exhaustion until she heard dogs barking in the street outside and then the door opening again. She closed her eyes but sensed his presence even before he was ushered into the room.

'Hello, Edward,' she said, opening her eyes. 'Could you close the curtain properly? There's a shard of light. It's too bright.'

'Rebecca was waiting to see you but I'm afraid I pulled rank. She said she'd be back tomorrow.' He closed the curtain and sat on a chair he'd pulled close to the bed, taking hold of her hand and patting it.

She stared at him. 'Please tell me what happened to the baby? I have to know.'

'We think we might have found a grandmother. I promise I'll let you know when we're certain we have the right person.'

She nodded. 'What was it all about, Edward? Why did it happen?'

He smiled sympathetically. 'It's somewhat complicated but I'll try to keep it simple, though really you should never have become involved.'

Belle hoped he wasn't going to call her a silly girl too and then, when he did not, tried to concentrate on his words. Apparently, it had all begun at the docks. Hundreds of Indian labourers employed to stow and unload cargo had gone on strike for better wages and Burmese men had been taken on to break the strike. Once the strike was resolved the Burmans were let go. These men had been accompanied to work by their wives who carried their lunch in baskets and had walked long distances to get there. As the Burmese were dismissed, the Indians made the mistake of laughing at them in front of their wives, and in so doing humiliating them. This contretemps led to blows, with Indians being killed and then thrown in the river. A rumour spread that some Indian men had cut off a Burmese woman's breasts, which led to thousands of Burmese going on the hunt for Indians to kill. Unfortunately, there had already been resentment brewing as too many Indians had crowded in from their impoverished villages and the Burmans looked down on them as little better than vermin.

'We've had no end of trouble,' Edward was saying. 'There have been hundreds of casualties and now the Indian population has barricaded itself in and won't come out. Most of the food shops are Indian so the city is running out of necessities. Not only that, it's Indian labourers who take away the city's night soil and the whole place is beginning to stink to high heaven.'

'What will you do?'

He sighed deeply. 'At least seven thousand Indians have taken refuge in the old lunatic asylum. Most of their homes were destroyed in the riot.'

'Riot? More like a massacre from what I saw. They must be terrified.'

He gave her a rueful smile. 'Indeed. There's not only been murder but looting too. So, to avoid a health epidemic, we are going to put them to work.'

'I hope they'll receive compensation for what they've lost.'

'Unlikely.'

Suddenly disillusioned, she frowned. 'But surely that can't be right?'

He shrugged. 'We don't have the means to help them further.'

'Nor the will,' she said, and he looked surprised by her sharp tone of voice.

'Look, Belle, things are tricky right now and there's much you don't understand.'

'Well, enlighten me then.'

'There has always been dissent between the races.'

'And whose fault is that? We brought the Indians here and now we don't care to protect them.'

'It was their own choice to come.'

'Lured by promises of jobs and money, no doubt.'

He shook his head, but Belle felt certain she was right. She stared at him, and knowing he was unlikely to say more, changed the subject.

'Why did the Burmese men paint those strange signs on their chests?' she asked.

'Makes them invincible. They believe the signs magically protect them. You may already have gathered how superstitious they are.'

She nodded. 'Yes, but I thought they were Buddhists. You know – peace-loving.'

'Buddhism mixed with animism and goodness knows what else. But there has always been violence here.' He sighed deeply. 'Anyway, about this river trip. I strongly suggest you go with Harry as soon as you are well enough. Do you think you might? There's likely to be civil unrest in Rangoon for quite some time, and you, my dear girl, have already suffered enough.'

He was right. She had. And, since she'd lost her chance with Clayton, the idea of the river trip had become tempting again. After everything she'd been through, it would be a relief to get away. Nothing would rid her of the persistent fear and the images that continued to torment her, but the further she was from Rangoon the better she might feel. She thought back to her arrival in Burma and how she'd been attracted to the golden coating of their Rangoon lives, but now she couldn't rid herself of Oliver's voice. He'd been correct about so much. Beneath the surface of this glittering colonial world lay tensions that would only become more pronounced and when it came to justice there was little for anyone who wasn't British. She hardly dared consider the abuse of power, the rampant greed and the terrible racial prejudice, and her compassion for the dispossessed Indians made her wonder if she was more like Oliver than she had ever realized.

33.

Diana, Cheltenham, 1922

I'd woken early knowing something special was going to happen but not remembering exactly what it was. But then, sweating and hot, ah yes, it came back to me. Now as I glance around my room checking everything is done I rehearse my words of departure. A solemn thank you and dry-eyed goodbye for ever or a face full of sorrow and regret? Although I feel anxious, I opt for solemn and dignified. For I know appearance still matters. My trunk has gone ahead so now it's just my personal items left, the bits and pieces that will accompany me in Simone's car: a few toiletries, my mother's silver hand mirror, my pills, my Parker pen and my diary. There's nothing much in there but I'd like to start writing again if I can. It seems the doctor thinks it will help too.

I am now to use my maiden name of Riley. Miss Diana Augusta Riley. It feels good. A farewell to loneliness. Although I still haven't set eyes on my cottage myself, Simone and Douglas have already furnished it and, of course, I'm curious. It's not without trepidation that I contemplate this change in my life and so I slip over to the window and grip the sill in the hope of one last glimpse of Annabelle. They don't want her to witness my leaving and it has been tacitly agreed that Mrs Wilkes will take her out for the day. Last night I sat on my daughter's bed and sang to her, some silly song I know she likes. After a moment she joined in and when we were done we both laughed and laughed – I'm not sure why, but it was happy laughter. She let me brush her hair until it shone and then I said goodnight and kissed both her velvety soft cheeks. She looked at me in such a way and when her forehead puckered I felt as if she had somehow deduced I was leaving. But then the moment passed.

'Night, night, Mummy,' she said, and I struggled to keep the tears from spilling.

'Night, darling,' I replied as I walked towards the door. 'Sleep tight.'

And then I hurried away from her room so she would not hear me weeping.

How will I cope with the loss of my daughter?

I'm not able to answer. Not yet. And the truth is, I don't know. Nor do I know if I'm doing the right thing. My mind wanders round and round in an unforgiving loop and I tell myself to think of something else. As Simone says, I am closing the door on the old me and opening the door on someone new. I must focus. This is something I must do, regardless of what I'm about to sacrifice, or how I feel about it. And I must also remember I'm doing this for Annabelle.

Simone says I will never have to pretend with her. That alone is a weight off my mind.

I put my cheek to the glass of the window and feel its soothing coolness against my cheek. It's June now and a sunny warm day and I wonder if I am overdressed wearing a twinset and linen skirt. I finger the pearls around my neck and my breath catches as, extremely suddenly, I see them. Two figures. Annabelle and Mrs Wilkes leaving via the front gate. Annabelle skips alongside the woman apparently with no sense of what is about to happen, and Mrs Wilkes is walking briskly as if in a hurry to leave. I raise my hand as if to wave and feel a moment of utter anguish. Is this really the right thing to do? I remember Douglas's arguments. What if the voice leads me to hurt my own child? Does he believe that's what happened in Burma? Is it why he's so adamant I should go? He's never said as much but it would explain an awful lot. I watch Annabelle until she disappears, but I do not cry. It is for the best. I am no use to her as I am, and nor will I escape from the guilt I constantly feel if I stay. She will be better off with Douglas.

There's a knock on the door and Simone walks in wearing a flowery summer dress beneath a lightweight cream raincoat.

'Will it rain today?' I ask.

She shrugs. 'It might. Are you ready?'

I nod and take one last glance around my room. Goodbye, room, I think. Goodbye, park. And in that moment I feel utterly bereft.

'Can you give me a few seconds?'

'All right. I'm parked just outside the gate, so it will only take a moment before we're in the car. You've taken your medication?'

I give her what I hope is more than a wan smile and hold myself together.

34

The riverboat, owned by the Irrawaddy Flotilla Company and captained by a Scot, was smaller than Belle had expected, but her first-class cabin was snug and comfy. After the relief at finding out from Edward that the baby she'd rescued had eventually been reunited with a grandmother, she'd packed a few things and boarded the night before. Edward had told her the child's name was Madhu, and that it meant 'honey'. Her grandmother lived in one of the villages not far from Rangoon, so the child would grow up safely and hopefully not remember a thing. But how much had the tiny little mite really witnessed? Aware that nothing could have prevented the child from hearing the screams as the murders happened, Belle forced herself not to picture it. But at least the little girl would be cared for, so something good had come of it, though how Belle herself would ever fully recover she had no idea.

The boat had been moored under a starless sky, so there had been little to see as she'd boarded, and she hadn't really cared. Although the light from the lanterns dancing on the water had been pretty she'd been tired and sick at heart. Refusing the proffered cocktail, she'd headed for her bed and remembered what the fortune teller had said. Well, he'd been right about the journey.

After an unexpectedly good sleep, she was woken by the engines gearing up and, wanting to see the river by daylight, dressed hurriedly. Then, as she climbed the slippery metal stairs up to the observation deck, taking extra care with her still-aching leg, she saw the wide river was wreathed in a hazy golden mist. Grateful for her mother's old cashmere shawl, she wrapped it around her shoulders.

When she'd requested time off, Fowler's usually florid complexion had turned completely purple, his square physique puffed up even more than usual and his eyebrows looked in danger of dancing right off his face. Belle had managed to conceal her amusement as he emphasized how problematic this would be. She already knew Gloria had put in a word for her and Fowler would not dare deny her request, but she had to go through the pretence of pleading and then thanking him effusively when he finally relented. Less than three weeks he'd given her, and she hoped it would suffice.

As she ate her breakfast – a strange concoction of sticky noodles with slices of chicken and an over-sweet sauce – she surveyed the few other passengers who were already breakfasting. A couple of well-dressed businessmen tucking into an English breakfast, three solitary Burmese men in traditional dress and one heavily pregnant Burmese woman, wearing a *longyi* of pink and green, and with flowers in her hair. She smiled sweetly at Belle and Belle managed a weak one in return. Comfortable rattan chairs and tables dotted the deck, interspersed with magnificent potted palms, and, at the bow, a row of canvas deckchairs were at the disposal of those who wished to sit in the sun.

In fact, the mist soon burnt off and, as Belle focused on the day, she saw that putting some distance between herself and what had happened in Rangoon had been the right thing to do. Spirits somewhat uplifted by the gorgeous morning with its sapphire blue sky and sunlight casting glittering diamonds across the water, she had a strong feeling this boat trip upriver might help. As a flock of herons took off, Belle took it as a sign of good fortune.

The boat slowly slid its way north. An hour or so passed and she found the peace soothing as she watched the sunshine enhancing the shadowy depths of the tall rain trees beyond the riverbanks. Even the grasses and bushes at the edges remained still and Belle, struck by the timeless quality of the scene, felt her jangled nerves calming. Here and there they passed villagers going about their daily tasks, preparing nets, washing clothes in the river then slapping them against the rocks. Others were cooking on open fires while their semi-naked children played in the mud and Belle found she was smiling. Life went on as it had always done.

An hour after that, Harry appeared, blurry-eyed and the worse for wear.

'Are you all right?' she asked.

'Stayed up late.'

'Coffee?'

He nodded and pushed his spectacles back up his nose.

She watched as other boats passed silently by. First an enormous oil barge carrying, Harry said, crude oil for the Burmah Oil Company, then another weighed down with timber for the Burmah Bombay Corporation. Smaller fishing boats moved at a leisurely pace and she spotted a steamer with a flat-iron floater in tow, on to which two motor cars were roped. Cargo boats laden with goods passed in the opposite direction: jade, bullocks, blue-grey elephants, bales of cotton and bursting sacks of rice. Harry pointed them all out, revelling in his role of guide, his hangover forgotten.

'Nothing enters or leaves Burma without a trip on the Irrawaddy,' he said.

She wondered if that applied to her sister too.

As if sensing what she was thinking, he raised a finger. 'Had a word with the purser about you, last night. Good chap. Likes his whisky. If you want a chat he'll be free for pre-supper drinks.'

'What did you tell him?'

'I said you were hoping to trace a family member.'

A volley of large black birds burst from a tree close to the water's edge, and Belle watched as a native woman, a red scarf wrapped round her head and using her *longyi* as a sling to carry her baby, raised her head to follow their flight.

She thought of Oliver and a wave of regret passed through

her, but she dismissed any ideas of seeking him out again. He'd shown his true colours and that was enough, and yet, still needing to unburden herself, she would have loved to have been able to talk to him. Tell him everything. The one person who might have understood. It had never been like that with Nicholas. She shook her head. No point thinking of either of them. She and Oliver were over. But the manner of their parting still hurt, and she couldn't talk herself out of that.

Other than during the white glare of the midday sun, she spent the day on deck reading or sinking into reverie as she surveyed life on the river, whistling in amazement whenever she saw a series of pagodas lining its banks. Sometimes she'd spot the red hair of a wild dog but, so far, had not seen a clouded leopard, a sun bear or a baboon. She'd heard sun bears could climb trees and make a nest to sleep in. Lunch, which she took with Harry, was Burmese, a tea leaf salad followed by something they called butterfish with some intensely fragrant rice. She noticed how much Harry liked a drink and wondered about it. He had not seemed to be a drinker when she'd first met him in Rangoon, accepting only a lemonade and turning his nose up at gin. In fact, there was something jittery about him now, and she wondered what was wrong.

As the day drew to a close, the iridescent blue of the water turned darker, the banks, lit by the low sun, shone golden, and the now lilac sky transformed the hills in the distance into a darkening smudgy blueish-grey. On deck the lamps were lit and, along with the salty, fishy smell of the river, burning oil wafted through the air. The river seemed rather spooky, as if voices were singing in the water, though it was probably sounds drifting from the villages beyond. In her mind's eye she kept seeing the blood of the dead woman lying on the floor with herself bending over and then finding the baby hidden in a blanket. She'd been brave, the mother, to protect her child like that. Belle halted every time she began to speculate what might have happened had she not found the child.

With the baby on her mind she watched as the people on board congregated in knots, talking and laughing as they accepted drinks from the smartly dressed waiters, but she didn't see the pregnant woman anywhere.

A small man, wearing a dark-green shirt with a discreetly patterned dark *longyi*, was smiling as he walked towards her. She rose from her chair, but he bowed and indicated she should remain seated. As he took the chair opposite her, he introduced himself as the purser and began to speak. His English was terrible, however, and it took several attempts before she could make out he was asking how he might be able to help. Feeling flustered, she glanced around, hoping to spot Harry who would be able to translate, but when she finally spotted him, he was deep in conversation with another man, a half-empty whisky bottle on the table between them.

After she'd explained about the rumour of a white baby having been seen with a Burmese couple all those years ago, the purser shook his head and she worked out he was saying it had been before his time. He did manage to convey that an archaeologist at Bagan might know something. He lived in the government rest house there and had been working at Bagan for many years. The rest house was a special place as it had been built in 1922 to house the Prince of Wales on his visit to Burma, though sadly he had never actually stayed there.

When Harry finally stumbled over she asked if she might be able to stay at the rest house too and he nodded.

'We have one night and a couple of days in Bagan,' he said, in a somewhat slurred voice. 'It's a wonderful site of extensive and partially ruined temples, so plenty to see. And in any case, they'll need to refuel and restock there.'

When they arrived at Bagan over a week later, Belle had become so accustomed to the slow pace of life and the routine of the days on board she no longer knew what day it was. It had made all the difference. Her memories were fading a little and, although she knew she would never forget, *should* never forget, she had stopped tormenting herself so often. It would take time. And the best thing to do now was to see Bagan, meet the archaeologist and find out whatever she could.

They had already made one overnight stop, where the crew had refuelled, although many of the passengers had remained on board including Belle and the pregnant woman who'd smiled again and said *good evening* in near-perfect English. Belle had then sat alone enjoying the night air and listening to the sound of tinkling Burmese music floating across from a nearby village.

Bagan was where they were all to get off.

Surprised by the makeshift manner of disembarking, she watched as the purser helped the pregnant woman. Belle then gladly accepted his offer to carry her small case so she could make her unsteady way across a narrow plank that traversed the worst of the mud. The riverboat itself, tethered to a stake hammered deeply into the ground, rocked gently in the water.

Harry accompanied her in a horse and cart along a dusty track to the rest house. She stared as the generous timber-framed place came into view, built as if it belonged in the home counties of England but with oriental touches here and there. They were met by a Burmese butler who led them to an airy reception room where they were offered a delicious juice of mango and guava, and where he explained that more and more visitors had recently been coming to see the ruins. After they'd registered he showed them to their darkened rooms on the first floor.

Once the butler had left her on her own, Belle stepped across to the shuttered windows, threw them open and surveyed the garden beyond. Enclosed by walls on three sides, all festooned with a riot of bright-purple bougainvillea, the garden itself was small but tranquil. In the middle a trickle of water suggested a fountain, though it looked unkempt and neglected. Birds swooped from tree to tree but the breeze ruffling their leaves wasn't enough to reach her stiflingly hot room. Although she'd enjoyed the river trip, she realized it had lulled her into a false sense of security. She'd almost forgotten what she was here to do and now it was time to meet the archaeologist, a certain Dr Walter Guttridge.

35

Diana, the Cotswolds, 1922

Douglas stands by the gate and I see he is stooped, staring at the ground beneath his feet as if in contemplation. I walk to him and he straightens up but still avoids my eyes.

'Well,' I say. 'This is it.'

'Indeed,' he replies, and now he looks at me.

I glance at his beautiful eyes. They are deep dark pools of confusion. Not harsh or severe, just rather lost. I see he is holding his emotions in, and there will be no sentimental farewell. I long to embrace him, for him to enfold me in his arms and for us to recapture the way we used to be. But it cannot be. Those days are gone. He has become good at hiding and now my husband is sprung so tightly he dares not allow himself to feel.

He grasps my hand and squeezes, then he lets go and steps back. I do what he expects me to do and I walk out of the gate wordlessly, without looking back, and without making a scene.

It's a glorious June day, the sky extraordinarily blue, and the sun tinting the tops of the clouds with silver and gold. I am silent at first as we begin the drive, unable to speak to Simone, but eventually I relax. We pass a riot of different greens still lacy with new life, drystone walls lining the road and far-reaching views across the Cotswolds, where fields dotted with sheep butt up against meadows in which horses nuzzle the fences. We make two stops at roadside inns to enable the car to cool down and to feed it with water and petrol. At one stop Simone encourages me to leave the car and take the air, but I remain where I am, so instead she brings me a cool lemonade and a sandwich for lunch.

When we eventually turn off to the left, passing deep woods on both sides, and then begin the descent down the hill to the valley, where the village of Minster Lovell lies, I feel my stomach clench. But after we cross the medieval bridge over the river I am surprised: I hadn't expected it to be so enchanting. Though narrow, and lined by enormous weeping willows, the river is flowing freely and as we turn right and away from the mill, we pass the pub on the left. Simone points out her cottage. Like several others it too is thatched, a long and narrow house of buttery Cotswold stone glowing in the sunlight, covered in wisteria and with a ditch in front of it. I notice how the ditch travels along the length of the lane to carry away rainwater and how a few of the houses are very close, in fact joined to one another. Simone catches the look on my face.

'Don't worry. Yours is detached and right on the edge of the village at the top of the hill.'

I hadn't noticed the gentle incline but see now that we are rising and am relieved to know I shall not be in the centre of things.

'There are only two houses after yours, both around the corner, and there is plenty of land between them.'

I'm longing to see my new home. When Simone pulls up she points to a beautiful cottage behind a drystone wall and, from what I can see, surrounded by pretty gardens.

She gets out of the car and then comes round to my side to help me. I feel my heart beating faster but my eagerness to see inside the house overrides my initial nerves and, within minutes, Simone is unlocking the front door and ushering me inside to the hall.

'I've arranged the furniture as I thought you'd like it and the curtains have been hung, but of course you must change anything you don't like. I shan't be offended.'

I smile at her, grateful for everything she has done.

She shows me around the house and I have to remind myself

it is mine and not hers. Up the narrow staircase, and off a tiny landing, there are three bedrooms and a bathroom. Two bedrooms overlook the road, but with a generous front garden that hardly matters. My bedroom, she says, is at the back, and when I step inside it I steer over to one of the two windows. From my vantage point I can see a well-stocked and well-maintained garden leading to dense woods beyond.

I spin round in gratitude. 'Thank you.'

'I knew you'd like it. When I came back from Burma after Roger died I needed to find peace and looked everywhere.'

'You found it.'

'But only when I came to Minster Lovell.'

'I love it. Really I do.'

'It's a special place. I always say the tranquillity here mended my broken heart.'

I reach out a hand to her and she squeezes it.

'I had your trunk brought up here. And, when I stay over, my room is one of the two at the front.'

We go back down and explore a sweet drawing room with a large fireplace, a cosy snug with a smaller fireplace, a dining room and a small kitchen with a pantry leading off it.

'When you are ready,' she says, 'I will take you to the doctor's house. You turn right just up from this house and go downhill towards the church. You only pass one house set well back from the lane and then his is on the right at the bottom.'

'I thought he would come to me.'

'If you prefer, I'm sure he will.'

I nod, feeling relieved.

'Mrs Jones from the village comes to cook and clean every morning. I've explained you've been ill and need peace and quiet, and as she's a sensible woman I don't feel she will be intrusive. She'll shop for provisions too and Norridge & Son take care of local deliveries in their specially built Ford T van. It's really comical actually, looks like a rectangular box on wheels.'

I shiver, suddenly cold. Although it's June, the late afternoon and evenings can still be chilly.

'All we have to do is light the fire,' Simone says reassuringly. 'Mrs Jones has set one here in the snug, but also in the drawing room and your bedroom. And she's made us a pea and ham soup for supper. For now, what about your cashmere wrap to warm you up? Didn't you bring it?'

'I left it behind. Annabelle might be glad of it one day and I want her to have something of me.'

I try hard not to cry at the thought of Annabelle.

'I need to go back to mine to collect my night things,' Simone says and touches my hand. 'Will you be all right? I can do it later, if you prefer?'

I tell her it's fine and, while she is gone, I think of home. After I said goodnight to Annabelle last night, I saw Douglas. He was softer than when I left this morning. He came to my room and we held each other for what seemed like a long time. I didn't want him to see my tears so pulled away and with my back to him dried my eyes. He saw through my little charade, of course, and knew I was crying. And when I looked at him I saw his eyes were sad too and his hands were shaking.

I inhale slowly. In and out.

I am here now and feel sure I will come to know every nook and cranny of my new home as well as every blade of grass in the garden too. The thought of it is strangely comforting. Maybe one day I will know the village as well. The world outside my window feels suddenly less flimsy, and my connection to it less fragile. Simone was right: there is something special about this place, but it has come at such a price and, more than anything, I wish Annabelle could have come too.

36

Belle's first meeting with Walter Guttridge, the archaeologist, was memorable. She had not expected him to be, well, so large – over six foot six – and well into his seventies too, with long straggly hair and a dark tan that served to exaggerate the deeply etched lines around his eyes. Judging by the look of him, he was still spry, but he had a strange habit of pulling his left ear when he was speaking.

'I was sent here in 1905 from the British Museum,' he said in a loud and strident voice after Harry had introduced them and he had agreed to take Belle out with him for the morning.

'Quite a culture shock, I imagine.'

He nodded his agreement. 'The government had recently decided to maintain and preserve Bagan. For more than thirty years I've been surveying the area, making recommendations, overseeing renovations and so on.'

They were walking and talking as he led her along sandy tracks towards the village, bypassing tall clumps of bamboo and wild banana and the secrets of the dense forest beyond. Harry had cried off with some excuse of work he urgently needed to do, and so Belle was on her own with this bear of a man who seemed so incongruous among the tiny Burmese and yet whom they all seemed to respect. He spoke to them in their own language and nodded and laughed as they replied.

Belle glanced up at him. 'You know everyone?'

'As I said, I've been here a long time.'

'Would you ever go home?'

'This is home.'

'Even when you retire?'

'I don't intend to ever retire. I shall continue to live and work and then I shall drop. Here.'

'The purser on the boat said you might be able to recall the story of a white baby being accompanied by a Burmese couple on their way to Mandalay.'

'I recall it all right. Back in 1912, wasn't it?'

'1911, actually.'

'Very curious it was . . . at the time.'

'And you saw the baby yourself?'

'Ah, no. That would have been my assistant.'

'He's here?'

'He will be. He's on his way down from Mandalay. Has family there.'

'I hope he'll be back before I have to leave.'

As they arrived she looked around at the village. At first glance, it appeared to consist entirely of wooden-framed houses, the walls constructed of intricately woven bamboo.

'Are they bamboo? The walls?'

'Toddy palm, actually. They cover the windows with bamboo matting.'

The first house, nestling amid the trees, built on stilts and with a thatched roof, looked cosy. In front and to the side of it, in an enclosed compound, a woman swept the earth, a child played with a ball, and several scrawny chickens pecked about in the dust. At the back two mottled goats were tethered to a spike and a dog lay slumbering in the shade.

'What do the people do?' she asked.

'Cultivation, fishing. They make farm implements and nets, ropes, sails. And some make lacquerware to sell to the pilgrims who come.'

She had worked out Guttridge was deaf in the left ear, the one he continually pulled as if to encourage it to function again, and so she made a point of always walking on his right-hand side. They passed three barefoot monks in saffron-coloured robes with two very young ones following behind carrying bowls. Belle asked him about them.

'Between the ages of seven and thirteen, the boys live together in the monasteries for differing amounts of time. Those who stay form strong bonds, become a family of sorts.'

'Do all the boys have to do this?'

'All Buddhist Burmese boys become novice monks for at least a few weeks, some for several months, some even for years, especially if they have no family.'

'Can they leave?'

'Of course. They can return to normal life at any time or they can stay on as a monk.'

'And the bowls are to collect food?'

'Yes. They can only eat what they are given. Sometimes it's just rice. They believe life always includes an element of suffering and the cause of suffering is desire. To end the suffering, you give up desire and attachment. Hence their simple lifestyle.'

Belle wondered about it. Certainly, her desire for Oliver had ended in suffering but, despite that, wasn't life all about light and shade? And she couldn't help thinking she'd prefer facing the challenges of such a life, with all its ups and downs, rather than existing in a lacklustre one. But then again, she was young, and knew she had a lot to learn.

She paused to watch a beautifully dressed woman wearing a *longyi* with a traditional shawl, her neck and wrists encircled by gold chains. Squatting on the compacted earth, she was grinding the wood she would then mix with water to make *thanaka* paste. Shyly, she held some out and with a few nods encouraged Belle to take it. Belle smoothed some on her hand, but it dried rapidly in the oppressive heat and began to itch.

At a small crossroads an Indian man was waiting with a horse roped to a carriage, or rather something that looked more like a cart with open sides and a straw roof, clearly intended to serve as a carriage.

'We are going in that?'

Guttridge nodded. 'Best way. You're welcome to walk but it'll get hellishly hot.'

As they reached the odd-looking vehicle he helped Belle up the one step at the back and then folded himself into the cart too.

'So, what are you doing today?'

'Checking up on a stupa over on the far side.'

'Stupa?'

'A stupa, sometimes called a pagoda, is the top of a huge structure, often with a relic chamber inside. During the Pagan kingdom's height between the eleventh and thirteenth centuries, there were over ten thousand Buddhist temples, pagodas and monasteries built in these plains alone. It was Pagan then, not Bagan.'

'How many are left?'

'Less than three thousand. You'll be able to spot the ones we've restored in recent years, mainly using Indian labour which hasn't always gone down well.' He shook his head. 'Some are sadly too far gone. You'll see them cracked and ruined, lost beneath the greenery strangling them. Mind you, the earthquakes haven't helped. It's a wonder so many have survived.'

'And the people live among them?'

'The way they have always done, although there's talk of moving them out.'

'What a shame. I like the idea that ordinary life is going on around the monuments.'

The carriage set off on its bumpy path, bypassing the occasional cow or sheep. With no springs to soften the ride, Belle was jolted, jerked and bumped as Guttridge's booming voice fought with the loud screech of metallic wheels. She spotted stupa after stupa, usually in the reddish colour of the earth upon which they stood, looking as if they were acts of nature and not edifices built by man.

'And what are all the trees?'

'Tamarind, plum, neem mainly,' he said. 'But to really understand the layout a hot air balloon is the only way to see it all. Are you game? I'm going up tomorrow. You have time. My assistant won't be back until later.'

Belle glanced up at the sky. Was she game?

'Constructed in England to the highest standards and brought over some years ago. Completely transformed what we do. I've trained the local lads as helpers, so it's perfectly safe.'

After a moment she nodded and began to feel excited. What did she have to lose?

'You'll have to be in the field by five in the morning. We always go up before dawn. Mark my words, seeing the sun rise over the plain is an experience you'll never forget.'

At the sound of persistent knocking Belle woke in complete darkness, her head still throbbing from the hours she'd spent in the cart during the unforgiving heat of the previous day. She fumbled for a light switch, glanced at her watch and saw she only had five minutes before she was due to meet Walter Guttridge in the hall downstairs. She climbed into a pair of loose-fitting trousers, threw on a long-sleeved white shirt and then, as an afterthought, added a woollen cardigan. It might be cold up there this early in the day.

Guttridge was waiting for her as she arrived at the bottom of the stairs.

'Ready?' he asked in a brisk tone of voice that brooked no dissent.

She nodded, wishing she'd had time for a cup of tea and slightly regretting she'd agreed to do this.

The driver of the bullock used a torch with just a suggestion of light to faintly reveal the track, though what he could see was a mystery to Belle. However, he succeeded in driving them to a place where her eye was instantly drawn to a brightly burning brazier. In the eerie silence, but for the sound of the fire, it took a while for her eyes to adjust to the gloomy field. Gradually she made out the shape of a huge balloon lying flat on the ground and saw dark figures were moving about noiselessly as they prepared the balloon for flight. She shivered, and by the time the gas was lit and had begun to roar, and the balloon had been raised from the ground, something was buzzing and thumping in her ears. The basket seemed so small and insignificant. Surely it couldn't be safe?

'Come on then,' Guttridge said. 'Time to climb in. I will be noting any changes I spot since I last went up, so I'm afraid I'll not be talkative.'

He went first, along with one other man. As she waited her turn she admonished herself. Embrace the experience, she whispered. You may never get another chance. She used the moment to settle herself before a helper stepped forward with a stool which she used to climb into the basket in a less than graceful fashion, feeling glad she'd worn trousers. From there she could now see five other men holding the balloon steady by pulling on long ropes.

Guttridge explained the rules. Then the basket bumped a little and began to rise, and she felt a thrill.

Before long they were high above Bagan, drifting in the cool, silent air. At first, when she saw the land wreathed in mist, she felt disappointed. But then the mist melted and as the sun gradually rose, it tinted the tops of the pagodas and stupas in shimmering shades of pink and gold. Her spirits soared as she witnessed the full magnitude of the ancient plain. The further the balloon floated on, the more she saw: smoke circling up from a lone farm, tidy regulated patchworks of fields, bullocks already ploughing, birds swooping, and the silence broken only by the ringing of temple bells or the bark of a dog. She hadn't expected the timeless tranquillity of floating in the air above the extraordinary expanse of so many ancient monuments. In the distance the sun streamed across the water of the Irrawaddy, turning it silvery-gold. She wasn't religious but there was something about this she could only call mystical. Full of the sense there was so much more to life than she'd ever known, her eyes dampened. She felt light, transformed, as if she too belonged suspended high up, sharing the air with birds and the gentle wind. That the world could contain such extraordinary beauty and yet such violence seemed incomprehensible, but she knew she would somehow have to find a way to understand and accept these extremes.

She felt she could have stayed up there for days but by the time Guttridge had finished jotting his findings in his notebook the ride was almost over.

Their descent was slow and the landing bumpy as they came back down to earth, the basket thumping several times as it bounced along the ground. Apart from that slight discomfort Belle had spent the time smiling with satisfaction. She would live her life differently now. She would stop dwelling on what had happened in Rangoon. She would see with new eyes and stop worrying about what she couldn't change. Never had she expected to ride in a hot air balloon in one of the world's most extraordinary and beautiful settings. But she had.

37.

Diana, Minster Lovell, 1922

Today I'm to see Dr Gilbert Stokes for the first time. I know little about him save that he was a doctor at Radcliffe Infirmary in Oxford for some years and afterwards he worked at the Radcliffe Asylum. When Simone told me I must have paled because it worried me terribly but, she assures me, he's now semi-retired and only maintains an interest in patients with special problems. Apparently, he's very forward thinking in his ways, has studied the work of Sigmund Freud, and I understand he believes in treating certain illnesses through discussion. I'm not sure what I think about that and, to be honest, have yet to be convinced, because really, how can talking help?

One good thing. I am in love with my cottage with its drystone wall marking the boundary, tall oak trees on either side, and its split limestone tiled roof. I'm also pleased some of the smaller and, I have to say, nicer pieces of furniture have arrived from our Cheltenham house: my mother's cream dressing table, a tiny chest of drawers which used to be in the nursery, my favourite Tiffany lampshade, a small semi-circular hall table and my mother's old desk with its little secret drawer.

I currently employ a gardener to cut the grass and undertake the weeding but ache for a time when I'll feel well enough to go outside and take care of planting and pruning myself. I don't know the village yet, but Simone says if you walk through the churchyard and come upon the ruins of Minster Hall and then go beyond them, you arrive at the glorious riverbank.

The sudden murmur of voices reaches me from outside,

though I can't see Simone or the doctor. They must be standing in the porch just out of sight and so I wait until they enter the house. When they come into my sitting room, I'm surprised by what I see. Gilbert Stokes is not what I expected. I think of psychiatric doctors as being thin and weaselly, always trying to trip you up with their clever ways, but he is a round, avuncular man with kind blue eyes and a shock of astonishingly white hair.

He holds out a hand to me. I shake it and can't help smiling. He claps a second hand over mine and squeezes gently.

'Mrs Hatton. It's an absolute pleasure.'

'Hello,' I say. 'It's actually Miss Riley now, but please do call me Diana.'

'Apologies. My mistake.'

Simone starts to back out of the room. 'I'll make tea,' she says with a smile.

I nod. We've already arranged this beforehand. It's a small contrivance to give me a chance to assess the doctor on my own and, I think with a wry smile, for him to assess me.

'Shall we sit?' I say and indicate the chair by the window.

I sit opposite it, so I can see the view of the front garden. He turns his chair to face me.

'I want to be sure you understand this process may be relatively slow, but that you are free to change your mind about it at any time.'

I nod. 'We just talk. Am I right?'

His eyes twinkle and he gives me a genuinely warm smile. 'Indeed.'

As I said earlier, I can't see how talking will really help but I nod and then, hearing the kettle whistle, I turn my head towards the door, wondering if it would be rude to go and help Simone.

As if he senses what is in my mind he says, 'Do lend your friend a hand if you'd like,' and I'm impressed.

Maybe behind his jovial exterior there lies a sharply perceptive mind, but if he is kind I can accept that. And I think by giving me permission to leave, I no longer feel the need to go, so instead of absconding to the kitchen, I stay where I am. As we talk a little longer about the village and he tells me about his house down near the church, I find myself relaxing. There is something so gently reassuring in his presence I'm a little disappointed when Simone returns with a tray and I no longer have him to myself.

After the tea pouring, the tea drinking and the biscuit eating is done, he wipes his mouth with his napkin, then rises from his chair. 'So, if you are happy to become my patient, Diana, we can make a start next week and maybe aim for two sessions, one on Monday and one on Friday. Both at ten. How does that sound?'

I get to my feet too. 'Thank you, Doctor Stokes. I'd like that.' And, as I show him out and then stand in the porch not at all worried at very nearly being outside in the garden, I am surprised by how genuinely I mean it.

38

Just before five as the day began to cool down and with an hour to spare before meeting Guttridge's assistant, Belle, feeling the need to distract herself, decided to leave the rest house and set off to wander on her own. With her boat's departure not due until eight, she had plenty of time, so she gulped down a glass of water and slipped some mints into her pocket.

A gentle breeze helped lessen the heat and, as she kept to the long shadows of the taller, bushier trees, she was able to keep relatively cool. She followed the dusty yellow track, listening to the crunch of her own footsteps and choosing to turn right at each junction, so that on her return she could retrace her steps by turning left. She almost stepped on a long-horned beetle with pom-poms on its antennae and stood for a while to watch its progress. She passed the same houses as before, only now the compounds were busier with entire families sitting out in the shade with the smell of fish sauce and onions frying on outdoor charcoal burners. Sunlight flickering through the trees threw shifting patterns on the dry ground and everyone seemed so charming and friendly as Belle waved hello and then continued to walk further and further from the centre of the village.

As a friendly dog followed at her heels, she listened to the birds chirruping and thought about Elvira. What would her childhood have been like had she grown up with a sister? Would they have shared secrets and protected each other in the way sisters did? Or would they have been rivals engaged in endless squabbles, seeking attention and never getting on? She imagined Elvira walking beside her now, their arms wrapped around each other as they pointed out this plant or that and laughed too loudly about some silly thing or someone they both found hilarious. And what about discussing boys in a giggling hush after their parents had gone to bed? Their parents. It was not without a lump in her throat that she wondered who her mother might have been . . .

She walked on deep in thought without really noticing where she was, until she looked around and saw she'd left the last of the houses behind and had arrived in some open scrubland. Wanting to get out of the still baking hot sun, she set out for a wooded area around one of the stupas and then, resting on the grass and sucking a mint, she gazed lazily at the low late-afternoon light with only a hint of pink on the horizon.

She checked her watch. Just a little longer. The gentle sound of temple bells drifted on the wind and leafy scents floating from the trees combined with the perfume of the sweet white flowers growing so profusely. She closed her eyes and relaxed against the sun-warmed trunk of a tree. She'd been coasting like this for some time, listening to the *tap tap tap* of something like a woodpecker in the trees when, wrenched from her reverie, she was startled by a deep moan. Her eyes flew open and she quickly rose to her feet. She brushed herself down, ready to make off, not knowing if she would still get back in time and berating herself for her stupidity. But the moans came again, only this time sounding even more agonized. Someone was in dreadful pain and so, despite a strong misgiving and hoping she wasn't being led into a trap, Belle decided to investigate. Acutely aware of her status as a woman and a foreigner, in a country she barely understood, she hadn't a clue what bizarre practices might be going on. Not to mention the deadly snakes and insects hiding in the undergrowth. Gingerly, she walked around the entire circumference of the stupa, keeping an eye out for trouble, and almost stumbled over the pregnant woman from the boat, now lying on her side with her legs drawn up.

Belle dropped to her knees and knelt beside the woman. 'Are you all right?' she said. 'I can go for help.'

The woman reached out a shaking hand. 'Please, no. Do not go. I am scared.'

'But why are you here alone?'

The woman gasped in pain before she was able to speak again. 'I wanted to bring the baby on. It is overdue. But I have to give birth on the boat or my husband will be angry.'

Belle frowned. Was this another of the outlandish superstitions she'd heard about? 'Why does it matter?' she asked.

'It is great good fortune to be born on a riverboat on the Irrawaddy. I have been up the river once already.'

'Where's your husband?'

'He is working at the Secretariat in Rangoon but could not get time off for a second journey.'

'So, you came alone?'

The woman let out an agonized wail.

Belle got to her feet. 'I really must get help. I know nothing about childbirth.' She didn't mention how the idea of it made her squeamish.

The woman pointed to a bag. 'I have brought turmeric to anoint the baby's body. It is to drive out evil spirits and we must find the astrologer too. There is one on our boat. I made sure before we left.'

'Do you think you can make it as far as the boat?'

The woman reached out a hand and Belle helped her up, but the poor soul immediately doubled over, clutching her belly and whimpering. Belle managed to help the woman to sit in the shade of a tree, but it was clear she wouldn't be going back to the boat any time soon.

'What's your name?' Belle asked, squatting down beside her and continuing to hold her hand.

'Hayma. It means forest. I was born in a forest.'

'You are not from Rangoon?'

'No, but I was born in a small hamlet not far from the town.'

She doubled over again, her face twisted, and Belle could see the woman was forcing herself to stifle a scream.

Belle's chest constricted in fear. 'I have to get help,' she said again, glancing at her watch, knowing she'd now missed her appointment, but also feeling terribly anxious for Hayma.

'Please, I beg you, do not leave me on my own.'

Belle acquiesced and for twenty minutes or so the woman remained relatively calm. She seemed more composed now Belle was keeping her company. But soon the contractions began again. Belle glanced around, hoping to seek out anyone who might take over the vigil. At first the place was deserted, but after half an hour she spotted a woman carrying a baby on her back while solemnly treading the path back towards the village. Belle beckoned the woman over and between contractions Hayma was able to speak to her. After a moment the woman spun on her heels and hurried away.

'She gets help,' Hayma said.

But the woman didn't return immediately and, as Belle tried to soothe Hayma, she felt it couldn't be long before the child would be born. She wracked her brain. What did one do with a newborn baby? She scratched her head, wishing there was somebody to consult, and then, at last, the woman who'd been carrying the baby returned with what looked like a large bundle of cloths and a jug of water. With a huge sigh of relief, Belle rose to her feet.

Before the baby arrived, the sun had begun to sink in the east, the sky had turned vermillion and then in a flash had transformed into a blanket of velvety indigo, dusted with the light of millions of tiny stars. Belle felt magic stirring in the woods and beneath the surface of their everyday world life seemed visceral and deep. Alive with anticipation, Belle held her breath. And then it happened. The strong night-time scents and the sound of cicadas singing fiercely as the baby girl was finally born brought a flood of joy. She watched a shooting star and heard the fruit bats babbling in the trees as if to welcome the child, and Belle knew she would never forget this moment. She stayed with Hayma, holding her hand, and made a little prayer until the baby let out her first indignant shriek. Good girl, Belle thought. Make your voice heard.

Then she reluctantly took her leave, but she left knowing life had given her this extraordinary opportunity to redress the balance. Yes, she had witnessed death, terrible violent death, death that would stay with her for the rest of her life, but she had watched the birth of a new life too and, above all, that was what she would hold on to.

After heading off down several wrong turnings, and with her hands protecting her head from bats flying close above and hoping to avoid any underground snakes coming out for food, she focused on the one track she could remember and eventually traced her way back to the rest house. It was now half past eight and she wasn't even sure if the boat had waited for her.

She soon found out, for the first person she came across was Harry Osborne. The livid expression on his face as he paced the entrance hall muttering belligerently to himself told her everything she needed to know. As soon as he saw her he stood still and glared.

'What the hell time do you call this?'

'I'm so sorry,' she said, trying to compose herself but still feeling overawed at witnessing her first birth. 'It really wasn't my fault.'

'You women are all the same. I wish I'd never taken this job on.' He bit his lip and looked as if he'd somehow said the wrong thing and then pushed his spectacles further up his nose in a nervous manner.

She could smell the whisky on him and frowned. 'Job?'

He didn't meet her eyes. 'I mean . . . um . . . I meant allowing you to accompany me. In any case, we've missed the sodding departure.'

'I really am sorry. I had to help a pregnant woman. It was . . .' But she couldn't find any words that could begin to convey how amazing it had been to be present at the arrival of a new life. And how, for a few minutes at least, it had been as if there could only ever be good in the world.

He raised his brows as if in total disbelief but didn't make a comment.

'So, what do we do now?' she asked.

He sighed. 'I've managed to get us two cabins for tomorrow morning.'

'Oh, that's wonderful.'

He gave her a wry look. 'You haven't seen the boat yet. Doubt you'll be calling it wonderful. Thank goodness we'll still arrive in Mandalay in time for your meeting with Alistair Ogilvy, the District Commissioner. My name would have been mud if you'd missed that. If anyone knows anything, he will. Anyway, Guttridge's assistant is in the lounge waiting for you.'

'Thank you.'

Although thirsty and longing to get out of her dusty clothes and sink into a bath, she made for the lounge. From the open door she could see the man inside had been sitting very upright on one of two sofas, but he rose as she entered the room and she saw he was tiny, with large ears and wiry grey hair.

As he made a little bow she smiled.

'I am Nyan,' he said. 'Please sit. You have questions for me?'

'Yes. I'm so sorry to keep you.'

'Keep?'

'To make you wait.'

He gave her the sweetest of smiles. 'Not a problem.'

'It was an awfully long time ago. 1911, in fact, but Mr Guttridge said you'd know about it.'

'He did explain and, yes, I do indeed remember. I was purser on the same boat to Mandalay and it was I who took the matter up with the captain.'

'So, what actually happened?'

'Not much. I can tell you the baby was small and looked European but the couple accompanying the child were from Thailand and not young. Even though I expressed my concerns, the captain didn't want any fuss and refused to become involved. He was a sluggish Scot due for retirement if I remember.' He paused, looking embarrassed. 'Do excuse me. I have the greatest respect for the many dedicated Scottish captains our river has seen over the years. He simply wasn't one of them.'

'So?'

'I questioned the couple, who claimed the baby was their grandchild. I had my doubts but became more suspicious when I asked them to repeat their story a little later the same day. This time they said they were taking the child upriver to be with its grandparents who were British. They said they had not fully understood my question the first time, but I feared misconduct and resolved to inform the authorities as soon as we laid anchor, with or without the captain's approval.'

'And did you?'

He nodded. 'I watched the couple disembark but by the time I reached the local police it was too late. I had no power to detain them myself and the captain washed his hands of the entire business.'

'And did the police follow through?'

He sighed. 'Yes. Initially a thorough search of the surrounding area was made but the couple had vanished. No one admitted to having seen them. But I knew about a baby's disappearance from the garden in Rangoon and feared the child had been kidnapped. It was in all the newspapers, you see, and so I still had hopes the police might be persuaded to extend their search.'

'But they didn't?' she said, feeling the disappointment.

'No. I am afraid they did not.'

'Do you know if the baby was a girl?'

'It was.'

39

Diana, Minster Lovell, 1922

We were never country folk. I say this because I'm adjusting so well to living in the countryside and it has surprised me. My mother's people had once been farmers so there might be something in my blood.

It hasn't been long, but Minster Lovell is perfect for me. I do miss Annabelle very much; and I feel a yearning for Douglas too, if I'm honest, but not so much I feel deeply unhappy. The missing is offset by the fact I can do as I please without any fear of upsetting anyone. I have Simone and Mrs Jones, who is a good soul, and of course I have Dr Gilbert Stokes, who is coming for our session in a moment.

Although I haven't yet sat down on a bench in the garden, I like to leave the front door open and stand in the porch. If anyone passes I do feel slightly panicky but I have learnt to wave and set my face into a smile. Today, you can smell the rain in the air, even though the sun is shining – so soothing this fresh air, so worth living for. The rain will be good for the lawn as we've had a long dry spell. As the scents of mown grass and the glorious early summer flowers drift over, I wait for the doctor.

His body is at an angle and his head is bent against the rise of the hill when I spot his shock of white hair. But at the top he lifts his face, sees me and waves. I return the gesture. I won't say I'm not nervous, but he is a kind man and I'm feeling hopeful.

Once we have shaken hands we make ourselves comfortable in my little sitting room where Mrs Jones has left a tray of tea and biscuits. She's off to market now, so we shall not be disturbed.

I can't articulate how deeply reassuring it is when he states I must let him know if any of his questions make me feel awkward. I had been worried about that.

So, for a while, we talk about my childhood. I'm not clear what he wants me to say, but he tells me there's no right or wrong and it's purely a question of starting somewhere. After he suggests I tell him what my father was like, I inhale sharply and then let out my breath slowly to give myself time to think. I think about how my father used to encourage me to 'be myself'.

The problem has always been I've never known how to do that. I express the thought and when the doctor gives me a gentle, encouraging smile, I notice the light in his blue eyes. 'Does it worry you, the not knowing?' he asks.

I chew the inside of my cheek, uncertain how much it is safe to say, but then I remember this man has no interest in sending me to the Grange or anywhere like it. I draw courage from that and tell him it makes me feel sad.

'And lonely maybe?' he adds.

I am uneasy, a lump growing in my throat, so stare at my feet and can't manage a reply. He tells me many people only begin to understand who they are near the end of their lives, or more realistically, who they have been or might have been all along.

I swallow the lump in my throat. For so long I've been made to feel I am beyond redemption, that whatever is wrong with me cannot be healed. This doctor gives me a little hope and I reward him with a generous smile.

I tell him I thought we'd be talking about what happened in Burma but when he asks me if I want to talk about that, I shake my head.

40

Harry was right about the boat, Belle thought as dawn approached. She silently surveyed the scene, but even before she'd managed to make her way up the muddy gangplank, she'd seen how crowded it was. Families were huddled together, wrapped in shawls and *longyis* and still asleep on the deck, though most of the women were already plaiting their hair and applying *thanaka* to their cheeks. While their mothers began to prepare their breakfast, some of the children awoke, blinking rapidly and wiping the sleep from their eyes, their thick, straight, chocolate-brown hair sticking up from their heads in disarray.

A group of monks stood together and Belle wondered if they were praying. She watched the sun rise, the sky deep blue at the top with wispy stripes of white cloud and the sun incredibly yellow. A royal-blue bird, perching on the rails, seemed to be watching too before flying off. Some of the men were stretching their legs and smoking. If not that, they stood gazing at the grey riverbank without speaking in those precious few moments before you gather yourself to face the day, when you're still partly in the land of sleep, of dreams and of forgetting.

Others still sat on the deck with dazed-looking faces, leaning against the sacks of produce making up part of the cargo. A fine layer of dust had settled over the deck. There were no miniature palm trees in tubs and therefore no shade either and there were very few rattan chairs from which to watch the world drift by. At least I have a cabin, Belle thought, though it might have been fun to sleep under the stars, if a little uncomfortable.

She and Harry were shown the way to their cabins and Belle fell back to sleep as soon as she lay on her bed. It was still early but, stirred up from the emotion of the birth, she'd slept badly the night before.

The journey to Mandalay passed quickly and, though not as peaceful as the earlier part of the river trip had been, it was more fun. As the sun streamed across the deck, Belle found herself constantly absorbed by the daily lives of her fellow passengers playing out in full view. They were mostly a happy, chattering bunch who seemed to take life as it came without complaint, although, of course, Belle was unable to understand anything Harry had not already translated.

While they stood leaning against the rails and looking down at the river, Harry also explained a little of the history of Mandalay. He told her whenever a new king took the throne all potential rivals had to be murdered to prevent the threat of anyone else seizing power. When Thibaw, the last king, had been crowned, at least eighty members of his family, including young children, were dispatched in the most horrific manner.

'Story goes,' Harry said, glancing across at her, 'they were tied up in bags, then beaten to death while an orchestra played to mask the sound of screaming. Afterwards their corpses were trampled by elephants.'

'Dear God,' she said, aghast at the thought. 'How utterly barbaric!'

'Indeed.'

'Yet the Burmese seem to be such gentle people.'

Harry raised his brows. 'Not only that but when the royal palace and enclosure was originally being built, many people were abducted and then buried alive beneath its walls to protect the city from evil spirits.'

Horrified by this, she couldn't help a feeling of foreboding descending on her. What might be about to happen in Mandalay?

Sunrise on their final morning was fiery and, as the sun

streamed across the water in a blinding shaft, Belle closed her eyes. When she opened them, it was to see the rippling water had been showered by sparkling silvery jewels. A little later, as they neared the city, dozens of golden pagodas situated proudly on the hills shone. How was it possible such magic and splendour could live alongside the brutality she'd heard about, and had witnessed too?

The bamboo huts lining the wharf were busy with people hoping to sell small trifles as they disembarked. Belle glanced across at the distant mountains on the other side of the river and wondered if that was where the baby who'd been on the boat had been taken.

Despite being besieged, they picked a path through the fishermen and vendors, then made their way quickly through the thronging streets by car. Soon Belle was settled in her hotel, one of only three frequented by British guests she'd been told. It was teak-built and her small room, smelling of lemon-scented polish, was comfortable with a window overlooking the Red River. Belle had a headache and so decided to stay at the hotel for the rest of the day.

Harry had told her he'd arranged for a meeting with the District Commissioner at ten the following morning, so after lunch, and with nothing else to do, she lay on top of her bed in her underwear and tried to sleep. But thoughts of the massacre infiltrated her daydreams, so she eventually gave up. Would she ever be free of what had happened? She watched a lizard creep up around the door opposite her bed. A brownish-green colour and small – an infant perhaps – it moved in short bursts as if it wasn't sure where it was going. A bit like her. The sounds of the city had quietened in the heavy afternoon heat and she could have sworn she'd heard the tread of footsteps coming up the corridor then halting outside her room. Languid and sweltering but also annoyed at the thought of her rest being interrupted, she didn't move to put on her clothes. In any case, she was sure she'd locked the door so whoever it was would just have to go away. She stared and waited, expecting a member of the hotel staff to speak. But instead of hearing a voice she was surprised to see the door handle turn infinitesimally slowly. Mesmerized, she watched it turn again.

'Who is it?' she finally called out, expecting a shy maid to reply. Hearing nothing and feeling irritated, she grabbed her robe and marched over to fling open the door. No one was immediately outside, but she glanced down the corridor and spotted Harry right at the end just about to turn a corner.

'Oh, it's you,' she said. 'Were you looking for me?'

'Sorry, I . . .'

'Harry, did you want something?'

'No. I . . . got mixed up. Sorry. My mistake.' And with that he turned the corner and was gone.

She shook her head and went back inside her room. The heat really did do odd things to people.

Once her headache had cleared she opted to take a rickshaw to explore the town where the tree-lined streets were buzzing with life. Although she felt lonely and a little bit sad, mainly about Oliver, it was a lovely day and she wanted to make the most of it.

She passed a temple where a few nuns with shaved heads and wearing pink robes knelt to pray. The pagodas and golden Buddhas on what seemed like every street jostled for dominance among the gracious stone-built British mansions. The upstairs verandas of these mansions were supported by huge pillars and gave shade to the walkways that had been formed beneath them. Next came the silversmiths, squatting in little courtyards in front of their wooden homes, a fire in the corner and their fabric bags of tools laid out on small benches beside them. Belle glanced at the exquisitely intricate work on items ranging from enormous bowls intended for the temples to tiny silver elephants and dragons. When she arrived at the huge walls of the palace and its pavilions, now used by the British for administration and the throne room a club, she gasped at the extent of it. She glanced through an open gateway and saw the lucky colours of red and gold everywhere, with ornate carving on the buildings and latticework above the doors.

As she rounded a corner close to a Chinese temple she spotted the silk bazaar and went inside to look for fabric. For a moment she stood still, then went further into the depths of the bazaar, where tightly packed stalls were teeming with people. She felt fine at first, happy to be there and enjoying the atmosphere, but after a few moments the hairs on the back of her neck began to rise. Something wasn't right. Could someone be following her? Was that it? She glanced back now and then. Had the ghost of a young Burmese man really slipped back into the shadows each time she turned? At first she thought she must be imagining it, but gradually she cottoned on. For each time she turned she glimpsed the red of his *longyi* and his pale-green shirt. More annoyed than genuinely frightened by this tedious game of cat and mouse, she continued to finger the delicate silks while the pretty Burmese stallholders watched her. After all, what could the man do in this busy hall? But still he persisted in following her and whenever she stopped, he stopped. Enough was enough. She spun on her heels and there he was, bold as brass, staring openly. Perhaps he was after money? Planning to rob her in a quiet corner? She clutched her bag tight to her chest and carried on walking, wondering where the nearest exit was.

Then she froze in fear.

Two grinning men – malevolent, dark-skinned men, covered in black tattoos – were striding towards her. Was it a trap? She knew the Burmese believed tattoos provided immunity to bullets and knives. Were they looking for her? When she glanced at their narrowed eyes she felt hemmed in and scanned the area. Could they smell her fear? The boy was still behind her and they were in front. As she wondered what to do, she thought about offering them money, but when they came close and then passed by, they simply nodded and continued to smile. She put a palm to her chest to help calm herself and felt ashamed that merely because of their dark skin she had automatically seen them as dangerous. The boy had vanished too. Horrified she'd so quickly turned into the worst kind of Englishwoman, she admonished herself for being suspicious. She took a deep breath and headed in what she hoped was the direction of the exit, wondering if she'd imagined it all.

For a moment the background sounds of the bazaar appeared to have faded, growing increasingly quiet as if from far away. Calmer now, she felt oddly detached. It didn't last. Suddenly the sound intensified, as if someone, in a successful effort to orchestrate the entire bazaar, had turned up the volume. The clashing, clawing sounds of this entire huge place rose and rose. She felt a surge of panic. Was she in danger of turning into her mother, too terrified to be outside? By the time the noise reached fever pitch, Belle felt she was going to be sick. The women's voices became a shrieking, horribly foreign sound, and the men's laughter wicked and alarming. The whole place vibrated with the clang and clatter of money changing hands and far too many voices. Her head began to spin. Now the previously polite stall-holders harried her, and the swarming crowds pushed past, jostling and hurting her as she bumped into them. When she tried to get away she moved with nightmarish slowness. Every single memory of the massacre was coming back to her. All the images she'd tried to push to the back of her mind and that she'd believed were fading now seemed as real as they had been when they were happening. It was as if her eyes had filled with blood. The unnatural deafening sounds pounded in her head and crushed her chest. She could not take in air, and everyone was staring at her.

And although she felt faint she broke into a wild, panting run, not caring who she jarred or jolted. She had to get back to the hotel.

By the time Belle reached the hotel her panic attack had faded. Maybe the intense heat had brought back the massacre? She wasn't sure. But calmer now, she approached the reception desk where the young man behind the counter was holding out an envelope.

'Miss Hatton?' he said, smiling politely. 'It's for you.'

Surprised, she frowned as she took it. Perhaps Harry had left it for her. Arrangements maybe?

The receptionist bowed before wishing her good day and then bent his head to study his appointments ledger.

Upstairs, Belle ripped open the envelope and exclaimed when she read the contents.

Think you are safe in Mandalay?

Her heart plummeted. It was almost identical to the anonymous note she'd received in Rangoon. She recalled the Eurasian man she'd seen leaving the girls' corridor at the hotel, a few moments before she'd entered her room and Rebecca had handed her the first note. Could the same man have delivered it? But why was someone trying to frighten her?

She hurried back downstairs to ask who had left the note and found out it had been a tall Eurasian man, although the receptionist hadn't asked his name. But yes, it might well be the same man. She felt sick with nerves as she climbed the stairs.

Flustered and ill at ease, she paced her room. She had no one here apart from Harry, and he wasn't exactly a friend. She didn't like Mandalay, not one bit. It became clear the best thing was to head back to Rangoon as soon as humanly possible. She would just meet with Ogilvy, the District Commissioner, as arranged by Harry, and then she'd go. So far, the story of the white baby on the boat had come to nothing. Why waste any more time here? In any case, her agreed time off would soon run out and if she wanted to keep her job she needed to get back. She had hoped finding Elvira might make up for what she'd felt had been missing in her life, but no one had seen what had happened. All she'd heard were wild suggestions. She sighed in defeat and made her way back downstairs to the hotel lobby.

As she leant against the reception desk and pressed the bell, hoping the clerk would be able to help her book a train ticket to Rangoon, Harry turned up at her side. She told him she was leaving the next day just as soon as she'd seen the Commissioner. She didn't mention the anonymous note.

His face fell, and she was surprised by how disappointed he looked. 'Oh, but I have specially arranged for us to go to a *pwe* tomorrow evening.'

'A *pwe*?'

'It's a *zat pwe*, a variety show you might say, with dancing performed outdoors accompanied by percussive instrumental music. You'll enjoy it, I promise.'

'I don't think –'

He interrupted her. 'You should come. Really. There's someone I want you to meet. He's an Anglo-Indian jade dealer who knows of a white toddler who was said to have been abducted and smuggled through the Shan States to China.'

'Did he say when?'

'No. But I really think you need to talk to him yourself. He speaks perfect English. Come with me tomorrow night and I'll assist you with trains the next day. What do you say?'

Belle hesitated. 'Let me think about it, Harry.'

Back in her room she noticed one of the window shutters was slightly open and a shaft of light fell in a straight line across the polished wooden floor. She walked over and flung open the shutters, and the room flooded with sunshine. In the bathroom she spotted one of the taps in the washbasin dripping. Had someone been in her room? The cleaner maybe? Lost in thought, she looked at the tap, then palm uppermost, placed her hand beneath it and allowed the drips to fall and collect in a pool. After that she turned the tap on fully and filled the basin before bending over and letting her hair fall into the water.

Once she'd washed and towel dried her hair, she slipped on a freshly ironed dress. She'd had to change her clothes twice a day since coming here but at least the hotel had a good supply of hot water. She combed her hair, put on some lipstick, then paced her room, thinking about what Harry had said.

At the start of all this she had been seized by the idea of finding Elvira, but the drive had suddenly gone out of her. It had become too difficult. And yet . . . What if this last-ditch attempt were to throw up something vital and she hadn't bothered to go? She ran her fingers through her hair, lifting it away from her scalp, so it might dry more quickly. She couldn't decide whether to go back to Rangoon or stay and go to this *pwe* thing with Harry. She argued with herself and sighed in frustration as she weighed the pros and cons. But then it came to her: whatever she might tell herself otherwise, the truth was she really couldn't stop looking. Probably never would. And if she did give up it would dog her for the rest of her life. Whatever had happened to her sister, she had to know.

At ten the next morning she knocked on the impressive carved door of the Commissioner's office. A well-dressed young Burmese man opened the door, bowed, and then ushered her in, asking if she'd like tea. The room, painted white, was flooded with light. Ogilvy stood with his back to her and seemed to be staring out of the large window, lost in thought. When he turned and walked towards her she saw he was a short, broad-shouldered man, with a large nose and smiling grey eyes in a round, very red face. He shook her hand and then indicated she should sit on a hard-backed chair on the opposite side of the polished teak desk from his own, to which he now moved. Once comfortable, he lit a cigar and then cleared his throat.

'So, Miss Hatton. My man has scoured our registry of births and deaths.'

'And?'

'Well, it isn't good news, I'm afraid. Or maybe it is, depending how you look at it.'

'I don't understand.'

He coughed before explaining there were no records of a white baby having died in Mandalay during January, February or March of 1911. 'So, you see, if your sister made it to Mandalay, it's highly likely she would have still been alive at the end of March.'

'She was three weeks old when she was taken. Could she have been passed off as someone's child here?'

'If a British or should I say European couple tried to pass her off as their own in this region, they would have had to register a birth. We're strict on that count, although, sad to say, it's not impossible to make a false entry if you know the right doctor.'

'And nobody registered a baby during that time frame?'

He sighed. 'Oh, indeed they did. Three babies were born in January. All boys, I'm afraid.'

'What about further out from this region? Maymo perhaps?'

He nodded. 'We are a small community here in Mandalay and even smaller there, but my man checked the Maymo registry too. Nothing useful, I'm afraid.'

'I was told you'd been here a long time and you would have heard if there'd been any gossip.'

'Quite right. And from time to time one does hear sad stories of children going astray, never to be seen again. In the furthest outposts of Burma, it's often a case of the child wandering off and getting lost. And, of course, there are wild animals aplenty.'

'Oh God, you mean . . .'

He nodded again and rose from his chair. 'I'm so sorry not to be more helpful.'

'Do you remember the time when my sister was taken?' Belle held her breath as she stood too and waited for his reply.

He puffed out his cheeks. 'Oh yes. Apart from anything else, it was in all the papers. We were all on red alert up here, on the lookout, you see.'

'Did anyone see anything?'

He smiled regretfully. 'Plenty of sightings. All led nowhere. Some of the women had nothing better to do in those days. A bit of drama brightened up their lives and nothing excites a woman as much as a lost baby.'

Belle held out her hand and thanked him but left feeling she'd reached the end of the line.

On their way to the *pwe* that evening, Harry and Belle passed small fires burning at the sides of the road with smiling people knotted around them and vendors selling coconut pancakes and fried rice cakes. Further on, at an outdoor area where a temporary roofed pavilion had been built from bamboo, Harry led Belle to a quieter spot at the back. The pavilion was about thirty feet long and twenty feet wide with an orchestra at the front and a large space in the middle lit by braziers set up around the stage. The noisy audience, seated in family groups on the ground where they had spread blankets, seemed in exuberant mood as the musicians assembled.

At a signal from one of the drummers some of the dancers began a prayer to Buddha.

'It's the most popular of Burmese performances,' Harry whispered in her ear in a moment of hush before the dances began and, as he did, she could smell the whisky on him.

She deliberated. Something about Harry was off and she couldn't work out what it was. He seemed nervous, jittery even.

'Are you all right?' she finally asked.

'Why wouldn't I be?'

'You seem troubled.'

He ran a finger inside his collar. 'It's just the heat.'

'I would have thought you'd be used to it by now.'

He didn't reply.

'So how long have you been a surveyor? That is what this trip is about?'

'Yes. I'm hoping to reach Nagaland, as I told you previously.' He spoke rather irritably, as if annoyed she'd forgotten.

'Tell me again,' she said.

'Well, the Naga are ferocious headhunters. That's what everybody always asks about.'

'And that doesn't worry you?'

He shook his head. 'They won't be interested in me. And, in answer to your question, I've been doing this job for twenty years. I'll only be there to survey the land.'

'And you live here all year round?'

'In Rangoon with Angela.'

'Angela?'

'My wife, of course.'

Belle had assumed he was a bachelor and was surprised. 'You never mentioned you were married.'

He frowned. 'I didn't know I had to.'

'What I mean is, I thought you might have said something before. Do you have children?'

He shook his head. 'We haven't been blessed.'

'Does she mind about your long absences?'

He gave her a quizzical look. 'What a lot of questions.'

'Sorry.'

'Well, the truth, if you must know, is that Angela would like to go back to England.'

'And you?'

He shrugged. 'It's rather a question of raising the cash.'

And then, with a loud clashing sound, the star of the show leapt on to the stage, dressed in a glittering colourful costume like one of the princes of old. He danced for ages like a frenzied gymnast, performing extraordinarily complex moves, accompanied by drums, gongs and oboes.

'These go on and on,' Harry said as the man eventually left the stage to rapturous applause. 'Won't end until sunrise.'

'Can we try and find the trader you told me about?' Belle asked, anxious to get on with it.

'Don't want to see more?'

'My head's pounding. It's the noise.'

'No problem. The man lives locally.'

'He's not here?'

Harry frowned. 'I gave you that impression?'

'Look, it doesn't matter. Let's just go?'

'Of course.'

They shuffled away from the dense group of people who were standing at the back, and then retraced their route, eventually pausing at a network of alleyways where Harry glanced about him, twisting his mouth from side to side.

'Are we lost?' she said, beginning to feel something was wrong. Fearing a recurrence of her previous panic, she hesitated.

He shook his head. 'Looks so different in the dark. I could have sworn this was the right place.'

As he stepped into narrower and gloomier alleys, she remembered Harry had been drinking. Did he even know where he was headed?

She followed him round a sharp bend and on to a wider alley, more like a street, and there he stopped in front of a grubby-looking house like all the others. 'I think this is it.'

He called out in English and a man replied, telling them to enter. Belle's hunch that something was wrong increased and she hesitated.

Through the open doorway she could see the room within was simply furnished with mats on the floor and one low table where an oil lamp threw the edges of the room into darkness. A single piece of patterned fabric, slung across the room from two hooks on the wall, clearly divided the space. As her eyes adjusted to the gloom Belle was able to make out the paraphernalia of food preparation piled up on another low table. This did not seem like the home of a prosperous jade dealer.

And then she saw the man himself.

The dark-eyed, heavily moustached man sat cross-legged on the floor wearing a simple black shirt and matching Western trousers.

'No,' she said, suddenly certain. 'I'm not going in. Take me back to the hotel, Harry. Now.'

41

Diana, Minster Lovell, 1923

Today is a special day as Simone and I are preparing to walk down the lane, not back to the village but away where it will be quiet. I don't know what tomorrow will bring but I am pleased with my progress. It's enough that I am here and that I trust Dr Gilbert. Anyone would trust a man like him, wouldn't they? And, after many sessions, during which we have been peeling back the years, I have started to knit my life back together. I do some work in my garden now. Only a bit of weeding and pruning but it makes me so happy I could weep for joy.

I cannot leave the doors unlocked, not yet, for fear that what is outside will worm its way inside and I will lose my sanctuary. Dr Gilbert would prefer me to work in the back garden while leaving the back door open, so I can observe if anything were to happen. But I worry something will sneak in, then fill up every nook and cranny of my home and I will not be strong enough to prevent it. I tell him it is my nightmare to be left alone and unprotected from all that is out there with no safe haven.

Nevertheless, I am improving. As well as encouraging me to take small steps beyond the house, he is also reducing the amount of medication I take, and I do believe there is a real chance I may one day be well again. We talk about everything, the doctor and I, including my shame over Douglas's unfaithfulness in Burma. Up until now I've only dared share this with Simone, always told myself not to think about it. But how can you not think about something when it's always there? For several of our meetings Dr Gilbert encouraged me to talk about what it had felt like. I knew, of course – the hurt, the fury, the impotence. At first, I was unwilling to say so, it seemed a weakness to confess, but when I finally did, I cried and cried. And when it was all over, and I dried my eyes, the shame had lifted as if by magic and I realized the true weight of the burden I'd been carrying.

As if a light had come on in my mind, I also came to see the shame should have sat fairly on Douglas's shoulders and not on mine. But when we lived in Burma, if a husband strayed it was seen as the wife's fault for not keeping her husband happy, and if he strayed while she was pregnant, well . . . men would be men. No wife ever spoke of feeling hurt or betrayed.

What interests me most about this process is the way the doctor asks me how I felt about something. Nobody has ever asked me how I've felt before, not even when I was a child or later when my mother died of the terrible influenza. Although I think my parents loved me in their way, as an only child I spent most of the time with my nanny. It was never my mother who comforted me when I fell and grazed my knee, or when I was sick and confined to bed. I only ever saw her for special outings, or when I was freshly bathed at the end of the day and dressed in my starched white nightdress and Nanny would bring me down to the drawing room to say goodnight.

Dr Gilbert even asked me what I would have said to my parents if I could have. I remained silent, but I knew. Love me, I would have said. Love me. But I didn't want to say, didn't want to make a fool of myself by weeping again. He asked how I had felt about the lack of love and I was shocked at how little I could really remember. I told him I had been loved. Nanny had loved me. The doctor suggested I visit my father as soon as I feel up to it and I might. Maybe there is a way to repair the sadness of the past. I should make the effort. It has been too long, though he writes a few times a year and I have invited him to stay at my cottage.

Ever since then I have been remembering more and more. And now, of course, I feel a devastating guilt in the pit of my stomach that my daughter, Annabelle, has experienced the same lack of love at my hands. I think of her jade-green eyes and coppery hair and realize I am missing her so much. He says we will talk of Annabelle soon and, although I've come to see how these sad and shameful things are better out in the open, I'm fearful too. The doctor tells me that when we do not face our inner darkness it has the power to make us very sick indeed.

So, because of all this, hard though the unravelling has sometimes been, my life has begun to feel real again. I have started to become real again and my heart swells with courage.

And now I must get ready for our walk. Simone has described it all. First, we shall walk uphill a little and then we will turn right and go down past the church and churchyard, through the remains of Minster Hall, and from there to the riverbank. She says it is a short distance and we shall be alone in the beautiful, comforting peace of nature. The doctor says nature heals, and I believe him.

42

Belle next saw Harry at a typically English breakfast of tea, toast, bacon and eggs. He seemed pretty subdued as he asked if he could keep her company and, when she said that he could, he pulled out a chair and shuffled into it.

'Sorry about last night,' he muttered. 'I must have got the wrong place.'

'What were you thinking, Harry?' she demanded, but he looked so disconsolate that although she'd been frightened by the sight of the *so-called* jade dealer, she decided to let it go.

Harry focused on his hands and then glanced up at her with a worried look. Belle felt the man was all nerves and growing more so as the trip progressed.

'I have bad news,' he said.

'Oh? I hope it's not too troubling.'

'For you, I mean.'

She raised her brows.

'I went to the station to book you a train ticket.'

'That's kind.'

'We agreed I would.'

'Indeed.'

He held his breath for a few seconds before he spoke. 'There are no trains.'

'What?'

'Some of the tracks have been blown up further down the line.'

'When will they be fixed?'

'They aren't saying. Could be some time, I imagine.'

'So, what do I do? Go back down the Irrawaddy?'

'It'll take two weeks.'

'By which time I'll have lost my job.'

'My contact is going to do what he can to find out about the state of the tracks. My advice is to sit tight and we'll hopefully hear something more tomorrow, though you might have to wait a while.'

Belle sighed. She did not want to sit tight. Mandalay was horrifically hot and the monsoon would be starting before too long. She didn't relish being stuck here for days on end.

She headed for the lounge where she planned to remain for the rest of the morning, relaxing beneath the relative cool of a fan and in safety from whatever might be out there. She picked up a magazine and watched the guests coming and going, but it was a tedious and deadly dull morning so she found a book in the hotel lounge and went outside to the small garden. With a delicate ivory hand fan she swept away the flying insects humming in the torpid air and when she reached a small pool she watched white lilies floating on the surface and goldfish swimming beneath them. As for her search for her sister, she felt frustrated and sad. She'd often wondered how it would be if she were to meet her sister now, if she really was still alive. She'd wondered what she'd say, what her sister might have looked like, how they both would have felt. Would Elvira's hair be like her own or more like their mother's? Would she be taller or shorter than she was? Would her eyes have been green too? Well, she thought resignedly, I may never know, and in any case, Elvira might well be dead.

At least if she gave up the search it would leave her free to concentrate on her career again. She was thinking about that and wondering about planning a new routine when she heard someone call her name. She spun round and couldn't prevent a gasp of surprise.

'Oliver!'

He nodded and remained where he was, looking unusually stiff and hesitant.

'I don't understand. What are you doing here?'

'I'm here because you didn't call me back. I left two urgent messages with Harry Osborne.'

She felt confused by the deluge of mixed emotion. She had felt such a burst of happiness at hearing his voice, yet she couldn't forget how they'd parted. 'How did you know I was here?'

'Tried all the hotels until I found the right one.'

She narrowed her eyes as she searched his face and hoped her feelings weren't too obvious. He gazed back at her with those candid blue eyes of his and she couldn't deny the attraction, even after everything. Tanned and strong, he remained very still. Even though she fought against it, she felt herself soften. She itched to run her fingers through his unruly hair and then pull back his head so that she might caress his neck . . . She reached out a hand but then withdrew it.

'Nobody said you'd called,' she said in a tight little voice.

'I left a message with Harry the morning you arrived, and then another. I phoned the reception and, as it happened, he was at the desk both times, so knowing you and he were together they passed the phone to him. I emphasized how critical it was and left my number for you to call me immediately. He said he'd pass it on straight away so I waited.'

'How did you get here?'

'Was lucky to get a fast overnight train.'

'I didn't know there were fast trains.'

He smiled. 'Rare beasts, but they exist.'

She frowned. 'But how? The tracks have been blown up.'

'Not on the north-bound line.'

'Did you see anything? Of the damage, I mean?'

He grinned. 'Nope. May have nodded off.'

'Why are you here, Oliver?'

They were interrupted by Harry entering the garden.

'I'll tell you later,' Oliver whispered before striding across to

Harry. 'Now look here, Osborne,' he said. 'Belle tells me you didn't relay the messages I gave you.'

Harry looked cornered. 'Didn't I? Thought I had.'

'You know damn well you didn't.'

Harry twisted his hat in his hands and glanced over at Belle. 'I am so sorry. They went clean out of my mind. I had so much to attend to, you see.'

Oliver looked annoyed but didn't speak.

'Look, why don't you let me make it up to you?' Harry continued. 'I know an excellent Chinese restaurant. It's where I was hoping to take Belle for a meal, but why don't we all go? Shall we say midday? My treat.'

Oliver raised his brows at Belle, who nodded.

'Very well,' he said. 'But it's one hell of an oversight.'

'Yes, sorry, I do realize.' Harry put his panama hat on his head and smiled nervously. 'Well, now. I just need to make a phone call. Do forgive me.'

Belle wasn't sure if he was still apologizing for not passing on the message or for having to leave to make a call.

Once Harry had gone Oliver stepped over to Belle. 'I wanted to apologize too.'

'Well, this does seem to be the morning for it,' she said with a smile, unable to conceal how pleased she felt that he was there.

'I was clumsy . . . back then. Truly, I didn't mean it the way it sounded. I want to say you're so much more to me than a story.'

'And you expect me to believe you?' she said, although in a gentler tone than before. Despite a nagging voice in her head, she so wanted to have faith in him she felt sure it must be written all over her face.

'I'm happy to help you and not print a word of it, if that will convince you.'

She stared down at the ground and there was a short silence while she thought about it. Then she looked up and as their eyes met something wonderful passed between them, making her feel so cared for she could not turn him down.

'I am very much in need of a friend right now, Oliver. But I absolutely need to know I can trust you.'

He nodded solemnly.

'In that case . . .' she said, then pulled out the second anonymous note from her bag and passed it to him.

He read it and looked up at her. 'Someone is trying to scare you. Do you trust Harry?'

'Of course. He's been very helpful. Though he took me to a weird place last night. Said it was a mistake.'

Oliver puffed out his cheeks, then exhaled slowly. 'I wonder what's going on?'

'With Harry?'

'No. I meant the note.'

She shook her head. 'Well, they've succeeded in scaring me. I've been afraid of my own shadow since receiving it, even before, actually. I had a panic attack in the market.'

'I've been worried about you. There's been trouble in Rangoon and the word is it's spreading, possibly to Mandalay.'

'Tell me.'

'The students have been rioting. It's the second university students' strike, this one triggered by the expulsion of Aung San and Ko Nu.'

'And they are?'

'Leaders of the Rangoon University Students Union. They refused to reveal the name of the author who'd written an article in their university magazine. It included a scathing attack on one of the senior university officials.'

'They were expelled for that?'

'The British reprisals for the riot have been ugly. As I said, the fear is it may spread to Mandalay, and soon. I phoned to warn you, but as you didn't call back I took the train here. I needed to be certain you were safe.'

'Shouldn't you be back there reporting on it?'

He took her hand and she felt the warmth of his skin making her own tingle.

'Already done, and there's not much more to say at present. In any case, I wanted to see you, and now I'm here there's no chance I'm going to leave you on your own. Whoever is trying to upset you will have me to deal with.'

At lunchtime Belle and Oliver met up with a very talkative Harry. He spoke about his job as they walked and told them of the dark recesses of Burma he still hadn't surveyed. He then went on to tell them about Angela, what a kind person she was, blonde and so petite but pretty with it. They'd met in London, married and travelled out to Burma together, though she hadn't really wanted to come. He led them on foot through the thronging backstreets of Mandalay as he continued his monologue, sounding a little edgy. Belle wondered again about Harry's nerviness, although she was becoming used to his odd ways. People were out conducting their business or smoking at little tea shops and food stalls. Belle smelt the dried fish stall before they even reached it and it was all she could do not to hold her nose. She paused beside a woman selling bowlfuls of odd yellow, orange and red things, looking for all the world like brightly coloured worms.

'Sweets,' Harry said, seeing Belle's puzzled expression.

Beyond that, vegetables and beans were piled high in baskets. Then came a stall packed with nuts and roots. The place was noisy and a little intimidating, as the three of them were the only non-Burmese in sight. But Oliver held her arm, giving her a squeeze from time to time, reminding her of his promise not to leave her alone.

Eventually they reached a quieter, more rundown area.

'Are you sure this is okay?' Oliver said.

Harry nodded emphatically. 'Yes, yes. Of course. It's a little out of the way, but I have it on good form it really is the best.'

'You've not been there before?'

'No. But I am assured.'

Oliver shrugged. 'If you're certain.'

They carried on into a terribly seedy network of streets deep in the Chinese quarter.

'Is it all right, do you think?' Belle whispered to Oliver as Harry crossed the street and stood in front of what must be the restaurant.

'I guess we'll find out.' He wrapped an arm around Belle's shoulders and they followed Harry through the door.

Apart from themselves, the restaurant was deserted save for a lone barman.

'Why so empty if it's supposed to be so good?' Belle said. 'I don't get it.'

'We're early,' Harry replied. 'I imagine it's only just opened.'

'But I can't smell anything cooking, can you?'

'Maybe not yet.'

'I could do with a beer,' Oliver said. 'But there don't appear to be any bottles behind the bar.'

'They probably store them in the fridges out at the back,' Harry said.

Oliver snapped his fingers at the barman, who nodded and then slipped out through a swing door.

'There you are,' said Harry. 'As I said. Out at the back. Now if you'll excuse me, I need to find the conveniences.'

While Harry was gone Belle and Oliver talked for a few minutes. He told her he'd missed her while she'd been away, and she told him about her thrilling balloon ride over Bagan. And yet, although he held her eyes, she was also aware that from time to time he was surveying the room as if in search of something. When, after a few more minutes, Harry hadn't returned, Oliver stood abruptly, grabbed Belle's hand and pulled her to her feet.

'I don't like this,' he said, his voice tense.

She shivered as she held on to him.

'Come on. We're getting out of here. Something isn't right.'

He pushed her out in front of him as they made a dash for the door. Once outside, he kept hold of her hand and they began to run.

With a blinding flash of white light, the blast rocked the street, the heat so intense Belle felt her bones had melted. Thrown back against the wall of a house, she was helpless to save herself and her heart hammered wildly at the sound of terrified screams. Flying debris and exploding glass forced her to crouch down and shield her head with her arms. In shock and disbelief, she tried to swallow but with a mouth full of grit her throat hurt badly and the taste of acrid smoke on the tongue made her heave. At first it was like charcoal but when mixed with the blood in her mouth it turned bitter and rank. She tried to call out for Oliver, only faintly aware she might have lost him. She could neither hear him in the deafening din, nor see him in the thick cloud of black ash billowing above and around the street. She closed her sore, dry eyes and became aware of a pain in her head, as if someone had punched her. When she opened her eyes, her vision swam. It was hot. Far, far too hot. She tried to scream but her throat, still raw from the dust and heat, made only a rasping sound. For a moment she felt she was floating. Then everything turned black.

When she came back to consciousness Oliver was squatting by her side, his brilliant blue eyes shining out from his dirty dust-streaked face. He's alive, she thought. He's alive. He stroked her hair and then sat down beside her. Dazed and horrified by what had happened, neither spoke. After a few minutes he seemed to collect himself, rose and then helped her to her feet too. Then they clung to each other, giving in to the overwhelming feelings of reprieve at finding themselves and each other still alive.

'Do you think you can walk?' he asked as they drew apart.

She nodded.

'I thought . . .' Numb with shock, her voice cracked, and she couldn't say the awful words.

'Me too.' And she could see his eyes were wet with tears.

He supported her as she hobbled to the side of the street, where she leant against the wall, her head pounding. Then he turned back to help anyone else he could to their feet. Some with minor injuries were already scrambling up, while other more seriously hurt individuals still lay on the ground. Oliver ensured an ambulance was on its way and did what he could for each of them before returning to Belle.

He reached out his hands to her. 'Let me look you over.'

Instead of taking his hands, she wiped a smear of black dust from his left cheek and then closed her eyes.

'Belle?'

She nodded, but feeling dizzy and light-headed, found it impossible to express the tumult going on within her. She wanted to weep so badly, but her eyes were dry and the unshed tears had somehow blocked her throat.

'Are *you* all right?' she asked when she eventually opened her eyes again.

'I'm fine. Now let me look you over.'

She was filthy from the dust and grit of the explosion and it was difficult at first to work out what was what, but after a few moments he deduced she only had a few cuts and grazes and no grave injuries.

He suggested they call a doctor to come to the hotel instead of traipsing up to the hospital where the staff would be overrun and the care mediocre. Belle's legs were still shaking as they made their way back through the winding streets, but she leant against him and he wrapped an arm around her as she took small shuffling steps, stumbling every so often. Finally they found a lone rickshaw.

As he supported her through the front door and into the lobby they met Harry hurrying down the stairs, carrying his suitcase.

His face lost all colour when he saw them and he tried to brush past, muttering something about being called away.

Oliver grabbed him by the arm. 'I don't think so,' he said, and glancing at Belle to make sure she was all right, he let go of her and half dragged the smaller man through to a snug at the back of the main reception area. Belle followed behind.

'What happened to you?' Oliver demanded, his face thunderous.

Harry stared and attempted to speak, but it came out as an incomprehensible stutter.

'Say that again.'

'I – I – I went out to the back.'

'Let me get this straight. You went out the back. Because?'

'To – to – the conveniences.'

'But you didn't return?'

Harry looked at his feet, then up at Belle, guilt written all over his face.

'Listen, you fucking rat,' growled Oliver, 'you nearly got us both killed. Now you tell me exactly what's going on.'

Harry, pushing his spectacles back up his nose again and again, looked terrified.

Oliver was gripping the man's arm and now he shook him. 'The truth, Harry.'

Harry still didn't speak.

'Do you really want me to break your arm?'

Harry shook his head. 'Please don't hurt me,' he said with a sob. 'I didn't know.'

'Didn't know what?' Belle asked as she sank into a chair.

'They said I had no choice.'

'Or?'

She'd spoken coldly and Harry blanched, his own voice coming out in a whisper as, head bent, he addressed his words to the floor. 'If I didn't do what they wanted they would hurt my wife.'

Belle ran a hand through her dusty hair and scratched her

scalp. Was he even telling the truth? Had Harry been responsible for the note she'd been given? Then she noticed a bleeding cut on her arm and, while Oliver watched, she dabbed it with her skirt. When she was done she scrutinized Harry's face; saw the shattered state he was in. And, despite feeling so angry and shaken herself, couldn't help feeling a trace of pity for this trembling wreck of a man.

'And what did they want you to do?' Oliver asked.

Harry glanced up and met Oliver's furious glare for the first time. 'I swear I didn't know it would be this bad.'

'So, how bad did you think it would be?'

'I thought they were just going to frighten her.'

Oliver spluttered. 'Well, that is big of you. Frightening a young woman who has done nothing to you is okay, is it?'

Harry bit his lip and looked at Belle pleadingly. 'They said they would hurt Angela. She already suffers with her nerves, you know.'

Oliver released his grip and roughly shoved Harry into a chair.

'I think you'd better tell us everything.'

Harry did not speak.

'Harry,' Belle said, leaning forward. 'You really do have to tell us.'

'I am sorry,' he said with a quick glance at her.

'So?'

Once again Harry didn't respond.

'Now look here, you little shit –' Oliver intervened, but then paused, pacing back and forth for a moment or two as he struggled to get his fury under control. Belle felt sure Oliver was itching to take a swing at the other man and beckoned for him to hold back.

'Who was it, Harry? Who got you to do this?' she asked.

Harry's face crumpled and his glasses misted up. 'Delay her, they said.'

Oliver turned on him. 'Who?'

'I swear I didn't know it would be a bomb. They said I had to call a number and tell them Belle was on her way to the restaurant. The barman said he needed to talk to me about something and we went to the storeroom at the back and he said we had to leave. I heard the blast and then I knew.'

'Right, Harry,' Oliver said coldly, 'I reckon this is what we are going to do . . .'

43

Diana, Minster Lovell, 1923

Dr Gilbert looks at me kindly from the sofa where he is leaning back against one of my feather cushions. 'You lived in Mandalay, I understand, before you moved to Rangoon?'

I nod.

He questions me, asks if there's anything I want to say about it. I take a moment before I speak and, as I do, I shiver at the memory of my husband's irrational rage, his face scarlet with fury. I tell him Douglas was terribly angry with me, although that barely describes it.

It was foolish, but I wanted a child so badly and couldn't seem to conceive. When I went to her the burning red sun had softened into a sultry Mandalay evening. The heavily made-up woman, wearing satin and silk, danced for me and the other women, almost in a trance. She drank beer and we all pinned banknotes to her shiny costume sleeves. The spirits liked a party, it seemed. When it was over she said the spirits had spoken, though she didn't reveal what they'd said. I tell the doctor how the people loved their spirit mediums. How they believed a Nat Gadaw, for that is what they called them, spoke to them and they thought the spirits could make wishes come true.

Douglas was immovable. He's a very rational man and was outraged I'd given in to one of their dark superstitions.

'Did it work? The spirit medium?' Dr Gilbert asks.

I nod. Instead of feeling helpless I had taken matters into my own hands. I felt different afterwards. Hopeful. The next day came, the sun shone, and before long I became pregnant with Elvira.

'And your husband forgave you?'

'Apart from once more, we never spoke of it again.'

'And does it still trouble you?'

There is a long, unsettling silence.

'The one time we spoke of it again, Douglas blamed the Nat Gadaw for the voices I began to hear.'

I find it hard to say anything more.

'A rational man, you say?' Dr Gilbert smiles at me oh so gently.

'Yes. Queer, isn't it? He said I had brought it on myself by dabbling in perilous superstitious practices.'

44

Oliver dragged Harry from his chair and narrowed his eyes. 'This is what we are going to do.'

Harry was shaking visibly, too scared to speak.

'I'm going to take you straight to the police station and tell them what you did. I will explain how you lured us into a deadly trap. Attempted manslaughter, at the very least, and who knows how many of the injured might not recover.'

Harry found his voice. 'They won't listen.'

'No kidding? And why is that?'

'Because . . .' He paused. 'It's the police who . . . who threatened me.'

Oliver stood completely still. 'And by the police you mean?'

'Er, not exactly the police.'

'Then who?'

'The Rangoon Intelligence Unit.'

'That's more like it. Who in the unit, Harry?'

Harry shook his head. 'I don't know his name. A tall man. Dark-skinned, with short cropped hair.'

'Nothing else?'

'He wore a linen suit. I can't remember anything more. He only said I had to delay her.'

Oliver and Belle exchanged glances, then Oliver spoke. 'Just get out of here, Harry. And I swear to God if you breathe a single word to anyone about Belle and me having escaped the blast with our lives, I will find you.'

Harry didn't need to be told twice and literally sprinted from the room.

'But we must go to the police, mustn't we?' Belle asked, still trembling from the devastation of the bomb blast.

Oliver looked scornful. 'Waste of time.'

'Because?'

'Corruption. If the Intelligence Unit were behind this, and I do believe Harry there, they have far-reaching antennae.'

'Oliver, why did they do this? I don't understand. Why did they want me hurt?' Her voice was shaky as she stifled a sob. Although she was trying to hold herself together she felt her face crumple. It was too awful to think about.

He placed his hands on her upper arms and squeezed. 'Not to put too fine a point on it, they attempted to kill you, my love, not hurt you.'

She looked into his eyes and saw his deep concern for her. 'I know,' she whispered. 'I know.'

There was a short pause.

'They tried to kill you too,' she added.

He gave a disgusted shrug. 'Collateral damage. But it's you the bastards want. This is about your sister. It's clear your mother had nothing to do with it, but somebody here is definitely involved.'

She took a deep breath and exhaled slowly to still her nerves. 'Were we right to let Harry go?'

'Harry Osborne is nothing. This goes much higher up.'

'Who?'

'I could make a guess but let's see what we can find out.'

'But, my God, what is it that they're hiding?'

He sighed. 'I don't know, but they're prepared to stop at nothing to keep it secret. And they see you as a threat.'

Belle rubbed her fingertips on her pulsing temples and wished she'd never started all this. An attempt on her life for heaven's sake! Somebody wanted her dead and the thought of it made her feel sick to her core. But it was more than that. She clenched her fists as anger began to grip her, and she longed to lash out at whoever had done this. How dare they? What right did they have?

'We won't go straight back to Rangoon,' Oliver said. 'I have friends in Maymo. It's about twenty-five miles west and a little north of here. We'll go there and work out what to do. It's cooler up in the hills, so we'll get some respite from this wretched heat.'

'How do we get there?'

'Train. Do you think you need to see a doctor?'

She shook her head. 'It's mainly dirt and small cuts on my arm. I have plasters upstairs.'

'Okay. Clean up and pack, but be quick. We'd better get our skates on.'

'They'll try again, won't they?' she said, unable to keep the fear from her voice.

'The truth?' he asked.

She nodded.

An hour later and they had just made it in time. As the train slid out of Mandalay, Belle peered through the window at tree-lined avenues and large British mansions. For a while the route remained flat but wooden shacks now dotted the dusty lane running alongside the track. The lane teemed with caravans of bullock carts heading away for the late afternoon, dogs lying fast asleep in the dusty air, pretty Burmese girls with flowers in their hair and carrying water pots on their heads, and men bobbing on bicycles as they rode over the rocky terrain. Oliver explained how his friends, Jeremy and Brenda, ran a small hotel or guest house and that he had called ahead to let them know. Although Belle had changed her clothes, there hadn't been time to wash her hair, leaving her scalp still itching and dry. The journey would take three hours and, shaken by the bomb blast and what they'd heard from Harry, Belle wanted nothing more than to sleep.

She leant against the window but the rattling sensation as the train gradually rose prevented sleep. She opened her eyes and felt a little distanced from herself. Agonizingly slowly, they passed villages where rain trees gave shelter from the heat, where banana palms grew profusely and where the hills in the distance glowed a deep hazy purple. The yellow acacia groves and green-carpeted foothills came next, but soon the track ran through steep rounded hills with rocky bases and deep vegetation beyond. Under the still blue sky they passed shrines and crossed a bridge over the valley, continuing to rise. She scanned the ridges of jungle, dark green close by, mid-green further on, then turning lighter and eventually becoming dusky blue.

For a while Belle leant against Oliver and managed to doze fitfully. As they drew closer to Maymo she woke, surprised to see how green it was. Oliver pointed out the fruit growing nearby: strawberries, damsons, grapes, lemons and limes.

'It's incredibly fertile,' he said.

She gazed at his handsome, rugged face and nodded.

He touched her cheek, and she felt something comforting about the simplicity of it. 'You all right?'

'I think so.'

Close to the station, cattle sleeping on the line delayed their arrival, but soon they were able to climb down. A porter ferried their cases to a waiting pony and cart and then, passing the usual stalls and a Methodist church, they made their way up into the higher ground. There, red-brick colonial houses with forest-green shutters, brown woodwork, porches and gardens nestled among the trees. Soon after Government House, the Government Administration Office and the Surveying Office, they climbed another hill. Oliver pointed out a grand half-timbered mansion.

'It's Candacraig,' he said, seeing her looking. 'The British club. They call it the Chummery. We're not far from my friends' place.'

As they arrived at the small hotel the sun was setting. Belle welcomed the cool breeze and glanced at the sky, now a deep shimmering coral shot through with violet.

'It can be cold here at night,' Oliver said, 'depending on the season. They even have fires.'

First Belle was introduced to Oliver's friends, Jeremy and Brenda, an older American couple, now retired apart from running the guest house. Oliver explained that he'd lodged with them during his first few weeks in Burma and they had shown him the ropes. They certainly seemed exceptionally fond of him, enquiring after his career and asking about his health and so on. Brenda was welcoming and friendly, and a terrific cook Oliver had told Belle, and they could most certainly look forward to a delicious supper.

They were taken to a room overlooking the front garden and, once they were alone, Belle turned to him. 'Just one room?'

'Do you mind? I thought it'd be safer. I can sleep in the armchair.'

She thought about what to do.

'Or I can ask for another room?' he said.

'Do your friends think . . . well, you know.'

'Would it bother you if they did?'

'A little. I wouldn't want them to get the wrong idea about us. About me.'

'Don't worry. I've explained about what happened. They understand we need to stay together. He's ex-military, nerves of steel and afraid of nothing, so exactly the right person to have on our side. It will be fine.'

'All right.' She paused, then walked across to him and touched his cheek. 'We'll both sleep in the bed.'

'Maybe a bath first and something to eat?'

'Maybe,' she said and looked into his shining blue eyes, then reached up to kiss him.

The impact of what had happened to them and how close they had been to dying had flooded them both with a need for comfort and safety. Later, as they lay on the bed after their baths and the delicious supper he'd promised but she'd hardly been able to eat,

Belle began to shake. Fear snaked through her again, reaching every part of her until it curled inside her chest. It felt like the massacre all over again. More than anything she longed to be held and told everything would be all right. But everything was not going to be all right. Not while she remained in Burma. And although Oliver did hold her tightly and she could feel his heart beating against hers, she also knew how badly he'd been shaken too. Then the tears began. It was delayed shock, he murmured, and she knew he was right because now the terror coursed through her, crushing her inside herself so she hardly knew who she was. She tried to speak but stuttered and stumbled over the words until she was gulping and choking and flapping her hands. He helped her to sit up and held a glass of water to her lips.

When she was calmer he asked if she was ready to talk about what had happened in Rangoon.

She looked at him in silence and then, at first haltingly, began to express her sorrow. She told him everything and all the fear she'd buried and never shared finally came flooding out. The atrocities she'd witnessed, the spilt blood, the animal brutality and wretched wasted lives, and then, gasping at the memory, she told him about the tiny baby she'd found alive. When she'd finished weeping, he stroked her cheeks and kissed her forehead with such utter gentleness.

'I'm scared,' she said.

He nodded.

'What are we going to do?'

He took her hand in his and squeezed. 'I don't know. Let's get some sleep and think about it tomorrow when we're fresh.'

After breakfast the next morning they cycled through the cool leafy town under a pale-blue sky. Oliver pointed out the various British governmental houses and the homes of dignitaries involved in running Burma. She took it all in, wondering at the luxury of their homes compared with the tiny shacks of the local people. When Oliver once again voiced his belief that one day Burma would be for the Burmese, she agreed.

'Not before time,' he added with a nod. 'The signs are everywhere.'

'You mean the unrest?'

'Yep. Right across the Empire. It'll change, and soon.'

They stopped at a flower market lining the edges of one of the main thoroughfares. The air, awash with the delicate scent of purple and white flowers, filled Belle with an odd kind of bittersweet delight. They slipped into the huge botanical gardens where they found a tall shady tamarind tree to sit and lean against. As she studied the teak trees in the distance, Oliver explained how the British had been drawn to Burma because of teak. They'd needed it for the navy and it had soon become a growing source of revenue along with gold and rubies from the Shan States, and jade found in the mines of the far north. And after the British exiled the last king of Burma to India, everything had been there for the taking.

He tilted her chin up. 'So. How are you feeling?'

'Still awfully shaken.'

He nodded. 'It might be best if I go back to Rangoon alone.'

'And I stay here?'

'Yes.'

'I'd rather come with you.'

'Jeremy and Brenda would watch out for you.'

She shook her head. 'I don't know.'

'Either that or we smuggle you down to Rangoon and sneak you on to an aeroplane.'

'I've heard there are passenger aeroplanes now.'

'Imperial Airways. Not many flights though. It takes eleven days to reach London.'

She thought about it.

'If I knew who was behind the bomb, I'd know where to start.'

'Who do you think it might be?' she asked.

'I think the whole thing may be political. In 1935 the Government of Burma Act ruled that Burma should be separated from British India. A new Senate and a House of Representatives would be created. Your friend Edward de Clemente is on the committee drawing up the final details of the constitution and the electoral rolls ready for general elections.'

'I didn't realize.'

'Everyone involved in this transition has to be above suspicion for the recommendations to be acceptable. So, I would guess someone high up is feeling under threat because of you.'

'And you think?'

'A cover-up. That's what I think. It's obvious someone has concealed the truth about what happened on the day your sister vanished.'

'Do you suspect Edward?'

'Not specifically. It could be anyone.'

There was a long silence. Belle listened to the buzzing of flying insects and the sound of the breeze rustling the leaves overhead. For as far as the eye could see everything was green.

'Let's walk to the lake,' Oliver suggested, and they wheeled their bicycles to another part of the park where swans slid across the silvery water.

'Did I tell you the doorman at the Strand said his father heard a baby screaming in the night back in 1911? He was a watchman.'

'A long time ago to remember.'

'Well, there was no baby staying at the hotel and when he reached the back of the hotel he spotted a car racing away. The episode stayed with him.'

'Did he report it?'

'I think he was persuaded not to.'

'Worth investigating.'

'You think?'

He nodded.

'In that case, I'm going back with you.'

'It may come to nothing.'

She looked at him. 'Oliver, I don't think I can leave Burma until I know what happened to Elvira, and I've got my house to think about too. I can't simply leave it to rot.'

'You can't go back to the hotel.'

'No.'

'Stay with me.'

She gazed at him. 'What will people think?'

'Despite the signs of scandalous goings-on here all the time, they will gossip and pretend to be outraged. Maybe some will be genuinely shocked, but in any case, your safety is the single most important issue right now.'

45

Diana, Minster Lovell, 1925

I've lived as if my whole life has been defined by one moment in the garden in Burma. I want to scream out *but that is not me*, and then I wonder if it's true. Maybe we all have one defining moment from which we can never escape?

The day I really do escape is a day like any other. The sun is attempting to shine through hazy clouds and I'm sitting in my usual chair.

I feel as if I'll drown when he asks me to picture the day I lost Elvira. He tells me I don't have to do it, but I know I must. I close my eyes. Time and time again I try but something keeps on stopping me, as if a solid wall prevents me from going further. I push against it, but it won't give way. He says I'm trying too hard and encourages me not to focus on the pram at all but to gently recall all the other lovely details of the garden. As I relax and begin to drift, the pretty summer house appears, although I don't see myself inside it. Then other images begin to stream through my mind. And when I picture the orchid tree with its heart-shaped leaves and flowers of white and pink, and the huge canopies where the monkeys swung in the branches, I smile. I can see the luminous green birds, smell the beautiful scented flowers: roses in June and July, huge poinsettia bushes with bright red flowers in December and asters surrounded by delicate white butterflies in spring. Slowly I sink back into the past and it really is as if I'm there in Burma, sweltering in the humid air.

As if from a great distance I hear him ask what else I can see.

I shake my head and feel my breathing quicken. *Only the pram under the tamarind tree*, I say.

Dr Gilbert does not speak again.

Then, when I feel I can't bear to look any more, I'm felled by a blurred image. I squeeze my eyes even more tightly shut as I try to focus. Or not. I'm unsure which. The image sharpens, and I make out a woman dressed in black, hurrying away from the pram and carrying a bundle. It is over in a flash and I wonder if I'm imagining it, but then I see her again as she turns to check if anyone has spotted her and for the briefest moment I feel as if I know who she is.

It was not I who harmed my baby girl. It was not I.

I open my eyes and see Dr Gilbert smiling at me. *Well done, my dear*, he says. *Well done*.

46.

They were to spend one more night in Maymo, and Belle could tell something fundamental had changed. Their relationship had tilted, become subtly different. She felt self-conscious as she undressed before him in tongue-tied silence, head bowed, full of an unfamiliar mix of feelings. Hope? Anticipation? Maybe even a little apprehension? Perhaps having survived such a close escape together had made her more attentive to her deepest feelings, maybe the peaceful day they'd spent had cemented their bond, maybe it was because she'd finally been able to talk about the massacre in Rangoon. Or maybe it was all of those things. Whatever it was, she felt she had lost the ability to communicate in words and the air in the room was alive with unspoken need. From the start there had been a strong pull between them. Now he didn't take his eyes from her and when she lifted her head and returned his gaze she saw the depth of longing there. Whatever it was that had drawn them closer, the time had come.

He undressed too and, as they stood naked before each other, it was as if, unguarded, they had tacitly agreed to unwrap their innermost selves, expose their flaws, their insecurities, their open desire. It wasn't cold, but she shivered slightly and held out a hand to him.

In the bed he commanded her to lie still. She barely moved as he caressed her body and, as he did, she felt every moment with such heightened sensuality that, still holding back a little, it was like exquisite torture. Each touch of his fingers – on her neck, her breasts, her thighs, her mouth – electrified her. Each brush of his lips left her gasping. And then it changed again. As the intensity soared she felt herself releasing all the tensions and

251

worries she'd been carrying for so long; letting go of the pain and fear too. Now she wanted him so much her mind dwelt on nothing else.

'Make love to me now,' she demanded, her voice urgent.

The sex itself was powerful, exhilarating, and it made her want to cry, though not with tears of sadness; these would be tears of liberation, and of joy, and then, before she'd realized what was happening, laughter began to bubble through her. It tipped and soared and became unstoppable. Such innocent, natural laughter she could not remember experiencing before. She felt childlike, free, like one of the birds she'd released at the Shwedagon Pagoda.

He laughed with her, then raised himself up on one elbow and searched her face, his focus absolute. 'If you knew how long I've been wanting to do that!'

She narrowed her eyes. 'How long?'

'Umm.' He twisted his mouth to one side as if considering. 'Since the first moment I set eyes on you.'

She grinned and felt the thrill all the way through her still-tingling body.

'Are you okay? I didn't hurt you?'

She dug him in the ribs. 'If that was hurting, please can you hurt me some more?'

'Right now?'

'Uh-huh.'

He laughed. 'You're a hard task master.'

This time they took it incredibly slowly and afterwards he told her he loved her and he always would. She took his hand and kissed the tips of his fingers, then snuggled in close to him, exhausted, but with her mind at peace.

The next day Oliver stowed their luggage in racks above their heads on what turned out to be a train to Rangoon with no first-class carriages. They shared theirs with a few sleeping Indian men and, intermittently, different Burmese women transporting fruit and vegetables further down the line. Apart from the smell of their cheroots, it wasn't too bad. But when a fish-seller joined them, Belle was forced to stand, wilting, beside a window so badly jammed it provided only the slightest hint of warm air. From there she could smell smoke from village fires and vendors cooking on charcoal beside the railway track. The smoke made her cough but was an improvement on nausea induced by the smell of fish.

Every hour or so hordes of vendors battered at the windows or traversed the aisles selling sticky rice and chilli noodle snacks. Why the train kept stopping and waiting, Belle and Oliver didn't know. In some cases, it appeared the tracks were still under repair, but other stops remained inexplicable and nobody seemed able to answer their questions about the delay. Whenever they halted, Oliver insisted she keep close to him as thieves were known to haunt the wilder and more desolate stations, ready to slip aboard and steal from sleepy passengers.

Now she was over the initial shock caused by the explosion, Belle felt happy and relieved to be with him again, although she wished the circumstances could have been different. Deep in the core of her she felt his presence. That he'd saved her life meant everything and she leant against him, drinking in the smell of his skin and praying nothing more would endanger them. Oliver, however, seemed on edge, constantly surveying the people climbing on and off the train as well as gazing out at the platform at every stop. He wore sunshades and a straw hat, making it tricky for others to spot what he was doing, but she could feel the tension in his whole body. She eyed any newcomers too but when half a dozen police officers boarded she relaxed a little.

After an execrable 386-mile journey taking three days, far longer than it should have done, they arrived back in the damp, clinging heat of Rangoon and headed straight for Oliver's apartment. With a sense of enormous relief, and no thought for what might lie ahead, they both lay back on his bed without even changing. He reached for her hand and immediately his breathing slowed. Belle, too exhausted to feel much, nevertheless knew what had happened between them meant something she'd secretly hoped for but had only ever vaguely understood. It had meaning, this relationship, meaning that spoke of the present, yes, but also of the future. And she knew the strength of the love between them would bring a completely different kind of life. She felt sure of that, if nothing else. Then she closed her eyes, curled into him and slept too.

Belle woke first to find they were wrapped in each other's arms as if their bodies had known what their souls needed even if they had been too tired. She touched the stubble on his chin, enjoying the comfort, the closeness, his warm breath on her cheek, and when he opened his eyes he smiled at her. She kissed him hard on the lips and felt again his hardness against her body. As she traced the contours of his dear face with her fingertips she saw how beautiful he was, his skin golden and glowing, his eyes blue and full of feeling. They made love, gently at first, but ending with such passion it made her shout out. He covered her mouth softly to stop her and whispered to be quiet. When the rise and fall of her chest had returned to normal she wriggled out from under his embrace and slipped into the bathroom for a wash. All her clothes were dirty now, so she rinsed out a blouse and a long skirt and hung them to dry above the bath.

When she emerged, her hair hanging wet and limp around her face, it was to see Oliver with his back to her, busily making coffee.

He twisted round when he heard her and smiled with such tenderness her heart literally missed a beat. To feel such love while in the grip of fear was beyond words.

'Sorry, there's no food,' he said. 'I'll nip out and get something.'

'I'm not really hungry. Coffee would be nice.'

'Come here,' he said, with an even broader smile brightening his face.

But suddenly harsh reality took over and with it the fear grew stronger. Her chest constricted as she whispered, 'Someone tried to kill me.' She remained where she was and inspected the floor. Anything not to have to think.

'It will be okay,' he said.

She raised her head to look at him. 'Will it?'

He gave her a nod. 'Come here,' he repeated.

She walked over to him and he held her close, gently stroking her hair. 'We are going to make sure it is all right. Together.'

She felt safer knowing he was there. This bond they shared was instinctive. It was an honest bond by which each declared to the other *I know who you are and what I don't know I want to find out*. The words 'a meeting of souls' came into her thoughts and although it felt like a cliché, it was the truth.

When they set out for the Strand Hotel and began to tread the familiar streets, Belle felt a throb of anxiety. Although it was busy and people were everywhere, if someone wanted to trail them she knew it would be a moment's work to slip unnoticed into the shadows. Oliver remained encouraging, but she feared another attack, worried every man they passed might be concealing a knife, or even a gun. She held tight to Oliver, but her eyes darted everywhere, and she was unable to corral her fears. Sensing her increasing unease, he steered her through the crowds and then quickly hailed a rickshaw.

At the hotel she left a letter of resignation at reception and was handed an airmail letter that had arrived while she'd been away. She stuffed it into her bag to read later, then hurried to her room to collect some of her things. The sooner she was out of there the better.

She didn't take long and had just finished packing some of her clothes and toiletries into a case and was getting ready to leave when Rebecca entered the room, her curves enhanced by a typically clinging red dress.

'Belle! Where have you been? You look terrible.'

Belle grinned at her friend and took in the tiredness in her eyes, and hair that needed a good brush. She looked as if she'd been out all night again.

'It's an extremely long story,' Belle said.

Rebecca flopped on to her bed. 'Well, at least tell me where you're going now. Is it home to England?'

'Not yet. I'm leaving the job and I'm going to Oliver's.'

Rebecca's eyes were huge with disbelief. 'Crikey. Well, good for you, but what about the gossip-mongers? They'll have a right old field day.'

'I really don't care any more.'

'But why leave? You're a wonderful singer.'

Belle met her friend's eyes and pulled a sad face. 'I'm really sorry I can't tell you now, but when it's all over I will. I promise.'

'Is this something to do with looking for your sister? Have you found out what happened?' Rebecca said, sharp as ever.

'Not yet.'

There was sadness in Rebecca's eyes as she nodded. 'I'll miss you.'

The two women hugged and then Belle joined Oliver in front of the hotel. The doorman agreed to arrange for her trunk to be sent to the station for storage and then Oliver asked him to repeat the tale his father had told about the baby screaming during the night. After accepting their assurance that they wouldn't reveal from where the information had arisen, he went into a little more detail than he previously had.

'The thing I did not tell you was this . . . soon after the incident, my father was dismissed on a trumped-up charge.'

'He was silenced,' Oliver said.

'Why didn't you say before?' Belle asked.

The doorman glanced at the sky then back at Belle. 'He was ashamed. I did not feel I should say. And I was nervous about my own job too.'

Belle nodded. 'I'm so sorry.'

The doorman shrugged. 'All so long ago, but it ruined my father's life. He was given no reference and found it hard to work again.'

Oliver blew out his cheeks. 'These people!'

They thanked the doorman and after they'd left the hotel they stopped to get some food supplies from a shop along their route. They then picked up a rickshaw while checking they were not being followed. When they arrived back at his flat he let them in and then explained he had a hunch and wanted to comb through a different newspaper's archives. She would have to be alone and didn't take much convincing to remain inside with the door locked.

'At least nobody knows you're here,' he said. 'So, you'll be left in peace.'

She grimaced. 'Rebecca knows.'

'Will she keep a lid on it?'

'Don't know. Maybe I shouldn't have told her. Or at least I should've told her to keep it to herself.'

'Can't be helped now. You'll be fine if you don't leave the flat but please don't open the door to anyone. Won't be long.' Then he added as an afterthought, 'Might be a good idea to keep away from the window.'

After he'd gone she made herself some toast and another cup of coffee before trying to settle down to read a paper. A few minutes later, too nervous to concentrate, she was back on her feet examining the spines of his books, and it was only then she remembered the airmail letter. She threw herself on to a chair, fumbled for the fragile paper, then opened and read it.

My dear Annabelle,

I hope this letter finds you in good health. I wanted to let you know I shall be visiting Burma soon. I always promised myself I would return one day and if I don't undertake the trip now I fear I may never get around to it. I'm hoping awfully much that we might meet. Of course, I don't know if you are still living in Rangoon, but I shall call at the Strand at the first opportunity.

Well, my dear girl, I think that's it for now. Do take care of yourself out there.

With kindest regards,
Simone

Belle read the letter twice then leant back in her chair, thinking about Simone. How extraordinary. She had never imagined she might meet Diana's old friend here in Burma, but what a fantastic opportunity to hear more about her mother. She'd been eleven when her father had told her they would never see Diana again and all Belle could remember was that it had been raining and she had just started as a weekly boarder at Cheltenham Ladies' College. Although she'd cried a little at the news of her mother's death, the tears had felt forced, her emotions scrambled and hard to fathom. Diana had not been spoken of again. Now Belle's feelings were even more confusing. Although she now understood how the loss of Elvira must have contributed to her mother's illness and consequent neglect, the pain Belle had felt as a child remained. The child in her still could not forgive and it left her with a feeling of sadness. She couldn't help thinking her mother might have found another way through the tragedy. Could have tried harder. As for Simone, Belle had no idea if she'd still be here to greet her mother's old friend.

As she was thinking this someone knocked at the door very gently and, before remembering Oliver's warning, she walked across. With her hand on the key, she hesitated, scolding herself. Stupid thing to do. Now whoever it was would have heard her moving. The knock came again, louder. Still she did not move, frozen in fear. She waited and after a few moments she heard a woman's voice.

'Belle, I know you're there.'

Gloria. She'd know that voice anywhere. Should she say something? Let her friend in?

'Belle?'

'Yes?'

'For heaven's sake, let me in. I'm worried about you.'

Belle leant her forehead against the cool teak wood for a moment and then unlocked the door, uncertain if she was doing the right thing. Gloria was Edward's sister after all and Belle was feeling increasingly doubtful about him.

Gloria marched in and began scrutinizing Belle's face as if looking for clues. 'What's going on, Belle?'

Belle felt wary, her colour rising. 'I don't know what you mean.'

Gloria seemed genuinely bemused. 'Come on. You've left your job, you're staying in the flat of a man I've already warned you is untrustworthy. This is madness.'

She flung herself down on the chair Belle had been sitting on. 'Got any coffee, darling? I'm gasping.'

Belle nodded and was glad of the chance to hide her inflamed face while she turned her back to make coffee. She knew people would gossip once it got out she was staying here but why should it matter to Gloria? Her friend didn't usually give a fig what other people thought, rather she prided herself on quite the opposite.

'Here's your coffee,' Belle said, forcing her face into a smile.

Gloria took the coffee, then pulled out a silver cigarette case and offered one to Belle.

When Belle declined, Gloria tilted her head. 'Oh, of course, your voice.'

'How did you know I was here?' Belle asked.

'Oh, you know, a little bird. Was it supposed to be a secret? I did rather press it out of her.'

'Rebecca?'

259

Gloria's eyes narrowed and she gave a small, satisfied smile. Then, as her face became sterner, Belle felt apprehensive. True, Gloria didn't like Oliver, but was there something else? Something she might know about?

'Tell me why you left your job,' Gloria said with a critical look that quickly turned to disbelief. 'Good God, he didn't ask you to?'

'Oliver?'

'Darling, you are being somewhat monosyllabic. Of course Oliver. This was his flat last time I looked.'

'I'm simply having a rethink. He didn't ask me to leave the Strand. I may go back to England.'

Gloria looked as if something about the news pleased her. 'But why stay with Oliver? You know he has a reputation. Don't go turning your back on your real friends.'

'What reputation?'

'Women, sweetheart. I said before. Getting on the wrong side of the law. We spoke of it, didn't we?'

Belle nodded but felt increasingly suspicious of Gloria's motive for coming here.

'You never know who he's really working for.'

'He's just a journalist.'

'So he says, but you can't trust him. And, of course, he's American too.'

Belle sighed in frustration. 'What's that got to do with anything?'

Gloria's eyes flickered and her mouth turned down at the corners. Just slightly. But it was enough to betray her prejudice. For all her rebellious posturing, Gloria was conventional under the skin.

'Think of the consequences of being with someone like him,' Gloria said.

'What consequences?'

'He'll let you down for one thing.'

'And the rest?'

Gloria tossed her head and shrugged as if Oliver's flaws were glaringly obvious.

Belle sighed. 'I'm fine, Gloria. And listen, I've now found out my mother had absolutely nothing to do with Elvira's disappearance.'

Gloria glanced down at her coffee cup, looking a bit nervy. 'How do you know?'

Belle hesitated and then decided not to say anything about the bomb. 'It's a long story.'

Gloria did not appear to be mollified and with dogged determination continued. 'Darling, don't stay here. You know how tongues wag once things get out. Come and stay with me instead, at least until you return to England. You'll be much more comfortable.'

'Let me think.'

'I'd prefer you came with me now.'

'Like I said. Let me think.'

'Then I shall return to pick you up later today. Now –' she glanced around – 'tell me all about your adventures in Mandalay.'

Belle enthused about the river trip and the ride in the hot air balloon but didn't say anything about Mandalay. She explained how the search for the white baby had come to nothing and, coupled with all the trouble in Rangoon, that was why she was considering going back to England. Gloria nodded and offered to enlist Edward's support in booking an early crossing if she was adamant about leaving.

'Whatever you decide,' she added, 'I'm sure Edward and I will do our best to help. But, Belle, I can't emphasize this enough. You must get away from Oliver. He's dangerous.'

'Is there something about him you haven't told me?'

'What more do you need?'

Belle flinched at the smug way in which Gloria assumed she was in the right, then felt her colour rising again, this time in annoyance. She'd had enough.

Gloria, seeing the look on her face, shook her head and, with an attempt at a placatory gesture, raised her hands. 'I only want you to be safe.'

One did not usually argue with Gloria, but Belle rose to Oliver's defence, the bond between them the only motivation she needed to stand up for the man she loved. 'You're wrong about Oliver. He's a good man. And I trust him.'

The two women held each other's eyes and then Gloria raised one eyebrow and sighed deeply as if at some recalcitrant child. 'Well, never mind. Let's not quarrel, and my offer is there. As I said, don't turn your back on your real friends.'

Belle looked away. She'd liked Gloria, admired her even. The woman had always been fun and ready to be helpful, but now Belle felt herself grow stiff with suppressed anger.

As Gloria drew out another cigarette, Belle retraced the course of their relationship, sifting through her memories and tracking back to their first encounter on the boat. She'd been flattered by Gloria's interest back then, but now mistrust flooded her mind. Had their friendship really been so innocent? Or had Gloria specifically cultivated their acquaintance once she'd found out Belle's surname?

Furious at Gloria's repeated insistence that Oliver was not to be trusted, she shook her head. She knew her trust in him was not a result of some awful lapse in judgement as Gloria had implied, and she would not allow the other woman to persuade her otherwise. She had no right to march in here like this and virtually demand Belle should leave.

'I think you had better go,' Belle said eventually, successfully hiding the crack in her voice and aware something between them had been broken. The truth was, she no longer knew who Edward really was or what he was up to, and the same applied to Gloria.

47.

Diana, Minster Lovell, 1928

I've lived in Minster Lovell for six years now. For the first year Simone lived with me almost all the time but afterwards, as I grew stronger, she went back home and only stayed occasionally. For the past two years I've lived alone. I go out. I greet my neighbours. Every day, weather permitting, I leave my cottage, the last in the village street, and then I take a few steps upward before quickly turning right and down Church Lane. The old vicarage, close to the bottom of the hill, is where the doctor lives. If I see him pruning or dead-heading his roses – he has a beautiful rose garden – we smile knowingly at each other, then exchange a few pleasantries as if he hasn't heard everything there is to know about me. The lane ends at Manor Farm, so there I turn right and walk through the grounds of the Cotswold stone church of St Kenelm. I like reading the names on the gravestones and imagining the lives of the folk who have gone before me. The first time I saw how many families had suffered more than one loss of a young child, as I have, it did not make me feel gloomy. Instead I felt an affinity with these people that roots me here in a way I have never felt so strongly before. After the church I usually slip through the atmospheric ruin of Minster Hall, then down to the path where the river Windrush flows, and as I walk among the delicate flowers, the place throbs with the sounds of wild birds, ducks and coots.

I often wonder how we know when we are happy. Is it the absence of worry or the absence of sorrow? Or, in my case, is it because I have found a wonderful, gentle rhythm to my life? The right beat that at last allows me to live with ease and able to appreciate the refreshing simplicity of things. Yet for all of us, happiness is fragile. I'd be a fool if I didn't acknowledge that.

Something inside me was broken. Maybe it still is. But now I know I can live with it. Before I could not.

I no longer live in a world of ghosts, apart from those who once inhabited Minster Hall and they are not mine alone. And, even though I sometimes strain to hear, the voice is extraordinarily silent. If it ever reappears my forward-thinking Dr Gilbert has taught me to talk to it. Don't be frightened, he says. He's taught me it is I who control the voice and not the other way around. It isn't always easy. Sometimes, when I'm alone in the thick dark night and I feel the dense foliage and the grasping branches of the trees in Rangoon, I fail. Then the past still has power over me, but when dawn curls around my bedroom, gradually lighting every corner, I find my way again. Overcoming difficulty is simply a part of life, the doctor says. For the first five years I lived here I saw him twice a week and there were many, many times I swore it was all a waste of time and money. Now I see him only once a month. He has saved my life and I can never repay his kindness and dedication. He, along with my dearest Simone, has been my greatest friend.

And now there is just one thing left.

I've been nursing feelings of guilt and loss over Annabelle for all these years and it's time to do something about it. I long to see her again and want so much to try to find a way to make up for my neglect of her in the past, if Douglas will permit it.

And so, next week, with much trepidation, I'll be travelling back along the road I came by. To Cheltenham.

48

As she paced the room, Belle felt hot and searched for the switch to operate the ceiling fan. She found it and flicked it but the warm air it shifted around didn't help. How desperate she was to see Oliver, hoping the feeling of connection between them would ease the reservations Gloria had planted in her mind. And although the need to believe in Oliver went deep, a tiny seed of doubt had crept in, even as she had defended him. What if there was the slightest chance Gloria could be right? But no, that couldn't be. She was just frightened and worried and didn't know how to feel any more.

When he did finally appear, carrying his briefcase, his eyes seemed impenetrable and she felt a wobble. I am scared to love you, she thought, and dipped her head so he might not see what was in her eyes.

'Something wrong?' was all he said.

'Gloria came.'

'But I –'

Belle interrupted. 'She said I shouldn't trust you.'

A look of irritation crossed his face. 'Why did you let her in?'

They stared at each other.

'Belle, it isn't me you need to worry about.'

'I know. But who?'

He shrugged. 'I don't know yet, but look, I have something.' From the case he extracted a yellowing scrap of newsprint that, judging by the blackened edge, looked as if the rest of it had been burnt.

'I found it by chance when I was looking up references to Golden Valley. It's just a tiny part of something longer but you can still see the date. Eight years ago, and only weeks before I arrived in Burma. Apparently, during renovations of a house in Golden Valley, a skeleton of a baby was discovered as they dug up the ground ready to build a summer house.'

Belle felt the blood drain from her face. 'My parents' house? Is that why my mother was digging?'

What had her mother known, she thought? And if it wasn't Diana who had buried the baby, who had? Lost in her thoughts, she didn't catch what Oliver was saying.

'Did you hear?'

She shook her head, spirits sinking.

'I said it doesn't say whose place it was, Belle. But it was number twenty-one, so not your parents' house.'

'But so close. Surely it must prove my sister is buried there?'

He nodded. 'Could be. As I said, I went through another paper's archives – a friend is editor there – and found it stuck between two other articles about building and developments in Golden Valley. There's nothing else about the skeleton. I reckon the whole thing was supressed. I found nothing more.'

'Do you think they informed my father about it?'

'Not sure. The case had been closed years before. Nobody followed this up, although someone obviously destroyed the rest of the article this scrap came from . . .' He paused. 'It must mean something. In any case, I'll do what I can to find out whose garden it was.'

'What's the point?'

'If it was Elvira buried there, don't you want to know who was responsible?'

An hour later they arrived at the Land Registry where they eventually managed to trace the family who'd been living at number twenty-one at the time. When it turned out to be George de Clemente, Commissioner of Rangoon Division, married to Marie, with one baby daughter, Oliver whistled.

'Did Edward ever mention anything about number twenty-one to you?'

She shook her head. 'He said he'd like to buy my house.'

Oliver raised his brows. 'Interesting.'

'This George must be a relative of Edward and Gloria's. It's an unusual name.'

'I'll check who inherited the house or who bought it.'

As he read on for a few minutes more, Belle could not understand why nobody had told her about a skeleton having been found buried in the garden of twenty-one. Had that been deliberate? Or was it simply someone else's dark family secret and nothing to do with Elvira at all? An unwanted pregnancy perhaps?

'Here we are. It seems the house was inherited by their nephew, Edward de Clemente, so there's your answer.'

'Gloria has a house in Golden Valley. I've never been, but perhaps she lives there. And if it is the same house, why did she never tell me about a skeleton having been found?'

'Exactly what I was thinking. Odd, isn't it?'

She nodded. 'What do you think Edward has to do with any of this?'

He pulled a face. 'I don't know. Maybe nothing. However, I've known for some time that Edward doesn't simply work as an advisor to the Commissioner.'

'Then what?'

'The Rangoon Intelligence Unit.'

Belle was horrified. 'You don't think he was behind the bomb in Mandalay?'

'Better not jump to conclusions. We'd need something irrefutable to be able to prove that.'

'So, what do we know about this George de Clemente?'

Oliver furrowed his brow as he considered her question. 'Well, it says they had one daughter. Of course, he and his wife might have had another baby. Perhaps twins, one of whom died.'

'But why bury it in the garden?'

'Stillborn?'

'That doesn't explain anything. Why not in the graveyard at the church? It has to be Elvira.'

'They may have had some other reason. Perhaps a servant's child?'

Belle bowed her head.

'First, let's establish what happened to this George chap. Find out where he is now.'

From the Land Registry they went to the governmental employees' archives to see if they could find anything in the few records available to the public. Admittedly much would be classified, but it was worth a chance. After half an hour their persistence was rewarded when they read a footnote to the paragraph on George de Clemente detailing how he and his family had moved to Kalaw in 1911.

'The year Elvira vanished,' Belle said.

'I know a guy who has worked at the Department of Health in Kalaw for years. He may tell us more.'

A small Department of Posts and Telegraphs had been founded in 1884 and, as a journalist, Oliver's paper had helped him acquire a telephone line early on. While he made some calls, Belle watched him, chewing the inside of her cheek and wondering about the de Clemente family. What on earth could be the connection between them and her dead sister? Belle felt exhausted by the questions whirling in her mind, but excited too. She hungered to know exactly what had happened all those years ago and why so much information had been lost or hidden.

When Oliver ended his calls, it was to tell her that the de Clemente family had left Burma to live in America but up until then they had employed a Chinese nanny who, after the family left, returned to Rangoon to run a small newsagent's shop. 'They weren't in Kalaw for any time at all.'

'That's odd.'

'Yes. Why go to Kalaw if they were bent on leaving the country?'

'Unless it was a holiday. It is a hill station, isn't it? A bit like Maymo.'

Oliver nodded. 'I think we have to go back to the Secretariat. I know the clerk at the Office of Trading Licences. If we can find the nanny, she might know something about the baby buried in the garden of twenty-one.'

Belle laughed. 'Because nannies know everything.'

'And, if she has a licence for her shop, we'll find her.'

'They know everything and *you* know everyone.'

He made a mock bow. 'All in the line of duty, ma'am. The British keep everything tight, so I have no option but to ferret out information however I can.'

She pulled a grateful face. 'Well, I'm jolly glad of it.'

'How British you sound,' he said, smiling back at her. 'But don't raise your hopes too much. The nanny may well have moved on, maybe even gone back to live in China.'

As they neared the Secretariat again, Oliver pointed out a small tea shop with chairs and tables placed outside in the shade beneath a wide awning.

'Best if you wait there.'

She shook her head determinedly. 'I'm coming with you.'

'Honey, I know the guy. Old school. Won't deal with a woman. If you come, you'll only raise suspicions. If I go on my own he'll just think it's something connected with a story for my paper.'

'Talking of your paper, shouldn't you be at work?'

'Leave of absence. Now, I won't be long, but do watch out. Whoever was behind the bomb may well see you.'

'Oh God.'

'It might not be a bad thing. Might help flush him or her out. It's too public for anything awful to happen here. If you sense the slightest hint of trouble, go inside the café and ask for the owner's help. He's a friend.'

Oliver left, and Belle made her way across to one of the tables where she sat close to a group of women, and then ordered a pot of tea. The day was hot with the promise of heavy rain and she felt herself wilting beneath the extreme humidity. In the distance the hum of Rangoon's busy streets went on relentlessly. All nerves, she sat eyeing the people milling about outside the grand Secretariat. Some, who weren't British, fretfully waited to be allowed in, while bustling self-important men entered and left the main entrance at will. She prayed Oliver wouldn't be too long. But how conscientious he'd been, leaving no stone unturned and fully proving himself as an investigative journalist.

The closer Belle came to knowing about the past, the more real it felt. How devastating it must have been to have been accused at the same time as dealing with overwhelming grief. She'd judged her mother for so long. She told herself she'd only been a child and couldn't have known any better. But it didn't help. *Sorry, Mummy, so sorry*, she whispered to herself. But it was much too late.

A voice broke into her thoughts and, squinting into the brightness, she glanced up to see Edward approaching her table. A shiver of fear ran through her and she struggled to steady herself. He looked uneasy, his skin redder than usual, as if he was troubled by the heat.

'Belle.' It was a terse greeting.

She swallowed hard but her throat had closed, so she flicked her wrist to indicate an unoccupied chair.

He didn't sit and, frowning, seemed to be studying her. 'I hear you've been making enquiries. You must be more careful to whom you speak and who speaks on your behalf. If you'd wanted to know anything you only had to ask me.'

'I –'

'Leave your tea, my dear, I'd like you to come with me.'

He'd spoken urgently and in a tone that brooked no argument but she shook her head and, with a thumbnail digging sharply into her palm, she found her voice. 'Sorry, Edward, it's absolutely lovely to see you, but I'm waiting for Oliver.'

'I thought *we* were friends, you and I.' He tilted his head to one side and now he did smile, but there was little genuine warmth in it and she noticed the dark shadows beneath his eyes.

'You look tired,' she said.

'It's the time of year.'

Although she knew what he meant, his grim face told her something different. She wiped her brow with her palm and prayed Oliver would get back quickly. 'It's so hot, isn't it? But as I said –'

'This is just a request, Belle. I wouldn't dream of forcing you, but really, I do need you to come with me. For your own good, you understand.' His tone had changed now, become more cajoling.

'But, Edward, the thing is, I don't understand,' she said, keeping her voice as light and conversational as she could, despite a nagging undercurrent of fear. 'What's this about?'

'I have a car waiting,' he said, without answering her question. 'I can't explain here. It's a small matter and won't take long at all. You'll be in and out in no time. We'd purely like to ask you a few questions. You won't come to any harm and I'll have you back in the blink of an eye.'

'Who is *we*?'

'My department, who else?'

Belle took a breath and then exhaled slowly. The heat had been building and building and now it had become unbearable.

While Edward took out his handkerchief and wiped his brow, Belle glanced to her left and spotted Oliver in the distance, now heading towards them. She hoped Edward hadn't heard the way her sharp intake of breath had given away the rush of relief she'd felt at seeing her lover. She remained seated and played for time by talking about how much she longed to see the monsoon. Inside, she was trembling. There wasn't any way on this earth she was going to go with Edward.

'How is Gloria?' she then asked.

'Gloria is fine, really fine. Thank you for asking. Anyway, shall we go? I'll have you back in a jiffy, there's a good girl.'

Patronizing, she thought, but he was definitely rattled.

When Oliver had almost reached them, Edward must have heard his footsteps because he twisted round to see who was coming.

Belle caught Oliver's eye, then she rose to her feet and picked up her bag to give the impression she was intending to do what Edward wanted, though her legs were shaking. She pressed down on the table with one hand to keep herself firm and hoped she could carry off the deception. 'Edward wants me to go with him. Says it won't take long. So, I'll just –'

'Is this police business?' Oliver asked the other man, interrupting her. 'Is she under arrest?'

Edward had no option but to shake his head. 'Of course not. Why would she be? I am simply trying to look out for her.'

'In that case, unless you do wish to have her arrested, she stays with me. I can do the looking out. Right, Belle?'

She nodded.

Edward turned to Belle and gave her a hard, regretful look. 'I can't tell you who to choose as your friends, I can only say you are making a grave mistake. I just wish you had listened to me.'

49.

Diana, Cheltenham, 1928

Cheltenham hasn't changed. Still the same elegant Regency buildings I've always loved, still the same tree-lined streets, still the same expansive parks. It's me who has changed and, as Simone draws the car up close to my old home, I turn to her.

'Thank you. I'll be fine now.'

She reaches out and squeezes my hand. 'I'll walk in the park for half an hour, then wait in the car.'

I get out, close the door and walk slowly up to the house with such new-found confidence I could never have imagined. For a few moments I do nothing, just allowing the fact that I'm there to sink in. But then, out of the blue, I think of the evening Douglas and I first met. I was eighteen. It was midsummer, one of those perfect warm nights. The kind that leaves you aching with the scent of honeysuckle and roses in full bloom and longing for the night to last for ever. My father had thrown a party for friends and neighbours as they used to do each year when my mother was alive.

I spotted Douglas before he even noticed me and inexplicably couldn't take my eyes off him. He was tall and academic-looking, certainly not the type to set a young girl's heart fluttering. But when I sat on a bench at the back of the garden, hidden away from the main crowd, he came across and asked if he could join me. His smile was sincere and there was a kind of expressiveness in his voice as he introduced himself and asked my name. My heart did flutter but I managed to reply and smile back. Once the rest of the party faded into the background and only the two of us remained, we sat for a long while, talking and laughing, and he asked if he might call on me the next day. I went to sleep hugging myself and knowing something special was going to happen. Whatever it was we both felt so keenly that first evening, it quickly grew into love, and I knew I wanted to spend the rest of my life with this man whose dancing eyes, behind his serious-looking spectacles, spoke of hidden passion.

The sound of laughter in the park brings me back to the present. I knock and wait. After what seems an interminable amount of time, I hear footsteps and then Mrs Wilkes opens the door. With raised brows she mutters an unconvincing welcome and ushers me in. It makes me wonder if Douglas has even told her to expect me. Then she indicates I should wait in the formal drawing room. I feel more anxious now I'm inside the house, but can't let myself succumb to nerves, so I don't sit but slip over to the window instead. I had forgotten how different the view is from down here. I can't see as much as I used to from upstairs, and what used to be my window on the world.

When Douglas enters I notice he's not smiling, and he looks much older.

'Won't you sit, Diana? Mrs Wilkes will bring us tea in a moment. So –' and now he gives me a brief smile – 'how have you been?'

I smile back at him. 'As I said in my letter, I'm enormously much recovered and longing to see Annabelle. Doctor Gilbert is a genius.'

He nods. 'I'm exceedingly glad to hear it.'

'And how is our daughter?' I say brightly.

'She's well. But this is rather tricky, Diana. You recall our agreement?' He has spoken noticeably slowly, and I wonder what it signifies.

'Of course. I was to stay away,' I say, still bright.

'Exactly.'

I give him a broad smile and keep my tone light. 'But I'm better now and that changes everything.'

He narrows his eyes and looks uncomfortable. 'No, Diana, I'm sorry but it changes nothing.'

I blink rapidly and try to ignore the first hint that this isn't going to go well. Surely, he can't mean it? I wait but he says nothing more, so I lean forward as if to encourage him. In the end it is I who speaks.

'Don't be silly, Douglas. I'm different now and naturally I have a right to see my girl.' I glance about in excitement. 'Is she here? In my letter I told you I wanted to see her today.'

'She is a weekly boarder at Cheltenham Ladies' College, so no, she is not here.'

'But, Douglas –'

He holds up a hand, and I sense a hesitancy he is trying to conceal. 'It really is quite impossible for you to see Annabelle.'

I feel as if he has punched me in the stomach. 'Why?'

He tilts his head as if scrutinizing me, then speaks carefully, enunciating every word. 'Let me finish. If you remember, we agreed that after some time had elapsed I would tell her you had died.'

'Don't speak to me as if I were stupid.'

'Diana, she thinks you're dead. I told her four years ago. She has adjusted to the fact. Got over it.' Now he's firm, decided, rigid, more like the Douglas he became later in our marriage.

My heart pounds in horrified alarm. Dear God, he can't mean it. He can't. I reel at the dreadfulness of what he's saying but will not let him browbeat me. 'For heaven's sake, I was sick when I agreed.'

'I'm sorry, my dear, she's thriving now, and I feel it would undo all the good work we have done with her if you came back, suddenly alive. It would be too unsettling for her after all this time.' His voice is hard, brooking no argument. But I will argue. I will. And I clench my fists.

'But, Douglas, this is insane! I'm her mother. We can think of something to tell her. You were mistaken about my death. Misinformed or something. There has to be a way.'

He shakes his head and speaks quietly as if to defuse my anger. 'I really must insist we stick to the letter of our agreement.'

As Mrs Wilkes carries in the tea tray, his words hit home. I feel myself beginning to shrink so to prevent it I get to my feet, stand tall, and take a few steps away to gaze out of the window again while calming my breathing. After a moment I glance back to see Mrs Wilkes pour us both a cup and then leave the room.

'Biscuit?' he says and holds up a plate. 'Do come and sit down again. They are Mrs Wilkes's favourite recipe.'

'I couldn't give a damn about her wretched biscuits!' I say, angry and staying where I am. 'I want to see Annabelle.'

He puts down the plate, gets up and walks across to me but I turn my back on him. 'You need to understand, Annabelle is fifteen now and very settled. I can't have her life disrupted. Surely you see that?'

I spin round. 'No, I don't see. You can't stop her seeing her mother. I won't move from this spot and if you force me out I'll fight it in the courts.'

'You're not thinking straight.'

I can't help snorting. 'That's exactly what you used to say if I disagreed with you on anything. Anything at all. You haven't changed, but I have. And for the first time in years I *am* thinking clearly. It's you who is not.'

He shakes his head and I can see his inflexibility growing stronger. How stubborn he is. I'd almost forgotten.

'You've been away for six years. You would lose your case and, anyway, think of the effect on Annabelle.'

I glare at him and raise my voice, though I know of old if I shout at him it will only make things worse. 'I won't be bullied. If you refuse to allow me to see her, I'll write to her at school! You can't stop me doing that.'

He almost laughs. 'Really, Diana, think how she would feel. And I can easily get the school to intercept her mail if it is in her best interests. And it is. You must see that it is.'

'No, I don't see. She's my daughter, Douglas. I've already lost one daughter.'

'We both lost Elvira,' he says more quietly but I won't respond to that.

'How could you make me agree never to see my child when I was so ill? It was utterly unfeeling.'

He's speaking fast now, animated, becoming angry, something he hates to be. 'Listen to me. It wasn't meant to be cruel. I thought it was for the best and I still do. Can you not imagine the distress when Annabelle is told her dead mother suddenly isn't so dead? It's taken so long for her to have become as settled as she is now.'

I feel my eyes heat up but then I straighten my back. I absolutely will not cry in front of him. 'And that's your final word?'

He nods. 'I'm delighted you're feeling so much better, believe me, but I'm afraid it has to be, at least while she is still a child. I'm sorry, Diana.'

I feel his tension as he carries on as he has always carried on, but the words I want to say die in my mouth. I think long and hard before I speak, remembering how it felt during the last few years I was living here. How trapped I'd been, going crazy all alone in my room. How disturbing it had been for our daughter. What an awful mess we all were in. Eventually I reach the conclusion that Douglas might be right. It hurts so much. I feel a stone lodging in my chest, twisting and turning and crushing my breath. I chew the inside of my cheek in the unlikely hope that this lesser pain will stave off the overwhelming sorrow I know will come. I do not know how I will ever bear it, but I cannot cause my daughter any more distress. She's been through enough, we all have, and, terrible, terrible thought though it is, maybe I really must relinquish my role as her mother.

'Diana?' he says.

'Well, I really am not the woman I used to be,' is all I eventually come out with. It doesn't go anywhere near articulating everything I've been thinking but it is true. I want to say we all change, don't we, become different from how we were, maybe even from day to day. I *am* different and glad of it, but Douglas can't see it. He wants everything to stay the same.

Instead of saying that, I nod, close to tears. 'I will accept your decision . . . for now, at least. But there is something I still need to ask.'

He places a hand on my arm and the physical contact brings on a storm of memories.

'Douglas, why did you have an affair while I was pregnant with Elvira? I never understood. We loved each other, didn't we?'

He looks ashamed, as if I've caught him out, his face blanching and his lips tightening in shock. He trembles as he speaks. 'You . . . you were expecting our child. I didn't want . . . well, you know.'

'You didn't want to touch me? That's what you're saying?'

'I didn't want to hurt you . . . or the baby.'

'And yet you did in a far worse way. You should have told me how you felt. You never told me how you felt.'

'I didn't know how,' he whispers.

But I am not finished. 'I always believed it was my fault. Something I'd done wrong. I carried that burden for years.'

He doesn't answer but he deflates further and won't meet my eyes.

'But it wasn't my fault, was it?'

He shakes his head and then he looks at me with such anguish in his eyes. 'I'm sorry. It shouldn't have happened. Not at all. I was arrogant enough to believe if I . . . if I met my needs elsewhere it would be better for you.'

'And yet you broke my heart. Why do you think I became so dejected?'

A short silence as I watch him struggle.

'And you still blame me for my illness?' I say, suddenly numb with grief.

He speaks softly when he replies. 'Not blame, Diana, not for that. Pity. That's what I felt . . . What I still feel.'

'Pity?'

'And an abiding sense of loss.'

I think about it. 'We both lost, didn't we?'

He nods slowly and as I witness the immense weight of sadness in his eyes my anger dissolves a little.

'Do you blame me for Elvira? Do you still think it was something to do with me?'

He shakes his head. 'No, I never believed that.'

'Do you remember nothing of how we once were?' I say. 'Do you remember us?'

His eyes soften still further and I see something of the man I used to love but I know he won't change his mind about Annabelle.

'Of course, you must know I do,' he says. 'But now I am sure you will place our daughter's needs above your own, as I must too.'

He touches my cheek, oh so gently, and I see his eyes are moist. I decide I must bide my time. Maybe one day, when she's older, I will see my girl.

'Have you a photograph of her as she is now?'

He walks across to the bureau and pulls out a folder, then withdraws a single photograph and hands it to me. Now I really struggle to hold back the tears as I hunger for my daughter. She has become the spitting image of me at the same age. I trace the outline of her face with my fingertips. 'Can I keep this, please?'

He hesitates for a second, then agrees.

I turn to leave but pause and hold out my hand. 'Goodbye, Douglas,' I say, and I don't know why but the poignant look in his eyes tells me I will never see my husband again.

50

Belle glanced at Oliver. 'Did you find an address for the nanny?'

He grinned. 'What do you think?'

She laughed. 'You did?'

'Come on.' He held out a hand. 'Better get back to the flat. It's looking like rain.'

'Shouldn't we look for her now?'

'It's getting dark. We're both tired and her business is in Chinatown, not a great place to be at night. First thing tomorrow. To be honest, I need a shower and I'm sure you must too.'

Belle felt damp inside her dress and, yes, she'd kill for a shower but . . . 'Shouldn't we get a move on?' she said. 'If she does know anything, someone might get to her before we do.'

'True. A bite to eat first?'

She agreed, so after a rickshaw ride to Chinatown they entered a small dimly lit restaurant bursting with Chinese folk.

'Always a good sign when a place is jam-packed with locals,' he said as they were seated at the last available table.

'I hope the service isn't too slow.'

'Relax. We have time and the Licensing Office is already closed so nobody will find out we know where she is.'

'Edward told me he knew I'd been making enquiries.'

'The Land Registry may have let him know.'

'Why would they?'

'A man like Edward has informants everywhere. But remember, apart from the familial connection we have no reason to link him to the bomb or to Elvira's disappearance.'

She thought for a moment. 'Except for what Harry told us about the Rangoon Intelligence Unit.'

'True. But a lot of people could be responsible, not only Edward.'

'Why are you defending him?'

'I'm not. I'm just saying we don't know.'

They stopped talking and listened instead to the sound of Chinese voices and the clang and clatter springing from the kitchen. Suddenly hungrier than before, Belle's mouth watered at the fragrant aroma of Chinese spices. She was glancing around the room at the other customers when a sudden burst of rainfall followed by thunder grabbed everyone's attention. All heads automatically swivelled in the direction of the window where the restaurant lights had turned a solid sheet of rain to red and gold.

'The monsoon,' Oliver said, and she could hear the relief in his voice. 'First rain of the season. Wonderful.'

She felt the wonder too. The gathering humidity had become intolerable and though rain made some things more difficult they needed the respite from the heat.

When they had finished their meal, Oliver borrowed an umbrella from the proprietor with promises to return it the following day.

The world outside had dissolved in the deluge, the rain discharging a thousand scents and odours into the air, some, like the fragrant flowers cascading from window boxes, enjoyable, others less attractive. Perhaps rancid oil and something sour from overflowing drains. The torrent obliterated anything they might otherwise have been able to see and, despite the umbrella, within a few minutes they were soaked. Oliver had a reasonable idea of where they were headed and kept glancing at doorways and into alleyways to identify their exact whereabouts. They spotted the shine of a car's headlights as it came crawling up the street and he pulled her back into a dark doorway until it had passed. Soon after, they reached an area where the shops were still lit up like hazy beacons shining through the wall of glistening rain.

'Let's ask,' he said as they eventually stood outside a news-agent's shop. 'I think this is it. I'm pretty sure I've been here before, although it's not a woman who runs it. I know the guy.'

He held on to Belle's arm, then opened the door. They both went inside, shaking the wet from their hair.

Oliver explained who they were looking for and the man stared at him coldly. 'Like I say the other man, she gone. I do not know where.'

'Come on, you know who I am. We are not the government and I believe the old lady might be in danger. We can help.'

The man looked confused.

'At least tell me what the other man who came looked like.'

'Tall man. Eurasian.'

Belle and Oliver exchanged looks.

'But other man with him. Older, British. Not too tall. Slim, grey hair coming here.' He pointed to his temples. 'He was boss, in charge.'

'Could it really be Edward?' Belle whispered, but then thought of the many British men who might fit a similar description.

'Look,' Oliver was saying, 'we are here to help the lady. Not cause trouble.'

The man shook his head but was looking increasingly worried and Belle wondered what to say next. 'Are you certain you don't know where she is?' she came out with.

'She give me the shop. All legal.'

Belle smiled at him and spoke gently. 'We're not bothered about that.'

He narrowed his eyes. 'So, what you want?'

'To talk. Are you a relative?'

He opened his mouth but just as Belle felt they were beginning to get somewhere he asked them to leave. She felt utterly despondent. There was nobody else who might know and now it looked like they'd never find out who had buried the baby, or why they had buried it at number twenty-one, or even who the child had been. She didn't want to admit it but in her deepest being she felt certain it had to have been her sister.

But right then, an old lady slipped through from the back. The man quickly gestured she should go back inside but Oliver was ahead of him.

'Liu Lin?' he asked, and the woman nodded without seeming to consider first. 'You used to be a nanny?'

She nodded again cautiously. 'A long time ago.'

'I think we need to talk.'

The man spoke to her in a Chinese dialect, but she waved whatever he had said away.

'I'll speak with you. Upstairs.'

They followed the old lady up a narrow staircase. At the top she pulled aside a curtain and then pushed a section of the wooden wall behind it. They went through what was clearly a secret door into what had to be the next house.

'My sister's house,' she said by way of explanation. 'Dead. Mine now and my brother has the shop. I am hiding here.'

She indicated they were to sit on cushions on the floor.

'What is it you wish to speak about?' she said, once they were settled.

Belle spoke first. 'I want to know if the baby who was buried in the garden of George de Clemente's house, where you used to work, is my sister.'

Liu Lin stared at her for a long time.

'Please, if you know anything?' Belle pleaded.

'Who was your sister?'

'My parents, Diana and Douglas Hatton, lived two doors away in Golden Valley. Their baby, my sister, a little girl called Elvira, vanished from the garden in 1911.'

The old woman shook her head. 'It was not her.'

'Then who?'

'They gave me money never to say.'

'Who? Please tell us.'

'The body in the garden of the de Clemente house was my mistress's child. Born without breath.'

Belle frowned. 'But why did it have to be a secret?'

Liu Lin bit her lip and paled.

'People must have known her baby had not lived.'

'Only me. I knew. The baby was a little early and I assisted with the birth. Mr de Clemente was still on his way back from Shan States and arrived three days later.'

'So?'

'Mrs de Clemente had gone crazy, told me I would be dismissed if I told anyone. She refused to accept the baby was dead, would not let me near, would not let me arrange a funeral, would not let anyone in her room. Just me. No one in the house knew the baby was dead. I told them everything was fine and Mrs de Clemente needed her privacy. A day later when she heard the Hatton baby crying and crying . . .'

The woman paused but Belle, mesmerized by the story, and feeling a lump in her throat, knew what was coming next.

'She slipped into the garden of number twenty-three, from a path that ran behind all the gardens, picked up the baby girl and brought her home. That night she told me to bury her own baby in the wild part of our garden where nobody went.'

'Oh, dear God,' Belle exclaimed as the truth of it sank in.

'I dug a hole and covered the ground with branches and leaves. I had to wait until the servants had gone home or were asleep.'

'Didn't anyone make the connection when Elvira went missing?' Oliver asked.

'No, because nobody but me knew Mrs de Clemente's own baby had been born dead.'

'What about a doctor?'

'She forced me not to call a doctor.'

'And what about her husband? Did she tell him the truth?'

'No.'

'He knew nothing about it?'

'When the police began searching for the missing baby I got scared and told him what had happened. I thought he would insist his wife give the baby back, but he said no. They would leave Rangoon instead. The scandal if people know his wife had stolen a baby would ruin him.'

'So, they went to Kalaw?'

'I went with them. They told everyone it was for a holiday but after a week passed we all came back to Rangoon at night. They paid me a lot of money never to speak of what had happened and then they secretly headed out of the country by car. I believe they were going in the direction of Thailand. Certainly they were never seen in Burma again. They said I'd die if I spoke and so I bought the shop and the two houses, one for my sister, one for me and my brother.'

Oliver looked incredulous. 'And you didn't think how the Hattons must have felt? You did not think to go to the police?'

'I tried to tell Mrs de Clemente it was wrong, but she yelled at me, and Mr de Clemente, he was worse. He threatened my family. I was scared.'

'They must have needed help to get away?'

'We came back to Rangoon from Kalaw in one car and then we met Mr de Clemente's nephew at the Strand Hotel.'

'Edward de Clemente,' Belle said in a very low voice, feeling sick.

'Yes, Mr Edward. He often used to come to the house for dinner. His uncle helped him with his career.'

'I bet he did,' Oliver said, his voice deliberately curt.

'This nephew had another car waiting ready for them.'

'So, my baby sister went with them and my poor mother was accused of hurting her own child.'

'I am sorry.'

'Why reveal all this to us now?'

'I am ill. It was a terrible thing. I do not wish to go to my grave with it still on my conscience.'

'Did Edward de Clemente threaten you?'

She nodded. 'He threatened my brother.'

'Recently?'

'A few months ago. I stayed up here, but I heard my brother tell him I had gone to China. This Edward de Clemente told my brother if people come asking questions to let him know or there will be big trouble.'

'Why didn't you leave then?'

'I planned to.'

'And your brother, he'd go with you?'

'Yes, but first I had to sell the houses. Without money, where would we go? I knew if we stayed we both might be killed. But I have not found a buyer yet and, as I said, I am ill.'

Oliver put a hand on her shoulder and spoke gently. 'Are you prepared to say all this to the police?'

The woman closed her eyes and didn't reply for a few moments but then she agreed.

Oliver gave her an encouraging smile. 'It would be best if you and your brother come with us and stay in a safe place until you have made a statement to the police.'

She nodded.

For a moment Belle felt shocked but gradually, despite hearing the truth of what had happened, a bubble of something like hope was rising and taking over from all her other feelings. If the de Clementes had gone to America, and if something awful hadn't happened to Elvira subsequently, then she might still have a real live sister. This was more than she had dared to imagine and her emotions swelled with possibility and hope.

She gazed at the woman before speaking. 'Do you know if the baby lived?'

Liu Lin and her brother were taken to safety and gave statements to the police. Early the next morning, Belle was alone at Oliver's apartment milling everything over, while he went out for food. There was a knock at the door and after a moment she heard Gloria.

'Belle, if you are there, let me in. For Christ's sake, it's urgent.'

Belle hesitated but felt so angry hearing her voice, she knew she had to see the woman face to face.

When Gloria came in Belle was shocked. Her face was a ruin. She wore yesterday's make-up and Belle could see how it had settled into the fine lines around her eyes and into the deeper grooves running from the sides of her nose to her mouth. She smelt of stale perfume and the whites of her puffy eyes were red.

'You've really got to help,' she said in a rush, not looking at Belle as she paced back and forth distractedly.

'What do you mean?'

Gloria stared at her as if she was stupid. 'This is your fault. They've arrested Edward and he's been charged with perverting the course of justice. If he's convicted he stands to lose everything. Career, reputation, friends.'

'Like my parents lost everything that really mattered, you mean?'

'I'm sorry, Belle, but it was such a long time ago. This is now, and Edward still has such a bright future. Surely you don't want to destroy it?'

Belle was amazed how Gloria could dismiss what had happened to her parents so lightly.

'I don't think you understand how much my parents suffered. And how much that affected me.'

'But you never knew your sister.'

'It drove my mother out of her mind. I think she came to believe she'd hurt her own child.'

'Edward was just helping out our uncle. He didn't take the baby.'

'He covered it up. A criminal offence, Gloria. And if I have anything to do with it he'll also be charged with aiding and abetting, plus obstructing the police in their enquiries. As will you.'

'I swear I knew nothing at the time. It was only later . . .' She trailed off as Belle glared at her.

Gloria lit a cigarette and then tried sucking up to Belle. 'Look, whatever you want, I'll do it. Maybe contact my cousin, Emily . . . Elvira that was? Could you help get Edward out if I did that?'

Belle stood motionless. Still alive. Finally, she knew for sure. Her sister *was* still alive.

And yet, now it had been confirmed, she hardly knew how to respond. After everything she'd been through, she stared at Gloria with mounting relief fighting against her rage. She steeled herself. Gloria and her brother had concealed her sister's existence and that could never be forgiven.

'Does she know? Emily, does she know the truth about what happened to her?'

Gloria nodded.

'When did she find out?'

'After her mother died, Emily discovered a letter . . . Marie had confessed everything.'

'When?'

'Just a few months ago.'

'And?'

'And what?'

'Does she know about me?'

'No.'

After a long silence Belle clenched her hands and snorted. 'And you think contacting her would be enough to make up for what you did?'

'Well, what would be enough? I have money.'

As Belle's anger turned icy cold she articulated her words with bitter precision. 'You mistake my meaning. *You* knew I was searching for Elvira. *You* let me believe it might have been my own mother who had hurt her.'

'I –'

Belle held up a palm. 'No! *You* don't get to speak. You encouraged me to go off on a wild goose chase with Harry where, I might add, I was very nearly killed. How convenient it would have been. And I suppose my little brush with death had nothing to do with you or your brother?'

Gloria shook her head. 'I don't know anything about it and I'm sure Edward doesn't either. Can you prove it was him?'

'Probably not, but our witness *can* attest to what happened twenty-six years ago.'

'Please, Belle. Edward was so young at the time, scarcely starting out on his career. I'm begging you to ask the witness to withdraw her statement.'

Belle stared at her in disbelief.

Gloria threw herself into a chair and, covering her face with her hands, began to weep. 'This will destroy our family name.'

'Listen, Gloria, I'll tell you what we are going to do. You are going to give me Emily's address and I am going to contact her myself. It's the least you can do.'

'And Edward?'

'Edward will get exactly what he deserves.'

She shook her head as she stared at Gloria and neither woman spoke, but something about the other woman's eyes, a knowing look, guilt maybe, made Belle's mouth fall open. Suddenly she felt as if her blood had frozen. 'It was *you*, wasn't it? You sent those anonymous notes. For God's sake, Gloria, why?'

She'd expected a vigorous denial, but Gloria didn't deny it. Instead, with a flash of defiance, her eyes lit up. 'It was for the best of reasons. I wanted to prevent you from getting too close to the truth. I was worried it would put you in danger if you dug too deep.'

'Danger from whom?'

Gloria ignored her question though Belle knew she was referring to Edward. 'I hoped the notes might encourage you to leave.'

Belle whistled. 'Oh my. That's rich! You're proud of what you did? You were looking out for me?'

Gloria nodded numbly. 'It's why I encouraged you to go to Mandalay. I needed time to think of ways to persuade you to stop searching, especially in Rangoon.'

'But you helped me at the beginning?'

'It would have seemed too obvious I had something to hide if I'd tried to hinder you.'

'Edward too?'

She nodded. 'Neither of us thought you'd ever uncover the truth.'

'And so you warned me off Oliver. You knew he had the skill and the contacts. You realized he'd know where to look.'

Gloria didn't move a muscle, her face frozen but for the mascara sliding down her cheeks. Belle felt no pity whatsoever.

51

Belle bent over the letter she was trying to write to Elvira, or Emily as she was now called. With too many unanswered questions clouding her mind, she'd already made five fruitless attempts. Would Emily want to know her? Would she be pleased at having been found and then contacted like this? Or would she still be so shocked at hearing about her origins that she was unable to contemplate anything more? Struggling to find the right words, Belle had scrunched each attempt at writing into a ball before tossing it aside. What did you say to a long-lost sister who still didn't know you existed?

She crumpled yet another sheet and flung it over her head in exasperation. Oliver, entering the room, caught it. 'Whoa,' he said, 'as bad as that?', then he came over and kissed the top of her head. 'Finding it tough?'

'It's awful,' she wailed, looking up at him. 'Everything I write seems clumsy. You're a journalist. Tell me what to say.'

'You know I can't, but my advice is to keep the story simple and straightforward.'

'It's hardly that though, is it?'

'Just stick to the facts. Avoid too much explanation. Give her the space she needs to react in whatever way she chooses.'

'What if she doesn't want to know?'

He raised his brows. 'Sorry, my love, but it's the risk you have to take.'

'Do I offer condolences about the death of the woman who became her mother?'

He shrugged. 'It's up to you.'

Belle hung her head for a moment, then glanced up at him again. 'Are you sure you won't write it for me?'

He laughed. 'Quite sure.'

As he left the room she picked up her pen, drew out a clean sheet of airmail paper and began again. This time the words began to flow.

Dear Emily,

You don't know me, but my name is Annabelle Hatton and I'm your younger sister, born after our parents left Burma. Your 'cousin', Gloria de Clemente, told me you recently became aware of the facts surrounding your birth and the first few weeks of your life. I imagine it must have been devastating to find out about what happened in the way you did.

On another note, I'm so sorry to hear about your loss. Sadly, my mother, Diana (your birth mother), died too, some years ago, but she would have given anything to know you're alive. I only found out about what happened to you when my (our) father died and I was astonished to discover newspaper cuttings reporting your disappearance. It had been silenced for so long and I didn't even know I'd had a sister.

As for me, I came to Burma to take up a job singing at the Strand Hotel but then spent many months trying to find out what had happened to you. I'd always wanted a sister and I'm so thrilled to have finally found you. You may not feel the same way, of course, and I will understand.

I currently live in Rangoon and have decided to remain here, at least for now, mainly because I am so enjoying restoring the house where you were born. If it's not too distressing I would love to hear from you and learn about your life. If you're interested in meeting I have plenty of room here and you'd be most welcome to stay. I shall, however, accept your decision if

*you'd rather not. I know that finding out about a sister like this
must be quite a shock.*

*I am to be married in four months' time to Oliver, an
American journalist and a wonderful man. There's so much
more I'd like to say and to ask but I'll keep this letter short and
will hope very much to hear back from you.*

With sincere best wishes,
Belle

Belle was aware that to avoid bitter disappointment she'd
have to keep a lid on her feelings of hope and anticipation, but
she couldn't help smiling. As she sealed up the airmail letter and
caught the tram into town, her natural exuberance spilled over.
Surely her sister would want to know her?

52

Belle – Rangoon, three months later

Belle carefully left her brush to rest on the lid of the paint pot, then stood back to admire the third bedroom she'd finished, mildew now gone and the walls as gleaming and fresh as the first. This room, with the veranda overlooking the garden, the one she was certain had been her mother's, was to become her own, although at present her creature comforts only reached as far as a camp bed and a stool to sit on. But at least the services had been reconnected, she had a bathroom, the floors had been repaired and the roof made watertight. Some of the walls had been plastered, the rudimentary kitchen now worked well enough for breakfast and tea, and the sitting room, though bare, boasted a sofa and two armchairs. She'd painted each room herself and gradually, as the white paint brought fresh life to the walls, she regarded her new home with immense satisfaction. Her only sadness was that her parents could not be there to see it.

All through the week she worked feverishly on the house, while weekends were reserved for her new job singing at the Silver Grill. It wasn't much but luckily the inheritance from her father stretched far enough to cover the work on the house.

As she washed out her paintbrushes at the Belfast sink in the little scullery at the back of the house, she heard the creak of the back door, now repaired, and Oliver came in.

'Your carriage awaits, ma'am.'

She grinned. 'You mean you've hired a rickshaw.'

He laughed. 'Spot on.'

'Just let me change,' she said and pointed at her paint-streaked shirt and shorts.

He came across to her, took the brushes from her hands and kissed the tip of her nose. 'You have paint there,' he said. Then he kissed her forehead. 'And there.'

While he kissed her cheeks, her neck and finally her lips, she tipped her head back, hoping for more.

'Stay at mine tonight,' he said, his face a picture of mock discomfort. 'I don't think my back can cope with sharing your camp bed for another night, especially as I usually end up on the floor.'

Belle twisted the engagement ring on her finger and beamed with pleasure.

'I need to be back early though. I've still got so much to do to get the place shipshape for Simone.'

He tilted his head and gave her a curious look. 'Anyone would think she was the Queen of England.'

Belle smiled cheerfully, pleased to have been able to write and fill Simone in on everything she'd discovered. 'Better than that. Anyway, last time I looked I think we had a king.'

'Guess what?' he said. 'I've spotted some lovely antiques in one of the Chinese shops near my place.'

'Expensive?'

'No . . . When I say antiques . . .'

'You mean junk.'

He smiled. 'Nice junk.'

She slipped her arm in his. 'I need new bed linen and an eiderdown.'

'Rowe's for those. But aren't you forgetting something?'

'I've already ordered the beds. They're arriving the day after tomorrow.'

She went upstairs to wash and change and afterwards opened the French windows to peer out at the garden and think of the day in 1911 when baby Elvira had been taken by Edward's and

295

Gloria's aunt. After she had posted the letter to Elvira, or rather Emily, she'd alternated between anxiety and excitement, and when the reply had finally come she'd opened it with trembling hands. She took it out now and read it again, possibly for the twentieth time.

My dear Belle,

I don't know what to say. I'm shocked. Flabbergasted in fact, but so, so excited to hear about you. I too never had a sibling but always wanted one. My mother – I'm sorry, I do have to call her that – well, she couldn't have more children. Sadly, she only gave birth to one. A stillborn girl.

I work in publishing here in New York, am married, and have a five-year-old boy called Charlie, your nephew of course. I would be delighted to come to meet you in Rangoon, though I will have to tie up a few loose ends here before I'm free to do so. There's so much I want to know about you and Diana.

You say you are to be married. If you can let me have the date, and I can make it in time, I'd love to be there, if I'm invited that is.

Until then and with my love,
Emily

Every time Belle read it, she felt her eyes moisten. Was Emily genuinely happy to have heard from her or was she being polite and saying what she thought Belle might want to hear? She knew it couldn't be straightforward for Emily to have to deal with what her parents had done, nor to come face to face with a sister she'd never even known she had. But she'd written back telling Emily it would be perfect if she could make it in time for the wedding.

She'd thought it best not to mention anything about what had happened to Gloria or Edward in her two letters but was annoyed Gloria had left Rangoon without anyone knowing where she'd gone. Strings had been pulled and Belle was infuriated that it seemed she was going to get away with what she'd done. Edward, however, had been found guilty of perverting the course of justice and now languished in Rangoon's jail, where he would serve an eighteen-month sentence. Everyone had thought he'd be released from police custody and sent back to England, his tail between his legs, but that hadn't happened thanks to a young and conscientious lawyer for the prosecution who could not be bribed. In any case, Edward's reputation was destroyed and his career lay in tatters.

Belle closed the windows then extracted a pair of red high heels from under the camp bed and slipped on some silver earrings. One last look in a tiny hand mirror to check her hair, then she was ready.

In the late afternoon two days later, Belle paced her hall admiring the newly polished marble floor. She'd bought a delicately painted oriental table and a pretty mirror from 'Oliver's' junk shop so now the place, though still sparsely furnished, looked more welcoming. The walls were white and the fragrance of fresh roses arranged in a glass vase on the table drifted through the air, masking the smell of paint. It had rained all afternoon and although it had stopped now, the sky remained bruised and brooding. She prayed the weather would not delay Simone's arrival.

Oliver, busy organizing the kitchen, was singing off-key. She'd been overjoyed to discover he was an excellent cook, not something she relished doing at all, and they had shared delicious meals together at his apartment. It had been after one of those meals when he'd surprised her by bending down on one knee, gazing into her eyes and proposing. Trying not to laugh, she had studied his dear face and the hopeful tilt of his head and had managed instead to smile and say yes. When he got up she called him a corny old fool, but they had drunk a bottle and a half of champagne, then made wonderful and utterly joyous love, and had been inseparable ever since. Her aversion to alcohol had, of course, been forgotten and she vastly preferred the more relaxed person she had become.

He'd also surprised her with a new cooker, saucepans, cutlery, crockery, glasses, provisions – all of it brand new and delivered by Rowe's. So they now had everything they needed to produce a first meal for Simone. Belle wandered upstairs to check Simone's bedroom for the hundredth time. The new and gratifyingly comfy bed was ready, made up with sparkling white linen and draped with a silky ivory bedspread.

So far, Belle and Oliver hadn't discussed the future in detail. He was worried there might be another war and, not at all sure how it would affect them in Burma, had suggested they move to America if things became tricky. But he hadn't objected when she'd expressed the desire to restore her parents' old house, with a view to living there if they stayed on in Burma.

As she was thinking this she heard a knock at the front door and with a rush of excitement ran down the stairs to open up.

A beautiful middle-aged blonde woman with amber eyes smiled back at her. Belle, so thrilled to finally meet this old friend of her mother, beamed at her and hurried down the front steps.

'Welcome,' she said, holding out both hands. 'I can't tell you how happy I am that you came.'

Simone stepped forward and the two embraced, then Simone held her at arm's length.

'So, you are Annabelle. How like your mother.'

'Am I?'

The older woman nodded. 'Look, I haven't been entirely honest with you.' She glanced to her left and, from just out of sight, another woman wearing an elegant pale-blue dress stepped forward.

At first Belle thought this auburn-haired woman must be her sister, but the woman was too old to be Elvira. She hesitated, her mind spinning wildly. No. It couldn't be. It couldn't. It was impossible. Belle could not look at the woman, nor could she look away. Deeply shocked and feeling as if the whole world had shrunk, she froze. Was she dreaming? Had she hit her head on something? Was this real? The silence went on and Belle felt she might never breathe again, but then, with an explosion of sound, the blood rushed to her temples, pounding and pounding. As if awakening from a spell she gasped, took a step back and fell against Oliver, who'd appeared behind her. A lump grew in her throat and she tried to swallow it, but instead her eyes grew hotter and an avalanche of tears began to fall. Silent and devastatingly painful. She felt dizzy, but Oliver kept her steady and upright, then passed her a clean handkerchief. As Belle wiped her eyes she continued to gulp back tears. Now she became aware of the whole front garden, its delicious scents released by the heavy rain, the loamy smell of the earth, the fresh green of the trees and the fragrance of the flowers that had survived the downpour. Apart from the haze of insects hovering over the shrubs now heavy with water, it had turned into a crystal-clear afternoon.

For a moment the woman angled her face to catch the warmth of the sun and Belle knew the familiar movement, oh so well. Then, unwavering, her expression calm, the woman gazed at Belle with bright clear eyes, looking as if she might be about to smile but was waiting for a sign. From me, Belle thought. Is she waiting for me? She shifted her weight from one foot to the other, then stared back at the older woman and, in that moment, she fully comprehended.

'Mother?' she whispered.

Diana nodded and took a step towards her daughter.

'But you're . . .'

'Douglas decided it was for the best.'

Belle waited to see the chaos of passion and obsession that had once raged beneath the surface of her mother's deceptively calm exterior. But there seemed to be none and Belle felt confused. This mother . . . this mother with her hair so neatly folded in a smart chignon, this mother with her clear eyes and flawless complexion, this mother who stood so still and dignified – who was she?

'But you never ever came,' Belle burst out angrily.

Her mother took a deep breath. 'I came.'

'When? When did you come?'

'You were fifteen. I had recovered from my illness –'

'You recovered? You recovered?' Belle interrupted again, the overpowering anger and hurt catching in her throat. 'But you didn't come back to us.'

'I wanted to see you, but your father thought it would be too unsettling for you, especially as he'd convinced you I'd died, and you had become used to that.'

Belle's tears came in a rush again and she swiftly wiped them away. 'You let him send you away? I needed you, Mother. I needed you.'

Her mother's face fell and though Belle could see the devastation in her mother's eyes she could not rein in her anger.

'I am so sorry, my love.'

'Sorry is not enough.' Belle turned to Simone and felt her cheeks burning. In the past she had not known how to cope with the wasteland of her mother's life. Was this really the same woman?

She stared at Simone. 'After I wrote to you, why didn't you tell me my mother was alive?'

'I almost did. She and I talked about it and I decided I would come to Burma to tell you in person. It was not the sort of news to deliver in a letter.'

'I insisted on coming too,' Diana added. 'I longed so much to see you but I didn't believe you'd want to see me. That's why I didn't dare try again. And then Simone told me you were over here.'

'I wanted –' Belle stuttered. 'I want –' And the tears started again.

Diana came straight to her daughter and Belle fell into her open arms. As both women sobbed, the world stood still and it seemed as if they might never stop weeping. When they eventually did, Diana smiled through her tears and wiped her daughter's cheeks, just as if she'd been a little girl.

'I am so proud of you,' she said. 'So proud. After you left school I sent letters to you in Cheltenham explaining everything. But you never replied, so . . .'

Belle's eyes widened. 'I never saw any letters.'

'Maybe Douglas –'

'Thought he was protecting me?'

Diana nodded.

Then, as all three women had moist eyes, and as a silence had descended, Oliver took over. 'I have champagne on ice. Who's game?'

Between laughing and crying, Belle managed to speak. 'Mother, meet Oliver, your future son-in-law.'

A month flew by and now it was the day before the wedding. The icing on the cake, if any more had been needed, was that a letter had arrived from Emily, and she was due in Rangoon today. Belle had already sent a brief letter explaining the wonderful news that Diana was in fact alive and also that she was currently in Burma. Oliver's parents, meanwhile, had already arrived, and had taken a suite at the Strand Hotel. Belle and her mother had toured the garden every morning before the rains came in the afternoon, talking and sharing everything that had happened during their long separation. At times Belle had been angry with her mother, and then angry with her father, and explaining the hurt she'd experienced as a child felt painful. She couldn't understand why her father had intercepted Diana's letters. When Belle asked about it again, her mother had simply said she and Douglas had loved each other once but life had changed them both. The look of sadness in Diana's eyes prevented Belle from pursuing it. The letters aside, and as far as she was able, Belle gradually came to accept things had been the way they had been for a reason. Diana had convinced her daughter that much of Douglas's behaviour, though perhaps at times misguided, had been to protect Belle.

'And you are really well, now?' Belle had asked, looking into her mother's green eyes when the rain had come and they had escaped indoors.

'I truly am.'

And when Belle had seen the wisdom and compassion in her mother's eyes she had known it was true.

Later on, as the rain abated and before darkness fell, Belle and Diana explored the fringes of the garden where roses clambered and cascaded in wild profusion. The whole garden, awash with moisture, shone from the monsoon rains. Diamonds of sunlight glittered on the wet grass and the sky shimmered in shades of lilac and pink. They breathed in the sweetness hanging in the air but neither woman spoke of Elvira. It was as if they dared not mention her name for if they did the magic of her being found alive might vanish and, with it, Elvira too. Instead they spoke of the wedding, the state of the country, what might happen in the future. Diana spoke of her path to healing and the gratitude she owed to Simone and Dr Gilbert, who had given her back her life. Belle talked about Oliver, and about her career. Although she'd initially come to Burma bright-eyed and hopeful for her career, things had turned out rather differently. She'd gained a mother and a fiancé, and was about to gain a sister. Singing was still an important part of her life and she hoped to continue but now she had a family too.

'You get your voice from me,' Diana said.

'And my green eyes and reddish hair,' Belle added.

Diana touched her daughter's hair. 'Yours is more golden than mine.'

But now Belle wasn't listening. She was gazing instead at the back door of the proud and lovely old house where Oliver stood with a woman Belle had never seen before. The woman was smiling and her hair, lit by the sun, was a brighter red than either Diana's or Belle's.

'Elvira.' Diana's voice came out in a hoarse whisper.

'Go on,' Belle said very gently and gave her a little push.

Diana turned her head, smiled at Belle, and then began to run, faster than she had ever run before, and with arms outstretched she reached the daughter she'd lost twenty-six years before and who she had believed was gone for ever. Belle followed behind slowly, wanting to give her mother those precious few moments alone with Elvira. She glanced back at the tamarind tree as she passed. Who would ever have thought it would turn out like this?

After a few minutes she walked up to Emily and Diana and came to a halt. Her mother stepped back and now the two sisters remained motionless, eyes locked. Bewitched and wanting to move forward but frozen by something that would have seemed impossible not so long before, Belle knew she had done this. She hadn't given up, not even when she had been terrified. Now, unable to do anything but drink her sister in, she felt her heart skipping a beat; it jumped and somersaulted until she had to put a hand to her chest. And then the spell was broken. Emily stepped forward and held out her arms and within seconds the two women were hugging each other, both laughing through the flood of tears.

There was so much to say, so much to resolve, and yet Belle found it impossible to speak. Neither of the sisters seemed to know where to start. The moment went on until they both eventually turned to Diana and then the three of them walked arm-in-arm towards the house in silence. Belle felt the past twist and turn as if it had suddenly sprung alive again and knew that, for now, some things were too deep for words.

At the door they all turned to look back at the garden, golden in the setting sun.

'I loved this garden,' Diana said in a whisper.

Belle found her voice. 'I knew that the first time I saw it.'

Emily stared at the ground before glancing at Diana. 'I'm so sorry for what happened here.'

Diana reached out and squeezed her hand. 'Plenty of time to talk. For now, I only need you to believe it's all in the past.'

There were a few moments of silence again.

'Changing the subject,' Belle said with a grin, 'I know it's rather short notice but, Emily, is there any chance you'd agree to be my bridesmaid?'

After the wedding, Oliver and Belle chose not to go away. How could they with Emily so recently arrived and with only three weeks to spend in Rangoon and so much time to make up for. Early one cool morning when the day was fresh and full of promise, Belle and Emily were sitting on a bench beneath the tamarind tree, listening to a gentle breeze ruffling the leaves above them and watching the birds swooping from tree to tree.

'This was where your pram was the day you were taken,' Belle said. 'Right here beneath the tamarind.'

Emily nodded but didn't speak.

They'd had so little time alone together and Belle didn't really know how Emily was feeling about everything. Was she truly happy to have been found or was a little bit of her begrudging having had her life twisted out of shape? Belle wanted to ask but wasn't sure how and then Emily began to speak.

'Marie was a good mother to me in her way, or as good as she could be,' Emily said, interrupting Belle's thoughts.

'Diana, too,' Belle said, tentatively. 'Though I didn't see it at the time. I didn't understand. I judged her. Blamed her.'

'You were a child.'

Belle drew in her breath and closed her suddenly smarting eyes.

'You have a chance to make up for it all now.'

Belle nodded and exhaled slowly, blinking the tears away.

'When I read about the way Marie had stolen me from this very garden, it was . . . well, I hardly have words. Nothing prepares you for a shock so life-changing.'

There was a short silence as Belle tried to imagine how it had been.

'I was so angry,' Emily continued. 'But I also felt sad and confused. My world had come crashing down around me and everything I'd thought about who I was had been a lie. Most of all I didn't want to believe it. I don't think I slept for a week. But it did make sense of the depressions and anxieties Marie had experienced throughout her life.'

'How do you mean?'

Emily shrugged. 'Guilt had been at the bottom of it.'

There was a long pause before Belle spoke.

'Diana was ill for years too. She was accused of harming you.'

Emily shook her head and her voice broke a little as she spoke. 'I'm so sorry for what Marie did and the way it affected your family. I don't know if I'll ever be able to truly accept it.'

Belle reached for her hand.

'As it gradually sank in I realized Marie had been tortured by regret over what she'd done. That's why she'd become so ill.'

'Diana too, though I feel blessed she's not only alive but well.'

'We've both found her again, haven't we?'

Belle smiled as her mother's image came to mind. 'She looks wonderful, doesn't she?'

Emily nodded but Belle caught something in her look and felt suddenly nervous.

'Can I be frank?' Emily asked.

'Of course.'

'Well, the trouble is I don't exactly know what to say to Diana. I feel terribly torn. I want to get to know her and I can't tell you how much it means to have met her. But on the other hand, and perhaps I shouldn't, but I somehow still feel protective of Marie too. What she did was inexcusable but, you see, she did love me.'

Belle nodded and thought about it before speaking. 'Diana's been through so much herself. I'm sure she'll understand.'

'I hope so.'

'What about your father? What happened to him?'

Emily inhaled sharply. 'Sadly, my father put a bullet in his brain about a year after leaving Burma. I was too young to remember anything about him but for some years my mother was beside herself with grief. I'm sure she blamed herself.'

'So much guilt.'

'Yes, but as I said, she did her best, and after she remarried a few years later, I ended up with a wonderful, caring stepfather and he made all the difference.'

'And now you have a little boy.'

'Yes. The light of my life. Truly. I can't wait for you to get to know him. I hope you and Oliver will come to New York soon? We live in a lovely old brownstone. There's bags of room.'

Belle grinned. 'You bet!'

Emily laughed. 'Goodness, I think you might be turning into an American too.'

Belle raised her brows in response and then laughed as well. 'You never know, there's a chance we might end up living there – though I'd be sad to leave here.'

'I can imagine.'

'I'm sure your feelings about what Marie did will eventually settle. I can't help but think her mind must have been terribly disturbed at the time.'

'Yes. She wasn't a bad person. Not really. Just a sick and

misguided woman who did a terrible thing and then paid for it all her life. The awful thing is, I still can't forgive her.'

'You will. In time.'

Emily hung her head. 'It hurts, Belle.'

'I know.'

There was a long silence and then Emily squinted at Belle as if she was considering something.

'What?' Belle asked.

'I wanted to say thank you.'

'For?'

'For all this. For finding me.'

'You're truly glad?'

Emily's eyes glittered. 'I always wanted a sister.'

'But there's something else, isn't there?'

'I still have so much to come to terms with. A lot to resolve, you know?'

Belle could see the sadness in Emily's eyes and understood. Of course, it couldn't all be plain sailing. Her sister would have to reframe her entire life, much as Belle had also had to do.

'You can always talk to me,' Belle said. 'I promise.'

'Yes, I've never had that before.'

As they smiled at each other Belle felt she would treasure this time for ever. It was a pause, this moment, a single beat in the crazy tide of life, that might permit the past to shift and fade as they sat together in the garden. Despite Emily's mixed emotions, it was special to share the newly rain-released scents of the profusion of flowers still blooming in the undergrowth, and watch the birds dipping in and out of the trees. Her sister was alive, and that meant everything. The gift of a sister. How lucky she was. How lucky they both were to have found each other, and she hoped they would have years ahead of them to become the best of friends. Years to get to know each other's hopes and dreams. Years to find out their flaws and fears. And years to support each other through whatever might lie ahead, even – given the uncertainty of things – the possibility of another war. Nothing could eradicate the loneliness they'd both experienced in the past, or the horrors Belle had witnessed, but she knew that in the marvellous way life gave as much as it took, the years stretching before them might eventually compensate for the ones they'd lost.

They would be a family and, given how fractured her childhood had been, Belle could ask for nothing better. She was a daughter, a sister, a wife, an aunt, and if everything went to plan, although Oliver was the only one to know so far, she too would be a mother . . . in about seven months' time. And it made her ache for Diana, finally dispelling any remaining reservations she might still harbour about the past. She already loved her unborn baby and could truly begin to glimpse the agony her mother must have felt at the disappearance of Elvira. She sighed deeply and then, lost in her thoughts, began to sing to herself.

Emily touched her on the arm very gently. 'What's that you're singing?' she asked.

Belle turned to her sister and smiled at a memory. 'Oh, just a tune from my childhood.' Then she glanced at the house.

'It's a lovely place,' Emily said, seeing her looking.

'It should be yours. As the elder.'

'No, Belle, it's yours,' Emily said, and squeezed her sister's hand. 'You deserve it. If it wasn't for you, none of us would be here now. You did this, and I couldn't be more grateful. I only ask that we never lose each other again.'

Belle's eyes filled up as she gazed at her sister and then her new home. It wasn't just a lovely house as Emily had said. It was the place her beautiful sister had been born, the place from which she had been lost, and now it had become the place where she had been found again.

'I was so frightened I would never find you,' Belle said, 'or that you were dead.'

'Well, you found me all right. And I am never going to let you go.'

They both stood and then they walked arm-in-arm around the garden, enjoying the moment Belle had so longed for but had also feared would never come. Her missing sister had come home at last. Thank you, she whispered as her heart filled with gratitude. Thank you.

Author's Note

Occasionally it's necessary to shift true events around to fit the timeline of the narrative in order to better serve the story. In the case of *The Missing Sister* one example occurs where I moved the massacre from 1930 to 1936.

The most crucial research took place while visiting Myanmar (Burma as it once was known) where I stayed in all the locations used in the book. In Yangon (Rangoon) the Strand Hotel was as luxurious as it is in my story, and it was easy to picture my characters there back in the 1930s. I also enjoyed a marvellous river trip travelling up the Irrawaddy from Bagan to Mandalay, just as Belle does. Time fell away as I watched the world go by and I could tell that it would have been virtually unchanged since her day. But the highlight came one morning just before dawn when we went up in a hot air balloon and drifted high above the ancient city of Bagan in central Myanmar, one of the world's greatest archaeological sites. When the rising sun painted the hundreds of pagodas pink and gold it took my breath away: a truly unforgettable experience. As a writer I found the entire tour inspiring and, hand on heart, one of the most exceptional trips I've ever been on while researching a novel. Other than my visit to Myanmar, the internet once again provided a wealth of detail, as did the many history books and memoirs which are far too numerous to mention here. I'm now looking forward to my research trip for book seven which will take place a little closer to home . . . Keep an eye on my Facebook page or website for news and, if you haven't yet done so, why not join my Readers' Club to be the first to hear about new publications and to enter competitions. (You can talk to me on Twitter too.)

www.dinahjefferies.com
www.facebook.com/dinahjefferiesbooks
Twitter: @DinahJefferies
https://twitter.com/DinahJefferies

Acknowledgements

Thanks once again to the entire team at Viking/Penguin and to my agent, Caroline Hardman. I've loved writing this, my sixth novel, and you've all been fantastically supportive as you always are. I'm very lucky. Thanks to all the friendly and helpful people I met during my visit to Myanmar from whom I learnt so much about the past and about the troubles of the present too. I'm also extremely grateful to the book bloggers who continue to do so much to help authors – where would we be without you? And, finally, I'd like to say a very warm thank you to all my readers.

FIND OUT MORE ABOUT DINAH JEFFERIES

For more information on Dinah Jefferies' novels, including competitions, publications and events, visit Dinah's Facebook page (www.facebook.com/dinahjefferiesbooks), follow her on Twitter (@DinahJefferies) or sign up for the newsletter on her website www.dinahjefferies.com.

We love stories.

Fact or fiction, long or short, exploring distant lands, imagined worlds or your own back yard – anything can be a story, and every place has stories waiting to be told. And we want to find them.

Do you have a story to tell? Want help cutting through the jargon, answers to your burning questions or advice from top authors, agents and editors across the industry?

Find out more about how to get published at:
www.penguin.co.uk/publishmybook